# Murder at the La Jolla Apogée

## A Bishop Bone Murder Mystery

By

Robert G. Rogers

Copyright © 2020 Robert G. Rogers

All rights reserved.

Also by Robert G. Rogers

**Bishop Bone Murder Mystery Series**
A Tale of Two Sisters
Murder in the Pinebelt
A Killing in Oil
The Pinebelt Chicken War
Jennifer's Dream
La Jolla Shores Murders
Murder at the La Jolla Apogee
No Morning Dew
Brother James and the Second Coming
The Taco Wagons Murders
He's a Natural

**Non-Series Murder Mysteries**
The Christian Detective
That La Jolla Lawyer

**Contemporary Dramas**
French Quarter Affair
Life and Times of Nobody Worth a Damn

**Suspense/Thrillers**
Runt Wade
The End is Near

**Historical Women's Fiction**
Jodie Mae

**Youth/Teen Action and Adventure**
Lost Indian Gold
Taylor's Wish
Swamp Ghost Mystery
Armageddon Ritual

**Children's Picture Story book**
Fancy Fairy

# DEDICATION

This book is dedicated to Chuck Ashford, a man very familiar with the business practices featured in the book. His suggestions were appreciated and very useful. Also, I want to thank Eva Abbo, Elsie Land, Elizabeth Patterson, Kathy Miller, Yarka Ondricek and the many others who participated in the editing process and offered helpful suggestions.

# CHAPTER 1

Phillip Marshall walked into Marcus Flint's office wearing racquetball togs. The leather bag draped over his shoulder held his suit and dress shoes. "You're not ready. Aren't we playing?" he asked Flint who had hung up the phone seconds before Phillip walked in but continued to stare at it as if mulling over what he'd just heard. His face had taken on a slight frown.

Marshall, in his mid-thirties, was Flint's chief financial officer. Marc was about ten years older.

Marc had deliberately forgotten they were playing and had worn a dark suit, his usual office attire, for the Saturday grand opening of their latest real estate project, the La Jolla Apogée, a few miles north of San Diego. According to Marc, who had come up with the name, it meant the best of the best. The Apogée was a mixed-use project with condos, single family homes and lots for those who wanted to build for themselves. Nothing was listed for under a million dollars and all had a view of the Pacific surf. It was La Jolla, after all, where the rich and famous lived. The higher the price, the more exclusivity La Jollans felt they had.

It was March and the weather was just right for an opening. Marc had put a little extra into the project by bringing in mature flowering trees. No matter where anybody looked they would see trees in bloom and in all colors. And, if their car windows were down, they could catch the sweet fragrance that floated on the breeze.

"Make 'em feel comfortable, like they're wrapped in luxury," Marc had said, "and they'll open their checkbooks."

Smiling real estate agents were already sitting on hundreds of reservations. So many, in fact, Marc was considering holding an auction.

\* \* \* \*

In fact, Marc and Phillip were scheduled to play on one of the project's racquetball courts. "We'll break it in," Marc had told him, adding, "Get its cherry." He had a tendency to be crude with his male associates but rarely with women.

Both men stayed in shape battling it out on racquetball courts twice a week. Phillip stood four inches or so under six feet. He had light brown hair, cut short, blue eyes and walked with a nervous gait. His face was somewhat narrow and longish with a nose showing a noticeable bow in the middle that told of some Indian heritage in his Irish lineage. He prided himself on maintaining a stoic demeanor. Behind his back, those who knew him would say, "When Phillip smiles, after an agreement is signed, you know that Marc got to you again."

While he and Marc played close, he'd never won more than one game. Lately though, he'd been coming closer and Marc correctly assumed he'd been practicing with one of the local pros.

Marc was a shade over six feet and like Phillip, was also in great shape. He walked with the ease and confidence of a predatory cat and only smiled when a smile might bring him something in return, something he wanted. Even though his smiles were like a down payment on something he was about to own, they seemed to come so easily that people were immediately captivated by their warmth and charm.

Women saw him as ruggedly handsome. Men considered him formidable and few crossed him physically. He had a full face, not unlike that of the long dead Cary Grant. His hair was dark as were his eyes and thanks to expensive dentistry his teeth were perfect and added luster to his smiles.

His mother had named him Marcus because she thought it was a French name and had taught him enough French to impress young girls. And, it didn't hurt him with the ladies when he got older. Along the way, he discovered that the name was more Italian in origin than French. Even so, sometimes he threw out a French phrase just for the hell of it.

* * * *

Seven years earlier, Marc had been the managing partner in a multistate law firm handling construction loans for a high risk lender headquartered in Florida. The lender's name was The New Opportunity Bank but Marc and all associated with him had shortened it to simply, "the lender."

Marc's firm had its offices near LA and Miami. The LA firm, which Marc managed, handled all loans west of the Mississippi. The Miami firm handled the rest.

The lender was listed on the New York Stock Exchange, but only made construction loans. Its army of MBAs scoured the country for high risk real estate developers looking for money for their next project.

A Master's in Business Administration or MBA was a requirement for anyone dealing with the financial ins and outs of the business world. By the time the candidates earned the degree, they were assumed to know the financial aspects and requirements of businesses from the front door to the back. An overly enthusiastic MBA could analyze a project from the get-go and write it up for the lender's loan committee like it was going to be a big success and in the very good times of real estate, the projects were.

MBAs were paid when the loans funded. Privately, their motto was, "Let's eat, get drunk, get laid and then go out and have fun."

Often the developers who borrowed money from the lender were not bankable by regular lenders, were willing to sell their souls to get money, and didn't hesitate to pay high rates of interest on their loans. They were often guilty of fudging the facts of their projects to meet their needs. As a result, notwithstanding what the MBAs wrote, some of the loans went bad before much of what they built was sold. And many more followed as the real estate market changed for the worse.

Marc and his firm of attorneys negotiated the terms before the loan requests were submitted to the lender for approval and afterward, re-negotiated the terms when the loans were conditionally approved.

The lender borrowed money from a number of banks who didn't want to bother with making and managing construction loans, especially loans that might not stand the light of a tight audit, but they did enjoy the profits the loans brought in.

Everything went well so long as the economy was growing. The developers who had borrowed money from the lender sold homes as soon as the certificates of occupancies were issued and sold the commercial developments as soon as they were eighty percent leased up.

Encouraged by the MBAs, the developers expanded to take on more debt and to begin even more projects.

Then the stuff that smelled began to hit the fan. The economy slowed and eventually ground to a halt. Developers could not make their loan payments and the lender, Marc's client, suffered the same fate. It could not make its loan payments to the banks it owed and worse, it could not make new loans to developers. So, things ground to a screeching halt for the lender and the law firms.

With no other choice, Marc sent the other attorneys in the LA firm packing and began searching for smaller office space for himself as he prepared himself for the onerous chore of building a new practice. He'd no sooner begun that task when he received a call from the chairman of the board of the lender asking for a meeting. He knew of the man, but had never met him.

"Can you meet me at midnight?" the man asked and added the name of his hotel. His plane was getting in about that time. He had some business he wanted to discuss. Marc agreed to meet him in the cocktail lounge of the hotel.

When Marc told his wife, Anne, about the request, she said, "Midnight! That's ridiculous! Why didn't you tell him to drive out here tomorrow? Did you tell him you're busy trying to figure out where our next meal is coming from?"

Anne was a natural blond and endowed enough to catch the eyes of men walking past. She was a little over five and a half feet tall and kept trim by watching her diet and by jogging daily. She had a degree in liberal arts.

She was born and raised in New Orleans though she had no French connections. Both her father and mother had been lawyers. They died young. Marc helped Anne wind up their estate and during that exercise, they fell in love. It didn't hurt that he occasionally used some of the French his mother had taught him.

They had a daughter, Cynthia, who had moved to New York after school to work for a public relations firm. Anne had taken up writing to stay ahead of the boredom that came with marriage to Marc. He was always out chasing rainbows or busy enjoying ones he'd caught and was away from home much of the time. She made enough money from writing to stay interested in continuing.

Marc laughed at her suggestion and said, "No, I didn't, Anne. When God calls and asks for a meeting, you don't negotiate." The man was held in that degree of awe with all who knew him.

\* \* \* \*

During the meeting, the man told Marc what he wanted him to do. "We'll sell you the stock of the developers whose loans are so far in default, they could never catch up," he said. When the attorneys closed a loan, they always took the developer's stock as additional collateral. And, when it became clear that a developer could not bring a loan current, the stock would be foreclosed on.

The chairman continued, "You'll become the owner and clean up their problems, financial and legal, so their real estate can begin throwing off money again. Right now, they're throwing off nothing. We'll pass the money to our credit-line lenders to pay down our loans and eventually – that's our plan anyway – exchange the projects for forgiveness of our debt. In effect, we're out of the lending business but we can avoid lawsuits and possible actions by the Feds if everybody leaves the table happy. If the plan works like I think it will, we'll get to keep many of our assets." He punctuated that with a slight smile which Marc noted in the dim light of the cocktail lounge. Ill-gotten assets, he thought, but kept it to himself.

"That's a good plan, but how am I going to get the money to cover the overhead of the companies I'm taking over? The companies I'll be taking over don't have a dime," Marc said.

"Get me a one year budget for each company we send you. Our credit-line banks have agreed, with a little arm twisting, to provide enough cash to run each company you take over until you can get them in a paying status," the chairman said.

He also said that their credit-line banks would allow Marc's client lender to subordinate their loans to any construction loans Marc may acquire to build out a project. In effect, an agreement to subordinate would put the new construction lender in a first lien position on the project. The lender's loans, which Marc inherited with each company he took over, would move into a second position; riskier but money from a new loan would make repayment of the lender's loan much more likely.

Marc knew that the subordinations would get him the construction funding he needed to finish out the stalled projects of the companies he'd be taking over. He was gambling that the real estate market would turn around, which it did, and enable his company to not only pay off the construction lenders, but his client as well.

"You understand that you're doing this on your own? You're not an employee. Right? We never had this meeting. And, one of these days, when you clean up the messes you're taking on, someone will call and ask you to deed the projects to various banks. I'm told you can be trusted. That's why I'm talking to you. When the time comes, I don't want us to end up in litigation."

Marc never saw the man again. A few days later, he opened an office in La Jolla, California and hired Phillip Marshall, as his chief financial officer, to make sense out of the books and records of the companies they took over. When Marc told him to make sense out of them, what he really meant was to use creative accounting to make the assets look attractive enough to convince a bank to lend them money.

At the time, Phillip was married without children. He and his wife, Linda, had a son three years later.

People in the business commonly referred to what Marc did in cleaning up a real estate developer's financial troubles as "working out" its problems. And, for the same reason, people called the company he had formed to do that, a workout company, to distinguish it from being a regular real estate developer. Of course, once the problems were cleared away, Marc's company, in effect, became a developer.

Most companies he took over were owned by rough and tough builders, who objected to Marc's demand that they give him the keys and leave. More than a couple went so far as to threaten him, forcing him to bring in the local police on those occasions to make sure his orders were obeyed without injury ... his. After the first few confrontations, he usually brought a big guy with him. He called him Lennie, a character he remembered from Of Mice and Men. If a borrower made a sound or move like he objected to Marc's request to clear out, Lennie stepped forward and the borrower shut up and began cleaning out his desk.

But, all that was coming to an end. Marc's client had negotiated a deal with its creditor banks and had told

Marc it was time to deed everything back. Marc had been stalling the process, but knew he had run out of time.

\* \* \* \*

Marc stood and told Phillip, "The lender is sending that Parsons guy out for the opening. He's the guy who's been after us for our financial records."

Phillip frowned. "Parsons? He's a financial analyst. They should be sending somebody with some kind of marketing background to see what a great job we're doing."

"I think our ride's over, Phillip. It doesn't matter what kind of job we've been doing. Parson's gonna stay after the opening and audit our books and records. The lender's banks want all our projects deeded back as soon as possible. We won't get the year I was shooting for.

"They've formed a liquidation committee to handle the takeover. According to a girl I know in admin down there, the committee's holding company will buy all the lender's mortgages, even pay a premium. The money from that will go to the credit-line banks to pay off the lender's loans. The girl says the lender may end up with a little extra. A pat on the back to us."

"A pat on the back won't pay my bills. I was counting on the year to get myself situated," Phillip replied.

"Yeah. The liquidation committee feels the real estate market is as strong as it's going to get and they want to, in effect, liquidate the lender now – that means us – and get their loans repaid."

"Damn, Marc! We just got the Palm Springs project going."

"I know. Looks like a sell-out."

Once a dead-in-the-water resort project, after Marc had taken it over, the city approved a zoning change to allow more units to be built. That had made the project immediately marketable with affordable units for buyers looking for weekend condos that included resort amenities. Kelly Smith, the ousted developer, had bad-mouthed Marc all over town, even claiming he'd made payoffs to get the zoning change. Marc didn't, but that's not to say he hadn't given someone money to do it for him.

And, as was often the case when Marc took over a project, it had been vandalized. Smith was blamed but nothing could be proven. The clubhouse had been torched and a couple of the wells for the golf course had been filled with concrete. Marc was able to laugh the damage off. The first thing he did when taking over a project was to increase the insurance to cover just such contingencies.

"Can you do anything? Negotiate?" Phillip asked.

Marc shook his head and said, "Je ne sais pas. The Tucson project is out for sure. The developer gave in to the lender's demands when they heard I was coming."

That often happened. When a borrower was told to expect a visit from Marc, they knew it was time to cut the best deal they could get or clean out their desks and hand over the keys.

"I suppose I'll be dealing with Parsons," Phillip said.

"Yep. You don't have to be overly cooperative however. We need to milk as much out of our projects as possible before the shit hits the fan," Marc said.

"Yeah. I get you." He shrugged and asked, "Well are we going to play or what? Parson's won't be in here today."

"Yeah. We'll play. My togs are in the bathroom," Marc said with a weary shake of his head. "I'm a bit under the weather. Probably from all the bullshit I've been catching. The pressure's been hell."

Phillip smiled. "Yeah, pressure! Hell, you used to say pressure was your middle name. You're just afraid I'll whip you! You barely lucked out last time."

Phillip's challenge got Marc's adrenalin up. "Yeah, babble on, cat shit. Somebody'll cover you up. Today, that'll be me. I can whip you blindfolded! Give me a minute to change."

Marc had not been stalling when he said he was feeling down. And, it wasn't from the pressure. He had just been feeling unusually tired for about two weeks, drinking water like it was going out of style, going to the bathroom much more than he ever did and eating energy bars which hadn't helped any. Finally, a few days before, he'd asked Phillip's wife, Linda, a nurse in a busy doctor's office to test his blood to see what she could find. The office had its own facilities to run a blood profile.

Marc and his wife often socialized with Phillip and Linda so he wasn't reluctant to ask the favor. "I don't want anybody to know anything," he'd told her. "Not even Phillip. If the word got out that I had something wrong with me, I'm afraid the lender might take a second look at its agreement with me."

She agreed but knew she'd tell Phillip anyway.

* * * *

The phone call Marc had finished before Phillip walked in was not from the lender's representative as he'd said. It was from Linda, giving him the results of his blood test.

"Your sugar levels are out of sight, Marc, over 600," she told him. "I think you have diabetes. Bad. You need to see a doctor and get a prescription for insulin to get that sugar level down. I can make an appointment for you. A doctor won't tell anybody. Ethically, he can't."

"I'll think about it, Linda."

"You'd better not think too long, or you could end up dead. Your sugar numbers are too high. I shouldn't do it, but if you can get by here, I'll give you a shot of insulin and bootleg you a few doses until you can get in to see the doctor."

"Okay, I'll finish the grand opening and call you."

"I'm telling you, it's serious. You could have a seizure at any time."

He was still thinking about the call. He really didn't feel like playing racquetball. His high blood sugar probably accounted for that. Hell, he didn't feel like making a speech to anybody either but he'd agreed to do it and people were expecting it.

He looked at Phillip. "Okay, I'll get dressed. This may be your lucky day."

"Yeah. Trying to sandbag me? It won't work. I know all your dirty tricks."

"Only the ones I've used, Phillip."

\* \* \* \*

Twenty minutes later, the two men were parking in front of the project's rec center. Marc had called Anne during the drive to tell her about his blood sugar tests results.

"What?" she said, "You'd better get yourself to the emergency room right now and get a shot!"

He told her he'd ask Linda to give him a shot after the opening. "I have to be there for that. They expect me to make a short speech."

"I'll make the speech for you. I've heard it often enough. Or, Phillip can. He can ad lib something. Nobody's going to care. You may not make it through the speech. You've been dizzy already. Please go to the emergency room."

"The people want to see the big man make the speech. I'm it. But, I'll take care of it, Anne. I promise."

She knew what that meant. He'd do it after the opening for which she was getting dressed to attend. She hoped she wasn't going to be drafted into making the speech.

To try and assuage his hunger, Marc had a candy bar before he got out of his tan, two- door Jeep with a soft top and roll bars. It also had lifters to raise it up for off-road use.

Marc liked the rugged feel and look of it when he drove out to a job site. He also felt it gave him a psychological edge over the construction crew to appear man enough to "whip their asses" if they crossed him.

Even though he and his wife, Linda, owned a new Audi, Phillip drove an old white Toyota truck they'd picked up from one of the companies they'd taken over. It had been outfitted for field use and had a metal frame on the truck bed for ladders and other construction gear.

The factory bumpers had been replaced by bumpers outfitted with heavy duty metal extenders, showing rust, to allow the truck, like Marc's Jeep, to be driven through brush on job sites without damaging the grill or headlights. Phillip liked it for the same reason Marc liked his Jeep, it made him feel rugged.

Marc chided him about parking the thing in public and made him park it where the subs and maintenance workers parked. The development also had a road for the subs and others so their old cars would not offend the wealthy looking to buy.

Marc thought, Damn, I am too damn tired to be playing. He felt a little dizzy as he glanced at his financial officer sliding out of his truck in the adjacent slot. Phillip waved his racquet at Marc and grinned.

"Out back," Marc shouted pointing at the truck. Phillip cursed but did as Marc requested.

Phillip smells blood. I'll give him some. His. He grabbed a bottle of water off the seat, finished it and waited for Phillip to return.

Marc paused for a look around the parking lot and the project beyond. He'd seen it before, but the flowering trees and shrubs, were still overwhelming. The March weather came with a soft breeze that felt warm on his face and brought with it the scent of the blossoms that surrounded them. Blooms, white and pink, danced in the wind like they were out for a frolic.

Damn, he thought, what we don't sell today will be twenty percent higher next week. That'll hold in the early buyers and stampede the timid to buy before the prices go up again. If we go to auction, we'll clean up.

In the distance, he saw brokers and agents chatting with lookers as they strolled from model to model in the complex. Sign 'em up. He also noted the security guards patrolling, some in uniforms, some in regular clothes. Phillip had doubled the number after somebody had turned the water on while the company was re-grading the building sites.

A big bluff had crumbled. A Caterpillar grader was ruined and a patrolling security guard severely injured by the mudslide. He and Marc figured it was the guy they'd kicked out, looking for revenge, but didn't discount the possibility that one of their subs had accidentally left the water on.

Marc looked up to see Phillip waiting by the clubhouse door, waving his racquet. "Let's play!" he shouted. "Quit stalling, old man."

Marc shook his head. Tired as I am, I have to beat his ass or I'll never hear the end of it.

They'd play on one of the tournament courts with glass walls and bleachers for spectators. Players often found the walls disconcerting initially, but they soon got used to them and were so focused on the ball they barely noticed those watching.

Marc's game plan was to go for quick kill shots to preserve his energy. His favorite shot, he had told Anne, was a drive serve down the middle caressed with an "almost" hinder. After crushing the ball against the front wall, he'd hesitate a split second before moving to let Phillip see the ball on the backhand side. It got him every time, at least three points a game. From the looks on his face, Marc knew Phillip wanted to call a hinder after the shots but wasn't quite certain enough to do it. If it had been a tournament game, Marc was certain most would have been called for the hinders and that would have resulted in a fault and a service change. But, playing like they did, it was cutthroat racquetball, where almost anything went.

They flipped a coin and Marc won. At first, he served to Phillip's backhand, a drive that came off the front wall, sometimes with a spin carom off a side wall, but sometimes he hit it hard and flat, maybe an inch off the floor. When he saw Phillip began to favor his backhand, he switched to the forehand. He won the first seven points before faulting and felt good. He hadn't had to use that much energy.

Phillip served high, defensive serves that looped high and dropped just in front of the back wall, forcing Marc to move. When Marc was near the back wall, Phillip dropped return shots just off the front wall so Marc had to work hard to cover.. He won 3 points before Marc drove a forehand past a diving Phillip. Soon the score was 10-6. Marc served the score to 14. Phillip, playing his "energy" game, got it to 14-8 before Marc finished it.

"Nothing's changed," Marc said. "I need to shower and get dressed for the opening." He glanced at his watch.

"Hell, we have over an hour. I didn't know you were a quitter," Phillip said.

"I had a long night, if you know what I mean," Marc said with a sly smile.

"Whose wife was it?" Phillip asked also with a sly grin.

"Ha. My own," he said.

"Must have been a slow week, having to sleep with your own wife."

"It happens."

"A hundred says I can take you in the next game," Phillip said slicing the air with his racquet.

Marc shook his head. He already felt about to drop.

"Maybe you want to default, give up," Phillip goaded him. "Hell, I understand. I won't tell a soul. Not many anyway!"

"Just everybody in town," Marc said. Hell, I can't let the little shit claim I chickened out. Probably give interviews to The Tribune. If he wasn't so damn good at what he does, I'd fire his ass. He sighed. "Okay. I'll take your hundred."

They played a second game. This time, it was Phillip doing the hard driving, spin serves, spin returns, drop shots and lobs, even an occasional hinder that Marc wanted to call but didn't. As hard as Marc tried, he couldn't overcome his fatigue and Phillip won 15-14.

"More like it," Phillip crowed. "The beginning of the end for you, old buddy."

"Bullshit," Marc said. "You caught me on a bad day and still only won by one fucking point. Not much of an end."

"Okay. Let's double down and play for the match," Phillip said, bouncing his racquet off the palm of his free hand.

Shit. I don't think I can stand, let alone play. But, there was no doubt he had to play the third game. He went outside for a big cup of water, came back and said, "Get ready for an old fashioned ass whippin'," he said. Now, I just have to figure out how to do it.

It was his serve. He took the pace off his first serves, causing Phillip to come in and hit high returns off the front wall. Marc would catch the ball in the air and drive it past him for a winner. He went ahead by three. Phillip then served and hit hard, drive serves that Marc was too tired to do much with and Phillip quickly converted to five points. Service changed a couple of times with neither scoring. Then, Marc used his hinder ploy for two points to tie the game.

Though he was dead on his feet, he scraped and returned almost everything Phillip threw at him. The score reached 10-10 and Marc was serving. He staggered into the service box, felt dizzy, even had to bend over to catch his breath before serving. The last was a bit of showmanship to lull Phillip into overconfidence. He hit his serve, with all the energy he could muster. It stayed an inch off the floor before bouncing in front of the back wall. He hoped it'd be a winner.

It wasn't. Phillip anticipated the shot and was waiting for it. He ripped it back, still just barely clearing the floor, against a side wall an inch off the front wall corner. The ball came off with a spin. Marc hesitated then stumbled to his knees with his back to the ball which was headed down his backhand side.

Phillip smiled and relaxed. Got you!

But, as the ball was about to pass Marc, who had always had great peripheral vision, stuck out his racquet. The ball hit it and softly bounced off the front wall for a winner before Phillip could recover.

"Son of a bitch!" Phillip shouted. "I don't believe it. You lucky bastard!"

Marc stood and forced a grin. "Not luck. Smarts. That's why I'm the boss. Didn't know about that shot did you? Good game Phillip, tired as I was, but not good enough. You owe me two hundred." His face had the pale look of a ghost.

Phillip grunted with a dismissive shake of his head. "Let's get dressed for the opening."

## CHAPTER 2

They walked into a clubhouse alive with dozens of engaging conversations spiced with laughter, signs that people were enjoying themselves. The women, all wealthy and looking like it, wore their best. Most were relatively young; second or third marriages for the men who'd brought them. The men, the ones with the money and their young wives, were dressed more casually. They had nothing to prove. They had the money.

Food from the best caterers in La Jolla was being spread on the long, white linen covered tables beside the clubhouse windows. Men and women servers strolled about with trays of champagne. A minibar had been set up near the food table for those interested in something a little stronger. A uniformed man stood behind the bar, showing lots of teeth and taking orders.

Marc waved at the mayor who was there with his latest. Thirty if a day. Blond hair from a hairdresser. Perfect shape, tits that probably set her back a bundle but they paid off with marriage to a politician with upward potential.

Also present were other politicians including a prominent state senator, glad-handing and smiling, trolling for contributions and votes. Marc wished his mother could have attended but the staff at the nursing home where she lived didn't think she was up to it.

He saw Derek, Anne's younger brother, lobbying one of the female brokers for a romp in bed, he figured. He didn't like the man and the feeling was mutual. He was blond and trim with muscles that showed he spent time in the gym. Women considered him "pretty" as opposed to handsome and fawned over him. He never had trouble finding one to take to bed. Forty and still surfing. Shit!

Marc had hired him, at Anne's request, as a marketing coordinator. His job, on Monday mornings was to report on the traffic – visitors looking to buy – they'd had over the weekend at all their projects, and especially all sales made. The report went to the lender.

Derek made sure advertisements got in all the newspapers, all billboard ads were timely placed and all marketing brochures delivered to the projects in time for the weekend open houses. That took no more that 15 or so hours a week even though he was on full salary. That left plenty of time for surfing, pumping iron and getting into bed with women.

Pushing Marc to the limits of his patience, he resisted "sitting a project" when someone was out. Sitting a project meant being behind a desk in the model complex on weekends to answer questions and hand out brochures.

"Too boring," he said. But, what really pissed Marc off was Derek's pathological need – as Marc described it – to sleep with every woman he met. And, if that wasn't bad enough, he'd knocked up one of the office girls. The company had to pay for her abortion and give her ten thousand dollars to forget it happened.

Marc had begun riding the man, pushing him to leave voluntarily. He watched the man walk the reluctant young broker into the back room.

He put Derek out of his thoughts and tried to do the same for the threat from the lender telling him to get ready for the end. It was not a time to let his angry thoughts show. This is a money event. The people expect me to be a happy camper.

Great scents, Marc thought, picking up the blend of perfume fragrances drifting about the room from the assembled ladies. Probably cost a fortune. The food smelled good too. He knew that cost a small fortune, but he'd get that back with sales if he could figure out how to hang on long enough. And, he wasn't sure he could.

Newspapers had sent photographers. Two guys also walked around with video cameras, taking pictures and asking questions. Television, Marc figured. Probably Phillip's doings. Should have been Derek's. But, he was pleased to see them. If not for this project, the next. If there's going to be a next, he thought.

He didn't see Parsons, the lender's man. Maybe he's not going to show.

The pressure from the lender had started him thinking about taking on more clients. But, he asked himself, are there any clients with problems these days? During boom times, all projects sold, even bad ones. No defaults and no need for workout companies; no need for him.

Phillip had drifted off to the side to be with his wife, Linda. Marc took notice of the younger woman's light brown hair, styled to perfection, her brown eyes and angelic, innocent face, always with a smile that he found intoxicating every time he saw her.

His wife looked great in an off-white sheath dress with embroidered flowers, a shade darker, that fit her like a glove.

Phillip is a wizard with numbers but he doesn't know shit from Shinola about women, especially his wife.

How in the hell can I get her away from Phillip long enough to give me the shot she said I needed? I'll call her after I make my little speech. Son of a bitch! I might pass out before I get through the damn thing. It's going to be short.

His eyes found Anne smiling and visiting with a group of prominent ladies whose faces he recognized. The names of the ladies she'd been with were always in the La Jolla Light supporting one cause or another. He knew Anne wasn't comfortable working the crowd, but he'd asked her to come and she agreed. Working a crowd was his forte. He felt at home surrounded by people and enjoyed knowing he was their equal and then some.

In keeping with her position as wife of the developer, Anne wore a fashionable gray suit and had had her hair styled at an exclusive hair salon. Looks like a million dollars, Marc thought. She makes me look better.

She had kept her figure over the years unlike a few of the older women in the room.

He wished he'd been more faithful, but the temptations were too many to resist, not that he tried too hard. For a fleeting moment, he wondered why. She has to be the most beautiful woman I've ever known. Why is it I don't feel completely comfortable with her? Why? He had a thought. The thought came with the face of his mother.

Damn, is it Anne's lack of warmth? I bet it is. Mom was always so warm and caring. Anne is just beautiful and wants to be told that every day. Ah, hell, maybe I'm just rationalizing to cover my dicking around.

He hurried over for a quick hug and kiss on the cheek. He pulled her aside for a quick talk. He told her he was going to leave after he addressed the attendees and called Linda for a shot.

"You should have done it already, Marc."

He agreed. "But, I didn't."

"Too damn stubborn. One of these days it's going to cost you," she said.

"Hopefully, not today. I'll get it as soon as I can get out of here." He was wrong on both.

He stepped away to speak to people waiting to say hello and to shake his hand. Most told him the same thing. "The La Jolla Apogée will set the standard for La Jolla developments for a long time to come. Congratulations!"

Marc agreed, but in his appreciative role – his name for it – he gave all the credit to people like whoever was giving him the compliment.

The guy representing the marketing company managing the sale of the La Jolla project headed for the mic at the front of the room when he saw Marc come in. He checked to see if the mic was working, caught Marc's eye and motioned him to the front. The man, Terry Wakefield, was about 5'6", about fifty pounds overweight from too many business lunches and too few workouts. He tapped the mic loudly to get everyone's attention.

Marc acknowledged Wakefield with a wave and smile and moved in that direction, letting his eyes search the room. Still no Parsons. He caught the eyes of two female real estate agents and smiled at them. They smiled back.

His visual sweep found Sarah Webster. She was wearing a captivating, rust-colored suit and floral blouse and standing beside her father, Ben Holliday, a huge man, over six feet tall but with a girth that put pressure on his belt. He was conservatively dressed in banker blue.

Sarah's suit complimented her brown hair and dark brown eyes. Her smiling, slightly oval, face brought a smile to his. Nobody is better in bed or more beautiful, he thought, well, Anne is, but ….

Sarah had a quiet confidence about her that he could not resist. And, when they were together, she showed a sensitivity and innocence that swept over him in a way he couldn't describe. He'd slept with her many times and enjoyed them all. If he weren't happily married, he'd marry Sarah in a blink. She was thirty-five, just the age he liked.

She managed the branch that made the construction and development loan for the Apogée project. Actually, it was her father who approved the loan. He was the director and major stockholder of the half a dozen or so banks in the California group. People called him "Banker Ben."

Marc knew old Ben didn't like him, but he couldn't refuse his daughter's recommendation. And, it had been a good one. Two alpha males butting heads, Marc thought, or maybe Sarah told him we were sleeping together and that pissed him off.

"Ladies and gentlemen," Wakefield said. "I thank you for coming to the grand opening of the La Jolla Apogée, the jewel in La Jolla's crown!"

He paused for applause.

Repeating what he'd been hearing, he added, "This development has set a high mark for all luxury developments in the future. And the man responsible for that is standing right beside me, Marc Flint!" He motioned Marc to the mic.

Marc stepped toward the mic, almost stumbling in the process. He chuckled, grabbed the mic stand and said, "The enthusiasm of the gathering has intoxicated me." He flashed his money smile and let his eyes catch the eyes of the guests in the room. He held his arms out then raised them high.

His smile broadened. "Mille fois merci, mesdames … messieurs. I thank you all a thousand times for your support and your interest in this development. Your encouraging words and best wishes kept us going through some difficult periods."

The guests responded with loud applause.

None of what he said was true, but he liked to pull people in, make 'em feel like they were part of what he was doing. Bond with them. He told Phillip that in an effort to get him to broaden his conversational horizons. It never worked.

Well, he told himself, I didn't hire him to be a people's man. That's my job.

He went on to say a few words about how the project had begun. Before he took over, earthmovers were poised to flatten hills and fill valleys to increase yields. "My vision was to keep the land in its natural state and build on it the way it was. And, I don't mind saying that I've never been more pleased with that decision!" He waved again over the crowd which had begun to look ever more blurry.

More applause.

The young broker Derek had taken out of the room re-appeared in the doorway, straightening her vest and looking a bit flustered. She merged into the crowd and joined the applause. Derek followed her in but immediately eased out the side door to where the musicians were getting ready to perform.

When the applause died down, Marc glanced about the room with a new smile. As he did, a man in back, wearing a worn suede coat with leather elbow patches, jeans and work shoes, pushed forward with his raised right hand in a fist and shouted, "You stole the project, Flint. Pure and simple. Cheated people out of their money ... what they had coming to them. May you end up in hell! I'd love to be the one to send you there!" He stormed out before the security guards could throw him out.

The speaker was Max Larson, the developer whose company had begun the project. Marc had taken over at the lender's request when the project stalled. All Larson's fault, Marc had said. The man had no taste.

Marc had spotted him during his first canvas of the crowd. Two money partners were by his side. Larson looked as tough as his reputation made him out to be, but he also appeared tired and weary. He'd been known to attack building inspectors who complained about something he was doing or should be doing in a project. His partners looked like they had become accustomed to the kind of life lots of money brought. Apparently they hadn't brought their wives or girlfriends, Marc had noted.

After taking the company's stock, and the property that came with it, Marc negotiated with the subs and suppliers that were owed money; got them all to settle for a few cents on the dollar.

Of course, the developer and his partners lost everything they had invested in the project and had a right to be pissed. Marc gave the man that. But, a fool and his money are soon parted, he thought, remembering something his mother had told him.

Larson had gone about the project all wrong, Marc thought. He planned it like it was a VA, FHA project for the masses, not the highly profitable luxury development it should have been, not the La Jolla Apogée it became. I don't mind a bit getting all the off-sites and street into the project for nothing.

He was thinking about the utilities, sewer, water, electrical, telephone and cable Larson had added to the project and paid for. It amounted to millions Marc didn't have to spend.

VA/FHA projects were considered low income housing because the loans were guaranteed by a government agency and required little or no down payment. There were also other advantages that made VA/FHA housing attractive to buyers, reducing monthly payments. Projects built in La Jolla didn't need VA/FHA backing.

Marc watched Larson stalk out the door. "I recall something from an old Clint Eastwood movie," he told the crowd. "A man's gotta know his limitations. Max Larson didn't. That's why he lost the project. Some people never face up to their shortcomings."

The man's financial backers stayed for the champagne and food and to exchange gossip with people they knew.

He thanked Sarah and her father for their financial support; singled them out for a round of applause from the crowd. Sarah's face turned pink but her father, taking it all in stride, briefly stepped into the opening, gave a subdued smile and an equally subdued wave.

Marc was pleased to have pulled her father into the project like he had and was pleased to get Sarah's response. As far as he was concerned, she only blushed because she loved him.

"I'll quit now," he said, "and let you all enjoy the rest of the festivities. Food, entertainment on the patio." He gestured to the group setting up to play outside, then toward the buffet table along the windowed wall.

He left to loud applause, hoping he wouldn't stumble and fall or pass out. He had to call Linda for that shot. She said I could die. I think she was right. Right now, I feel so bad, I'd have to get better to die. He was feeling dizzy already.

Linda was standing beside Phillip. Marc stared in her direction hoping she'd look his way. She didn't. Instead, Phillip was talking on his phone and she was watching him. He said something to her, and headed toward the door Derek had just taken.

Probably some last minute glitch Derek messed up. No matter, he'd call her from the Jeep and began walking toward the door. Damn. He stopped and spoke to some people between him and the door. He smiled and shook their hands.

After Ben Holliday had completed his moment in the sun, a moment he neither wanted nor needed, he looked at Sarah tenderly and asked softly, "Are you still seeing that son of a bitch? He's little more than a used car salesman. I can't stand the man, playing to the crowd like that."

Then, as if a thought had just then streaked through his consciousness, he pointed toward her and said, "You know, don't you, that your iniquities have separated you from God. Your sin has caused Him to hide His face from you. He will not hear your prayers, Sarah. You will go to hell."

Sarah turned a shade red and answered, "I love him, Dad. I don't believe God would turn His back on love. And He would never turn His back on an innocent child."

"How do you know Flint gives a damn about you? All he wanted was the construction loan. He'd make love to a tarantula if he needed spider eggs."

"Be fair, Dad. I don't think the loan was a mistake, do you?" She gestured at the crowd. "They have reservations for all the units and the lots. Marc says they may hold an auction. That'll bump the prices up even more."

"Hmpt. Lucky. Hell, I could sell doghouses in La Jolla for a million."

"Come on Dad! Don't be a grump. It's a great project."

With a shake of his head, he concurred and asked, "What about the take-outs?" He was asking about mortgage financing for the buyers. Holliday's bank had issued a letter indicating their interest in making loans to the buyers.

Sarah frowned and said, "I'm not sure. Marc was talking about putting the mortgages in an investment package and selling interests in the package to investors. They'd participate in the interest collected on the mortgages."

"That crooked son of a bitch. He'll do anything for a buck." He brushed a strand of gray hair off his forehead and added. "I have to give the bastard credit for that idea though. That's a damn good plan. Hell, I might be interested in picking up a piece of that investment myself. La Jolla mortgages are as good as gold."

"He has investment bankers putting the vehicle together. They already have enough subscriptions to take us out."

"Probably female investment bankers," her father speculated with more than a trace of sarcasm in his voice.

Sarah laughed. "Only three."

"Probably sleeping with every damn one," he said. "One of these days, somebody's gonna kill the son of a bitch. Hell, if I had a clean shot, I'd do it myself."

A guy strolling past, heard the remark and laughed. "I heard that Ben. You'll have to stand in line."

Ben slapped the guy's shoulder and laughed.

He looked at Sarah without speaking and then asked, tenderly, "Does the philandering bastard know you had his baby?"

"I didn't tell him. I knew he would never leave his wife. He told me that the ... well, up front. He loves me though. I can tell. I told him I was taking a leave of absence from the bank to take care of mom ... get her into a home that could better look after her."

"Your poor mother. I'm glad she's not here. It would have broken her heart." His wife had passed away some years back.

"Maybe not, Dad, but this is a new age culture and Mom was fairly progressive."

Her dad looked away and wiped away a tear. "Yes. She was. I miss her. She's with the Lord now."

She nodded. "I miss her too."

"Should have adopted it out, but it's a beautiful baby. Almost two now, you're going to have to tell Flint sooner or later."

"I know and I will. Right now, I'm just enjoying the heck out of my boy. Every day. He's my joy, Dad. I named him Marcus."

Her dad cursed.

"Your name's in the middle," she said with a smile and nudged him with her hand. "Benjamin. It has a nice ring, don't you think? Marcus Benjamin Webster."

"It would ring a hell of a lot better if you were married."

"I tried that once. All I got out of it was a new name."

"What do you think an illegitimate baby's going to do to your chances to marry somebody decent? Who's going to marry you with an illegitimate baby?"

"Somebody who loves me, Dad."

He cursed under his breath.

"By the way, changing the subject, I'm buying one of Marc's condos, one with a great view."

"What! Why the hell are you doing that? You have a great condo in Banker's Hill!" Banker's Hill was considered a desirable area near downtown San Diego.

"And, I'm keeping it as an investment. I thank you for helping me get it. And," She smiled and playfully touched her finger to his coat. "I'm getting this one at a discount. Eight hundred thousand as opposed to the list price of one million."

Her father's mouth dropped open. "Hell, he must love you. I'd buy two at that price." He owned a unit in the Seville, one of the more prestigious developments in La Jolla. He owned another home, a townhouse, near downtown in the Banker's Hill community. He and his wife had lived there during her last years. He bought the unit in the Seville after she'd died in an effort to escape her memory.

If he had bank business downtown, he stayed in the Banker's Hill townhouse. He smiled and added, "He'll get a surprise if he shows up and finds little Marcus Benjamin Webster running around."

She laughed. "I imagine he will. Right now, I have a sitter taking care of that."

He looked at his cellphone to check the time. "Well, on that note, I'm taking my leave. I have plenty of food in my fridge." He left out the side door.

\* \* \* \*

Outside, Marc turned to see if anybody had followed and noticed his wobbly weave along the sidewalk. No one had. He figured Anne would have to stay awhile longer before she could break away. This was the biggest opening he'd had since he'd been in business and the only one she'd attended. Wakefield had had handled the others.

He mumbled to himself. "Have to get that shot of whatever Linda said ... insulin?"

He got into his car and punched in Linda's number. It rang a number of times before a voice came on and asked him to leave a message. He did.

"Son of a bitch! Her damn phone is off. I'll drive home and lie down. Maybe I'll go to the office instead. She can come there. Probably easier."

He managed to get the Jeep out of the lot without hitting any of the parked cars. He felt light-headed and ready to pass out but forced himself to concentrate. "Five minutes," he said. "Five minutes and I can lay down. I can do that."

\* \* \* \*

The police found his Jeep upside down at the bottom of a ravine along the coast, a few minutes from his office. He was dead.

At first, it was thought that he'd had too much to drink and passed out but no one at the opening had seen him drink more than a few sips of champagne. That prompted a full blown autopsy which revealed that he'd probably suffered a diabetic seizure and lost control of the Jeep which tumbled down the embankment. The consensus was that he was likely dead before it left the road.

His funeral was attended by his wife, Anne, his daughter Cynthia, her husband and their daughter, Phillip Marshall and his wife Linda, Terry Wakefield, the real estate broker who handled sales for his company and Sarah Webster. She didn't bring the baby.

The funeral was reported in the La Jolla Light as being well attended. Someone was overheard saying the report was accurate except for one word: well.

Cynthia and her family stayed on for a few days to be with her mother.

# CHAPTER 3

Bishop Bone sat in a rattan chair on his screened-in back porch drinking an afternoon beer and watching the beavers work in their pond on the other side of Indian Creek that flowed past his backyard. It was April and the mosquitos were getting active but the screen kept them out. Otherwise, the temperature was just right, one of the best seasons in south Mississippi.

For his afternoon exercise, he'd dragged his old wooden boat into the creek and rowed across to jog three times around the pond before returning to his reward, a glass of cold beer. Ordinarily, he played tennis with Seth Campbell, a shopping center developer, and his granddaughter Sonja. They always knew somebody they could call for a fourth. But, it wasn't a tennis day so he had to fall back on a jog around the beaver pond for his exercise. Sometimes he cut his grass or cleaned brush from around the larger trees on his land.

He owned twenty-two acres and an old log cabin on stilts overlooking Indian Creek. The stilts were insurance against the so called 100 year-flood which hadn't happened since he'd been there.

The creek almost divided the property into equal parts. On the far side of the creek, the beavers had built a dam across a small branch that fed into the creek to create a pond for their stick-mud mounds that poked up here and there from the pond's surface. The interstate marked one boundary of his property, a waterfall down the creek marked the other. He had bought it after arriving in Lawton, an old lumber town, and had never considered leaving.

Before coming to Lawton, he'd consulted with banks about their bad loans and properties, mostly commercial, in California. He was a lawyer and doing very well until one day he got blindsided in Los Angeles by a crooked borrower and a bank manager the borrower had bought with a few two martini lunches and a couple of five minute rounds with an expensive hooker. The borrower claimed Bone had agreed, on behalf of the bank client, to accept a lowball offer to settle their dispute. In exchange, Bone was to get an under the table payoff.

The bank manager backed the borrower and after a long litigation which Bone lost, he left California in disgrace, no wife, no legal practice and no way to start a new one. He ended up working for Seth after rescuing Sonja from an assault by two thugs in a rough bar where Bone went now and then for a late night beer. She'd been dumped there by her boyfriend at the time, after an argument. That rescue got Bone a job working in Seth's campaign for governor, a campaign he lost. But, Bone observed, his heart was never in it anyway.

Seth's business at that time was building factory outlet centers all over the south. However, that business had more or less dried up so he returned to his beginnings, building commercial buildings, some on spec, some on contract. It didn't much matter if he worked or not since he'd inherited a ton of money from his family, timber and oil, but he had too much energy to do nothing.

Bone, in his early sixties, stood a shade over six feet, with almost no flab, a consequence of staying in good shape. His face was rough and showed the beginnings of age lines. He had light brown hair that was showing some gray here and there and a thinning spot at the back. He only shaved when he was seeing Kathy, his very close friend – to say the least – and when he was handling an assignment from a bank.

Thanks to one of Seth's friends, Rooster, Bone was able to develop bank contacts around the state and handled their field work, usually inspecting small businesses with bank loans, getting current financial statements and reporting on how they were doing and making recommendations when they weren't doing well as they should.

The work didn't make him rich, but that and other income from his later settlement with the crooked developer and bank officer gave him as much as he needed. Just having the conspiracy officially acknowledged meant more than the settlement anyway, but he had no notion about not taking it.

Their fraud had almost killed him. But, on the plus side, he ended up in Mississippi as a result and had taken to the kind of laid-back easy way of life Mississippians enjoyed.

In addition, his work for the Mississippi banks gave him a sense of satisfaction; handling negotiations, doing the documentation and exercising some creativity in solving the problems of the borrowers he came into contact with. He'd passed the Mississippi bar so he could represent himself as a lawyer and take cases when the need arose.

He glanced at his watch. Kathy had said she'd come out after she got her mother situated in front of the television for the evening. Her mother had been sick and needed help taking care of herself just then. But, Kathy wasn't due for another hour and had promised to bring food. He relaxed and took another drink of his beer. It was still early.

He'd met Kathy at the library which she managed. Instead of buying his reading material, he'd begun checking it out. They eventually talked and discovered they were mutually attracted. Like Bone, she'd been married before, for a short time. She lived in an old Queen Anne home with her mother in the better section of Lawton.

She drove up as the sun was disappearing on the back side of the beaver's pond and had cast an orange sheen over the pond waters. He went out front to greet her.

The front steps of his cabin were shadowed in twilight which gave her face an intriguing glow as she bounded up holding a bag containing a barbequed chicken and baked potatoes. The smell reached his nose before she got to the top.

"Smells good," he called to her.

She wore long jogging pants and a warm pullover that she filled in the right places. And, not an ounce of anything excessive showed. She kept in top shape, jogging practically every day. Though April was warming from the cold of February and March, she had dressed for the chilly night. She knew they always ended up on the porch.

Her lips flashed a smile as she saw him. It gave him a lift on the worst of days and sent him into a dream state on the best of them. He pulled her close, kissed her hard and enjoyed the fragrance that came from the embrace.

"I'm overjoyed every time I see you, Kathy. I love you, sweetheart."

"Thank you, Bishop. I love you too."

Her face was more round than narrow, but pretty and it didn't come with an ego, he liked to tell himself, like some did. She was a brunette with sparkling brown eyes. The beginnings of gray had lightened her hair just enough to add a kind of mysterious charm to her appearance. She was in her early fifties, some ten years younger than him.

She put the chicken and potatoes in the oven to warm while they sipped wine on the porch. Bishop had turned on his outside lights. The ones he'd anchored in the creek turned the water an emerald green and added a special kind of warmth to everything.

They watched the mosquitoes bounce off the porch screen as they tried to get inside for a bite. Her eyes caressed his face as if searching for something. She reached over and squeezed his hand.

"Mom's feeling better so I don't have to get home early." She smiled.

He kissed her again. He liked what she said.

\* \* \* \*

Over dinner, he told her about a call he'd received that afternoon from Anne Flint. "Her husband, Marcus Flint, a kind of real estate developer, just died. I didn't know him but I heard his name mentioned last time I was in La Jolla. Most people just called him Marc. Kind of a California custom to shorten a name. He took over companies in financial distress and worked out their problems."

Bishop had stayed in La Jolla with an ex-client while he finished negotiations with the people who had ruined him some years earlier. That was when he'd heard Flint's name mentioned. At that point, his visit was mostly about getting the last settlement check. They were stalling so he had gone out to make sure they paid it.

While he was there, he became involved in a murder case in La Jolla; two murders actually. Two women who had been part of an amateur musical group were killed and Bone ended up being asked to investigate one of the murders on behalf of his ex-client who was afraid the police would come after her. He ended up clearing her.

"I may have told you," he continued. "La Jolla is a wealthy enclave along the beach just north of San Diego, where the rich and famous live."

"I think you did tell me," she said, recalling what he had said about the musical soiree murders, his description of them.

He laughed. "Getting old," he said. "Telling my stories twice. Anyway, a banker I knew from the old days had called earlier to tell me the guy had died in a car crash. The guy worked for a lender in the east someplace, maybe Florida and had projects all over California. He said the guy was extremely bright but equally arrogant. He disguised his arrogance with such a charming persona that nobody noticed until it was too late to get back what he had taken from them. Well, what he'd talked them out of. "

"Don't tell me his wife called to ask you to take over for him or something," Kathy said.

Bishop laughed. "Not likely. No, but the banker had talked to the widow, Anne, after the funeral. She asked him about having someone write her husband's memoirs."

She laughed. "Not you."

He twisted his head with a grin. "'Fraid so. As you know, I was involved in real estate work when I practiced out there. The banker knew I had worked construction and developments problems and wrote reports. Lots of legal work comes out of sick real estate projects. Banks, borrowers, subcontractors and suppliers, not to mention buyers, all fighting it out and all needing lawyers. That's how I got to know the banker. He had called me in a few times when things at his end got hot.

He told her what I had done for him and what he knew about me. That's why I got the call from her."

"She wants you to come out there?"

"That's what she said. She offered a fee of ten thousand, more if I wanted more. Evidently, her husband had left her reasonably well off," Bishop said.

"Wow! Ten thousand! What'd you tell her?" she asked.

"I told her I'd have to talk to you first. So, I'm talking."

"Do you want to do it?" she asked.

"I have to say it's an inviting proposition. Yes, I think I do," he told her.

"How long will it take, do you think? I'll miss you."

"That's the problem. I like my life with you here. But, now and then, I think of the old days, shouting across the table at attorneys and borrowers. But, I figure no more than a couple of weeks, maybe three, to do the investigation. Then I'll come home to do the writing. If necessary, I'll fly back later," he explained.

"Well, do it. I guess I can stand two weeks or so. Mom wants to go to New Orleans for a few days when she's able. I could use the time to do that."

She gave Bishop a sly smile and said, "However, I don't want you being taken in by some wealthy California woman, looking for a replacement."

"That's why I told her I had to discuss it with you first. To let her know I was happy with my situation here."

With that assurance, she gave her approval. He would call Anne Flint the next morning.

"You can read what I write," he told Kathy. "Flint was apparently a tremendous success story. Built a huge house perched on the side of a cliff in La Jolla, overlooking the surf in La Jolla Shores. It should make an interesting read."

She'd be delighted.

He promised to call every day, but in consideration of the time difference, he'd call in the mornings after he got up.

They enjoyed the dinner she'd brought. He provided the wine.

Mendelssohn's Violin Concerto in E Minor played through his outside speakers during dinner. Bishop had installed speakers in some of the trees at the edge of the woods so the music surrounded his cabin. Afterward, he left it on to compete with the chorus of nature coming from the woods while they enjoyed the last of their wine on the back porch.

He finished the projects he had undertaken and notified his bank clients that he'd be out of town for a couple of weeks. They had his cellphone in case of emergencies. He was in La Jolla four days later.

\* \* \* \*

He rang the bell at the massive front door of the Flint's impressive home. Even from the street, he could see the whitewater surf rolling over the sandy beach of the La Jolla Shores Mata Park far below. Surfers were out in force, paddling out and catching the waves back in.

The home, connected to the sidewalk by an eight-foot-wide walkway, was contemporary in style; lots of glass with a structurally curved roof line about sixteen feet high at the highest point, maybe ten at the lowest.

"Bishop Bone," he said when Anne Flint opened the door. He had called from the airport to alert her that he was on his way. That was after he'd called Kathy to let her know he had landed.

Damn, he thought when he saw the beautiful woman standing in front of him. She was in her casuals, jogging shorts and a pullover shirt with tennis shoes. Her dishwater blond strands lay casually over her shoulder as if she hadn't had time to do anything about it. She wore no makeup, but didn't need any as far as he was concerned.

She has the natural beauty some women spend fortunes trying to imitate. Haughty beauty, he decided. From his experience, he'd come to believe that such women somehow knew they were beautiful when they were born and over the years acquired an arrogance that overlay the beauty.

He wondered to himself how a woman of her arrogance and beauty, and apparent intellect, had agreed to play second fiddle to a man like Flint, every bit as arrogant apparently, bright and appealing to women. That was part of what the banker had told him. He'd also said that Flint wasn't so much handsome as he was rugged. That made him attractive but probably the reason he had so much success with women was the power that came with his status as a developer.

Bishop agreed. He had noticed that over the years. Some women gravitated to men in power. Power seemed to turn them on.

Maybe there's another side to the proposition of an irresistible force meeting an immovable object. Instead of destruction, maybe something like a merger results. Well, that's not my problem and not why I'm here.

Her perfume didn't go unnoticed either. Bishop wasn't into names, but knew impact when it hit him and hers had impact. He'd had the same reaction the first time Kathy bounded up his steps for dinner.

"I'm Anne," she replied to complete the introductions.

They exchanged nods and the customary quick hug in the doorway. Thanks to the description from his banker associate, he knew about what she looked like. The man hadn't done her justice, he decided in a flash as he wondered how many men – ones expressing an interest – she'd killed with the contemptuous look he knew she must have.

Bishop also marveled to himself at how well Anne looked considering the recent loss of her husband. Though understandably, she did look a little stressed and tired. Based on what he'd been told, she was probably forty at least but could have easily gotten away with claiming thirty five. Hell, maybe thirty, he thought.

Looking through the house out the back, he could see that indeed, the home was anchored to a hillside overlooking the shores. The inside was a continuation of what he'd seen outside: glass, stone and metal, something home magazines would love to feature. Not a house Bishop would have picked for himself, but nevertheless still very impressive.

And the view was stunning, especially with the windows along the back wall framing the beach and the coastline down below. At her request, he moved his rented car into the large, three car garage. She gave him a garage-opener.

After he returned, she explained her house rules. "I usually go to bed around eleven. If you want to eat here – and, you're welcome to – let me know before you leave every morning. A lady comes in the afternoons to cook dinner. I'll probably stop that, but I don't know when. I did it for Marc. He had fixed ideas about what he wanted to eat." She punctuated that with a twist of her head.

"I show up in the kitchen around seven in the mornings, have coffee and a roll or whatever is handy and go downstairs and start my day unless I have some kind of social engagement. I try to keep those at a minimum."

"Me too. They eat time," Bishop said.

"Yes. I enjoy writing children's books. Tom Sawyer adventures with girl and boy characters. I snack for lunch."

"My banker friend told me you wrote. He said you are very good," Bishop told her.

"He may have embellished a bit, but I make a living for myself. Not big money, like Marc made, but enough to make me quit looking for tall buildings to jump off. Watching Marc go through a day and sometimes a night, working B.S. like only he could, made me think I needed to do something for myself. That's why I got into writing," Anne explained.

"I'd like to read them," Bishop said. "Leave a couple in the room. I loved Mark Twain's books when I was growing up."

She smiled. "I don't think my books compete with his or J.K. Rowling's but I get decent reviews and they're sold in bookstores." She smiled and added, "There's a bookcase in your room. My books are the only ones on the shelves. I don't encourage competition."

He chuckled.

"You're probably wondering why I don't write Marc's memoirs. Well, it's because I wanted somebody with a fresh perspective to do it. I was afraid I'd get bogged down by … feelings."

Bishop said he understood.

She showed him his room. Like all the rooms in the house, it had the surf view. Bishop was impressed and said as much.

"Marc built the house so every room would have the view ... and a bathroom," she said. After he dropped his bags, she gave him a strolling tour of the house, explaining as she walked.

At one room, she stopped to say, "My brother, Derek, moved in after Marc ..." She gave a nod of her head without finishing the sentence. "This is his room. He's at the office now. He was Marc's marketing manager. I needed his emotional support. He'll be home this afternoon. You can meet him then."

He was taken by the softness of her voice, the confidence and ease of her presentation. Like she has always lived a life without strife and conflicts.

He'd only met a few such people in his life. Most had to overcome something in their childhoods before they could get on with their lives. The "overcoming" often left noticeable scars.

The front of the house was attached to the edge of a rocky cliff and built on stilts anchored in the bedrock of the slope. There was no yard except for slope below the house where Marc had planted trees, all dwarfs so they wouldn't block the view. Most bloomed in the spring time; others at different times during the year.

"He loved nature," Anne said without emotion when she saw Bone taking it in.

Under the main floor of the house, was an exercise room and two offices, one for Marc and one for Anne. The exercise room came with a Jacuzzi. That level was accessible by stairs or a two person elevator.

She glanced at her watch – something expensive, Bishop noted from the jewels. She said, "Coffee ... or something stronger?"

It was almost noon in California so nothing was off the table. In some circles nothing ever was.

Bishop opted for coffee, black. She had one of those grind-to-order machines from Switzerland, two actually, one for regular and one for decaffeinated. He went with the regular. She had wine, a red. It suited her somber mood. They sat out back on a deep balcony shaded by a roof overhang.

"When do you want to start Marc's memoirs?" she asked, showing a faint smile. "And, what approach will you take?"

He gave her an overview. He'd interview as many people as he could who knew or had anything to do with him. After he'd finished those interviews and any follow-ups for things that usually cropped up later, he'd sit down and make an outline of what he wanted the history to show, the focus. He'd discuss that outline and anything else he felt was relevant with her before proceeding in case she wanted to call it off. Who knows what he'd find out? She might decide to bury his past with him, leave his legacy a mystery.

"So, let's start with you. Just tell me about him, about the both of you. How you met, that sort of thing," he said as he took a drink of coffee. "Good coffee, by the way."

She thanked him and stared out toward the Pacific as if in thought about what to say. Except for the faint smile she showed now and then, her facial expression never changed much.

Like a beautiful porcelain doll, Bishop thought.

Finally, she began the story. Marc had opened an office right out of law school and handled everything that walked in the door. She skipped to how they met and got married when he handled her parents' estate.

Along the way, he decided real estate was going to be the field with the most potential for income in the future, and the most challenging, so he took the time to get a master's degree in real estate and finance.

"I'll tell you a story about that," she said. "I thought it was kind of funny."

Marc had applied late to a prestigious law school for their fall term. When he went in for an interview, one he'd requested because he felt they were stalling for some reason, the lady told him that she didn't think his application would be approved. They were full up and had no seats left. And besides, she told him they had had exhausted their grant money.

His reply was priceless, Anne said, "Too bad, I was going to pay cash."

The school made room for him.

"The American way," Bishop said.

She explained how he connected with his Florida based client, the New Opportunity Bank, and moved from being an attorney into the business of cleaning up the messes some real estate developers had made of their projects. "Over the years, Marc had shortened the name to simply, the lender," she said.

Bishop got a real laugh when she told him how "God," the lender's chairman of the board, launched Marc's career into real estate, his new life, during a midnight meeting.

# CHAPTER 4

The lender's assignments to Marc of the shares of stock of the borrower companies in default made him the owner and led to him becoming a developer as he successfully cleaned up their problems and made them worth something. Then, when the economy turned around, he took advantage of it and made money.

"Marc had a deadly charm about him," Anne told Bishop. "He could get people to do things for him, especially the ladies."

Bishop nodded knowingly.

She looked Bishop in the eye and said, "I know he slept around, he told me about most of them but in some strange way I knew he loved me. Even so, I didn't like it. We sometimes had words about it."

He thought he saw a little fire in her eyes when she said that. Most likely understating her reaction. She was more than likely pissed, very pissed. A woman like her is not likely to take that kind of shit lightly.

Bishop mumbled agreeable words without adding judgmental comments or intonations. In reality, he didn't know enough about their relationship to comment, one way or the other. I doubt it'd work for me, but maybe I'm old world. Hmm, maybe just old.

She looked into her wine glass, pensively, then looked up and said, "I think there were a couple of women he didn't tell me about. One worried me, Sarah Webster, the bank manager he convinced to loan him money for the La Jolla project. Her branch is part of a chain of banks owned by her father, Ben Holliday. We invited them to the house for dinner a couple of times after the loan was approved. I wanted to see her. She was impressive. Still is. Has looks and intelligence."

Wanted to check out the competition, Bishop thought.

Holliday didn't try to hide his dislike of Marc, she told him. Anne thought it was equally obvious that Marc and Sarah did like each other. She couldn't keep her eyes off him, always smiling and laughing at everything he said.

"She was in love. That was clear. That's probably why he didn't include her name as one of the ones he slept with. He felt something for her. Another one he didn't tell me about was, well, is married. I may be wrong about her. I know her. I may tell you more about her later. I'm not sure I want her name in print however."

Anne said she warned Marc not to see Sarah socially again, translated to mean, don't sleep with her again. "He acted indignant, but I knew."

I bet she warned him. The woman was threatening her world.

She sighed and stared outside pensively for a second before continuing.

"At the opening," she said, "Holliday smiled and acted like he was all for the project. Marc introduced him … and Sarah, let the man say a few words. I think Holliday was putting on a show for the La Jolla crowd. Most of them probably bank at one of branches of his bank. However, as soon as Marc headed for the door, he did the same."

"I'd guess he would have been in favor of the project at that point. I understand that it was a great success," Bishop added.

"The La Jolla Apogée is going to be a big success but banks were reluctant to lend Marc money to get it going when he took over the project. Once a real estate project fails, it gets a bad reputation and lenders shy away. Marc went around Holliday's back, after Holliday had turned it down, and convinced Sarah to recommend the loan to the bank's loan committee. Holliday had to go along. That's probably why he didn't like Marc."

Anne talked a little bit about the impressive umbrella of banks Sarah's father had built over the years and how, even after Sarah had pushed the loan through, he had laid-off some of the loan to banks in the east to reduce his bank's exposure should the project fail, as he was certain it would. After Holliday saw the reservations for units, backed with money, he wished he had kept it all, Sarah had told Marc.

All the prominent people in La Jolla attended the opening, plus politicians, and some not-so-prominent came. Max Larson was on the list of the not-so-prominent. He wasn't invited; just showed up with his financial partners who probably were invited. She described Larson's outburst.

"Larson left before the security people could throw him out. Marc left right after he gave his little welcoming speech. He was feeling very shaky. Linda, Phillip's wife – she's a nurse – had called him with the results of his blood work. She told him he should get a shot of insulin. He was going to call her as soon as he got into his car. Unfortunately, she had turned her phone off for the opening and apparently he went into a coma before he could get reach her."

Not all the women he slept with were single, she told him, and now and then a husband would call or send a letter threatening to beat him up if he did it again. But, Marc was big enough to take care of himself and, he never backed away from a fight. Most of the time, the husbands did the backing away as did most of the tough developers whose companies he'd taken over.

"Some of them wanted to fight Mark," she said, "but he was only doing what the lender asked. I have to say, however, he loved every minute of every confrontation he had. God, he loved to scrap … and, I think, he loved for women to get dreamy-eyed when he smiled at them. He said he never did it for love. I'm not sure that's true - I told you about Sarah - but I believe one thing he said. He said, if he had to sleep with a woman to get something he needed, and there was no other way, he'd hop into bed in a minute and when it was over, he'd smile and tell her she was the absolute best. I accepted that."

"Sounds like a high energy man," Bishop said. Among other things. I think Anne took that country western song, "Stand by Your Man," to heart. Not many would have.

She nodded. "He … his mother told me – she's in a nursing home now, still lucid, but frail – that he'd always been competitive and never gave up on anything. He'd had a couple of things he had to overcome when he was young. Apparently nothing serious. But the boys bullied him and the girls ignored him. Once he got past that, whatever it was, he found a way to be everybody's friend. Personally, I've always thought he came up with his talent for charming people as a reaction to the bullying. Some kind of psychological compensation. Who knows? I'm not a shrink. Regardless of the reason, he has sure used it. He can … could … spread the BS on."

"Good observation. I'll use it if that's okay with you."

She didn't mind. In fact, it seemed to please her.

She gave him the name of the mother's nursing home. He'd never heard of it but made a note to remember it because he wanted to at least touch bases with the mother.

"Who's running the company now?" he was glad she was able to talk about her husband's death, even if inferentially.

"Phillip. He knows enough to do what's necessary right now. The company's being shut down. Not much to do. When he came in, he made the company's financial statement look like it was ready for listing on one of the stock exchanges. That made it possible for Marc to get loans to build projects out. Marc took Phillip's financials to the local banks and with his bullshit the bankers took their checkbooks and made him loans."

He could tell she was proud of her late husband even if he did fool around.

Could be, he thought, accepting her husband's infidelities was a better alternative than getting a divorce and starting over with somebody inferior to the one she had. Marc Flint sounds like he was one formidable son of a bitch.

"You said the company's being shut down. Has something happened?"

She shook her head, no. "I don't suppose you could know. The lender, Marc's client and source of real estate projects over the years, is in a friendly liquidation. A liquidation committee contacted Marc and asked for all the projects, every asset the company owns, to be transferred to a holding company for distribution to creditors of his lender-client, mostly other banks in their credit line. That was his agreement when he began taking on distressed projects."

Marc had first estimated that they'd have a year. That didn't turn out to be the case, Anne told him. A representative from the lender was at the opening and would be doing an audit of the company's books.

"That's the only thing holding up the transfer now," she said.

"Damn," Bishop said. "I can imagine that was a shock."

"It was. Marc's been stalling the process of course, hoping he could make contact with other banks or attract partners and stay in business. He enjoyed developing real estate. Every sick project he took over became a success. He had an instinct for it, I think."

"Sounds like it," Bishop stood. "Tell you what, I might as well get started. I'd like to take a look at where Marc's car went off the road, just to get into the story from where it began for me. I know a police detective in San Diego. I think she can get me into their storage yard for a look at the car. I'll want to describe it."

She wasn't up to showing him where Marc had crashed, but told him where it had taken place. He understood.

He turned to leave but stopped to say, "I'd like to invite you … and your brother, to dinner tonight. Barbarella's in the Shores. Say six o'clock? I try to get by there at least once when I'm in town. It's the best Italian restaurant around. Barbara makes it a point to go around and greet her customers during dinner. She adds a delightful ambience to the restaurant."

She hesitated and said, "Our cook is preparing a Middle Eastern dish tonight, lubi, bites of beef in a tomato sauce over rice. It's very good. But, listen, I'll call her. We can have the lubi tomorrow night. Getting out might snap me out of my depression. I'll let Derek know. He'll probably bring a date."

\* \* \* \*

Bishop easily found where Flint's Jeep had left the street and tumbled down the steep incline into a pile of rocks. The Jeep's passenger side front tire left black skid marks a car length or so along the curb.

Damn, looks like he tried his damnedest to keep it on the street. Poor bastard. I guess he died like he lived, fighting for what he wanted. In this case, it was for his life, he thought.

Bishop stumbled and slid his way down the slope following the path of the rolling Jeep from the curb to a pile of rocks where the Jeep eventually stopped. He figured, from the indentations the top of the Jeep made in the ground, that it rolled over four times before coming to a rest. Roll bars likely collapsed as it rolled.

Anne had said it was tan. Bishop's old Jeep was brown and no doubt much older.

The tumble most likely broke Flint's neck, Bishop thought.

He had Ellen Wasserman's number and wanted to call but decided to wait. She probably wasn't involved because it was an accident, but she might know something about it. They had worked together on the La Jolla murders he was drafted into the last time he was in La Jolla, the ones he'd told Kathy about.

\* \* \* \*

He decided to talk first to Flint's mother. He found her nursing home. As were most in La Jolla, it was expensive and looked it both from the outside and inside. Mothers knew more about their children than anyone else, even their spouses. He didn't call ahead but felt it wasn't required. Most seniors in such facilities welcomed visitors and company.

He found the prestigious building the nursing home occupied and parked in front. A female attendant in white took Bishop into their library where a frail lady with white hair sat in a chair reading. She introduced the lady as April.

Bishop told her his name and explained why he was there. "Do you mind if I ask you a few questions?"

Indeed, she seemed pleased that he'd was there, like a visit from an old friend. He guessed that most occupants of nursing homes felt abandoned and were just putting in the time until they had none left to put in.

He sat in the chair she'd offered and said, "I've just come from Marc's home. Anne and I had a long talk about him." He told her what Anne had said about Flint's accomplishments, embellished as much as he dared though there was not much he could add to Anne's recitation.

"He was a dear boy," April said and wiped tears from her eyes as she did. "If he saw something he wanted, he just reared up and went after it. He never let anything stand in his way. He always said that being told no just got his juices flowing."

She said he never got to know his father. He had died soon after Marc was born. "I was worried that might hurt his emotional development, but it didn't seem to. His emotional development made everybody stand back and watch." She laughed.

Bishop gave her a "sounds like him" retort.

He was going to ask what precipitated the bullying from the boys but she was already glossing over the period before he could.

"At that age, boys did anything they could to make themselves feel good at somebody else's expense. If they could make somebody else look bad, they figured that made them look better to the girls. He didn't have a father figure to tell him what to do. He took the bullying for a while. Never complained. But, by high school, he had grown big enough to take care of himself, even with them ganging up. Somewhere along the way, he reckoned he could talk anybody into anything ... or, maybe out of anything and didn't have to always fight. He had a talent for it. It just bloomed somehow. But, if talking didn't work, he didn't mind mixing it up."

Anne might have been right. Why fight if you can talk your way out of it?

They chatted awhile longer before someone came by and told her it was time for her medicine and to take a nap. One of the nurses walked with him to the door.

"She seemed glad to see me," he said.

The nurse smiled. "They love visitors. Most children dump 'em here and forget they exist."

"How about April? Does she get many visitors?"

"Her son, Marc and his wife, Anne, used to come by every week. I heard he died. That's too bad because she loved to see him. He was a nice-looking man, but that wife of his looked like a movie star to me."

"She is a beautiful woman."

The nurse agreed. "When Marc came by during the week, usually just a short visit, another man came with him. Phillip, I think was his name. I believe he worked for Marc. They usually didn't stay long. I could tell Phillip wasn't comfortable. He fidgeted the whole time they were here."

"I'll try to get by again," Bishop promised with a glance back at Flint's mother.

He drove back to Flint's home, wrote in his notebook, showered and got ready for dinner at Barbarella's. Anne appeared pleased to be getting out. She'd been more or less cooped up in the house since Flint's funeral.

During the drive to the restaurant, he told her what he'd been doing. He asked what would happen to Flint' mother. He asked subtly but was wondering who was going to pay. He assumed she would, but she had no legal obligation.

She told him that Marc had set up a trust fund to cover her expenses until her death. At that time the residue would revert to her.

* * * *

"Derek will be joining us. With a date," Anne told Bishop as the parked in front of the restaurant. He had driven her Tesla, at her request. He liked the way it drove. No way would he ever afford one, however.

He was glad Derek was joining them. He could ask him questions about Flint. That would save time later and he always welcomed the opportunity to do more than one thing at a time.

As they came closer, Bishop saw a tallish man in a blue blazer and off-white slacks, smiling and talking to a young, thin girl standing near the front of the restaurant. His hands touched her playfully as he talked. Derek, he figured.

The girl wore jeans, a pale blue sweater, had her hair pulled back in a kind of ponytail, looked half his age, was pretty and at least a foot shorter.

Boobs she's still paying credit card interest on, he decided as they got closer, but, they look good, especially without a bra.

He quickly made an assessment of Derek. Late thirties. Spends time in the gym, pumping weights. Not a line in his face. Sun-bleached blond hair laying where it was when he got up. Blond hair must run in the family. Probably considered gorgeous by women.

Derek's smile disappeared when he saw Bishop and Anne approach. Bishop noticed. Has to be me he wants to bite. Anne's hand is the one that feeds him.

Bishop stuck out his hand, "Bishop Bone. You must be Derek. Anne said you'd be joining us. Thank you."

Derek smiled faintly. "Yeah. Eating is one of the important things we have to do." He winked at the young girl by his side as if to say, that's not the only thing, however. She smiled.

"This is Evelyn, my good friend. We surf together. She clerks for a law firm. Goes to night school."

"Impressive," Bishop said. "Has to be hard."

It was, she told him and gave him a quick hug. Bishop gave one back with a friendly smile.

\* \* \* \*

Inside, they ordered drinks. Bishop ordered a mug of the house beer as did Evelyn. He'd remembered it from the last time he'd eaten there. He'd never tasted better. Derek and Anne ordered wine.

"So, you're going to write old Marc's memoirs." Derek said, looking at Bishop after a glance in Anne's direction.

He continued before Bishop could respond. "I hope you won't sugarcoat the son of a bitch's life. He was a hypocrite! I'm not sorry he's dead." He looked at Anne again.

"Sorry Anne but I have to say it. The bastard was trying to force me to quit. He humiliated me in front of everybody, every day I was there. Said I was a lazy bum!"

Anne looked into her wine glass as though it contained an answer but said nothing.

He turned his face toward Bishop and continued. "He accused me of getting some girl pregnant. I mean announced it in front of everybody. It wasn't mine! Hell, I've got better sense than that. If anybody's, it was his. Hell, his zipper stayed open. Excuse me, Evelyn... Anne."

Both women shook their heads as if agreeing, though Anne frowned as she did.

To try and take the edge off, Bishop though and forced a laugh. "I think I can safely write that you and Marc didn't get along."

"I think you can." He glanced at Anne and added, "Just say we had differing opinions."

Bishop nodded. He'd write what he had heard. That was how he saw his assignment. Anne could censor it. That was her job.

The waiter took their orders. Derek and his friend ordered something from the menu that Bishop called steak bites. He and Anne had the fettuccine, Bishop's favorite. It was always great.

For dinner, he went with the wine Anne selected. He felt it was a bit dry for his taste but he was no wine connoisseur and didn't want to get into a discussion that'd end up showing his ignorance. He drank it slowly and managed to get through dinner without a refill.

Most of the dinner discussion was about Flint. Bishop steered it that way. Evelyn, who'd never met the man, said very little but seemed to enjoy the food and drink. He mentally calculated her age at something less than thirty, maybe younger.

Derek found an opening and recounted the nasty look Marc had given him at the open house. "I could tell he didn't want me there. I was asking one of the brokers, a female, how sales were going. Probably one of his regulars, if you know what I mean."

Anne, apparently tired of hearing her husband being bad-mouthed by Derek, took over the conversation at that point and talked about the good things he'd done and his plans for the future once the lender's liquidation committee took everything back.

She said Marc had been arguing with the committee about an interest he'd carved out for himself in the mortgage fund he had set up for the La Jolla project. The lender wanted it. Marc said no but knew he didn't have much of an argument. His agreement with the lender's chairman of the board regarding projects he was given was broad enough to include everything of value linked to a real estate project he'd acquired.

Marc had told her he was using it as a negotiating wedge to get some other concessions. She figured the negotiations ended when Marc drove off the street. If they wanted the interest, they could have it.

"Any chance I can talk to anyone from the lender while I'm here? I'd rather not fly to Miami," Bishop said.

"Smart," Anne said. "Marc flew me down there one time. Once was enough. Phillip is the one you should talk to. He'll know when somebody will be in town. I'd be surprised if someone ... in fact, I know. The lender sent someone to the grand opening. He didn't show up until after Marc had gone. I'll call Phillip in the morning and tell him you'd like to drop in for a visit."

"Good," Bishop said. "I'll talk to Phillip as well."

Barbara, elegant as always in black, strolled by their table mid-dinner to ask if they were enjoying everything. Their compliments brought a smile to her face.

After dinner, Bishop and Anne drove home. Derek and his friend went someplace else. Bishop, joking to himself, assumed they had gone to do the other important thing Derek had alluded to earlier.

Anne offered drinks to end the day on the porch. She continued with wine. Bishop settled for his favorite, a glass of beer. They watched the cars along the streets below and could even see people strolling along the beach walk in Mata Park.

"Tell me about his diabetes," Bishop said. "The banker who recommended me said he'd just found out he had it."

She agreed. "He had. For a week or so, longer I guess, he'd been feeling tired, had lost weight and had had a couple of, what he called, dizzy spells. Even so, he'd been playing racquetball with Phillip and winning. It had gotten harder though, he told me."

"When did he know it was diabetes? Or did he?" Bishop asked.

"He only found out the day he ... died, I think. Phillip's wife, Linda, had tested his blood in the doctor's office where she worked. She told him his blood sugar reading was so high, he should see a doctor and get a shot of insulin. She figured it was diabetes. He called me and I told him he should go to the emergency room and get it treated right away.

Stubborn as he was, he wanted to wait until after the opening and call Linda for the insulin shot. He never made it."

"Too bad," Bishop said.

"It was. He said they were expecting him to make a speech. He didn't want to disappoint them and Phillip was nagging to play racquetball on their new courts. Marc tried to beg off the racquetball but Phillip wouldn't let him. He wanted his pound of flesh for all the beatings Marc had given him."

"I know the type," Bishop said. "Too bad he didn't call Linda."

"Right before he left the opening, he told me he tried, but Linda had apparently turned her phone off and didn't get his call until later."

"Damn," Bishop said. "He was that close to saving his life."

She nodded and looked away to dab at her tears. "Yes … that close."

They called it a night.

# CHAPTER 5

Bishop made notes of everything before getting into bed. Anne had left a laptop in his room. He'd later transcribe his notes onto a memory stick to take back to Mississippi for editing.

The phone rang as he was falling asleep.

"Who in the hell can that be?" He knew it wasn't Kathy unless some emergency had happened. It was past midnight in Mississippi.

"Hello," he said.

The muffled voice at the other end said, "You're no better than the bastard you're writing about. Don't get caught in my headlights." That was followed by a buzz as the caller hung up.

"What the hell?"

Somebody must have read the stories in the papers and have transferred their hate for Flint to me. So much for putting my number in the story for people to call with useful information about Flint.

He lay down but had a hard time getting back to sleep.

* * * *

He had a breakfast of coffee and roll and a view of the Pacific washing the beach on the La Jolla Shores. No one else was up.

Afterward, he called Ellen Wasserman, the black police detective he'd worked with the last time he was in California. At an ex-client's request, he'd gotten involved in two murders in the La Jolla Shores. The ex-client was afraid she might be charged and wanted Bishop to make sure she wasn't.

"Wasserman," the woman said, bluntly as if expecting a fight of some sort.

"Ellen," Bishop replied. "This is your old cornbread and turnip greens buddy from Mississippi. Oh, I forgot, pepper sauce on top of the greens."

"Bishop Bone! You old redneck son of a gun. Why the hell are you callin' me? Wait a minute. I bet you're out here because of that big shot developer who rolled his Jeep in La Jolla."

"I never told anybody you're weren't sharp as a tack, Ellen. I'm impressed!"

"I'll confess. I read his wife's interview in the La Jolla Light. She said she'd asked a Bishop Bone to write her husband's memoirs. The story got picked up by the Times and the Tribune. Hell, you got enough press to kick off a political campaign. That's gonna be a high profile assignment, old buddy, but hell, you never could keep a low profile."

Bishop laughed. "I always think I'm low profile until I hear the bullets whiz past my head." He told her about the phone call he'd received the last night.

"Count your blessings that you're hearing the reactions, not feeling 'em."

"You put things so succinctly, Ellen. This time I am low profile, though. I should be anyway. I'm not sure what the phone call was about. However, there are no murders and no suspects. Just collecting a fee for writing about the man. "

"Enough of your bullshit,. Bishop, What the hell do you want? If this is a social call, it'd be your first."

He laughed. "You got me, Ellen. I wanted to see Flint's Jeep. I assume it's still in one of your storage yards. I'll probably say something about it in my opening chapter. You know, how his brilliant life ended in a crumpled Jeep. May include a picture."

It was still around. Eventually, it'd be sold for scrap. Flint's wife had already given her release. She gave him the address and said she could meet him there about lunch time.

"Maybe we could grab a bite of lunch afterward," he said. "There's a place not far from there, Bread and Cie. Great soup and grilled cheese sandwich."

"I wasn't angling for lunch, Bishop Bone, but since you're insisting, sounds good to me."

After the call, he remembered the newspapers on a table in the bedroom and picked one up, the La Jolla Light, to see what Ellen had referred to. The Light carried the story about how he'd been selected to write Flint's memoirs and a photo. Most of the stuff about him had come from his banker friend.

Afterward, Bishop called Phillip who answered the phone and identified himself.

"This is Bishop Bone, Phillip," he said and explained that he was writing Flint's memoirs at Anne's request and was interviewing people Flint knew or had worked with.

"I know," Phillip said. "Anne said to expect your call. When do you want to meet?"

"How about fifteen minutes?"

Phillip would make time and Bishop was in luck. A representative from the lender was in their conference room reviewing financial statements. Phillip said the man should be able to make time for a few questions from Bishop.

"I told him Anne had hired you to write Marc's memoirs. His name is Stan Parsons, a mean little shit, if you don't mind me saying," Phillip said.

"I don't mind. Forewarned is forearmed. Also, if you can, I'd appreciate the names of the more vocal borrowers whose projects you guys took over."

Phillip laughed. "Why don't I give you the ones who actually threatened to kill Marc? None of them were very happy but only a few made threats."

\* \* \* \*

The company's offices were in a residential area off Girard Avenue that was changing from residential to office. Bishop parked on the street and walked into the clapboard, half Tudor-styled home. It had been refurbished and looked practically new. What he assumed was a company truck sat out front, a white Toyota with a ladder rack and bumpers that could take out a small tree. Anne had said Phillip drove the thing.

Inside, Bishop introduced himself to a young girl out front and told her Phillip was expecting him. The front room of the converted house was filled with empty desks and computers, evidence that the business was being liquidated.

She directed him to Phillip's office at the back of the building. The door was open. Next to it was a closed door bearing the name Marcus Flint. That tells the story, he thought. Flint's not in now and won't be in tomorrow.

Bishop walked in and introduced himself. Phillip gestured at a chair in front of his desk. He wore glasses. Bishop refused his offer of coffee figuring it had more than likely simmered down to sludge consistency by then.

An old coat, brown tweed, hung from the back of his desk chair. His tie had been loosened to give him a frazzled look. Maybe it's a relaxed look, Bishop conceded.

Files lay on top of the desk; a calculator sat near Phillip's right hand along with a notepad. His eyes were bloodshot.

"I'll let you ask the questions and I'll tell you what I know," Phillip said. "As you can see, I'm up to my asshole in work. I'm trying to get things ready for the transfer."

"Yeah," Bishop agreed. "Can't be easy."

He recited what Anne had already told him about how they got into business, what they had been doing and what they were about to do – go out of business, more precisely, being forced out of business.

Phillip grumped under his breath, "Yeah. The shit's flying back at us, me, anyway."

Bone ignored his complaint and asked, "What can you add to what she told me?" He opened the pad he'd brought for notes.

"Not much." But, he did fill in some of the blanks Anne had left and finished by saying, "As Anne told you, the lender – our client – wants us to deed everything back to them or some company their credit-line banks designate to wrap things up, a liquidation committee. They want it done as soon as possible. We thought we had a year or so, but they want to take the projects back while the market is hot."

"I can understand," Bishop said. "But that doesn't make it easy for you."

Phillip shook his head. "Maybe Marc could have squeezed them for a year. I don't know. He did have some clout. I sure as hell don't. The lender's people asked me to prepare legal documents to close the deal by the end of the month. Our attorneys were in here last week to pick up what they needed. A marketing company hired by the liquidation committee has already taken over our sales and marketing. Except for the girl out front, who's next, I let everyone go this morning. Derek included." He cracked a smile. "No loss there."

"I saw the empty desks as I came in."

"Yeah. Kind of like dying. We own the building. The liquidation committee wants that as well. They want every dollar we have. They've offered to sell us – that'd be me, Anne is not interested – a couple of trash properties if I can get a loan or bring in a partner. Low income housing, VA, FHA, multi-family. Low profit margins. Anne says I can have the company after we close. A couple of builders may be interested in the company and the land. I'd get a fee if they take it. The company has some value though without Marc, not much. He was the big dog. I'm nothing to anybody, just a numbers guy with a calculator. Hell, I'm not even sure about my wife." He laughed.

Ignoring his comment, Bishop asked, "Would you stay on? Run the company?"

"God, no. My resume is with a headhunter. Marc did that, run the company, and loved it. He had a broker's license and a contractor's license and could do it all, in the office or in the field. Marc could blow smoke up your ass if he wanted something or wanted to give you a pat on the back for doing something that helped him, but he could kick your ass in a hurry if you screwed up. I lost two good people because of that. The last one about a year or so ago."

He shook his head as if remembering something.

"One girl, really good," he said, "missed a hundred thousand dollar item in a budget Marc wanted for a takeover. He reduced her to tears. She quit. Her husband stormed in the next day, cursing and shouting like a little dog. You know the kind, barking their heads off. Anyway, Marc heard him and came to see what was going on. The little guy faced him and began cursing. Marc listened a little before he bent over and laughed in the guy's face. He poked him in the chest with his finger, told him to shut his mouth and get the hell out his sight before he did something the guy would have to lie about where he worked. The guy shut up, blinked, backed up a step, then turned and left."

Bishop gave the story a chuckle. "Anne said there was a dispute about a mortgage fund."

His eyebrows raised. "Ah, yes, there is. They want our ... well, Marc's interest. It was in his name and Anne's. Our attorney says they'll get it. I think Anne agrees. Maybe she already has signed it over."

"What will happen to Anne?"

He shrugged. "She has some money but, who knows, she may have to go to work unless she sells the house. That'll be a new experience for her. She makes some money from her books, but not nearly enough to support that house, I don't think. With Marc out of the picture, who knows how many books she'll sell, anyway? He helped her get going."

"He made enemies, didn't he?"

"Plenty, mainly the developers whose companies we took over. Most of them were fighting mad. Some called him ruthless and heavy-handed. A 'ruthless thug' was what one builder called him. Hell, we did the guy a favor by taking over his mess. He'd never have survived anyway. I think deep down they all knew they were finished, but they resented Marc's lack of compassion. He seemed to enjoy seeing them squirm. That's what I've heard."

"Did he have fights with the developers?"

"Only one, Max Larson. Marc gave him the pitch about buying the company stock from the lender and asked him to leave. Knowing Marc, probably ordered him. He owned the company and wanted Larson out."

"The guy was in about the same situation as you are now."

He answered with a grim smile, shrugged and said, "That's right. Just to finish the story, Max, frustrated out as hell, rushed Marc and started swinging. Marc gave me the details. He sidestepped and knocked the man down. Max got up, cursed a blue streak, and charged again, swinging like he was in a barroom brawl. Marc, ducked and hit him in the stomach. That doubled Max over. While he was trying to catch his breath, Marc hit him with a couple of shots that put him on the floor for good."

"Did he leave?"

"No. Marc said he had somebody drag him out to the street and leave him in the gutter. He then took the stuff from his desk and poured it over him. Of course, anything valuable, Marc kept for himself."

"Sounds like he could take care of himself."

"He could. Usually, he took somebody with him when he was taking over a company but didn't for Max's. I don't think he was expecting trouble. He took a big guy he called Lennie most of the time. If anybody made a loud noise like they were going to cause trouble, Lennie would step forward and that was the end of it. They did curse and threaten but didn't swing or throw anything."

He handed Bishop a list of names and telephone numbers of all the developers whose companies they had taken over including Max's.

"Anne said you'd want them," he said. "I've added notes beside the ones Marc said made threats. Not as many as I'd thought. Two or three."

Bishop thanked him and put the list in his briefcase.

"Thanks. By the way, I heard that a couple of husbands got after Marc but thought better of it once they saw him. Anne told me."

"Yeah. I'm surprised that somebody didn't take a shotgun to him. He took what he wanted, when he wanted it. It didn't matter who owned it. More to the point, whose wife it was. If he wanted somebody's wife, he figured she was his."

"His diabetes did what nobody else could do. It said no and he couldn't talk his way out of it."

"I guess it did," Phillip said. "I hadn't thought of it that way, but I think you're right."

"That reminds me. Anne said that your wife ran blood tests for him and told him he probably had diabetes. Linda, right?"

"That's right. She called him before the opening and told him he needed a shot of insulin. He'd asked her to keep it a secret, the blood test, but she'd told me. So, I knew."

"I'd like to talk to her if that's okay."

He frowned. "Why? I just told you all you need to know about Marc's diabetes and I assume Anne told you. What else do you need? She works full-time. Right now, I need for her to keep her job till I get situated. If you screw that up -"

"I'm not going to screw anything up. I just don't like to write secondhand info. It's called hearsay. I'll only take a minute or two. She must eat lunch. I could do it then. Hell, I'll buy lunch."

"You're almost as pushy as Marc. Must be something they teach you in law school. The newspaper article said you were a lawyer. As an aside, if you don't mind me saying, I think this memoir thing is a damned nuisance. A memorial to a guy most called an asshole and I can't say I disagree. He was about as self-centered as anybody I've ever known."

Bishop was a little surprised. "Didn't you get along?"

"I arranged to. The pay was good and to be fair, the guy had a genius about him. Some people said he was simply lucky. But, nobody's that lucky. He got things done."

"Maybe that's why he was a success."

"I guess you're right. He wanted to be the top dog in everything he did. Racquetball, projects, women, you name it. Anything competitive, he got in line and usually finished on top. I never beat the son of a bitch."

Phillip wrote his wife's name and cellphone number on a slip of paper and handed it to him. "I'd appreciate it if you'd keep your questions to a minimum. Marc's death, no matter that he was an asshole to some, has been hard on all of us. And, now, the damn company is about to be shut down. Lots to absorb. Linda's feeling it too."

"I'll be quick," Bishop said and shoved the paper into his shirt pocket. He had brought his khakis with him from Mississippi and was wearing them. They always made him feel comfortable.

"I'd be in your debt if you wouldn't tell Anne what I said about Marc .I may need her as a reference someday."

Bishop shook his head, but didn't promise anything. Hell, he was writing a memoir. Good and bad impressions were part of that history.

"Moving on," Bishop said. "What about the girl who got pregnant? Derek said Flint likely did it but blamed him for it."

He gave a dry laugh as an answer then added, "It wasn't Marc's. He tried to screw every good-looking woman who smiled at him, even ugly ones if they had something he wanted, but he drew the line on employees. You have to remember, he was a lawyer and he hated lawsuits. It was Derek's doing, no matter how much he says otherwise."

"Anne said Flint was sleeping with the young woman from the bank ... the one that backed the La Jolla project."

"Yeah," Phillip said. "Sarah Webster. At first, she didn't want to have anything to do with the project – Banker Ben, her father didn't like Marc at all and she knew it. But, after Marc got started with her, she was totally behind it. In fact, I think he wrote the loan submission that went to their loan committee. Of course with numbers help from me."

"A man among men," Bishop said.

"Some people, including me, think he might have been born in hell with Lucifer as a father." He looked at his watch and sighed.

"If you want to talk to Parsons, now's a good time," he said, rubbing his hand over his hair as if that would erase the memories he'd been reciting or the troubles that lay ahead for him as he wound up the company.

Bishop recalled from Phillip's earlier conversation that Parsons was the lender's representative from Coral Gables, Florida, where they had moved their offices for the liquidation, known otherwise as the settling of their accounts with their bank lenders. He glanced at his watch. He still had two hours before it was time to meet Wasserman.

"Introduce me," Bishop said.

## CHAPTER 6

Parsons had the Flint company files spread out all over the tables in the conference room. His laptop was open beside him. One hand was punching away at the keys while his weary face stared into a file. He looked up when Bishop and Phillip walked into the room. He frowned, obviously displeased. From the tired look on his face, Bishop figured he was about burned out.

Bishop calculated his age as the late thirties. He had dark hair, a small round face that looked permanently frozen in an angry scowl. He was also thin and probably no taller than five six or seven, about like Phillip, shoulders permanently slumped forward.

Bishop remembered Phillips comment, "A mean little shit." From a glance, that looked about right.

Phillip introduced Bishop and gave the reason he was there. "Marc's wife wants Mr. Bone to do Marc's memoirs. He once practiced law out here. I told you he wanted to talk to you but I think you were distracted. I don't think you were listening."

Parsons blinked, didn't stand or offer his hand, as if not comprehending what Phillip had just said. "Memoirs?"

"Marc's life history."

Parsons shook his head. "I vaguely recall you saying something about it, but hell, I'm up to my asshole in this shit audit for the liquidation committee and Flint's wife wants me to talk to some guy about how great the man was. That's bullshit!"

"I suppose it is, Mr. Parsons." Bishop said as he walked forward and stuck out his hand. "But, I won't take much of your time. I'm an attorney and very familiar with what you're doing. Very boring stuff."

The man shook his head in agreement and took Bishop's hand as a reflex but quickly released it as if it were dirty. "An attorney?"

"I worked for banks out here. I'm licensed in California and Mississippi where I now live. Thirty minutes should be enough for me. We've already taken five."

Parsons sighed loudly, flipped the file shut with a loud flap and stuck out his arms in resignation. "Ask!"

"How would you characterize your relationship with Flint? By you, I mean the lender Flint worked for. However, if you had a personal relationship, I'd like to know that as well."

"Okay. The chairman of our board, now resigned, brought Flint in to handle the western workouts. We had a shit-pot full of problems. I had recommended the man for the job, based on the number of loans he had closed and got funded. He was damned fast. Made the lender a lot of money, at the time. The chairman thought Flint was King Shit. He didn't take time to read the economic forecasts. None of us did. The real estate market was about to turn around. It did and Flint took all the credit for it."

Parsons went into some detail about how the lender had made a number of high dollar, very risky loans, all with big front end fees. When the loans went bad, the lender tried fanciful bookkeeping to cover up the defaults. But eventually, not even fanciful bookkeeping worked.

That was when the chairman came up with the plan to have Flint acquire the distressed properties encumbered by the lender's loans and clean them up. Flint got lucky and the plan worked, but it didn't save the chairman. He was given a choice, either resign or face charges. He resigned but by then, Flint had a huge portfolio of the lender's loans to clean up.

"Hell, it was a free ride for the man. Our bank arranged operating capital and when the market turned around, Flint looked like a hero. Yet, he had no investment in anything. No risk whatsoever!"

"Just his time was all," Bishop observed.

"I suppose. He had been stalling the liquidation process. Wanting to milk things as long as possible. Hang onto his power. I think he was as crooked as a snake and just about as deadly. I never got a straight answer out of him and I can't find an answer here."

He tapped the file open in front of him and waved over the others.

"The Lord only knows how much he stole from the lender while he was taking over companies and cleaning up their problems. That's why I had to come out here. God, you can't go into a bar around here without getting high on something they're smoking. And, every woman you look at thinks you want to go to bed. I can't stand the place," he said with disgust.

"I can't say I've noticed that, but I don't go into that many bars," Bishop said.

The man grunted and added, "If the chairman were still around, he'd most likely have objected to the liquidation and Flint would still be in business, but he's not and our credit-line banks, through the liquidation committee they set up, want to wrap it all up by the end of the month."

Bishop made notes as the man talked.

Finally, Bishop looked up and said, "I understand what you're saying, but I'm not sure what the beef is, or was, with Flint. Didn't he do what the chairman wanted, what the lender wanted? Maybe he got lucky with the market turn-around, but he did clean up the problems and got the lender in a position to settle with its banks. Maybe he objected to the liquidation. Who wouldn't? Nobody wants to be forced out of business. Not even your head man, I think you said. Flint did invest his time. He could have been building a law practice. If he hadn't died, he'd be looking for a new job, starting over."

Parsons wagged his head wearily as if to agree.

Bishop continued, "Knowing human nature as I do, I'd say it was a hell of a lot easier to deal with one man, already agreeing to cooperate, than with a bunch of tough-assed developers. They would have fought you tooth and nail."

Parsons stared at Bishop for a second, grimaced with a slow nod of his head and agreed. "I suppose. Right now, I'm staring at documents and wondering what the hell I'm going to do when it's all over. Our credit-line lenders, a bunch of big banks with big teeth and lots of influence in Washington, got together and worked out the liquidation plan we're trying to implement. They're pushing us to get it done right away and I'm feeling the pressure."

"It won't last forever."

He laughed. "No. We were hung up on the mortgage fund Marc had set up for his La Jolla project. He wanted to keep an interest he'd carved out of the fund for himself. We said it was ours under his original agreement and our attorneys agreed. That's a dead issue now so we can move on."

"So, what's left to do?"

"Not much. Having him die saved us all a lot of grief. He had been balking about the early liquidation. He wanted more time. Also, I think he siphoned off funds from the company to build that big-assed monument he called a house overlooking the surf. However, his wife swears she put the money her family left her into the thing. Could be, but I have a hunch that every contract Flint issued to a sub included a gentleman's agreement to spend some time on the house."

"I'd be surprised if that were not the case, but what can you do about it?"

Parsons shrugged and tapped the file in front of him. "Probably nothing. I haven't been able to find how he did it. Everything was most likely verbal. Maybe if I had more time. Anyway, I'm going to ignore the damn thing. It does not appear as an asset on any of the files I've reviewed. And, if I can't find it, nobody can. Neither Flint nor his wife show up as owing the company anything, so in the interest of keeping the liquidation clean, simple and moving, I'm not going to bring it up."

"You said you recommended Flint."

"His track record, when we were making loans, blinded me to his tactics. Hell, I now think he was a crook, slick and glib. But, I have to admit, everybody in Miami where we had our offices before we went bust, loved him. From what I've heard, with the exception of the developers he booted out and a few husbands, everybody else loved him as well. He was one smooth son of a bitch and smart as hell. I sure as hell wouldn't have wanted to play poker with the bastard."

Bishop smiled as he made notes. "Glad to get your honest opinion. Maybe you're being too hard on yourself. In your world, maybe the Marcus Flints rule."

"You may be right. Is that all you need? I want to finish up, write my report and get back to Coral Gables, to my wife and family and start looking for a job."

"How long have you been here?" Bishop asked.

"Out here, off and on about three weeks but the liquidation process has been ongoing longer. Marc made things difficult. We were trying to do as much as possible from Coral Gables, but, as I said, he was stalling and I think using the time to hide or squirrel away assets ... cover his tracks." He shrugged.

"But you can't prove that, I take it."

"No, I can't. I was at the grand opening of the La Jolla project. He'd sent us an invitation. I came late and didn't stay long. I didn't want to give him the impression that I was in anyway backing him but he was leaving when I walked in. I knew I'd be digging through his books and records for anything untoward to hit him with."

"But, so far, you haven't found it. Right?"

He shook his head, no.

"I doubt you were sorry he died."

The dark haired man, rubbed his hand over his hair, shook his head tiredly and said, "I'd be lying if I said otherwise. It has made our negotiations a hell of a lot easier. He'd told us all we had to do was call and he'd immediately transfer everything back to the bank. He forgot that."

"I think your timing, for the liquidation, must have surprised him. He was expecting a year."

"Hmm."

Bishop said his goodbyes to Parsons and to Phillip but promised he'd be back. It was time to meet Ellen at the police storage yard.

He checked his phone for messages. He'd heard a "ding" during his meeting with Parsons. There was one. It read, "If you try to glorify Flint, you'll end up like him, dead."

Damn. I wonder if that's the same person who called me.

\* \* \* \*

Ellen greeted Bishop with her hands on her hips and a scowl on her face. She had lost a little weight since he'd last seen her. "You always find a way to stretch the facts into something ass backwards, Bishop Bone," she said. "And then you screw around until it turns out the way you thought. So, forget the bullshit about writing some big shot's life history and tell me what's really on your mind."

Bishop gave her a hug and laughed. "Come on, Ellen. You read the newspaper story. That's all there is. I'm going to write the man's memoirs and collect a healthy fee. No hidden motives. Well, that's not exactly true. It gives me an opportunity to visit with my old crime-solving buddy."

She chuckled and slapped his back in a friendly gesture. "Yeah. Just wanted to check you out, Bone. Let's go look at the man's car. What's left of it, anyway. By the way, I got a promotion since you were here. I'm a damned lieutenant now. How about that shit?"

"Damn! Congratulations! Somebody decided to recognize your talents."

"That they did, my man. That they did."

He told her about the hate call and text message.

She laughed. "They can't kill Flint 'cause he died, so you're the next best thing."

"Looks like it," Bishop replied.

"Be careful. I don't want to be investigating your murder."

"That's the last thing I want, Ellen," he joked.

"Yeah. Some Flint hater blowing off steam, I'd guess. Come on."

He followed her through the gate and past a line of cars until they came to Marc Flint's twisted wreck, his Jeep.

"Damn," Bishop said as he did a walk around. "That son of a bitch took a beating. No way anybody could have survived that, seat belts or not."

"They had to cut him out but he was dead, dead. That's why the top of the Jeep's gone. They say he must have been in a diabetic coma. Probably didn't feel a thing as he tumbled to the bottom of that ravine."

"Needed a shot of insulin, his widow said." Bishop continued his walk around the Jeep. He paused first at the driver's side, bent over for a look at the door, then at the tire rim. He went around to the passenger side and did the same thing.

"Sounds right to me. Hell, I have to take pills myself," Ellen said.

"You got it? Diabetes?"

"Not a bad case, but any case is bad enough."

He mumbled something with a sympathetic tone, pulled out his iPhone and took pictures of both sides.

"We took some shots with a good camera. You want some? We don't need 'em anymore. The man died because he didn't have enough sense to take care of himself."

"Yep. Looks like it." He walked around the mangled Jeep one more time, pausing as he had previously done.

"Looks like it. What does that mean? You looking for something, ain't you? You sneaky crook. What the hell's bothering you, Bone?"

"Nothing really, Ellen. But, there are a couple of things I don't like. You know how he fought to keep the car on the road. I saw the tire marks on the curb."

"Yeah. I saw 'em too. So what? That's consistent with being about to pass out."

"I agree, but look at the driver's side fender and the driver's side tire and rim. Got some damage. An argument could be made that somebody sideswiped him," Bishop said.

"That woulda played hell with their car, Bone," she said with a grin.

"Maybe. I haven't checked all the cars and trucks on the road, but could be one of them might have been able to push against the man's front tire without causing a lot of damage. Why don't you have one of your forensics experts look at the front tire rim? See what they say."

"Bone, you can be a pain in the ass sometime. I ought to call in the white coat guys to cart you off to a pill facility. The Jeep coulda hit rocks or stumps as it rolled down that hill. Caused that damage," she said with a touch of sarcasm.

"Hmm, not many rocks or stumps that I saw, but let me add something. If you look at practically every real estate project Flint took over, you'll find somebody with an axe to grind. He had at least one fight and several people threatened him. Max Larson, the guy he'd taken the La Jolla project from, stood up at the grand opening and wished him to hell. I'd say that was bordering on a threat."

Ellen exhaled loudly. "Shit fire, Bone, and save matches. When bad guys die, they end up in hell. Don't you read your Bible?"

Bone chuckled to himself at the "shit fire" expression. He heard it often in Mississippi but had rarely heard it used in California.

Bishop smiled and said, "Just sharing my thoughts, Ellen. I can't tell you how to do your job."

"Okay, okay, I take your point. I'll talk to some people and see if they'll let me do a study on the Jeep. I'm not promising anything. But what the hell do you expect me to do if they agree with you?"

"I'd say you look at some people's cars. The guy I just talked about, Larson, left a minute or so before Flint. He might have followed him and driven him off the road. Assuming Flint was fighting a diabetic coma, it wouldn't have been too hard."

"I knew you'd be trouble when you called. You just can't accept reality, can you?"

"Let's get some lunch," Bishop said with a big smile.

\* \* \* \*

At the Bread and Cie, he ordered his favorite, a bowl of tomato soup and a grilled cheese sandwich with a cup of cappuccino. Ellen followed suit.

She talked about her family mostly, their troubles, their victories. He told her about sitting on the back porch of his cabin drinking a beer in the afternoon and watching the beavers work in their pond.

They talked a bit about the La Jolla Shores murders and burglary case they worked on the last time he was in California.

"I'm gonna come down to Mississippi to see you one of these days. I gotta see your beavers. Maybe we could have a little beaver stew with some fresh collard greens. That's soul food, collards," Ellen said with a laugh.

"Sounds good to me, except for the beavers. They wouldn't like for me to cook one."

"Hell, maybe we could find a beaver road kill. You guys eat road kill down there don't you?"

Bishop laughed.

\* \* \* \*

He thought about calling on Max Larson. His house was close to the Hillcrest area where he and Ellen had lunched, but decided to phone first or drop in after breakfast before the man could get going to wherever he went these mornings.

So, he went to the Flint house and walked in on Anne dusting a bronze sculpture in the foyer of the house. It was a baby seal with a baby's face and feet instead of flippers.

He stopped. "That's one of Marsha's, isn't it?" He said.

Anne turned sharply, looked surprised, if not shocked. "You know her work?"

"We met the last time I was here," he told her.

"Marc bought it for me at an auction. She's doing very well. Tours all over the world."

"She lost a baby," Bishop said. "I kind of figured the loss of the baby was the source of her inspiration to put babies' faces on her sculptures."

In a flash, he thought, Kind of like Flint sculptured himself as a person with deadly charm after being bullied during his childhood. Both had become success stories in their own right.

She accepted his offer for a briefing of the morning's investigation after he'd taken off his working clothes and put on his evening casuals, what he called his invisible clothes. When he was in those, whether pajamas or tennis togs, he was off duty and able to relax.

She was on the balcony patio when he returned, a glass of red in her hand. A mug of beer with foam sliding down the side of a frosted glass waited for him on the table. He saw the beer and thought, early days for a beer, but what the hell, when in Rome.

He picked it up as he sat down and looked out at the view.

The orange sun had begun its daily slide under the horizon and covered the sky in shades of orange and red. The clouds were dark on their eastern side, pink and purple on the western side. The ocean picked up all the colors as well. Surfers and beach lovers were all over in the water and on the sandy beach at the Shores.

She told him it changed every day. "You never get used to it." she said.

He reported Phillip's apparent resentment of Marc's attitude and Parsons' likely envy of Marc's achievements with what Parsons called a free ride at the lender's expense.

"People like to take potshots at anybody strong enough to be a leader. They resent people who can do what they can't," she said between sips.

He agreed.

"By the way," she said, "a reporter from the Light called to see if you'd begun Marc's memoirs yet. I told her you were already at it, interviewing and inspecting. She said the Light would run an update of their original story in their next edition. It might give your investigation a bit of clout."

Recalling the hate call and the text message made him wonder. *If I'm not careful, I may not get around to asking people anything.*

## CHAPTER 7

The next morning, Bishop called Linda Marshall to see if she had time to talk to him about Flint's life. Reluctantly, it seemed to him, she said. "Sure, what time would you like to come over?"

It was her day off and she was at home. One day a week, she explained, she stayed home to give their son's sitter the day off. Their son, Eli, going on four, wasn't quite ready for daycare, she volunteered.

He'd be there within the hour.

The Marshalls had a home in La Costa. It was one, Phillip had told him during their talk, the company had acquired with one of the companies they'd taken over. He'd bought it from Flint's company at a discount. Fortunately, he used outside financing for the purchase so the lender would not learn of the transaction.

Bishop parked on the street in front of a long, ranch styled house with dormers to catch the morning sun. Nothing spectacular, Bishop noted, just a comfortable looking house.

Linda opened the door seconds after he'd rang the bell. She was in a casual, morning wrap, pink with darker pink flowers and slippers. A nice-looking, dark-haired woman with dark, sparkling eyes and an innocent smile, Bishop decided. Her hair was cut short and nicely styled to barely brush against her shoulders. She was tallish, somewhat slim but not lacking on top. From the look on her face, he decided she was an intelligent woman.

I imagine Flint took a second look, he thought as he introduced himself.

"I'm Linda," she replied. "Excuse my appearance, please. On my day off, I kick back and take it easy. Mostly, I play with Eli."

She touched her hand to the shoulder of the little boy standing beside her, holding her leg. Bishop noticed a gauze wrap around his head and right eye. On top of that was a black patch.

She glanced down and said, "Come on in. This is my little pirate, Eli. Say hello to Mr. Bone, Eli."

"Hello ... Mister Boon. I'm a pirate," he said shyly.

Bishop laughed.

She gestured for Bishop to follow her into the living room at the rear of the house, talking as they walked. "Eli's just had eye surgery. Had to correct for ... what they call a lazy eye problem he was born with."

Bishop shook his head. Lazy eye was a first for him. "I don't think I know about lazy eye."

"A child is born with one eye weaker than the other, the lazy eye, which may see blurred images. We tried to correct it with drops and the eye patch to make the weak eye stronger but it wasn't working very well so we went ahead with surgery to correct the condition. He likes to wear his pirate's patch. Don't you, Eli?"

The boy looked up at Bishop with a smile and said, "I'm a pirate."

"We didn't know anything about lazy eye either," she said. "Until we noticed that something was wrong. The doctors say it was likely inherited from Phillip's side of the family. Phillip doesn't remember having the problem but it could have been somewhere along his male family tree, we don't know. Just what the doctors said. It doesn't matter. He's our boy and he no longer has the lazy eye."

Bishop gave that a nod.

"That's why we've kept him out of daycare. We didn't want the other kids making fun of him or some instructor writing him up as retarded or something."

"I don't blame you. Kids can be rough. Instinctive, I think. A herd mentality."

She offered coffee. He declined, having had his fill earlier.

She sat down. He took a chair facing her and pulled his notepad from the briefcase he'd brought. "You want to know about Marc, I assume," she said.

"Yes. Anne said you drew his blood and told him he needed a shot of insulin. The day of their grand opening, she said."

"Yes. His blood sugar reading was very high. I figured he had a bad case of diabetes and told him he needed to see a doctor immediately to get it treated. He wanted to wait until after the opening of their new project and asked if I'd give him an injection of insulin to tide him over until he could see a doctor. I had the results the day before but we had plans so I waited until the next day to call him. If I had called him right away, he might still be alive. I feel guilty about it."

He said he understood how she might. "You were friends?" he asked.

She agreed with a shake of her head. "I think Phillip and I were their only true friends. Marc didn't get close to anybody unless they were part of a plan he had. Marc wanted me to keep the blood test a secret from everybody, but I told Phillip anyway. I didn't think telling Phillip would matter. I knew he wouldn't let on anyway."

At his request, she gave him her impressions of Flint and Anne. Anne, she said was very sophisticated and talented. Also beautiful.

"She was a little, what I call, stuck up, but once we got to know each other, she was okay."

Just okay.

Marc was the most charming and talented man she'd ever met.

Join the club of everyone else who'd met the man, but was he charming because they were friends, or because he wanted something. Bishop took another look at her and wondered if Flint had added her to his list of conquests. He wanted to ask, but her son was within earshot.

"From what I'm hearing from everybody, he was a fierce competitor. Determined to have his way in everything he set his eyes on, including women." He felt safe putting it in those terms. The boy was not likely to catch his inference.

She blushed. "Phillip has said as much, but if you're looking at me." She shook her head. "We were all just good friends. I think Marc preferred it that way. He was more a hit and run kind of guy, according to Phillip. But, his charm was mesmerizing."

Bishop made notes.

"I understand that he tried to call you right before he apparently passed out and tumbled down the ravine."

She looked down at her hands. The wistful smile left her face. She shook her head slowly then said, "I wish I had left my phone on. Phillip asked me to keep it off during the opening so I did. I … I'm so sorry. Two times I might have saved him and I blew it both times."

Bishop shook his head. "You can't get yourself hung up on hindsight."

She agreed but didn't sound convinced.

Bishop asked about what they were going to do now that the liquidation committee was taking everything away.

"Fortunately I'm working," she said. "Phillip isn't sure what he's going to do. He's looking at several options. One is to find a buyer for the company or a partner and keep doing what he's doing. Unlike Marc, who could do anything, Phillip is most comfortable making spread sheets look like gold."

Bishop acknowledged that Phillip had told him as much. "I think people who know Phillip are very impressed with his ability," he added to give the man a pat on the back. He figured she'd pass it on and that might grease the skids if he needed more information from the man.

"How are you getting on with Marc's memoirs?" she asked.

"Reasonably well. I think I have a point of view. I'm going to pick up on his childhood, what impact it had on him and carry that forward to his death. I've seen his Jeep, what's left of it. It looks like he was desperately trying to save himself. The police detective who showed it to me, figures he was going in and out of a coma and knew he was in trouble."

She lowered her head and wiped tears from her eyes. "Too bad his life had to end that way. I think he would have preferred something more glamorous."

"You're probably right."

He wished her and Phillip luck in overcoming the trauma of having the company yanked away. And, he wished Eli, the pirate, luck in winning his next great sea battle.

"Hit 'em with a broadside, me mateys," he told the boy at the door.

Eli said something he didn't catch and waved goodbye.

Linda said goodbye with an angelic smile he considered devastating. Good friends. I bet. Flint wouldn't pass that up. Few men with an undisciplined urge would

However, he would only write what she'd said. No need to cause marital problems with his cynical speculation.

It was still early so he drove down the street and parked to call Max Larson, hoping to work in another interview. A woman answered his call. Bishop had hoped the number was for Max's cellphone. He explained who he was and why he was calling. She told him she was Max's wife. Max was on a job.

"We know who you are, Mr. Bone. It was in the papers. You're going to write how great that Flint guy was."

He smiled and said, "I don't know about that. I write what people tell me. That's why I want to talk you, well, your husband. Get his side of things."

That softened the woman's attitude, Bishop thought.

"Max will tell you. He didn't like the man one bit!"

She asked Bishop to call back around three o'clock when she expected Max to be home.

He said he would.

\* \* \* \*

Bishop drove to the Flints' home to add to his notes while what Linda had told him was still fresh in his thoughts. Anne was out as was Derek, but he was glad to have the time to himself.

He had another text message on his phone. You're on my list, it said. He wished he could trace it but assumed whoever it was had taken steps to prevent tracing. He hoped Ellen was right. Just somebody blowing off steam. Pissed off developer, subcontractor or husband. All have reasons to be pissed at Flint.

"But nobody has reason to be pissed at me," he said. I'm just trying to write a damn story. I haven't screwed anybody. Hell, I'm not even sure Flint did."

He put the text message in the back of his mind and began calling developers on the list given to him by Phillip. He shied away from calling the ones who had made threats. He'd call them, but later. Who knows, maybe one of them was behind the hate messages. If so, he hoped they'd give themselves away.

Most of the ones who had gone quietly when Flint showed up were not experienced developers. They had property that could be developed for housing of one sort or another. Usually the property had been left to them by their families. The suede shoe MBA's had somehow gotten wind of their situations and came calling holding out big money loans.

Almost as soon as the loans funded, they were in trouble. Most were relieved when Flint called to tell them he'd bought their company and would be by shortly to take control.

A little after three o'clock, he called Max Larson.

"Hello," a gruff voice answered. "This is Larson. I assume you're that Bone guy who's going to write Flint's life history. As far as I'm concerned, you've stepped into a pile of shit. I hope you're getting paid enough to buy your way out of hell if it comes to that."

Bishop gave his comments a chuckle and said, "I am doing just that, Mr. Larson. My hope is that you'll talk to me about your experiences with the man. I don't intend to sugarcoat anything I'm told, if you're wondering."

"I'm damn happy to hear that. That son of a bitch was evil as far as I'm concerned. I've got some time in the morning, around nine if you want to drop by the house. I'm damn glad I didn't let the bastards put a lien on my house when they made me the loan. At least I got to keep that."

Bishop said he'd be there at nine the next morning.

He thought about calling Sarah Webster but decided to save her and her father until the end of his investigation.

Phillip called to tell him that Parsons had completed his audit and had found nothing that would stop the takeover of the company and all its projects by the liquidation committee. The lawyers had been told to proceed with the closing. It was set for the end of the month, about three weeks away.

When she was told, Anne held a board meeting to approve of everything and to delegate authority to Phillip to sign all documents necessary to complete the takeover. Once that was done, she said she'd sign the stock over to Phillip. The liquidation committee didn't want the company because they were wary of any litigation that might be lurking about. Phillip would inherit that contingency if he kept the company.

"Flint's rise to fame and fortune streaked across the sky like a meteor and is now plunging into the sea as a ball of burned out ash," Bishop said as he made his way to the Flints' wet bar for his afternoon libation.

Anne was already there. "I saw your car," she said. "But I thought you were busy. Won't you join me?"

He said he would and poured himself a mug of beer.

On the patio, he brought her up to date on what he'd learned that day. "Phillip's son just had an operation on his eye. He had something called lazy eye."

Anne looked puzzled. "Lazy eye. I think they may have said something to us about it. Maybe not. A bit strange. Lazy eye. I've heard about that. So, he's okay now, is he?"

The boy seemed to be, Bishop told her.

"I've been getting some hate calls ... text messages mostly, but definitely hate. Somebody had transferred their feelings against your husband to me."

"I'm sorry. Maybe I shouldn't have put your telephone number in the story."

"No, I think it was the right thing to do. Encourage calls with information about Marc, but who would have thought somebody would have reacted like they did?"

She said the usual and told him to be careful. "If you feel threatened, you can stop and go back to Mississippi. I'll get somebody else to write it and next time I won't put it in the paper."

He was staying.

"Looks like the takeover will be completed by the end of the month. Phillip told me. What will you do?" he asked. "I understand you have a mortgage on this house."

She smiled. "It's not much and I'll have money coming in as soon as the La Jolla project sells out. I also have the money Marc had been putting aside."

"I don't know about money from the La Jolla project," Bishop said. "The interest Marc carved out for himself is being transferred to the liquidation committee or their designee, I understand. Didn't you agree to it?"

"Marc had agreed and I didn't object. Marc knew they'd pick up anything in his name and want it. He argued about it because he figured that's what they would expect. Then, he capitulated and told them they could have it. What they didn't know and you can't put this expressly in the memoirs, was that Marc had another interest in the name of a Delaware company. I'll have a decent income from that. I also have money my family left me. So, I won't starve."

Parsons was righter than he knew. Her family money did not go into the house.

She also explained how Marc had bought thousands of her first book through the company and had given them to libraries all over as charitable deductions. The bean counters who only looked at numbers thought her book was a great success and stood in line to publish the next one. Marc did the same thing with that one as well and her success as a writer was assured. Not big money, as she had already told him, but enough to motivate her to keep writing and to keep her in good wine.

Derek strolled out with a glass of wine and a wet towel wrapped around his neck. "Hi sis!" he said and sat in a chair next to Bishop's.

"Bone." He gave Bishop a nod.

"I was wondering when you'd show up," she said.

"Good surfing today," he said with a big smile. "Surfer girls all over. Looking for action."

"Bishop says they'll be shutting the company down by the end of the month," she told him.

"Hell, they've already shut me down. I'm halfway through my severance check. I've applied for unemployment already. What's for dinner?"

"I don't know. I let the cook go this morning. I'm having dinner with a friend. You and Bishop have to fend for yourselves."

"A friend?" Derek asked.

"My publisher. He wants me to go a world signing tour. Not bad for having actually only sold a few hundred books on my own." She smiled.

"Congratulations," Bishop said. "Take success any way you can get it."

Anne agreed with a turn of her head.

She turned to Derek and said. "I think you'd better be thinking about your future, brother. The gravy train ended up at the bottom of the ravine."

He grinned. "I thought you would support me, Sister."

"I guess you thought wrong, Brother. You can live here, but no support. I may need rent sooner or later."

He cursed and changed the subject, asking Bone how he was getting on with the memoir writing. Bishop told him about the same thing he'd already told Anne including his hate messages.

"I'm not surprised. Marc had more enemies than you could shake a stick at including yours truly."

"Not my enemies," Bishop said. "I didn't take their companies."

"Maybe they don't give a rat's ass. The taker of their companies is dead, long live the guy writing glorious things about him until he's dead also."

A gruesome thought, were the words Bishop let run through his mind.

Derek finished his wine and left without saying where he was headed.

A few minutes later, Anne did the same. "Will you be okay?" she asked Bishop as she left to dress for her dinner date.

He assured her he would. "I'll get a hamburger or something out."

When she was gone, he called Kathy with a report. His morning calls were little more than "Good mornings."

After he'd finished telling her what he had done, she told him about her trip with her mother to New Orleans and lunch at Mr. B's.

When they'd finished, he scoured the Flints' refrigerator for food but found nothing he recognized.

"It's a Denny's night," he mumbled to himself and reached into his pocket for his keys.

## CHAPTER 8

He got into his rented car, backed out and turned the car on the street toward Pacific Beach, the location of the nearest Denny's he knew about. He hadn't moved ten feet when his rear window shattered.

"Damn!" he shouted and ducked below the steering wheel but nothing else happened.

The nearest neighbor came running down the street. "I heard a shot," he said.

Bishop hadn't heard the shot, but knew that's what must have destroyed his back window. He called the police who were out almost immediately. It was La Jolla after all, and a call from its important people demanded a quick response.

They took his statement and found the spent bullet. They also took pictures. He told them he knew Ellen Wasserman. They knew her also and would pass on the information.

Since the car was drivable, he drove to Denny's for one of their senior breakfasts.

No sooner than he'd ordered and had been served a cup of fresh coffee, his phone dinged. The text message said, "I missed on purpose. Next time I won't. Get your ass back to Mississippi and let that dead son of a bitch go to hell without a glorified send off from you."

"You bastard," Bishop said to his phone. "Next time may be my time not to miss."

He enjoyed his senior's breakfast but his thoughts were on getting shot at, even if it was a deliberate miss. Who did it?

"I wonder where Derek was?" he mumbled to himself. "Hell, does he even know how to fire a rifle? I'll ask Ellen to give him a call. Parsons hated Flint, presumably, but how would he get a rifle? Max? Who knows? Could have been anybody who reads the papers, anybody involved with Flint."

* * * *

When Bishop got back to the Flints' house, Derek's car was in the garage as was Anne's. Neither were visible in the house as he would have preferred. He'd have liked to get their reaction to having been shot at. He'd try to do it the next morning. Likewise, he'd do the same with Max Larson when he interviewed him.

He called and left a message with the car rental company that he wanted another car delivered to the Flints' address the next morning.

The reps were pulling up out front with a replacement car when he got up. He gave them the old keys and took the new ones after explaining what had happened. It didn't appear to bother either of the men who came. It wouldn't, but they weren't in the car, Bishop thought.

He went back inside and found Derek and Anne sitting at the breakfast bar having coffee and croissants. A platter of the pastries sat in the middle of the table along with butter and jam. He got coffee and sat down to join them. Neither showed anything that indicated they knew about the shooting.

"I had a bit of excitement, last night," he said and told them the story of the shooting.

"What?" Anne asked when he had finished.

Derek said, "No shit." Like he didn't care much one way or the other. "Missed you, huh?"

After they had kicked that around for a few minutes, Anne gave Bishop the news she'd gotten from her agent. He'd set up a book tour to begin in Hawaii, the setting for one of her books. After Hawaii, it would move to

California. Then, she'd take a break until December, the gift buying month, and resume in major cities around the country. After December, she'd take a break until spring time.

Bishop indicated how impressed he was. He didn't add that he was glad it was her and not him. He had never liked living out of a suitcase. Derek, on the other hand, was lobbying to come along and help for a fee. He hinted strongly about the fee. Anne was noncommittal.

The doorbell rang. Derek answered it and brought Ellen Wasserman back.

"Ellen," Bishop said and got up to greet her. "Sit down and have some coffee with us and I'll tell you about last night."

She did just that and listened to Bishop's recitation of the telephone warning and text messages he'd received, especially the one after the shooting.

"Maybe somebody is afraid I'll find out something incriminating while I'm writing his memoirs," he said.

"That man made enemies, everybody says, while making money and love. Not a surprise. You make 'em just showing your face," Ellen said.

"Rub it in, Ellen."

"II figured you'd stir things up, Bone. You seem to have a knack for it. I'll give you something to chew on. My forensics team kind of agrees with you about the Flint Jeep. Looks like somebody might have tried to run him off the road. They got that from the marks on the tire rim and slight damage to the fender."

"Yeah," he said.

Anne seemed aghast. "You mean somebody deliberately pushed Marc off the road?"

"It's possible," Ellen said. "He may have been unconscious at the time, but it looks like somebody ran their tire into his and sent his Jeep over the curb while he was conscious or about to pass out. Murder."

The forensics report figured a driver with any skills at all could have rammed his front tire into Flint's without doing much damage to their vehicle since Flint's tires were exposed because he drove with the lift suspension in operation.

"Wasn't me," Derek said. "I wish I could claim credit, but I was still at the opening."

Later, Ellen would tell Bishop that no one could confirm that he was still there. He had left the meeting room prior to Flint and no one saw him come back.

"I'm outta here," she said. "Now, I have a probable murder to investigate, maybe another one about to happen. Yours." She pointed at Bishop. "I'm gonna hate missing that mess of collards you've been promising me and I've been countin' on."

Bishop laughed and said, "Hell, I'll be around. You'll get that mess."

He walked her out. As they walked, he suggested a check of the cars and trucks owned by Max Larson. He'd look at Derek's on his way out, to see if it had any damage on the front passenger's side. He also asked her to see who left the opening at the same time as Flint. She said she was already on it.

She paused in the foyer to say, "Glad to have the privilege of visiting the digs of the upper class. I only get to do that when you're in town, Bishop. I hope you stay alive long enough to do it again."

"Thanks, Ellen. I'm glad to have brightened your day."

"Don't give it a second thought. Hell, if I solve this one, maybe I'll get another promotion. These La Jolla people know which side their bread is buttered on."

"Stay in touch," he told her at the door.

"You too."

He went back inside and commiserated a few more minutes with Anne before getting ready for his interview with Max Larson. Derek had already vanished.

\* \* \* \*

He parked in front of Larson's house and walked up the sidewalk to the front door. It was a nondescript dwelling, maybe farmhouse in style if it had any style at all. He rang the doorbell, hoping it was working. It was. A large, rough looking, balding man with huge hands yanked it open. He was as tall as Bishop but much wider. The man doesn't miss many meals or bottles of beer.

"You Bone?"

He was.

"Come in." He gestured with a jerk of his head toward the rear of the house down a narrow hallway. He hurried in front of Bishop to a small Formica-topped table off the kitchen, yanked out an aluminum chair with a torn seat and plopped down. Bishop followed suit.

"Okay. You want me to talk about the son of a bitch that ruined my life. Let's get at it."

Bishop stared at the man for a second before saying, "Somebody took a shot at me last night."

The man laughed. "No shit. I guess they missed you since you're here. That falls in the pot with that old saying. You lay down with dogs, you get up with fleas. You get friendly with assholes, you get what they should be getting."

"Did you do it?" Bishop stared hard at him.

The man stared back. "If I had shot at you, you wouldn't be here."

"It was a warning shot."

"I don't give a shit about warning shots. When I shoot, I mean to hit something. I don't waste my lead."

"I don't like to be shot at," Bishop said.

The man practically leaped out of his chair and clinched his fists. "You accuse me, you better have something to back it up!" He took a step toward Bishop who had jumped to his feet when the man had.

"Take another step and I'll put you on your ass, Larson," Bishop said. "You're slow, overweight and too old to be screwing around."

"I've brought down bigger than you."

"That was then and this is now."

The man stopped and looked hard at Bishop as if trying to decide if he could "whup him." Slowly he fists loosened. He decided no, backed up and sat down. "Okay. Ask your fuckin' questions. Just don't accuse me of shooting at you. I don't know where you're hanging out."

"I asked. I didn't accuse."

"Okay, okay. I'm short-tempered. I have high blood pressure. Let's get on with it. I have to make a living, thanks to the guy you're writing about. I'm back to supervising a job site."

"That's better than sitting on your ass, Max. Okay. I want to know what happened between you and Flint from the first time you met until the last time you talked."

He told him. Flint had called the day before he was coming out. Larson didn't take the call but got the message. Flint hadn't said anything about coming to take over, just that he was coming out. Larson knew he was in trouble with the lender but was talking to investors about putting money into the project. They were in the process of deciding. He thought that was why Flint was coming to see him.

"I thought he was going to tell me I had more time," he told Bishop.

But when Flint walked in, the first thing he did was order Max out of the building. Max explained that he was within a few days of raising enough money to cure his default but Flint said it was too late. He'd had almost four months to cure it. Now, he had thirty minutes to clear out his desk. Max said he lost his temper when Flint told him that and came around the desk.

"I wanted to go eyeball to eyeball with the guy, try and convince him to give me more time. I wasn't looking for a fight. But, my phone rang and when I turned around, the asshole sucker punched me. Next thing I knew, I was in the gutter with my desk stuff on my chest. I tried to get back inside, but Flint said if I tried, he'd have me arrested. His company owned the building. That's the last time I talked to him."

"Except at the opening," Bishop said. "You threatened to send him to hell or words to that effect."

The man stared at Bishop for half a second then answered. "Hell yes. I wished him to hell. That's where people like him belong."

"Your investors lost money. They must not have liked that much."

"They didn't. They liked the project. We were going to build houses for the middle class. There're too damned many rich dogs living in La Jolla already. Why not bring in some people who have to work for a living?"

"Did your investors think that?"

"Hell yes! It was their idea."

"They must have lost a bundle."

"Over two million. Nothing to them. They just wrote it off. A loss against a gain on their taxes. They have more money than me or you could count."

He talked some about why the project went into default. Basically he blamed the overruns on the city for constantly changing what they wanted for off-sites and to complete the street into the project. He thought he had an understanding with the city planners. Turned out he didn't.

"You should get everything in writing before you spend money. How much did you lose?"

"Hell, I had every dollar I owned in the project."

"I imagine you were happy to find out he'd died."

"You can't know how damned happy I was. I just wish I'd been there to see the look on his face when he knew he was going to die."

"You left the opening early ... well, you were practically thrown out after you'd made a fool of yourself. Did you run him off the street? Were you there?"

He bolted from his chair again. Bishop followed suit. This time the man grabbed a knife from the top of the table and came around swinging it.

As Bishop had said, he was slow. He took a back swing but before he could let it lose, Bishop had already hit him full in the jaw. That staggered the man. But, when he tried to swing the knife again, Bishop hit him in the stomach. The man dropped the knife and fell into the chair, dazed and gasping for breath. Bishop kicked the knife away, grabbed what little hair the man had left, pulled his head back and shouted, "I asked if you were there!"

The man was shaking his head when Bishop heard a tell-tale click behind him. He knew what it was and turned to face the man's wife holding a shotgun pointed in his direction. A woman with a heavily lined, weary face and about as wide as Larson was, pointing a shotgun in his direction. Her worn print dress, two sizes larger than she was, had faded to a barely visible blur.

"Quit hittin' my husband" she ordered, her jaw set tight.

Bishop looked at her and released Larson's hair. "Ma'am, I'm not hitting your husband. He attacked me and I defended myself. I warned him not to but he did it anyway. One thing I need to tell you though. If you shoot that shotgun, it's going to tear me and your husband into pieces."

"Quit hittin' 'im. He's been sick. Got high blood pressure. Had one stroke already."

"I'm not hitting him, Ma'am. I said. If you put that gun down, I'll step back and get out of your house."

The woman blinked as if trying to figure out what to do. Finally, she lowered the shotgun and propped it against the wall. Bishop moved away from Larson and backed toward the front door.

At the door, he paused and said, "I thank you Mr. Larson for taking the time to talk to me. Sorry it had to end like it did. You should know that regardless of what you thought of Flint, he was only doing what the lender told him to do. He had no alternative but to take over your company."

Bishop hoped the man would think about what he'd said and accept responsibility for what had happened. It was not Flint's fault that the project was in default. It was not Flint's fault that he was late finding other investors.

As he drove away from the Larson's house, he felt not only relief but regret that the gun his wife held was not a rifle equipped with a scope. So, he had to think about what, if anything, he'd learned from the visit and then, he wondered why he even cared. All he had to do was write something nice about Flint, collect a fee and go home to Kathy.

But, how can I write something that's not the complete story? If somebody killed the bastard, and Flint probably was a first class bastard, THAT should be part of his memoirs. And, if I'm not willing to poke around to find out, I might as well pack my bags and go home.

"Right now," he said out loud, "that sounds like a damn good idea."

Just then another thought struck him. "Son of a bitch! I forgot to check Larson's truck or even see if he has a truck."

Hell, that's Ellen's job. He called her.

"Bone," she answered, seeing his name on her phone screen. "What trouble are you trying to stir up now?"

He told her about the ruckus he'd just had at the Larson's, the fight and the shotgun threat.

"So, what you want me to do? Arrest them both?"

"No, but I'd like for you to check the man's truck. See if it has damage to the passenger side fender area. I'm assuming he has a truck. I've never seen anybody working construction that doesn't."

"I'll do it, not for you, even though I like you, Bone, but because this is a kind of murder investigation. We're not totally convinced it was murder but it could have been. Probably was. That's the best I can get out of the forensics people. Aren't you supposed to be writing the man's memoirs? Why are you involving yourself in his possible murder?"

"I asked myself the same question." He gave her the answer he had given himself.

"I guess I buy that. I'd add the shot at your car as extra incentive."

"Yeah. I'd forgotten about that."

She'd let him know if they found anything then asked, "What's next on your list?"

"I'm grinding my way through the list of people he knew in this phase of his life," Bishop said.

"I've got somebody doing the same thing, Bishop, but I'm limiting it to the people who were at the opening. It'd be too much to assume somebody would know where he'd be and wait for him to leave. More likely somebody at the opening – somebody with an axe to grind - might have noticed how wobbly he looked and followed him out."

"Good approach. I'm looking at the developers whose companies he took. Eventually I want to talk to everyone who knew or dealt with him even if it's only a phone call. I wish I could interview the kids who bullied him at school – his mother told me – but I doubt anybody even knows them today. I may go back and ask the mother more about that phase of Flint's life."

"Best to keep it simple, Bone. Why stir up trouble for yourself? Write a plausible story, collect your fee and get home to your beavers. They don't shoot at you, you know."

"Yeah, Ellen. I agree. Like an old buddy of mine said, 'There ain't no flies on you.'"

"I've heard that expression. I think it means, I ain't dead. I hope to stay that way," she said.

"I had a thought."

"Tell me in a hurry, Bone. I got guys waving at me to go with them someplace. They wouldn't care if I was about to get a confession out of an axe murderer, they think they're entitled to their pound of flesh when they want it. Lord knows, I have plenty of pounds to give them. Shoot."

"It's ironic. If the person who pushed Flint's Jeep into the ravine, had waited, the man most likely would have fallen into a diabetic coma and died anyway. No murder. Isn't that a kick in the ass?"

"I'll remind the murderer – assuming there is one – when we catch the dumbshit. Causing me all this damn trouble. I could be reading cold case files and drinking coffee."

"Go give your pound of flesh."

She laughed.

\* \* \* \*

Bishop's thoughts turned to Kelly Smith, the guy with the desert project Flint had taken over. According to Phillip, he had bad-mouthed Flint all over town and the project was heavily vandalized after the takeover.

Back up a minute. I may be barking up the wrong tree. Maybe Flint was killed for some other reason. I think I'll interview Smith later. Anne said Flint might have been serious about Sarah Webster. She should be interesting and I doubt she will have a shotgun.

He called her.

"Sarah Webster, Eden Bank," she said. Her voice was pleasant and confident, all business. I'd open my account there, Bishop told himself, joking. He told her who he was and why he was calling.

"I've been expecting you. I read the story about you in the Tribune. Writing Marc's memoirs."

"I could meet you after banking hours if you'd prefer."

There was a pause. "No. I think here would be better. I'll block out some time."

Another pause. "In fact, I have time right now."

He'd be there in fifteen minutes.

# CHAPTER 9

The bank was in a downtown corner building a few blocks off the interstate. Bishop parked in the adjacent parking garage and walked into the bank. She was in a glass-windowed office at the rear of the bank, bent over her desk studying something. He knocked to get her attention.

She got out of her chair, smiled and approached him with her hand out. She wore a charcoal sheath dress with a dark vest that fit her perfectly. Her brown hair was cut to frame her face.

Bishop was impressed. What a combination. She's the morning mist in the forest before the early sun touches it. Innocent and without blemish. Her eyes greeted him with a smile as did her lips. There's a sexuality about her that reaches out and grabs you. Damn. There's no way Flint could escape her appeal, even if he wanted to. Anne was right. I'm betting they had a serious affair.

He introduced himself and added, "I assume you're Sarah."

She was. She gestured toward a chair in front of her desk, started toward hers, but stopped to close the office door. "We might as well have some privacy."

"Good idea."

She sat down. "I'll tell you what I know about Marc Flint," she said and proceeded to tell him how the Eden Bank came to loan his company money for the La Jolla project. He first went to her dad at the main branch but he turned the project down, almost without looking at it. When Marc proposed the project to her, she didn't know her father had already turned it down. Even so, at first she was leaning against it, but after some study, accepted it and proposed it to their loan committee. Her father tried subtly to derail it, but the other members of the committee were in favor of it and Sarah was pushing it so it was approved. Besides, two well-known real estate groups were predicting sales of at least 30 units a month. They were wrong. The project was, in effect, sold out in three weeks after the signs went up. The grand opening was more a celebration than a sales event.

"He drove me to the site and described what was going to happen, how it was going to look. He was so enthused I got caught up in it. I think he sold it to me. He was a born salesman, very charming, but very direct. I never got the impression I was being sold anything. Nevertheless, once I got back to the bank, I was sold on it, the way he described it. I didn't see how it could fail."

"Apparently it is a great success. His wife says they have more reservations than they have units," Bishop said.

"Yes. Marc said they're going to auction off the units. Maybe they have. That'll greatly increase the value. Dad's pleased even though he won't admit it."

"Anne told me you and your father had dinner with them."

She looked down as she agreed with a shake of her head. "Dad's wasn't at his best, but it was pleasant."

"Anne said your father didn't like Flint ... Marc. I suppose it must have showed."

She sighed. "Yes."

Bishop saw the picture of a toddler on the cadenza behind her chair. "Your baby?" She wasn't wearing wear a ring and from what Anne had said, wasn't married. That immediately raised a big question in Bishop's mind. Plus, he'd noticed the slight baby bump a woman often had left after giving birth. And, most had a difficult time getting rid of that final little bump.

113

"Oh, yes. That's uh ... that's my little boy. About two now."

She was going to give his name but backed off. Wonder why?

"Since I'm writing Marc's memoirs, I have to get into something, probably personal. I've been told that you and Marc were having... do they still call them affairs? Anyway, you and Marc were having a relationship." He pointed at the picture.

She breathed out loudly, looked at him and said, "Well, you've done your homework. I don't see how you found out but it's true. That's my little Marcus. I didn't think anybody but Dad and my sitter knew. I hadn't even told Marc. I went away to have it."

Bishop replied with a non-committal response. "Hard to keep those things a secret."

She shook her head. "We were in love. I know I was and I think he was. He was married and he told me up front he would never get a divorce unless Anne asked for one. They had a very ... understanding marriage. I know he slept around. He did it when he wanted something. That may be how ours started. I know he wanted a loan, but our ... affair continued long after the loan was approved. Usually, his dalliances were one night stands."

"From what I've heard about your dad, he was too straight-laced to condone anything like that. He would not approve anything not sanctioned by the Bible."

She grimaced and said, "He didn't approve at all. Mother's dead. But, he loves my baby. He comes over every chance he gets. They sit on the floor and play."

"What are you going to do?" he asked.

"Nothing as far as Marc's death, Mr. Bone. Nothing I can do. I'm getting on with my life. I'm going to buy a unit in the Apogée. Marc set one aside for me. I'll sell my townhouse in Banker's Hill to pay for it. I'll raise my boy in La Jolla. Dad doesn't live far from the Apogée so he can visit as often as he likes."

"I have also heard that your dad still harbored resentment, to put it in its best light, toward Flint." He embellished a bit on what he knew – what he was guessing – to get a response. "Two alpha males butting heads."

She shook her head. "I ... you're right. He did. Dad's old fashioned. You might have guessed from the name he picked for the bank, Eden. He lives by the Book. He reads his Bible every night and expects everybody else to do the same."

"Let me tell you this," he said and looked at her face to get her reaction. "The police think somebody ran Flint off the road. He didn't die of a diabetic coma as was announced. He died when his Jeep was pushed into the ravine."

Her hand went to her mouth. "What? You're saying he was killed! I ... I don't know what to say. Are you thinking Dad might have done it? No way! He's tough and can be abrasive when somebody crosses him, as Marc did, but there's no way he'd kill him. He lives by the Bible. Thou shalt not kill."

Bishop nodded. He decided to do a logical extension on a premise he'd been developing about Banker Ben. "Well, the thinking is that he felt Flint had debased you and that aroused his primitive instincts to redress that debasement by running Flint off the road. He did leave about the same time as Flint and both would have been headed in the same direction. And, he was driving one of the larger Jeeps. The police think his Jeep was pushed off the street by another vehicle. They'll be checking the vehicles of anybody with a grudge against Marc, for damage."

He looked at her facial expression to get her reaction.

She was still shaking her head, no, and frowning in today disbelief. "There's no way it could have been Dad! No way!"

"Also, somebody shot out the back window of the car I had rented. If somebody killed Flint, they may be worried I'll stumble onto something that'll tie the murder to them."

"That's ridiculous. Dad would never do anything like that. Shooting your window out. That's almost laughable. He's not exactly nimble. You may have noticed." She said and touched her stomach to support what she'd said.

She continued. "Besides, he doesn't even have a gun as far as I know. I know something about you, Mr. Bone. You have a good reputation. I'm surprised you'd even suggest my dad had anything to do with shooting your back window out or running Marc's Jeep off the road." She scoffed and looked at her watch.

"I'll tell you something else," she said with another look at her watch. "If you put anything like that in Marc's memoirs, Dad's lawyers will be all over you and Anne. Dad's good name means more to him than you can know."

"I'm a lawyer. I know what I can get away with," Bishop said. "I won't be libeling your dad."

"That's a wise decision." She picked up a file then put it down.

She's tired of this interview. She's right. I was reaching when I suggested that her dad had anything sinister to do with anything. Regardless, I would still like to talk to him for the memoirs.

He looked at Sarah and said, "I'd still like to talk to your dad. For Flint's memoirs. Do you think he'd talk to me?"

She didn't know, but considering what Bishop had just said, she felt he would. "He'll laugh at you if you suggest he's involved in Marc's death or your window. You don't know how honorable my dad is. He makes the Pope look a little off-center, if you know what I mean."

He did. "I had him on my list to call anyway. He was someone Flint knew, socially and in business. I thought a paragraph or two in Flint's history would make sense."

She picked up the phone and called her dad. Without going into as much detail as Bishop had, she asked if he'd make some time to talk to him. "As a personal favor, Dad." Bishop figured he had already been saying "No."

"There's more to it than that, Dad. I don't want to go into it just now, but the police believe somebody ran Marc off the road up there. Killed him. I think Mr. Bone will tell you."

She held the phone obviously listening. "They have. What'd they say?" A pause. "Okay. We'll talk more tonight. Okay?"

She hung up and said, "He'll talk to you. Call him. The police were there to see him. They told him the same thing you just told me. Not your back window, but the running off the road thing. They'd checked his car for damage but it didn't have any. One of the neighbors or the garage attendant told them he was driving a Jeep the week of the opening. They gave it to him on consignment. They wanted the bank to finance their car loans in case they needed a backup source. He'll tell me everything they said tonight. We eat dinner together a couple of nights a week." She wrote her dad's number on a pad and handed Bishop the sheet.

Ellen's been busy. Bless her. I'll call her later. I'm sure she checked with the dealer to see if the Jeep had any damage.

He thanked her. "If you don't mind, I might call again. As these things go, I may need to ask for clarification or more details before I finish Flint's memoirs." She didn't mind.

\* \* \* \*

It was noon so he drove to the Flint home to see if he could scavenge anything from the refrigerator. He parked in the garage. Derek's car – he assumed – a VW hatchback was in the third stall. He inspected it even as he admitted to himself that it didn't nearly have the weight or power to push Flint's Jeep off the road. And, there were no scratches anywhere on it.

Might have borrowed somebody else's car. But, I'd need more facts than I have to go far with that. That'd mean premeditation and how could Derek – how could anybody – know he was slipping in and out of a diabetic coma. Still, it was a loose end that had to be checked.

He went inside. Derek was sitting at the table with half a sandwich and glass of wine reading a newspaper. Dressed in his surfing togs. They looked dry.

After they exchanged greetings, Bishop went to his room to leave his notepad and returned to see what he could find to eat. He found leftover rolls from breakfast, got out the platter with butter and jelly, cranked out a mug of coffee from their fancy machine and sat down at the table for a snack.

Derek looked up. "Still chasing the rainbows that hovered over old Marc's head?"

"I have."

"I'm surprised somebody hasn't taken exception to you," Derek said.

"How do you know they haven't?"

"Serves you right, then, Bone. Anne says when she saw you that first day at the front door, her first reaction was that you were Marc, come back to haunt her. Better watch out. You'll be warming her bed."

Bishop laughed. "Not likely. From what I've been hearing Flint was a world unto himself. I don't think I would fit into it."

Derek leaned back. "Not true, she may be right. Both of you have a kind of roughness to you. Pushy lawyer personalities. I agree with her."

Well, I guess I have to put Derek on my list. He hated Flint, so now he could have reason to hate me. What if I moved in with Anne? What would that do to his cushy situation? That'll never happen, but he doesn't know it.

He mumbled and began eating the breakfast roll he'd warmed.

"Police came by to see me," Derek said. "Did you sic 'em on me?"

Bishop looked up. "I knew they'd be nosing around talking to anybody who was at the opening. What'd they ask you?"

"That detective rattled my cage. She's about as pushy as you. She was the one who came here the morning after your back window was shot out."

"Ellen Wasserman. We're friends from way back." He embellished a bit, but did it deliberately.

"Oh yeah. Why doesn't that surprise me?"

"Did she ask you when you left the opening?"

He looked surprised. "Yeah. Did she tell you?"

"We talk," Bishop said with a shrug.

"I told her I stayed almost to the end. I went home with Anne. She backed me up."

Bishop looked at him, feigning surprise. "Is that so? I thought ... well, somebody said you left for a while and came back. Drove somebody's car to the opening, not your VW." He decided to run a little bluff. See if Derek was as smart and quick as he thought he was.

"You bastard." Derek bolted out of his chair.

"Somebody else cursed me," Bishop said calmly, "and they ended up on the floor. Are you trying to join the club?" He pushed back from the table.

Derek eased back down.

I guess he doesn't want to join the club. Too bad.

"Son of a bitch. I guess that means the detective will be back ... to ask about the car I drove. I'd forgotten about it. I had borrowed my girlfriend's car. An old Chevy her family gave her. Mine was in the shop."

Bishop pulled his chair closer to the table and said, with raised eyebrows, "They'll wonder how you could forget something like that. Police are a suspicious lot."

"Had a lot on my mind. Marc was trying to fire me. Some girl at the opening ...offered to check out our chemistry. I couldn't pass it up." He smiled

"They know all that too." He was still bluffing, and Derek was still buying it. "Apparently there was another time you went missing. Ellen told me. I don't think I'm supposed to talk about her investigation."

"Yeah. I had to go outside and see about the entertainment. Make sure they all got there and were ready to play. I guess I'd better call that bitch. Otherwise she'll think I'm hiding something."

"Good idea."

I'll still pass the info on to Ellen in case he forgets to call. She'll want to have a look at the Chevy. Maybe ask the entertainers if Derek was outside checking them or inside checking someone's chemistry.

Derek got up and left without saying anything.

Bishop got a second cup of coffee and a second roll to finish what passed for lunch. He heard the garage door open and close. Derek going out. Probably has a surfing date. Hard life.

Anne came in as he was washing his mug and saucer. She walked over and said hello.

"I think I'll sit on the porch and relax with a glass of wine. Will you join me? Catch me up with your progress."

He was about to call Sarah's father to set up an interview, but Anne was his client so he agreed so long as he could sip a beer. It was early, but for ten thousand dollars, he could make an exception.

Do I tell her Flint spawned an illegitimate child? I should do a little research to see if the boy has any rights against the man's estate. With today's medical technology, it'll be an easy matter to prove that Flint fathered him.

He decided he had to tell her. His reasoning being, the information belongs in Flint's memoirs so she would have to be told sooner or later.

Bishop briefly covered his interviews with Larson and Derek, pausing for sips of beer. Anne nodded at appropriate intervals and drank wine. After he'd finished with telling her that, he paused and looked at her, trying to decide whether to tell her or not. She must have sensed his dilemma because she looked over her glass and asked, "What? Have you discovered something you're wondering if I should know?"

He sighed and said, "Yes, I did."

Her head shot around. "What? You sound serious."

"I am." He couldn't keep the seriousness out of his voice. It was his way of preparing her. "I met with Sarah Webster this morning. We talked about the La Jolla project and how Marc finagled her dad around to get the loan. He back-doored the submission and her dad had to vote to approve it. She also confirmed what you strongly suspected. She and Marc began having a serious affair. He did tell her that he'd never divorce you."

"I knew that already, so, why the gravity in your voice? He told me on a number of occasions, if we got a divorce, I'd be the one who filed for it. That gave me some satisfaction."

He looked at her squarely and said, "Right. Did you know that they had a son together? She named him Marcus. She never told Marc. The boy's almost two. Sarah's father knows."

"What! Marc had a son? Are you sure? I can't believe it. I can't."

"I think he did. You could always run some tests on the boy to be absolutely certain, but my read is that Marc is the father. Sarah doesn't strike me as the type who'd lie about something like that. She knows a DNA test would easily show whether she was lying. I'd guess there's something of Marc's around here you could use for a DNA analysis"

Anne slumped like the air had been let out of her body. "Marc had a son. He always wanted one. I knew he was sleeping with her. I knew it! She must have told him she was on the pill."

"I didn't get into that. But the information should be in his memoirs. That's why I'm telling you. I'll be meeting with her father, probably tomorrow. I'll bring it up again. He left the opening about the same time as Marc. He was driving a Jeep. He had it on consignment from a dealer who was trying to get his bank to finance their sales if they needed a backup bank. He didn't keep it long. I figure the police had it checked for damage but I haven't had time to ask them what, if anything, they'd found out. Just off the top of my head, I think a Jeep could have been used to drive Marc's Jeep off the road as sick as he was," Bishop said.

"You think Sarah's father might have done it? Ben Holliday? He's a banking icon in this state. Most people say he's as honest as he claims to be so I doubt he did it," she said.

"I don't know, of course. Just a possibility. Avenge his only daughter's disgrace by a man he thoroughly disliked," Bishop said.

"I don't know what to say. I'm going to have to let what you've said sink in. I'll ask our attorneys what my legal position is relative to the boy. Does he have a claim against Marc's estate?" she asked.

"Good idea to ask. He probably does not, but it might ease your mind to check," he told her.

She picked up her glass and drank half. "Any other good news? Maybe this memoir thing wasn't such a good idea after all."

"I can't disagree. The police have been talking to anyone who left the opening around the time Marc left and anyone who had dealings with him and who was at the opening," Bishop said.

"To see if they harbored some kind of grudge and might have run Marc off the road?" she asked.

"That's right. They talked to Derek."

"He was at the opening after Marc left. I saw him around. And, he drove home with me. He seemed normal, not excited or anything. I was ... I don't know tired from all that busy talk with people I didn't know so I asked if he'd drive home with me. He went back for the car later," she said.

"I see. Even so, he was missing from the opening a couple of times. Once he says he left to have a go at a woman he'd met and a second time he said he went out to make sure the entertainment made it on time," Bishop said.

"He owns a VW," Anne told him. "I can't see him running Marc's Jeep off the road with that thing. It's too light for one thing and it'd be beat up if he tried."

"I agree, but that day he was driving his girlfriend's car, a Chevy. He forgot to tell the police but told me he'd call and let them know. I'm sure they'll check it out."

"Damn. It's raining dog shit," she said. "I'm sorry, I don't ordinarily use such crude language. Marc did and now and then, but it seems to fit the situation."

"It doesn't bother me. I do the same now and then, when the spirit moves me. Derek said somehow I remind him of Marc. For some reason I haven't been able to put my finger on, I don't think he likes me much. Maybe he has ... transferred his dislike of Marc to me. In fact, I've been thinking he's the one behind the calls and text messages I've been getting," Bishop said with some hesitation. "I wish there was some way I could trace the calls. The caller probably has one of those throwaway phones from Wal-Mart."

Ellen had offered that bit of information when he called her.

Anne was speechless for a second or two before saying, "If he is the caller ... he'd also be the one who shot out your car window."

Bishop nodded. "Yeah."

"I can't believe he'd be that full of hate for anybody. I think you're totally wrong."

"Does he have a rifle?"

She didn't know. "I haven't seen him with one, but he was in the Army for a time, a medic. I guess they taught him how to shoot."

Bishop agreed. "Well, you're the only one I've told. It's supposition based on what he said. I don't intend passing it on. And, I don't see any reason to put that in Marc's memoirs. They're about Marc, not me. As a matter of fact, though, he told me you had the same reaction to me. I reminded you of Marc."

She stared out at the blue Pacific way down below and said nothing. "I was missing Marc. There is a resemblance. Neither one of you look like you'd walk away from a fight until the other guy's flat on his back."

Bishop laughed. "I don't know about that but I'm a lawyer and I have a habit of trying to fit puzzle pieces together. Sometimes that rubs people the wrong way. Right now, I'm going to speculate a little more. If you don't like what I say, you can tell me to pack my bag and leave."

"What is it? It can't be as bad as what you've already told me."

"Suppose this. Derek, even if you do love him as a brother, is something of a freeloader. I'm sure Marc felt that way also. And that, in part, has to be why he wanted to fire Derek from the company."

"You're saying Derek is afraid you'll move in and, like Marc, would want to get rid of him. No more free ride. No more living in the lap of luxury."

"Yeah. That's what I was getting at," he said.

She finished her wine before saying anything. "Well, well. Maybe you and Marc were cut from the same cloth.

That's more or less what he was saying. You may be right about Derek. I just don't know. Derek is my brother. I promised my parents I'd look after him. I don't know how far my duty extends however. I don't think it does anybody any good to be given a free ride. People need to have a purpose. That's why I write books. I didn't want a free ride even though wives usually get one. It comes with the ring."

Bishop shook his head and drank his beer.

"I agree," he said. "Be that as it may, that's about the extent of my day."

"You've hit me with a big pile of ... stuff to think about. Larson and his wife threatening to shoot you." She shook her head in dismay. "I'm sorry. I had no idea having you write Marc's memoirs would be dangerous. I'm going to rethink my decision about whether to continue, Bishop. I'll sleep on it for a couple of days."

"I'll continue until you tell me otherwise. I will talk with Sarah's father. And, I want to drive out to Palm Springs and talk to Kelly Smith. He threatened Marc and probably had someone vandalize the desert project Marc took from him. I thought I'd mention it in what I'm writing as the kind of thing Marc had to contend with when he took over projects."

"Okay, but I'm still going to think about it." She stood, bent over and kissed him on the lips. "Don't get the wrong idea, Bishop. I just wanted to thank you for sticking your neck out for me ... doing what I asked. And, I do like you. You do remind me of Marc, but you are nicer."

"Thank you Anne. I've tried to keep my mind on what I came out here to do, but you do have a mesmerizing aura about you. I won't say more. I have a friend in Mississippi, a good friend."

"I understand. I wish Marc had had the same convictions."

"I do too."

She left and didn't return.

# CHAPTER 10

Bishop finished his beer and went to his room to enter what had happened that day in his notepad. He also called Sarah's father and arranged to meet him the next morning. He had a townhouse in the same complex as Sarah. The man wasn't rude or even hostile during their telephone conversation. Just told Bishop to show up.

Kelly Smith popped into his thoughts so he called him. An answering machine picked up. "I'm not here. If you have money, leave a message and I'll meet you, even buy you a beer. If you want money, I'm never here."

A wag.

Bishop decided he'd drive out and wait in front of the guy's house early until he left for wherever he went. He had to make a living somehow. He'd follow the man to wherever that was and nail him.

He also called Ellen to tell her what Derek said about driving his girlfriend's car and driving home with Anne. Bishop didn't think Flint's illegitimate son was any of the police's business just then.

Ellen said she'd check out the girlfriend's car and talk to the musicians to see if anybody saw him nosing about. She gave him a little more on the Jeep Sarah's father had driven on consignment to the opening. He told them he turned it in because he didn't think it was suitable for him to be driving something like that. "Not the image I try to convey. I'm a banker, not a cowboy."

The Jeep had some scuff marks on it, according to the dealer, but it had been out on consignment twice since the banker had driven it; a promotion approved by the manufacturer. It'd be sold as used later.

The service department told her the scuff marks could have been put on by the subsequent drivers or even a prior one. She also asked the DA what he thought about it. He told her no jury would buy that as evidence of anything. He would not spend the taxpayer's money on a case that weak. So, she closed her file on the banker.

Bishop couldn't disagree. He walked back to the kitchen to see if he could take Anne to dinner. He wasn't sure how much cooking she did.

She was sitting on the balcony with a second glass of wine. He walked outside and invited her to dinner. He knew a place that served great Japanese noodles and hot sake.

She mulled over his invitation. "Derek's with his girlfriend. Why not? What time?"

He told her about six. She'd be waiting.

A hot shower helped him put the day behind him. He dressed in his other khakis. On trips, he brought two sets, one with a long sleeved shirt for casual evening wear. Afterward, he called Kathy to tell her all that had happened including the possibility his assignment might be cut short. She was pleased to hear that.

"I've been missing you."

He'd been missing her as well. He didn't tell her he was taking Anne to dinner. It meant nothing to him and would only worry Kathy if she knew.

They said their goodbyes and he went down the hall to see if Anne was ready. She was coming out of her bedroom as he approached. She saw him, turned and held out her arms. "Please hold me, Bishop. I need to feel somebody caring next to me. I know that you care. I can see it in your eyes."

He reached out, put his arms around her and pulled her close. He felt her warmth and had to admit it was enjoyable. It had been awhile since he'd felt a woman.

"You are a wonderful lady, Anne. Marc was blessed to have you as a wife."

She pressed her face against his chest. "Thank you for indulging me. People think I'm made of iron. Beautiful and stuck up but I have feelings just like everybody else."

"I know," he said. He didn't, but it felt like the right thing to say. "I know."

He held her until she released him and they went to the noodle house for dinner. It was a decidedly blue collar place, but the noodles and hot sake were excellent and they both enjoyed them.

During the dinner, she described what happened when she told Derek about Marc's child with Sarah Webster.

"I told him he had an illegitimate nephew." She laughed.

"What'd he say?"

"He didn't laugh. In fact, I thought he got a little upset. He said he didn't like the idea that the boy could make a claim against Marc's estate and take some of my inheritance."

Most likely thinking the boy might take money he could con Anne out of.

"What'd you tell him?'

"I told him our attorneys said the boy didn't have much, if any, claim against the estate. I called them after our talk."

"I haven't looked at the inheritance laws lately, but from what I recall, I think that's right. However, I had the sense, the last time I looked, that the law has been moving in the direction of giving illegitimate children more inheritance rights, but I'm not up on the current state of judicial decisions to say where the law stands now. I think Sarah's father has enough clout and enough money to push a claim for the boy if he chooses to do it, but why would he? I'd think the boy would have plenty of money from his estate. And, Sarah isn't exactly impoverished," Bishop told her.

"That's kind of what my attorney said, as well. I told Derek not to sweat it. That kind of calmed him down. He laughed about the father's dilemma, Banker Ben."

"How so?" Bishop asked.

"It's well known that he lives by that worn-out old Bible he carries around with him. The notion that he has an illegitimate grandson probably sent him to a shrink. That's what Derek was laughing about."

"I don't doubt it. Derek strikes me as getting a kick out of other people's misery."

She didn't respond, preferring to think only good things about her brother.

Bishop looked about him at all the patrons enjoying noodle dinners. He picked up his sake cup and toasted Anne with a click. "To more good times," he said.

"To more," she said. "Marc and I let all this pass us by. We got so tied up in the luxury that came with his work, we never stopped long enough to ... what is it they say?"

"Smell the roses."

"Yes. That's it. Smell the roses. Get out and live. Marc's job consumed him. He was just playing a part and I think somehow it killed him."

Bishop didn't know enough to respond, but figured it was possible. Living high on the hog might not have been a good diet and that might have led to his diabetes. More speculation. At any rate, it didn't seem like she expected an answer so he didn't give one.

Just then, for some reason, Bishop figured he knew who the married woman was; the one Anne had alluded to the first time they talked. But, he didn't bring it up. Maybe later when she wasn't depressed.

\* \* \* \*

He parked in front of the townhouse Sarah's father had directed him to. It was obviously an expensive, conservatively styled Mediterranean building with a red tile roof and wrought iron balconies in an exclusive section of the community people called Banker's Hill.

"Appropriate for Banker Ben," he said.

He knocked on the door and Sarah's father opened it. "Come in," he said. "You must be Bishop Bone. I read about you in the Times. It showed a picture but it was so small I couldn't tell anything about it. Even so, I knew it was you knocking."

I guess. I had an appointment.

Bishop thanked him for taking the time to talk about his relationship with Flint.

"I'm doing this for Sarah. She asked me. I love my daughter and would do anything for her. You know, of course, that the police at least wondered if I ran Flint off the street. I think they decided I hadn't."

"I see. I can't say I knew they suspected you. I know they are looking at anybody with a grudge against him, somebody with an opportunity to kill him. Knowing what I know, I'd say you could satisfy their requirements."

"That sounds like what the detective said. Fortunately for me, the Jeep I was driving wasn't damaged. I shouldn't have been driving it. I didn't like it. More Flint's style than mine." He smiled.

They walked down a wide hall into the cozy living room. The hall floor, aged oak, like that of the living room was covered by rugs that were old and worn. The living room had a fireplace. Real as far as Bishop could tell. A few old masters hung on the walls. Bishop assumed they were prints. On the mantle sat a photo of a woman with dark hair that hung a few inches above her shoulders.

His wife, Bishop decided. He sat in the chair the man pointed to. Like the rest of the furniture in the room, it had an aged look to it.

The man saw Bishop looking and said, "My late wife. I loved her. She died a few years ago."

"Tell me how you met Flint, your impressions then and later after you'd approved the loan and now. I understand you and Sarah socialized with them, the Flints."

He talked first about the dinners with the Flints, how he was rude and how he regretted it. "It was a sin," he said. "The Bible says I should treat others like I want to be treated. But, I let my prejudices tell me what to do. I should have followed the teachings of Jesus."

He rambled on about Flint, his problems in dealing with him. "It is hard for me to deal openly with people who are arrogant. I've been around so long that I've had to deal with all kinds like that. You know they're trying to con you into something and you are inclined to ignore what they are saying just because of that. You don't even consider the merits of what they're saying."

Bishop said he could imagine.

He explained how Flint went behind his back and "sweet-talked" Sarah into recommending the loan. The submission was one of the best, he said. Absolutely without a flaw. And, he admitted it was a great loan.

"What about the affair he had with Sarah? I assume you know about that."

The banker frowned. "That! I didn't like it one bit! I didn't know it was going on until we began funding the loan. If I had, I might have pulled the plug and let the lawyers fight it out."

"And, you know about the baby."

He swiped the air with his right hand. "Yes, I damn well know about it! I love the little rascal but I hated Flint for it. What kind of man would do that, knowing he was not going to marry the mother of his child? He most likely ruined her chances of ever marrying a decent man. Who's going to marry a woman who's had another man's illegitimate child? I ask you."

Bishop said he didn't know.

"The Bible tells us that whoever commits adultery destroys himself. Flint did just that and he died for it. It was the Lord's work."

From what I read and what I know, lots of men are out destroying themselves every night, Bishop thought. And few die from it.

"At least the boy will have a good home. Sarah loves him and, I assume, has enough income to support him. I suppose you'd help if it came to that," Bishop said.

He shook his head with a frown. "I think Flint's estate should step in. Flint's sin brought the boy into this world. His estate should help see him through it. Sarah doesn't seem to care, but it's my nature to look at everything. I've told my attorneys about it. They going to study it and let me know. They were not encouraging."

"You obviously hated the man for it," Bishop said.

"I did. I'm ashamed to admit it, and I hope the Lord forgives me, but I did hate the man. I get some satisfaction, another sin I think, knowing that he never knew what he had done. He never knew he had a son. From what Sarah has told me, he always wanted one.

That's why she went off the pill. She was going to tell him but ... he died before she could."

"Makes you wonder if he would have married her if he had known."

He looked hard at Bishop then said, "You may be right. I might have ended up calling him son. I don't know if I could have stood it."

"But, for Sarah's sake, I suspect you would have."

He shook his head. Bishop wasn't sure it was an agreeing shake or a disagreeing one.

"Do you mind if I ask what happened after you left the opening?" Bishop said. "As you probably know, the police figure somebody pushed Flint's car off the street up there and it rolled to the bottom of the ravine. They tell me a Jeep would have been the perfect vehicle to do that. And, you were driving one." Ellen hadn't said that but he deduced that, from the Jeeps he'd seen, it was possible.

He shook his head. "I know. I know. I told you the police came by here and by the bank, asking the same questions over and over. Like I was going to forget and tell them something incriminating. I can never do that because I didn't run him off the road. They checked the Jeep and found nothing. Besides, it was the Lord's vengeance against the man for his sins."

Bishop ignored the last bit of diatribe and said, "That's what you said. However, the man did debase your daughter and force you to make a loan you didn't want to make, in fact, one you had already declined to consider. A case could be made that you came up behind him, saw him weaving and some primitive instinct took over and you rammed into his tire and forced him over the curb."

"When that policewoman, Ellen Wasserman, told me that's what they figure had happened, that thought passed through my mind. I wondered whether I would have done just that, had I come up behind him. I knew he drove a Jeep. He had driven it to the bank when he first tried to get me to make the loan. Regardless, I would have recognized him if I'd tried to pass. That didn't happen though. So, I don't have that sin to atone for."

"Somebody's been sending me hate messages and most likely that same somebody shot out the back window of my car."

As Sarah predicted, he laughed and it didn't appear to be a staged laugh. "If you're suggesting that I had anything to do with that, you should seek help. I can shoot a rifle. I don't have one however. I do have an automatic handgun which I keep for protection. Sarah doesn't know about it. And, I haven't sent you any hate messages. Until a few minutes ago, I didn't even know you. Why in the world would I ever shoot out your window? Sarah told me she thought it was ridiculous. I concur with her. That's the most absurd thing I've ever been accused of. I might foreclose on widows if their late husbands hadn't paid their debts, but I've never shot at one yet."

They talked a little while longer, mostly about the boy. He was walking some. Still not potty trained so they had to have a sitter. And, he wasn't talking yet either but he was sweet and, he thought, very bright.

"I just hope he doesn't grow up to be like his father, glib, smooth and arrogant."

With that, Bishop decided the interview was over. He hadn't found anything definite about who might have killed Flint and wondered if he ever would. I may have to finish my investigation, write the memoirs and leave that part open.

He figured he would have plenty to write about without having to worry about who killed him. Sure, it would make a nice ending to be able to include the killer's name, but not knowing might be a good ending also. It'd leave the reader with something to think about.

## CHAPTER 11

Bishop stopped at Starbucks for a cup of cappuccino and a roll after leaving "Banker Ben." He called Ellen with his impressions of the man.

"I think he hated Flint for fooling around with his daughter. He didn't like Flint going around his back to get a loan approved that he'd rejected out of hand because he didn't like him. The man's one of those Bible people and I think he believes what he reads. I don't think he thumps his, but he taps it," Bishop told her over cappuccinos.

"Right. I don't need to remind you, Bone, since you're living in the Bible Belt, that lots of so called religious people are zealots who kill regularly when somebody does something they think violates their Bible."

"No comment on the Bible Belt crack, Ellen. But, no you don't have to, I'm just giving my impression. You can keep him on your list. I still have Larson on mine."

"Larson. I meant to call you. We checked his truck. It has some scratches and bangs, on both sides. The ones on the passenger side could have been made running somebody off the road or driving on an undeveloped job site."

"What did he say, besides curse at you when you asked?"

She laughed. "You know the bastard. I threatened to drag his sorry ass to the jail if he cursed me one more time. He shut his mouth. Anyway, he said it gets banged up on the job sites he works. What else would he say? He said the latest ding came from sideswiping some boulders on a job in Escondido. We couldn't verify it but the DA says we don't have enough to charge him."

"I'm going to the desert in the morning to interview Kelly Smith. He's another one who threatened Flint. After Flint took over, the project suffered some major vandalism."

"Good luck."

"I was wondering if you wanted to come. I have to leave around five, I figure. I'm going to stake out his house and follow him to whatever job he's working."

"I ain't fixin' to get out of bed that early. Let me know what you find out. And, try to stay alive. You make work for me, Bone."

"Lunch at Denny's?"

"Not even that's gonna get me out of bed at five."

Try ten thousand dollars, Bishop thought.

Just before he climbed into bed, his phone rang. He knew before he punched "on," what the call was. "You should get on a plane while you can." The voice was obviously disguised. It could have been a man or a woman. He made a note to reference the hate calls in a kind of prologue to Flint's memoirs. If I'm around to write them.

\* \* \* \*

Bishop got up at four-thirty, had a quick cup of coffee and a roll. He wanted to be parked in front of Smith's house by seven. A cold call would prevent Smith from getting ready for him or having his wife hide behind a door with a loaded shotgun. Bishop didn't want to be on the terminal end of the death of the messenger.

He parked across the street one house away from Smith's at seven sharp. A light was on in the house but he could see no movement. Like most he'd driven past, the tract was primarily the California standard; ranch style houses with white stucco, already cracking. Garages facing the street and as close together as the building codes allowed.

Seven-thirty came and left and no car or truck came out of the Smith's garage. He chanced being seen by getting out and looking through the fixed windows in the garage door. Though almost dark inside, there was enough light to show a car and a truck.

He went back to his car and waited until eight. Still no sign of Smith. So, Bishop slid out of the seat and walked toward the front door, pad in hand. He rang the bell and waited. No one came so he rang it again. That time, he gave it a triple push. It opened. A woman wearing glasses and nearing her mid-sixties opened it. She was still in her nightclothes but had an apron wrapped around her waist. In her hand was a knife.

"Yes?" she asked with an angry tone. "What do you want? We ain't buying anything."

She reached to close the door but Bishop stuck his foot out and said, "I'm not selling anything, Mrs. Smith. I assume you are Kelly Smith's wife. My name is Bishop Bone. I want to ask Mr. Smith some questions about his experiences with Marc Flint. I've been asked to write something about Mr. Flint. I'm talking to everybody who had any significant dealings with him."

"So, you're the one his wife picked to write about the crooked son of a bitch that took my husband's life's savings from him. We barely had enough left to live on. That's the same as taking his life, as far as I'm concerned. Another month and he woulda been all right on that damn loan. Houses started selling but you think Flint would give him another month. No! He threw him out without so much as a how do you do."

"As I understand it, Mr. Flint was under orders from his client, The New Opportunity Bank to, in effect, foreclose because your husband was in default. As I recall from what I've read, your husband didn't have anything to sell at that time, did he? And, I should point out to you that Flint didn't have the right, certainly didn't have the authority to give your husband any time."

"Flint was a crooked bastard. He didn't have a soul."

"Maybe so, but I think you're getting mad … got mad at the wrong person, Mrs. Smith. You and Mr. Smith should look at why the project went bad in the first place. Flint didn't cause that, did he?"

"And, he sure as hell didn't try to help, did he! Just barged in like King Shit and took over."

"I've made a mental note of what you've said for what I'm writing." Including the King Shit crack. It'll spice up the memoir. "Now, where is your husband? His truck is in the garage. I'd like to speak to him. Ask why he vandalized the project after Flint took it over. He did quite a bit of damage. Do you know why he did that?"

She slammed the door in his face. Bishop heard voices from inside but couldn't make out anything that was said. One though was definitely male.

He pushed the doorbell again and kept pushing until the woman opened it again.

"If you don't stop pushing my door bell, I'm gonna call the cops and have you arrested."

"I know Mr. Smith is in the house."

"He ain't done it. He's in … Colorado working a job site. Now, you git. Unless you're planning to beat me up like you did Max Larson. You're no better than Flint." She stepped back and stared a few seconds. "Good God. Are you that bastard's brother? Kind of resemble each other from what I remember. I seen him around. I worked in the clubhouse after he stole the project from my husband."

"I didn't beat up Mr. Larson. He did attack me and I defended myself. What'd he do, call you? Maybe his wife did."

Must be a hate Flint club. All the members being developers whose projects Flint took. Larson or his wife must have warned them I might be calling.

"Poor man on his last legs and you beat him up. Don't push my doorbell again. You hear!" She slammed the door again. Bishop heard laughter from inside the house as he walked back to his car.

I left a warm bed for nothing. Good thing Ellen didn't come. I'd never hear the end of it.

Bishop sat in his car for a few minutes and made notes of the woman's remarks including his supposition that Smith was inside the house listening. His suspicion was supported by the fact that his truck was in the garage and he heard a man's voice.

He drove around the block and parked some distance away but close enough to keep an eye on the Smith's garage door. Sure enough, fifteen minutes later, the garage door opened and a white pickup backed out. In the driver's seat was a man wearing a billed cap. That was about all Bishop could make out.

Bishop followed the truck to a construction site. It looked like somebody was building a fourplex. Smith, he assumed, parked the truck and hopped out. He was a relatively short man with a mid-section that flopped over his belt. He wore denims that looked worn. He began walking the job site, pausing to talk to men working. When he'd made his way around and back to the front, Bishop got out of his car and walked to where he stood.

He had to pass the truck as he did. Like most construction vehicles, the truck was spotted with dings and scrapes. The ones that interested Bishop, however, were the ones near the front of the truck on the passenger side. The fender was pushed in. A sizable scrape showed.

A rifle rack was affixed to the back window but no rifle was in it.

Well, well. Maybe that's why he didn't want to talk.

Bishop walked up to the man, stuck out his hand and announced himself. "Sorry I missed you at your home, Mr. Smith. I'd like to ask you a few questions, if you don't mind."

The man's mouth dropped open. "What the hell're you doing here? Did you follow me you creepy shit? You're invading my privacy. That's stalking. I'm calling the police. He shouted to three guys framing a wall. This asshole is stalking me. Can you help me out?"

Bishop took out his phone, pretended to punch in a number and said, "Palm Springs police. I'm being attacked by four men holding hammers." He gave the address and shoved the phone back into his pocket.

"Better hurry. Cops are on the way. You'll spend time in the jail tonight. Probably get three to five years for attacking me. Felony assault. More if I die. Lots more. But, I don't think that's gonna happen." He reached behind his back where he might have had a gun.

The men stopped, looked at his hand then, looked at each other. One guy said, "Kelly, it ain't our fight. We're sorry. We really are, but we got families to feed."

To Bishop's everlasting joy, the sound of a siren was heard in the distance. He wasn't sure what had saved him, the warning, the siren or the fake reach for a gun, but he was grateful.

"Okay, call 'em off," Smith told Bishop. "I'll talk to you."

Bishop punched in a number and said. "Yeah. This is Bone. I just called. You can cancel my call. We've worked things out."

The siren sound had already begun to fade away. But, it had lasted long enough to get Bishop out of a tight situation. Now and then, the law of averages comes down on your side, he decided with a grateful smile.

Smith down sat on a stack of lumber and waited for Bishop to talk.

"Tell me what happened ... the takeover. You were in default. You had no money to complete the project and you'd already spent what you'd borrowed. Also, you had no other collateral to put up to get more money. Is that about it?"

The man shook his head. "Houses started selling after he took the project from me. Not too long after the bastard threw me out of my own building."

That was your company's building. You mortgaged it when you accepted the loan.

That's what Bishop was thinking but he kept it to himself. No need to get Smith started again.

Bishop recalled what Phillip said. "I believe the project had to be reworked completely. If houses started selling, it wasn't because of anything you'd done."

"Mine woulda sold."

"They weren't built, as I understand it."

He ignored that and said, "I lost everything I had in the project. Everything!"

"So, you poured cement down the wells and burned down the clubhouse. You could spend a long time in prison for that."

"Nobody says I did it."

"That was because Flint let it go. You have him to thank for that." Bishop was bluffing a little but thought it might help Smith put it behind him. How long can anybody live life looking backward? Larson and Smith.

Smith stared at Bishop, as if trying to assess what he'd just said.

"I never saw the man again. My wife did. She worked out there. I had to go back to working construction jobs to make ends meet. She still works here and there."

"Any comments you want to make about him?" Bishop asked.

"He was cold-hearted. A hard man. Never said a kind word to anybody according to the wife. He didn't care a damn bit about what I said, what I needed. I drank a six pack the day I heard he'd died. Celebrating. I was damned glad," Smith said.

"You weren't there? I thought somebody said you were."

"What the hell! Fuck that! Whoever said that was lying in their damn teeth. I was working a job, not two miles from here. Ten people'll swear to that."

"You have a gun rack on your truck. You must have a rifle," Bishop said.

He looked toward the truck. "Damn rack's been there since I bought the truck. Flint tried to take the truck but it was in my name, not the company's."

Not much worth writing down was said after that. Bishop was more or less satisfied that Smith had not run Flint off the road. As with other conclusions he'd reached about Flint's death, he wasn't certain but didn't see any other ravels he could pull just then but he had some things he could put in Flint's memoirs.

Bishop told the man goodbye and found a Denny's for breakfast and hot coffee. While he waited for his senior breakfast, he called Ellen with a report.

She answered on the first ring. He told her what had happened.

"I don't know if it's worth your while to talk to the man. I'm pretty sure he vandalized the project but Flint's financial officer said it didn't hurt them much. The damage was covered by insurance and the clubhouse needed taking down anyway. I doubt he ran Flint off the road, but I can't be sure. He has a gun rack but I figure if you check it out, you won't find a rifle in his house."

"Well, I've got better things to do anyway so I'll put him on a back burner for now. I will tell you this, Bone. Smith and Larson got their educations in the school of hard knocks, just like I did. In that school, if you get crapped on, and you got the cojones, you crap back. Justice is served. Nobody runs around feeling guilty. That's one reason I got into law enforcement. I get to be the crappor for crappees who are too weak to be a crappor for themselves," she said and added a chuckle.

"Good point, Ellen, I think. I forgot about that school. It's right around the corner from the law of the jungle. I've been out of life's loop too long, I guess. Smith's wife said as much. Flint took her husband's life-work when he took his company. I imagine Larson feels the same way. Not much I can do though. I'll write what they said and let the readers think what they want about whether either one killed him. Or, maybe by then, you'll have solved the case and they'll know."

"That's right," she answered.

"So, did you check out Derek?"

"We tried. We talked to a bunch of the people who were at the opening. Most of them, in fact. Rich people,

Bone. Rich and famous. They said Flint looked pale and was wobbling when he worked the crowd, shaking hands, backslapping and swapping stories. The Marshall guy who worked for him, Phillip I think is his name, said Flint'd been complaining about being tired, but he figured his boss was sandbagging him before they played their game. The security guard who saw him leave said he almost hit a car as he drove out. He was stumbling when he came out the clubhouse door. That's why he watched him drive off."

Hell, Phillip knew Flint had raging diabetes. His wife had told him the day before. I guess he was going with the story she was telling; that Marc didn't want anybody to know he was sick.

Some thought pushed to get into his consciousness but it slipped away before he could catch it. It'll come back, he told himself.

"Anything interesting on Derek?' he asked Ellen.

"I'm getting to Derek! Damned if you ain't a pushy son of a gun. Okay. Derek. He was in and out. Nobody knows for sure how long each time. We talked to the female real estate broker he disappeared with. People noticed that. He was gone about 20 minutes with her. She said he had something to show her. You can imagine what that was. She apparently didn't like what he showed her so they had an exchange of words and she returned to the party."

"Derek said he left another time to check on the entertainment people."

"He may have," Ellen said. "Some people said they saw him go in that direction. They didn't see him come back, but Anne Flint said he was at the opening until it ended. He caught a ride home with her."

"Yeah. They told me. Anything else?"

"You rushing me? I'm telling my story in my own damn time. Okay?"

"Sorry," Bishop said.

"Accepted. Okay, the Marshall guy, Flint's financial man, went out once. He told me. The beverage guy called him to say they had a delivery of champagne and needed help. He asked Derek to help. The beverage manager confirmed that two men showed up to unload some cases of champagne."

I guess I can tie a knot in that loose end.

"Good job, Ellen. I wonder if anybody saw them come back."

"Well, they must have if they brought the champagne inside. Thirsty bunch like that, they'd have been screaming for it."

"Yeah, I guess."

"The police were waiting at the Flint's house to tell Anne Flint that her husband was dead. I guess it was a good thing her brother was with her."

"I can imagine what a blow that must have been. Flint had just given a speech to put the finishing touches on the best project he'd done and bam, he dies," Bishop said.

"Yep. Woulda put me in bed. Anyway, later on, Derek picked up his girlfriend and drove her back to the clubhouse to pick up her car. They stayed at the Flint's house with the wife that night. We checked the car out. It had some damage but our so-called damage experts couldn't say for certain how it might have been caused. The girl said it was there when she got it. It didn't look like anything that'd run Flint's Jeep off the road."

"I suppose you called the entertainers to check on Derek's story. Dotting the I's and crossing the T's," he said.

"My middle name, Bone. We tried. They're on tour and we couldn't reach them. We left word for them to call. Who knows when that will be? So, all we know is Derek was seen going in that direction and helped take in some champagne. We don't know how long he stayed or if he went anyplace else, as in the street where Flint's Jeep was pushed over the side."

"Not much to go on," Bishop said. She mumbled her agreement.

"Well, it's not my problem," Bishop said. "I'm just writing the man's memoirs."

"I couldn't have said it better myself. Just write what you know or heard, Bone. That's all you're getting paid to do. I get paid to solve crimes. I'll do my job. You do yours. You're getting paid more than me anyway."

"Yeah. Frankly, I'm about ready to whip out a draft and leave it with Flint's wife. I don't have much else … well, maybe I do have a couple of things. I think I'll talk to Larson's money partners and Flint's outside marketing guy, Wakefield. He was at the grand opening. That'll just about wrap it up for me. I don't guess you know the money guys, do you? I don't want to go back to Larson with a question. His wife might still have an itchy trigger finger."

"I might have their names. We got names and numbers on everybody there. I'll email it to you, okay?"

"Okay."

"Good luck with your job, buddy," she said.

Bishop laughed. He knew what she was saying. She was ordering him to stay out of her patch. He said, "And, good luck with yours, Ellen. Oh, give me the girl's name and number. Derek's friend. I may want to talk to her."

"I believe that'd be messing around in my patch. Don't you? She didn't know Flint and wasn't at the opening. Didn't have the social standing, did she?"

"You're right, Ellen. I forget myself now and then. Just the others."

Bishop finished breakfast and drove back to La Jolla. Nobody was home at the Flints' so he lay down for a nap. It had been a long day already. He dozed for about an hour, got up and walked to the kitchen for a cup of coffee.

Anne was on the balcony facing Mata Park and the beach. He didn't figure she was enjoying the view so much as just staring at things moving down below to try and stay ahead of the depression she'd been fighting. Her glass of wine looked untouched.

He took his coffee and sat down at the table beside her.

She greeted him. "How'd your interview with the Smiths go?"

He gave her the blow-by-blow exchanges at the house and the almost real blow-by- blow at the job site.

"Quick thinking," she said about his fake phone calls.

"I had to come up with something. I wasn't up to taking on four guys, three with hammers."

"Not many men would be, Bishop." She reached over the table and softly put her hand on his forearm, and looked into his eyes with her faint smile. "I was just remembering when you hugged me in the hall. Thank you. That helped me."

"You're more than welcome. I enjoyed it too. You're a beautiful woman," he said.

She didn't follow the conversation with anything else and he was glad. What the hell would he do if she did? He made the decision to cut it off and leave. She was beautiful but so was Kathy and he wasn't looking for a one night stand.

"The other night you told Derek he might have to fend for himself. Did you mean it?" Bishop asked.

"Oh yes. I did. Of course, I won't let him starve, but it's time he made something of himself. Mom and Dad felt that way too. They said he'd always taken the easy way in life," she answered.

"The police aren't sure he was at the opening the entire time."

"I know. They talked to me about it. I told them every time I looked around, I saw him so I don't think he had time to drive Marc off the street. What would he have used anyway?" she asked.

"He was driving his girlfriend's old Chevy and he had a motive. Marc was trying to fire him and had been humiliating him at the office."

"I know, but Derek isn't … how can I put this? He doesn't have the will to kill anybody. That'd mean he'd have to make a decision. That's his big flaw. He can't make decisions. That's why he's never been able to hold a decent job for long."

Bishop had to admit her reasoning made sense. However, he recalled an old cliché. Every man has his breaking point. Was the pregnant girl's humiliation Derek's breaking point?

But, he'd write it like he'd heard it. Nobody wanted his opinions in Flint's life story.

After they'd finished their visit, he excused himself and went back to his room to begin writing a first draft. Mostly, he wanted to see how it flowed. He started with Flint's death after the grand opening of perhaps the most significant achievement of his career, the La Jolla Apogée.

Then, Bishop flashed back to Flint's childhood. For that, he used what Flint's mother and Anne had told him. He thought it flowed well.

By the time he'd finished, it was too late to call anyone. He went into the living area of the house. No one was around. He checked the garage. Anne and Derek's cars were gone. He wondered if they were out together or on separate dates.

"I'd be surprised if Anne didn't get invitations. By now all the eligibles know she's available. Maybe her publisher stayed in town a few days."

Everybody believes California women are liberated and always at the ready. A smile is as good as an invitation to the bedroom.

So, he went to dinner by himself. It was a hamburger night. He picked the In 'n Out Burger place. He'd never had a bad hamburger there and didn't have one that night either.

While there, he caught Kathy up on what he'd been doing. He promised to email her his first draft after he'd read it the next morning. That's when all the errors and inconsistences would jump out at him.

Neither Anne nor Derek were in when he returned so he typed more on his draft and went to bed. He had about 30 pages of decent material with more in his notes. His goal was 100 pages. He was almost to the point of finishing up at his cabin with Kathy visiting.

He sent an email to Terry Wakefield, one of the few for whom he had an email address, asking if he had time to meet the next day. Terry dealt with Flint day in and day out and should be able to give a decent impression of the man.

Jackson Irvin and Carson Adams were also on his list to see. They were Larson's money partners. Bishop wanted to see if they had formed any opinions of Flint. To a certain extent, they traveled in the same circles as Flint and may have known him socially. He was curious to know what they thought.

Bishop also wondered why they hadn't stepped forward when Larson needed more money for the project. If they had liked it in the beginning, why wouldn't they still like it? Larson said they had plenty and wouldn't blink at the amounts they had lost.

But, Bishop had been around long enough to doubt Larson's assessment. People with lots of money hated to lose it as much as people who didn't. But, it was a loose end that he wanted to tie up.

\* \* \* \*

Wakefield's reply was on Bishop's iPhone the next morning, asking him to call which he did over coffee on the Flints' balcony. No one was up except him. He decided he was still on Mississippi time, two hours later than California time.

"This is Terry," the man said when he answered.

"Bishop Bone. I'd like to meet with you today and talk about Marc Flint if you have the time. That sort of thing. I want to get your impressions of the man and listen to any stories you want to share for his memoirs. I assume you know I'm writing them for Anne."

"Sure I know. It's been in the papers but I knew anyway. Maybe Phillip told me. I may have some stuff for you. It'd be business. I didn't know him socially. How about breakfast?"

"Sounds good to me. Where would you like to meet?"

He liked a popular place off Girard called the Brick and Bell. "We can get a breakfast sandwich and coffee and eat it outside. Great coffee."

Bishop remembered the charming used brick cafe. "What time?"

Wakefield paused for a second. "Well, how about eight or eight thirty? I have a couple of calls to make. That should give me time."

Either was okay with Bishop. They settled on "around eight."

Bishop finished his coffee.

## CHAPTER 12

He called Kathy before leaving for the Brick and Bell. She was doing okay but was missing him.

"I miss you too, Kathy. I think I'm about to wind things up. Or, it could be that Flint's wife, Anne, might want me to stop. I've run into some problems."

She asked so he recounted the phone calls and text messages and the shot out window of his car as well as his confrontations with Larson and Smith. He didn't mention the one he almost had with Derek, thinking he might be lurking around. No need to create more animosity.

Bishop parked a block away and walked to the café. It was already busy but there was one empty table, covered by an umbrella, in front. As Bishop approached, a short, heavyset, younger man in his forties, hurried up and sat down. He was wearing a suit without a tie. Had a neat haircut, dark hair and wore no glasses. Plus, his shoes were newly shined, unlike Bishop's. His tennis shoes didn't require shining, ever, and the khakis he word never needed pressing as far as he was concerned.

Bishop bet he was Terry Wakefield. The guy kind of looked like a real estate broker, all business and always with a smile. They hadn't set any guidelines for identification but since he hadn't gone in directly, he must be waiting for someone and that might be me, Bishop thought.

He walked up and stuck out his hand. "Bishop Bone," he said. "You must be Terry Wakefield."

The man took his hand for a firm handshake. "Be damned! How'd you know?"

"Just a guess. How do we order? How are we going to hold this table?" Bishop asked.

Wakefield took off his coat and hung it over the back of the chair he was on. "People around here accept a coat as evidence of ownership for the time it takes to have coffee and a bite," he said with a broad smile. "Longer than that and I'll be looking for another coat." He laughed.

Bishop added his and followed him inside to order a breakfast wrap and coffee. Wakefield paid.

They took the food and drink back to their table. "You asked for this meeting," Wakefield said with a gesture and a smile. "Fire away." He chowed down. Bishop matched him chomp for chomp but managed to ask questions in between.

Bishop asked him how he'd met Flint, his first impressions and later ones. How was he to work for, easy or hard? What kind of business man was he? Did he cut corners or make payoffs? And finally, were all the stories about Flint's womanizing true?

Wakefield told him that Flint was always fair to him. "But, I didn't give him any reason not to be. I did what he asked, when he asked and how he asked. If he said jump, I said how high?"

He said Flint was a shrewd business man. "He had an instinct about when somebody was bluffing or serious, when somebody wanted to deal or not. He knew people. And, as far as I know, he never cut corners and never made a payoff. For sure he never asked me."

"Would you have if he had?"

He shook his head. "Most likely. I know how to do it in such a way that if somebody wants to say no and start screaming bribe, I know how to leave myself enough wiggle room to be indignant and deny it. Most of the people I work with would take the money, however. Everybody can use a little extra." He grinned.

"How'd you meet?" Bishop asked. His sandwich was down to its last bite and his cup was empty. He left Wakefield to ponder the question and to catch up on his breakfast wrap while he went for refills for both. When he returned with the coffees, Wakefield said, "I was a junior real estate salesman sitting tracts on weekends. He stopped by the model home complex where I was working to see what his competition was doing. Most developers do it. I saw him out of the corner of my eyes, watching me give my spiels to interested lookers. He made the rounds and came back toward the end of the day and asked if I had time for a beer."

"I did and followed him to his house. He had just finished it. Like a museum. Beautiful. Anyway, we got to talking and the next thing I knew, I was agreeing to head up a real estate company for him and sell all his homes, all over. He had put his broker's license in the company. I'd own the stock. I executed an agreement to pay ten percent of the net commissions each month into a trust."

"I think I know about that," Bishop said. That'd be for Flint's mother "What happens now that he's dead?"

"Well, he was a lawyer so the agreement provided for that contingency, his death. I don't think he expected to die, but he covered it in the agreement. As I said, he was a lawyer, a good one. If he died, the company and I would pay the trust a termination fee of one hundred and fifty thousand dollars payable in monthly installments of five thousand dollars each."

That's how he made sure his mother would be cared for, Bishop decided, and nobody would ever find out. I guess the man was shrewd.

"Did his wife know?"

"I don't think so. He never said, but he kept things like that to himself. His lawyers will likely tell her. They have the agreement."

"Are you going to do it? Pay the money?"

"Sure. I signed the agreement. Hell, I have fifteen salespeople working tracts all over, not just his. We have listings from all over as well. But, I haven't forgotten how I got started. I owe it all to him. I've been told I have to bid on his projects going forward but I don't see that as a problem. I can undercut the competition and we know the product better than anybody else."

"Womanizing? Is it true?"

He laughed. "I don't know how that started. I think to begin with, he was more interested in getting his projects to marketability. But, some women waved it in front of him and he took what was offered. That started the reputation. It just grew and pretty soon, sleeping with Marc gave a woman bragging rights. It meant they were highly desirable if Marc wanted to have sex with them. He was considered rugged with great sex appeal."

"Anybody ever want to kill him over it?" Bishop asked.

"What? Kill him! Hell, not that I know. A couple of men got pissed enough to kind of threaten him, but they backed away when Marc came after them. He could knock heads. He never backed away from a fight or a threatened fight, I should say. He didn't have that many, though," Wakefield said.

"Do you think he was himself at the opening? Was he sick?"

"Well, I heard the story about the diabetic coma and all. Looking back, I can say that he looked sick, acted odd. I didn't think much of it at the time. Hell, we all overdo sometimes. I just figured he'd had a big party the night before."

"Did you stay until the end?" Bishop asked.

"You're damn right! I had salespeople answering questions, I had to be there in case they needed answers or support. The La Jolla bunch wants to be stroked. It comes with money. I don't mind. Stroking pays well. I drive a Tesla now, thanks to Marc. Got myself a new wife. She doesn't give a shit if I look like a sausage as long as her credit card bills get paid."

"You're living your dream," Bishop said, more tongue in cheek than truthful.

Wakefield laughed. "I'd say."

Wakefield started to get up, but sat down and asked, "Has Phillip said anything about those two guys I sent his way? The guy with the limited partnerships was excited. Hell, he could take the tax losses Marc had squirreled away and make his investors happy. Marc once told me he hadn't paid a dime in income taxes since he'd gotten into the business."

Bishop did a quick take on what Wakefield had just said. Apparently the companies Flint took over had been suffering losses. That made sense. Flint merged the companies together and kept the losses available to offset gains his company had when his projects became profitable. So, if someone bought the company and merged it with theirs, they could continue to use the tax losses.

Phillip hadn't said anything about the tax losses. He had only talked about the two properties the company had been offered. "Trash properties," he had called them.

Bishop said, "Phillip mentioned something about it when he was telling me about two trash properties the liquidation committee had offered to sell the company.

Kind of a don't make trouble offer and you'll get a going away present."

"Yeah," Wakefield smiled. "Marc had me write a marketing report about both pieces. I went heavy on what it would cost to develop the properties, the off-sites and permits. And I went light on the marketability of any units that could be built on it."

"Are they bad or what?" Bishop asked.

"Truthfully, the parcels aren't all that bad. I figure the company could build seventy to eighty units, VA, FHA of course, on both properties, sell 'em all within six months and make a nice profit."

"So, the guy with the limited partners looking to maximize the returns to the partners would love to have some way to not only eliminate his income taxes for a time but also to have some marketable inventory. A merger with Flint's company could provide both," Bishop said.

"Hell, Phillip said they still had around a million in tax losses. I told him he could probably clear four hundred thousand, give or take, if he sold the company with the loss carry forwards and the properties."

Bishop cursed instead of the usual whistle at such a deal.

"Yeah. He'd owe me a finder's fee, of course," Wakefield grinned. "He signed a fee agreement."

"I'll be seeing him. I'll bring it up," Bishop said.

"I'd be surprised if they didn't get together."

"I imagine he's waiting until he closes with the liquidation committee and has the company in his name," Bishop said.

"I guess. I was just curious about the negotiations. If Marc was handling the negotiations, they'd be wrapped up by now and he'd have the money in his pocket."

"No doubt. Phillip isn't as skilled as Flint but he seems to know his way around."

That was the end of breakfast. An interesting meeting, Bishop concluded.

However, as Wakefield walked away, Bishop had another question and chased after him. "Terry," he called the man's name. "I had one more question."

The man stopped and turned with a smile. "Ask away. If I know, I'll tell you."

"I was wondering if you knew anything about Jackson Irvin and Carson Adams. They were Max Larson's money partners for the La Jolla project Flint took over."

Wakefield frowned as if thinking. "I know a little. Both are rich as hell. Adams got his from his wife. Her husband died and left her with a bundle. Adams moved in and started spending it. From what I hear, not everything he touches turns to gold like her late husband. That man could make the money. Adams likes to play rich.

"Now, Irvin has money. He earned it from investments. A couple of months ago, he invested heavy in a startup software company. I don't know what it does, just heard a little. Something to do with medical records. That's about all I know."

Bishop thanked him and let him go. He walked back to his car to drive back to the Flint's home.

\* \* \* \*

As Bishop drove, he talked to himself. "I wonder if Phillip told Anne about the tax losses and how much the company could be worth. A significant amount, really. I have to tell her. I work for her and what I just learned would definitely be something I'd put in Flint's memoirs. The man never stopped thinking."

Phillip had said she was giving the company to him. However, Bishop was not sure whether she had given it or was going to give it after the close and document signings with the liquidation committee.

"I'd think it'd be after the close, but I'll ask. In any case, if he made false pretenses, she could probably file an action to void the gift." So, Phillip stood to gain from Flint's death. Puts a new slant on things.

When he walked into the living area, she was giving instructions to a cleaning lady about how she wanted something done. Bishop fiddled around with the coffee machine until the instruction giving was finished.

"Won't you join me?" he asked. "I'll bring you up to date on what I've learned today."

She looked at him with a frown. "I don't really have the time, Bishop. I was about to take a shower and go out. I have an appointment at the hairdressers. My publisher has asked me to dinner. Can you make it quick?"

He told her what he'd learned during his meeting with Wakefield. Marc had set up Wakefield's company and had put his broker's license in the company until Wakefield could qualify for one.

She said, "Marc was satisfied with the way Wakefield handled sales. Wakefield did pretty much what Marc wanted."

Bishop told her about Flint's fee arrangement with Wakefield. How the fee was deposited into the trust account used to pay for his mother's care at the nursing home.

"He didn't tell me about that. That means I don't have to scrap around for money to do it. Thanks for that bit of news. Marc's attorneys would probably have told me eventually. I haven't met with them about Marc's estate. I've been putting it off until after the closing."

"I did learn one more thing, I'm not sure if it's important or not, but it could be," Bishop said.

He talked about Wakefield finding at least two companies interested in acquiring Flint's company. One of which, the one with the limited partners as investors, seemed seriously interested.

"They would develop the two pieces of property the liquidation committee is selling the company."

"Good idea," she said.

"They'd be able to cover any profits made from sales of the units built on the properties with the tax loss carry forwards of the company. Marc had ... well Phillip had made sure the losses from the companies they acquired over the years stayed intact and could be used to offset profits from operations."

"Marc never told me any of that. Just as well. I don't understand any of what went on at the company. Tax losses. Might as well be talking Greek."

"Wakefield said the company might be worth three or four hundred thousand if sold as is."

She looked surprised. "That much?"

"That's what Wakefield said. When Marc knew the lender, through the liquidation committee, would be taking everything back, he signed a fee agreement with Wakefield to find someone to buy the company or partner with him so he could stay in business. Someone who could use the company's tax losses. I don't know why Parsons didn't find them. Maybe he did and just didn't care," Bishop said.

Anne touched her fingers to her lips and said, "I told Phillip he could have the company after the close.

Marc's attorney is preparing an indemnification agreement for him to sign. We talked today. He asked how you were doing with the memoirs. I told him you were about to finish up."

"What will the agreement say, otherwise?"

"Not much. He'll agree to hold me harmless from any lawsuits that may crop up in the future. He'll pay me a hundred dollars for the stock. We'll agree that the company has no value to speak of. The property the liquidation committee is virtually worthless because of what it'll cost to develop it. Maybe in the future it'll have value but not now. Phillip is looking for a builder who can hold it until then," she said.

"So, you haven't actually transferred the stock to Phillip yet."

"No. Now, I'll have my attorney talk to him about the … what'd you call it, Bishop, the tax losses. Four hundred thousand dollars is a lot of money for a company I was led to believe would have no value."

"It might not have value but for the tax losses and the two pieces of properties," Bishop explained.

"I'll call and ask them to talk to Phillip."

"I will put that in Marc's memoirs. It shows how Marc thought about business, how he always kept an eye on the bottom line," Bishop said.

She shook her head in agreement, obviously lost in thought about what he'd just said. She finished her coffee and stood.

She started to say something but Bishop interrupted and asked, "By the way, during our first interview, you said Marc might have been interested in another woman, besides Sarah Webster, a married woman. She said you might tell me along the way."

"Yes, I might have said –"

"It's Linda Marshall, isn't it?"

She looked shocked. "How'd you ... did she tell you? How?"

"I've kind of developed a pattern for the kind of women Marc liked. What they looked like, their personalities, their ages. He liked the little girl, innocent look. Smart and not cynical. Linda fit the pattern. Sarah did also."

Anne was already shaking her head in disbelief. "Hard to believe he was that transparent."

"I can't say he was. It's just that in talking to them, it kind of jumped out. Especially after you'd told me about him. Also what you'd said about Sarah."

"Well, you're right. I was talking about Linda. He seemed to gravitate toward her. Like he did Sarah."

"Did Phillip know?" Bishop asked.

"If he did, he never said. I don't think Marc told him and I doubt Linda did. Most married women keep their affairs private," she said.

She looked at her phone, the time. "Gotta go. We'll talk more. I have to call our attorney. I'll see you this afternoon."

After she'd gone, he wondered if he'd opened a can of worms for Phillip telling Anne about the tax losses. He decided he'd done the right thing.

"It sure as hell looks like Phillip was trying to pull a fast one. Letting her believe the company had no value when with a little bit of work, it could be worth almost half a million dollars. That might not seem like much to the typical La Jolla resident, it sure does to me. And, from Anne's reaction, it did to her as well. Not my problem, though. I was hired to write the man's memoirs."

He went to his room to make notes of his meeting that morning with Wakefield and his subsequent meeting with Anne. He had begun typing his notes onto his computer.

"I'd be curious to see if Flint kept notes of what he was doing ... what his plans were," he said to himself. "Anne said he had an office on the lower floor. I'll ask if I can have a look around. Maybe he had a computer. I'd like to check his files."

After he'd finished his updates, he called Jackson Irvin and Carson Adams. Irvin was out of town, but Adams could meet with him that after lunch at his home in the Farms on the view side of Black Gold Road. The Farms was an exclusive residential area near UCSD. The view homes looked down on Black's Beach, known for sunbathing. Visitors could let it all hang out on Black's Beach or just look at what others were letting hang out.

A Hummer was parked in Adams' drive way. Naturally Bishop inspected the passenger side. Indeed, it had a scrape.

He rang the doorbell. A tall, thin guy with bushy brown hair answered. "Come in," he said. "You must be Bishop Bone. I'm Carson."

Bishop assured him that he was and shoved out his hand for the customary hand shake. Afterward, he followed him to the living room at the back of the house. Bishop did the expected and admired the view and "wondered how in the world anybody could ever get used to it."

Adams replied that he never had.

They sat down in soft chairs facing each other. His wife was out.

Bishop said, "I'm writing the memoirs of Marc Flint. You may know that."

He did. He'd read about it in The Light .

"I know you were an investor in the La Jolla project that Max Larson lost to Flint. Do you mind talking about that?"

He didn't. Although he and Irvin had wanted Flint to get them more time, he knew it wasn't likely and that they were going to lose their investment. "Human nature to kick somebody when they get down. Larson got down and he got kicked. Unfortunately, we got kicked with him."

He blamed Larson for beginning the road construction and the utilities before they had written approval from the city. A consultant without authority told Larson that everything looked good, but the planning department hadn't agreed. By the time Larson had made all the changes, they were out of money and the lender had stopped funding, because their construction management department didn't think there was enough money left in the loan to complete the project.

The lender had asked for an additional investment from Adams and Irvin but neither man offered any and Larson was totally out of money.

"Irvin was getting into some kind of software company and frankly, I didn't have any money left to invest. My wife and I pass judgment on investments and she didn't feel that Larson was a safe bet so we told him no when he asked for more. That was a mistake, but …" He shrugged.

Bishop thought, his wife made the judgments about investments according to Wakefield. Adams just enjoyed being a wheeler dealer with his wife's money.

"Larson said you and Irvin could afford to lose the money. You'd just deduct it on your tax returns."

Adams laughed. It was a nervous laugh. "That's not exactly true. My wife lets me made the investments but she makes me accountable for the results."

"You were at the opening."

"Larson asked us to come. Give him some moral support. We didn't know what he was going to say, but figured he'd say about what he did."

"Did you stay until it was over?"

"We stayed. We danced and enjoyed the food and drink."

"Did you leave for a time?"

Adams looked puzzled. "Leave? Why? No, I didn't. I don't think Jackson did either. Once the music started, I lost track of him."

"I saw your Hummer outside. Did you drive that to the opening?"

"Ah, that's not my Hummer. It belongs to my wife's son. I did use it though. I drove it to the opening. How'd you guess? My car was in the shop. Her son lent it to me."

"I couldn't help notice the scrapes on the passenger side."

"I caught hell for that. I can tell you. That damn car is bigger than my little car and I ran into a tree when I parked it."

"It didn't do the fender any good," Bishop said.

"You should see the tree. I hope nobody sends me a bill for it."

"The police think somebody might have run Flint off the road with a car like a Hummer."

"No shit! Damn, now I wish somebody had seen me. I didn't run Flint off the road. He left long before I did. Right after he said his few words. He looked pretty damned shaky at the mic. I wasn't surprised when they said he'd passed out and ran off the road. You're saying that's not the way it happened."

"Apparently not."

"I didn't see much of Jackson after the music started, but he was around. He drives a Mercedes. I can't swear it, but I think he was around for a good hour after Flint left."

Bishop thanked him.

## CHAPTER 13

On his way home, he called Ellen and told her about the Hummer and the man's story. It was up to her what she did with it. She said she'd send somebody out to talk to him.

Bishop decided not to bother with Irvin and crossed him off his list. He knew enough from Wakefield and Adams to include him in the memoirs with a one sentence comment.

\* \* \* \*

He drove back to the Flints to record his notes. He had sixty pages of decent material. Around six, he came out of his room and went into the kitchen to see what he could find to eat. Derek was doing the same thing. Anne had been picked up for her dinner at the La Valencia.

"Find anything?" Bishop asked.

"Not a damn thing. She just left. Didn't leave anything to eat. Crappy. I don't have people picking me up for a big night on the town. I'm practically on welfare."

"Well, I'm thinking I'll have a hamburger and fries. You can be my guest."

Derek hesitated, frowned as if wondering if Bishop had anything up his sleeve. Of course Bishop did. No way would he buy Derek anything unless he expected information in return.

"Yeah. Why not?" Derek answered. "Where'd you have in mind?"

"How about the Public House? They have a pretty good burger and fries. Take your pick of beer or ale," Bishop said.

"I'd want wine. I'm not into beer. To common for me. I'll look at the menu for something decent."

"I'm sure you'll find something you can stand, Derek. It is kind of blue collar but it's comfortable and I love it. Relaxing atmosphere."

"Okay. Let's go."

Bishop drove. They parked in front of the red shiplapped wooden building, farmhouse style including a charming porch, with the quaint sign on the roof.

Bishop ordered a beer the waitress recommended. Derek asked for one of their award winning ales, though reluctantly, Bishop thought. They got an order of crab cakes for starters and when the waitress brought their drinks, they placed their regular orders. Bishop ordered a regular hamburger without onions and cooked well done. Derek ordered their blackened fish.

"What are you doing with your time?" Bishop asked. "I imagine you're getting pretty bored."

"Not really. I surf to stay in shape. Evelyn joins me when she can. She works in a law office and goes to night school at Cal Western. She'll graduate next year. The firm where she works has offered her a position."

"Congratulations to her."

"Yeah. I'm thinking about marrying her."

Why not, she'd be working, bringing in money.

"You haven't told her?"

"No. I didn't want to worry her while she's working so hard. She's law review and is under a deadline to finish an article."

"Must have good grades," Bishop said.

"She'll be a good lawyer. Won her Hale Court competition."

Bishop knew Hale Court was a kind of mock trial that let students play lawyer in a real case environment.

"You shouldn't let her get away."

"I'm not."

They drank their beer and made small talk about nothing in particular until the food came. It was steaming, and smelled great. And, after the first bite, Bishop proclaimed, "I've never had a better hamburger."

Derek was less enthusiastic but did give an endorsement for his blacken fish. More telling was the enthusiasm with which he devoured it.

"Other than getting married one day, what else are you planning? Your unemployment checks won't last forever. You strike me as a people person. Maybe you should look for something that'd let you use those skills. Maybe something in sales."

"I have a liberal arts degree. Anne helped me get through San Diego State. I guess I am friendly, well not always. I apologize for getting on your case when you showed up. You looked like Marc, you weren't married and Anne seemed to like you. I could see you moving in and kicking me out. I didn't like it."

"I figured. Is that why you called me? The hate calls to warn me off writing Flint's memoirs? Shot out my back window. You were in the Army for a time. You'd know how to shoot."

His face became a mask of puzzlement. "Uh, no. I didn't call you. Ever. I didn't like you like I just said, but I didn't call you and I sure didn't shoot out your car window if that's what you're thinking. Hell, in basic training I got more Maggie drawers than anything on the firing range. That's why I ended up working as a medic." The range officers waved something that looked like a pair of women's drawers when the shooters missed the target completely.

"You have a rifle?"

He didn't. "You're free to search my room."

"You might have stashed it with your girlfriend."

"Not likely. She hates guns. One of those antigun nuts. You can look if you want. I'm sure she wouldn't mind."

He seemed sincere enough, but Bishop never completely let anybody off the hook until he was absolutely certain.

Derek said, "I'd heard of you when Anne said you were coming out. You got involved in some murders in the Shores. I saw the write up in the Light."

"I did."

"That bothered me too. I figured Anne might go for you because of that."

"Not likely, Derek. She's too smart for that. Your sister is a very attractive woman. I'd have to be blind not to notice, but I love someone in Mississippi."

"It doesn't matter now ... about you. Now, she's fooling around with somebody else. Her publisher. Probably a crock of shit guy, but he most likely took one look and decided to go for it. She gravitates toward important people ... well, men."

Bishop shrugged.

"How do you get on with Terry Wakefield?" Bishop asked. "Maybe he'd give you a shot at selling for him. Good place to use your people skills."

"I've thought about sales. I'd rather go into business for myself. I hate working for other people. They're always telling me what to do. Rubs me the wrong way."

*Especially with a chip as big as the one you have on your shoulder.*

"You have to have something to sell to go into business yourself. And, for that, you'd need working

173

capital. Do you plan to ask Anne for money?" Bishop asked.

"She'd say no. She's already told me I have to find something to do. I have a couple of ideas."

"What?"

"I'd rather not say. It seems to me that as soon as I tell somebody an idea, it goes away. I'll wait until I'm ready to say anything."

"Good luck."

They finished up and drove home.

Anne came in a few minutes after they did.

"How'd it go?" Bishop asked.

"It wasn't bad. Got me out of the house. The food was okay. Something gourmet. Paul kept asking how I was doing, my plans, kept the ball in my court. I wanted to hear about him, see what made him tick. I still don't know enough about the guy to know if I like him or not. He publishes books. Well, he works for a big publisher in New York. That's all I know. I know more about you than him."

"Maybe I'm not trying to hide anything," Bishop replied.

"That's what bothered me during dinner. I began to wonder if the guy was married. You know what I mean. Looking to score with a lonely widow." She laughed. "He said he was staying at the hotel. I let that go. I knew what he was suggesting."

Bishop laughed. "I wouldn't be surprised. You are a very attractive woman. Desirable doesn't do you justice."

She reached over and put her hand on his arm as she'd done once before. "A little more of that kind of talk and I'll ask for another one of your hugs. Not even

Marc was that ... understanding. If you know what I mean."

He did. Some men kept their feelings to themselves for fear of overinflating a woman's ego to the point that she wants more and goes looking. He smiled and looked into her eyes. She seemed pleased but said nothing more.

They walked down the hall toward the bedrooms. Indeed, as they reached hers, she turned and kissed Bishop full on the lips. He instinctively responded but immediately caught himself.

"Thank you. It isn't often I get a kiss from someone most men would kill for. I'll probably think about that one for a while." He smiled and turned to leave before she could say more. He didn't want his resistance tested.

She touched his nose and smiled knowingly.

He was relieved to close his own door behind him. He opened his computer and entered his notes.

Sleep wasn't easy that night. He kept remembering Anne's kiss. He knew she wanted to be friendly and he knew he didn't want that to happen.

He called Kathy the next morning. She asked if he was about ready to come home. She missed him. "I'm lonely here, Bishop," she said.

"Same here," he replied. No way was he going to say anything about Anne. He had hoped she would decide to send him home without finishing writing her husband's memoirs. That didn't happen.

"Maybe you could fly out here," he said and immediately ran through how that'd work. One good thing he figured. Anne would probably fire him as soon as she met Kathy.

Kathy put an end to his speculation. "No, I can't. Thank you though. Mom needs me here."

He'd try to finish in a week and get home.

\* \* \* \*

The thought of a fresh cup of coffee brought him to the kitchen the next morning. That, and a warm croissant. No one was in sight but a plate of croissants was on the table with jam and butter. He put two on a saucer, got a coffee and went outside to take in the view and to think about what he could do next.

Derek was probably on the beach for a morning surf with Evelyn. Anne had said something about an early Garden Club meeting with breakfast. Later she had a deadline to meet with her latest book. The cover was giving her some problems.

As he had his breakfast, he asked himself, "So, what do I do next? Maybe I should be thinking about winding things up. I have enough to glorify the man."

Phillip, he thought, I should see Phillip about the tax losses before I close my books. Why didn't he tell Anne about it? I want to read his face as I ask. Was that enough money to motivate him to kill his boss?

Bishop usually figured a million as the kind of money that would motivate murder. In La Jolla, three or four hundred thousand wasn't big money among the high rollers.

"It's not even my problem anymore. I've told Anne. But, I guess I'm curious."

He showered, dressed in his working khakis and headed toward the Flint company offices, soon to belong to the liquidation committee.

He parked in front of the building. Phillip's old truck was parked on the street. He opened the door to get out when his cellphone rang. It was Ellen. "Ellen, it isn't often I get a call from someone I like."

"Enough of your bullshit, Bone. I've been out doing the work you gave me. Talking to Adams. The guy who drove his stepson's Hummer."

"I do recall telling you about that."

"Yeah. Big favor. We talked to the man. Got the same story you got," she said with more than a touch of sarcasm in her voice. "Went to the clubhouse parking lot. Found the tree about where the man said he left it. It was scarred up, just like he described, but still alive. To make sure we covered our tracks, we called the security service. They remembered the Hummer. It was the only one at the opening. And, they didn't see it leave. So, Mr. Bone, can we close our books on Mr. Adams?"

"You do very well, Ellen. I'm gonna put a star beside your name."

"Yeah. Well, we still don't have a suspect for anything that'd lead to jail time or a promotion for me. Any other bright ideas?"

"I'm always working, always thinking, always keeping you in mind. As I stumble over clues, you're the first person I think about."

"I wish you'd do a little more thinking, less stumbling and a lot less calling."

"I hear you. I'll keep in touch only if what if find is glowing."

"I may be out of town, extended leave. Leave a message."

Bishop laughed.

"Before you punch off, Bone. One more bit of news for you. The manager of the touring musicians that played at the opening called. Derek did come out to see if everything was okay. Right behind Derek was another man who was putting his phone in his coat pocket as he walked up. He and Derek talked but the manager couldn't hear much. He thought the man with the phone said something about "help." Wore glasses and a black suit. They walked away together."

"The other guy was Phillip Marshall. He worked for Flint as his chief financial officer. He drives the old pickup."

"The manager didn't see either man after that. So, that's the end of what I had on my plate. I'll be seeing you ... if I can't avoid it." She laughed.

"I like a woman who tells it like it is." He thanked her for calling.

* * * *

Bishop didn't bother ringing the bell at the front door of the Flint company offices. He just turned the knob and walked in. It wasn't locked. Bishop saw Phillip at his desk in his shirt sleeves pouring over a file. Phillip looked up when he heard the front door open. There was no smile on his face.

"Bone," he said, as Bishop approached. "What brings you here? Linda said you came by to see her. I guess you know all our family secrets now." He forced a smile.

"Most likely not all," Bishop said. "May I sit down?"

Phillip gestured, palm out toward a chair. Bishop took it.

"I came to see you about tax losses," he said.

He thought Phillip's face turned white. He took off his glasses as if something had suddenly clouded them over. Then, he put them back on.

"Tax losses? You've lost me."

"I doubt it. I'm talking about the tax losses you and Flint hid from Parsons and to get to the point, from Anne. Correct me if I'm wrong, but I believe you've been saying the company has no value. That's what you told Parsons and Anne. Now, as I recall, failure to disclose a material fact when you know someone will rely on that failure to their detriment, might be called by some as fraud. It's been awhile since I wallowed in the gutter about duplicity, but that's my recollection. What do you think? Would three to four hundred thousand be a material fact?"

Phillip pushed back in his chair, straightened his glasses and picked up the pen he'd been holding when Bishop walked in. "You've been digging around, I see."

"Anne is paying me to write memoirs. I'm just doing what she's paying me to do. I found out that you've been negotiating to sell the company to a developer with limited partner investors for four hundred thousand dollars. That'd include the two pieces of land that you've been calling worthless. I understand that the land is not worthless. I'd call that another material fact."

Phillip looked around the room as if searching for something. Bishop figured he was searching for an answer. Finally, he looked at Bishop and said, "I'm not a lawyer. I'm an accountant. Marc started this process before he died. I'm just following through. I know this much. In the business world, you can't count the money until it's in the bank. The possibility that the tax losses might be worth something is just that, a possibility, until a buyer puts money on the table. Nobody has done that yet."

"Good thing I'd say," Bishop replied. "Until the closing, you don't really have anything to sell. Anything of value belongs to the liquidation committee. Right?"

"Right. Marc had a handshake agreement with the lender's chairman. If he asked for everything back, Marc would give it, no arguments. Later, they reduced that to a one sheet agreement, just as broad. There was nothing in it that required Marc, now me, to speculate about value. They're taking back everything that has tangible value as of now, not some speculative potential. They agreed to sell the company two pieces of land Marc had studies run on by a reputable real estate company. Those values were accepted and the company will get those properties with a mortgage equal to the values reported," Phillip said.

"Speculative potential? You know the value of the tax losses. Nothing speculative about it."

"They're only good for a company in the same business as we were in, as I understand it. The liquidation committee isn't in any kind of business."

Bishop breathed loudly. "However, the liquidation committee might have contact with a builder like you that could use them."

"Maybe. I'm not paid to think for them, Bishop. They audited the books and records and didn't find anything of value."

"But, you're negotiating to sell something. I think an argument could be made that you only negotiate if there's something of value to sell," Bishop said pointing at him.

Phillip shook his head. "Nobody's talking real money until after the closing. That'll be next week, the lawyers told me yesterday."

Bishop laughed. "Do you honestly think anybody would believe that? What are you using for value, the report Flint asked for?"

"Uh, well, actually, we haven't talked numbers at all. The guy, the builder, is just kind of looking things over to see if he might be interested."

"Listen, I know you dangled the tax losses in front of him. So, let's cut the bullshit. What I don't know is what value you are assigning to the properties."

"I don't know about that. Marc did all that kind of thing. I'm ..."

"Just a numbers guy, Phillip. Yeah. You told me. And tax losses are numbers. Assuming you work out something with Flint's wife, you'd better get some help. You don't know shit from Shinola about developing real estate or putting a value on it."

"Uh, would you mind not telling Anne any of this?"

"She knows. That's why I'm here." He didn't say how she knew.

"Damn. Damnit to hell." He did his look around the room again, collecting his thoughts.

The man would never make a poker player, Bishop thought.

"I was going to wait until after the close to tell her. I wasn't going to sell anything unless she agreed."

"Why wait? She might have some ideas for ... her company. Or were you going to wait until it was your company to reveal how you accidentally discovered the tax losses that Flint somehow hid from the liquidation committee?"

"Ah, hell, Bone. You're a bastard. You know that. You're just like Marc in your own way."

"You mean he was always after the truth?"

Phillip stared at him and said, "Something like that. I'll call her this afternoon and let her know what I've been doing. I figured if she didn't know anything about the tax losses, she couldn't be held responsible if somebody finds out later. That's why I haven't said anything."

Right, and people in hell get ice water daily.

"She might cut you a finder's fee. Who knows? Also, who knows what the final value of the company with the tax losses and the two pieces of property might be. You need an engineering study to see what it will cost to develop the property and how many units you can put on it. You'll need another study to see what kind of units are selling where the land is, and at what price they will sell. The engineering company can probably give you some estimate of what it'll cost to build the units. With that information, you can back out the value of the land."

"That's what Marc did. My lawyer, well, the lawyer Linda recommended I use, somebody she knows, has just been knocking numbers back and forth. If the builder says one thing, he doubles it."

"I call that instinct negotiating. Figure the other side will offer low so you counter high and get a reaction. Risky, but in a pinch it'll work."

"I didn't want to spend money doing anything until I own the company."

"Right now, I'd say, if you own the company." Bishop said he'd call Anne.

Bishop got up to leave, hesitated and asked, "What about that old truck outside?"

"It belongs to the company. Technically it belongs to Anne. I've been using it since we got it. We have an Audi but Linda drives it. Marc drove his Jeep. I drove that thing. It's in good shape. Marc didn't like it but we used it to inspect undeveloped property we were looking at. It plowed through almost everything. He always made me park it out of sight if I drove it anyplace respectable, however."

"Like to the opening?"

"Yeah. I had to park it at the rear of the clubhouse, out of sight. Good thing too. The beverage caterer brought more champagne and needed help getting it to the clubhouse. I asked Derek to help. We loaded the cases onto the truck and unloaded it at the back room. I think every bottle was used up before the opening was over."

Well, that ties two knots in one loose end. No need to call Ellen. She pretty much already knows.

"I'll leave it up to you to explain the business about the tax losses to Anne. I'm not working for the liquidation committee so I don't care what you tell them or don't."

"As I said, I don't think I'm withholding anything. The tax losses would have no value to them."

Bishop left.

## CHAPTER 14

Bishop wondered what Anne's substitute cook was preparing for dinner that evening. Anne probably wouldn't keep her, but would enjoy the evening dinner. The lady was laboring away when he walked in. No one else was around, preferring to stay out of sight so as not to interfere with her. Bishop found out from her that she was preparing something called coriander salmon with spaghetti and fresh tomatoes. It smelled good and later, he'd find out if it tasted as good as it smelled. It was served with a salad and wine. And, it did taste as good as it had smelled.

Over dinner, Anne discussed her phone call with Phillip and his revelation. Derek asked what she was talking about and was told.

He said, "Damn, that's a windfall, sis. That son of a bitch was going to keep it for himself!"

"I don't know Derek. You can't just say that."

"Bullshit! I knew he was a bastard when he took Marc's side against me when that girl came in pregnant and pointed a finger at me. I didn't do it."

"You should have insisted on a DNA test," Bishop said. "Phillip said Marc didn't do it. You say you didn't do it. A DNA test would have settled it."

"Nobody said anything about DNA, they were too busy pointing a finger at me. Phillip and Marc. And the girl. Hell, she'd say anything. Sure I slept with her, but that's all. That bastard was going to cheat you! I wouldn't trust him a foot. Don't give him anything."

"I'll see what our lawyers say," Anne said.

"No money yet, Derek," Bishop said. "I don't think anything'll get done until after the close and the liquidation committee has left town with all the documents of title they need."

"He's right, Derek," Anne said. "I'm not going to give Phillip anything now, anyway, until after the close when I've had a chance to look at everything, including the tax losses."

She said Phillip told her he had kept it to himself in case the liquidation committee found out about it and wanted to make trouble. If they did, he'd be the one they looked at. She thought that was admirable.

"Admirable my ass!" Derek practically shouted. "Bullshit is what I'd call it! He was covering his ass. Got caught and said that to cover it up."

Bishop didn't say anything one way or the other, but he did wonder how he was going to write it up. He decided he'd tell it like he'd heard it and let the readers make of it what they wanted.

Anne looked at Bishop and asked, "I don't suppose you had anything to do with any of that, did you Bishop? Phillip's call."

"Ah, well, I did discuss it with Phillip to get his read and to see if he needed my advice. I can't say he did. He said nothing was going to happen until after the closing which was set for next week. I told him he should tell you in case anything happened to him. How'd you leave it with him?"

"I thanked him for calling and told him I'd pass it on to our lawyers. I told him that the money involved put a different light on the company. It obviously has value," Anne said. "He said he'd call me as soon as the man made contact, if he did, after the close."

"I bet that sent him home for a headache pill," Derek said. "His pretty nurse wife could give him one. Maybe she'll draw my blood and give me a reading, like she did Marc." He grinned like he'd said something funny.

Bishop mentioned the Marshall's boy and his operation to correct his lazy eye condition. "I think he's recovering. I should drop in and see, I guess. You meet people and find out they all have problems."

Nobody said anything else about it. They finished dinner.

"Damn, good," Bishop said.

For dessert the new cook served something Anne described as an Italian custard, panna cotta covered with sliced strawberries, with freshly brewed decaffeinated coffee.

All agreed it was delicious.

Bishop was glad she stayed to serve and clean up afterward. Of course, the Flints had a dishwasher. When Kathy gave a dinner party at her house, he felt obliged to clean up and wash the dishes and pots and pans. She didn't yet have a dishwasher but had promised to get one. Something about the old plumbing was holding her up.

He joked with her about cooking. He'd ask when she was going to be finished and she never knew. He finally developed a system. When every pot and pan she had in the kitchen was dirty, he knew the cooking process was over. He tried to wash the pots and pans before the guests arrived to lighten the load afterward. That way, he would have more time to spend with Kathy.

After dinner, Anne, Derek and Bishop enjoyed an after dinner drink on the balcony and watched the lights below. Bishop figured Anne had told Derek the publisher turned out to be a dud, looking for a one night stand, so Derek probably put Bishop back in the picture. Bishop figured that must have caused Derek some inner conflicts, having made his peace only to see the rationale for that peace destroyed by a dud publisher.

Bishop wasn't bothered, generally, since he knew he was never going to be part of their lives. However, he was concerned that Derek might not know that.

Bishop called Kathy before leaving his room the next morning. All was well. She wanted to know if he was still researching Flint's memoirs. In other words, when was he coming home? He told her he was almost finished. He was going to wait for the closing, a big event since that would signal the end of the Flint empire, such as it was. The closing was scheduled in three days.

Though it had not been mentioned, he wondered if the survivors of Flint's company, Wakefield, Phillip, Derek and Anne, would get together for a celebration or, maybe a wake. He wasn't going to bring it up and hoped he'd have his plane tickets bought, and would have an excuse not to stay. On the other hand, such a celebration should be included in the memoirs as the closing chapter. He could get the details from Anne.

He went to the kitchen for coffee. Derek and Anne were at the table; Anne listening, Derek talking animatedly. From what Bishop could pick up, he was still railing about Phillip's plan to steal money from Anne.

When Bishop sat down with his mug of coffee and roll from the table platter, Derek was vowing to fix the crooked bastard's wagon. He didn't say how and Bishop figured he was blowing off steam to more closely bond with his sister. His bills still had to be paid.

Bishop inquired about their plans for the day.

Derek, already dressed for it, said he was going to catch a few waves with Evelyn.

Anne wasn't sure. There was a Circle meeting she had been called about. She wasn't in the mood but might go.

Bishop wondered if Derek might have had something to do with her mood. Before Bishop had finished his coffee, she had decided to go, and left to get dressed. Derek left seconds later.

That left Bishop to enjoy a second cup on the balcony pondering what, if anything, he had left to do. He decided to call Linda and check on his pirate mate, their son.

"How's he doing?" he asked Linda after the usual greeting.

"He's fine. The bandage is off and the doctors think the surgery was a complete success. You aren't going to say anything about Eli in the memoirs you're writing, are you?"

"No, I can't see why I would. Unless Marc did something for Eli when he heard about the problem?"

"What? Of course he didn't. Why would he? It was our problem."

"I guess he knew about it though," Bishop said.

"Sure. We told him. "

"What'd he say?"

"He was sorry. That's about it. Well, he did give Phillip a generous bonus the year we discovered it," she said.

"That tells something about the man's character. I should include it in his memoirs," Bishop replied.

She didn't respond right away. Finally, she said, "Yes. I guess you should." She sighed. "The doctor says we can put Eli into a day school in a month. We'll let our sitter go and save some money that way. Phillip may be without a job for a while. His headhunter says he'll have him a position in no time though. That's our good news. He probably should have been looking weeks ago when we first found out Marc was going to lose the company."

"He was probably busy winding things up," Bishop said. He knew otherwise but obviously Linda didn't.

"That's what he said. I think he was hoping somehow to keep the company and stay in business. Maybe bring in a partner, a builder type to take Marc's place. He'd stay on as the chief financial officer. That's what he does best, pushing numbers around to make them look their best. He's enjoyed his work. Marc wasn't always easy but they managed."

"He tailors numbers like a sculptor works clay, a creative effort," Bishop said.

"Yeah. Thanks. I'll tell him."

"Maybe it'll still work out, Linda, his idea to bring in a partner."

"I doubt it. He thinks Derek, Anne's brother, will take over the company and try to run it. He thinks that would be a disaster. He blames him for something that happened at the office. A girl accused Derek of sexual abuse and Phillip took Marc's side. Derek hasn't spoken to him since."

That ended the conversation. By implication, Bishop had learned that Phillip had accepted the fact that he wasn't going to get a big windfall from the company after the close and had to look for a position elsewhere.

Must have been a depressing realization. Poised for a big pay day only to see it yanked away. Hmm, that'd be me doing the yanking. Maybe Ellen is right. I do cause trouble.

I don't think I'll be on Phillip's Christmas list this year. But, I can't see how that's my fault. I didn't try to steal money that didn't belong to me. If he had told Anne up front, he might have been able to negotiate a big fee for himself. Now, she'll probably still give him something but it'll have a taint on it.

He suddenly had another thought. I haven't had a hate call in a while. Maybe the caller died or is in the hospital. Or, maybe he or she thinks I've gone to Mississippi.

He typed more on the draft of Flint's memoirs. It was up to sixty five pretty good pages.

"Flint's office. I should plunder it to see if he left anything that'd look good in his story. The Flint story or book, I should call it. I don't suppose Anne would care if I looked around, assuming the door is unlocked."

He walked down the stairs. The door to Flint's office was open so he went inside. With the entire wall in glass, he didn't need a light.

The desk was the first thing he looked through. He found nothing worth including in the book. The file cabinet contained mostly files about loans on projects the lender might ask him to take over and on projects he had taken on. None held anything he thought would interest a reader. A laptop was the desk but it needed a password. "I wonder if Anne has one."

He opened the pencil drawer to check for numbers or characters Flint may have used for a password. "Maybe the date he took over his first project," Bishop said.

He slid the file on the project Anne had said was Flint's first and punched in the date of the takeover in the password slot. Be damned. It worked!

Bishop quickly scanned the file list and saw nothing more than business correspondence. He was more interested in emails, but was equally disappointed. There was nothing interesting. In fact, there were only a few junk emails.

I shouldn't be too surprised. A man as careful as Flint with as much to hide, would have never left any embarrassing emails for anybody to read.

He closed the computer, left the office and went upstairs for a late morning coffee.

\* \* \* \*

Anne came into the breakfast room where Bishop was sitting. She was looking weary. "Run one for me, would you?" she asked. "Having to talk to old ladies who can barely remember their names tires me out. They mean well, but right now, I don't have the patience to deal with them."

Bishop's reply was more an acknowledgement than anything meaningful. *Hell, I'm old too. I'm not sure I even mean well.*

They sat at the table and drank coffee without saying much. Finally, he said, "I'm about finished with my research. I think I will take my notes home and finish a draft for you to look at. If I need to, and I expect I will, I'll come back out."

Her face fell. She frowned. "I … I didn't think you … well, for some reason I assumed you'd write it out here and I'd read it bit by bit. Why can't you do that?'

Before he could answer, his phone dinged with a message. He looked at it. It was a text message. "Write anything good about that bastard and you'll join him in hell."

He showed it to Anne who gasped. "Who's doing that? And why? Marc wasn't that bad. He was a business man, not a saint. He had to make hard decisions. Most of those were made for him … in Florida."

"It doesn't make a lot of sense. And, why send me hate messages? I didn't do anything."

"Have you told the police?"

"Yes. They know, but they can't trace the messages and so far, the only threat came from the blown out car window. The rest has been hate mail more than anything. This one is a threat however. I'll show it to the police."

"I can see why you might want to finish it in Mississippi. I doubt anybody will follow you down there. Once it's finished, you'll also be in Mississippi so what will the sender gain from all this?" she asked.

"Maybe the sender doesn't know I plan to finish it in Mississippi. Or maybe they think I'll be scared off."

"Even I know you better than that. You're too much like Marc to be scared off. Anybody threatening him, ended up regretting it."

Bishop shook his head. "I'll do the same if I ever catch up with whoever it is."

He thought a couple of seconds then added, "It seems to me that whoever is sending me these messages is blinded by hate. They hated your husband so much, they aren't thinking clearly."

"Do you suppose they killed Marc?" she asked.

"That's the way it looks, Anne. I'd say for emotions to run to hate, Marc must have done something terrible to whoever it is. A woman he spurned, perhaps? A husband with a broken marriage he blames on Marc?"

She looked out in thought. "I'll have to say it like this. I've told you all the women Marc's bedded. Until now, not one of them has said anything. So, why would they start now, after he's dead? As for broken marriages, I don't know of any."

"Somebody sure as hell is upset," he said. "I thought about this once before. I ended up thinking Marc's murder might have been for some reason other than one of his take-overs. It's beginning to look like that is the case. So, let me push it a bit. Let's suppose Marc was murdered for revenge. But, now, I come on the scene. No one would logically want to take revenge against me. No sane person anyway. So, why?"

"To shut you up. They should know that's not going to happen," she said.

"Maybe they don't. Suppose they don't. If that's the case, their only option is to kill me, too. That'd end up stopping me from telling some secret Marc took to his grave."

"What secret?"

"I wish to hell I knew. And, I've finished my investigation. I haven't found a damn thing that'd bother anybody. And, I don't have a clue about his murderer."

"What are you going to do?" she asked.

"I'm going to ship the dilemma off to my subconscious and let it have a go. I won't go to Mississippi for awhile yet. I don't want whoever it is to think they've scared me off."

"Don't take any chances, Bishop. I didn't hire you to get killed. I just thought it'd be a nice tribute to write about my husband's life. Regardless of what some people might think about him, he accomplished things."

"He did." Also stepped on a few people in the process. Slept with a few women as well. And somewhere along the way, made somebody very, very angry.

She excused herself to go to her office. "A book to finish," she told him. "Don't go out without telling me. I don't want to be told that you ended up at the bottom of a ravine."

He laughed. "Fortunately, I'm not fighting off a diabetic coma. Anybody trying to push me off the road had better watch out. I push back."

She smiled and turned to leave, but came back to give him a full body hug.

"If that doesn't keep me safe, nothing will," he said.

"Marc couldn't have said it better."

He called Ellen to tell her he'd finished his research and was about to catch a flight to Mississippi when he got the latest hate message. Since it was the first one to actually threaten him, he thought she ought to know.

"Bishop, how in the hell can one man stir up so much trouble? How do you do it? There are folks out there born with the ability to play the guitar just by listening to the music. Other folks paint pictures that show up in magazines. I don't like 'em, but people who are high learnt rave about them. Now you, you were born with the God-given talent to cause trouble. Pure and simple. You just walk in a room and people immediately start thinking about killing somebody. They were probably good Christians before you walked in. How do you do it?"

"I think it's the California smog, Ellen. A chemical thing. It gets into people's blood and somehow when they see me, it triggers a killing reaction."

"Okay, I hear the bullshit, Bone. What the hell do you want me to do, assign a policeman to follow you around?"

"No, Ellen. I just wanted to let you know in case I stop calling you and people stop getting killed."

"That's what I call a good deal. You stay in touch, you hear me. Really. Call me now and then. Hell, I'll buy lunch. Good Lord, did I say that?"

"I'll give you a call. Call me if you come up with anything worthwhile," he said.

"Same back at you. Let me know if you do the right thing and fly out of here. I can take some people off overtime, searching for dead bodies."

He went to his room and typed on his computer. Rereading some of the stuff at the beginning made him change some things to focus more on Flint's life. Now and then, he let the material drift off to whoever he had interviewed without keeping it referenced to Flint.

He saw something interesting. Phillip's old truck. He'd used too many words to describe it in his first draft. I need to pare it down. All those rusted iron bars for bumpers and for hauling ladders on the truck bed. It had intrigued him because the truck was so unlike anything an intellectual like Phillip would drive. Now though, a different thought surfaced. It was one he tried to have before but it got away before he could.

"Phillip's truck would be the perfect vehicle to push somebody off the road. With all that iron for bumpers, it'd be easy and the truck wouldn't show any damage."

He decided to have a look at the truck. He knew it'd be parked in front of the company's building. If Flint were still around, it'd have to be parked in the back but he was dead.

He parked a block away and walked to where the truck sat. Phillip was not around. Bishop walked slowly around the truck. A streak of the rust on the passenger side iron bumper had been scraped away. It's what he'd have expected if the bumper was ramming into a tire, say, Flint's Jeep tire. That wasn't evidence that the truck had run Flint off the road, but it was evidence that it might have been used to do just that.

He took a picture with his iPhone.

His call to Ellen to gain access to the storage yard where Flint's Jeep was kept wasn't met with enthusiasm but she agreed to call the guard to let him in.

He showed the guard his driver's license. "Ellen called you," he told the uniformed man.

"Yes sir. She said to stand away from you at all times. You were a walking bomb. Something to that effect. I think she was joking. Wasn't she?"

He assured him that she was.

He found Flint's Jeep. It had not been moved.

It had already begun to rust. Bishop cursed. He was hoping to find rust from Phillip's truck bumper on the driver's side of Flint's Jeep. There was some rust, even some on the tire itself as well as the rim. The tire was flat and the rim bent but he'd seen that the first time. He hadn't noticed the rust, but he hadn't been looking for it. Even then, he could hear the defense attorney objecting to any testimony about rust inasmuch as the Jeep had been exposed to the elements for over a month. Not only that, who could say for certain the rust hadn't been left from the tow?

"It may not be evidence, but it's sure as hell suspicious." He took iPhotos to be printed.

He thanked the guard for letting him in.

Before driving away, he called Ellen. The Jeep had rust on the tire and the rim, he told her. And, before she could point out the time lapse and the possibility that the rust may have come from the tow truck, he told her as much.

"I hear what you're saying, Bishop. Yeah, it sounds good. Yeah, the Marshall guy is a prime suspect. The tax losses he hoped to run away with could have given him a motive. Plus, I think you said Marshall wasn't exactly a fan of Flint."

"True," Bishop said.

"So, you have a suspect, Bishop. I don't. I have to convince a DA we have enough evidence to convict the man. You're a lawyer. Am I there?"

Bishop had to admit she wasn't.

"When you're sure I need to be, give me a call. When we get to that level, I will buy lunch."

"Would you at least send some forensics people out to look at the truck and do a study to see how the bumper would match up with Flint's Jeep tire?"

"I'll see if anybody has the time, Bishop. Only because it's you would I even consider it. I can't overlook your track record for dumb luck."

"I knew it'd come in handy one day."

## CHAPTER 15

Bishop had some thinking to do. He figured a beer might relax him just enough to do that. So, he drove back to the Flints' house to get a beer and hopefully, to do some thinking.

Ellen was right. So far all he had was guesswork. How could he get from guessing to something real? "I wish I knew," he said to himself.

Phillip's truck was the first decent thing he'd found since he been interviewing for Flint's memoirs and it wasn't conclusive, just a pointer in Phillip's direction.

"I'd hate to leave La Jolla with the suspicions I have and let the case be closed because I was too lazy to see if there might be some truth to back 'em up."

Bishop's thoughts were miles away when he walked into Flint's home from the garage. Anne was in the kitchen presumably thinking about dinner since the new cook was not about. They exchanged hellos.

He told her. "I'm not going to Mississippi until I have thought through a possibility about Marc's death."

"If you do your thinking on the patio," she replied. "I'll bring you a mug of beer and if you don't mind company, I'll join you."

He went outside. Minutes later, Anne appeared with a mug of beer and a glass of red. She leaned over the small table to set the beer in front of him. She was wearing a thin blouse. The upper buttons of the blouse were not fastened and when she leaned over, since she was not wearing a bra, Bishop got a double barreled view of what the bra would ordinarily have been covering. She held her position over the table longer than Bishop figured was necessary. She looked him in the eyes and smiled. It was the smile of a woman looking at a man she wanted. He got the message.

Damn! What the hell do I do? That was the problem. He knew what he wanted to do. And, he knew he couldn't do it. Son of a bitch.

"Anne," he said, shaking his head. "Anne, you are a very attractive woman. You know that. To say that you are desirable would not do you justice. You are every man's dream. I know that. Hell, I feel it. But, I made a promise to a

lady in Mississippi that I would be true to her. She made me the same promise. If I can't keep my word, I wouldn't be worth a damn. Please understand. I am a human not a machine. Can you give me a break?"

She straightened up and gave him her regular smile, the haughty one, like Bishop had just earned a place on her all time shit list.

"I'll accept that, Bishop. I don't think you should be that strict on yourself, however. I won't come to Mississippi and tell your friend. She's a lucky woman."

"Thank you, Anne. I think I'm a lucky man."

She nodded and sat down with her wine. "Okay, now that we've dealt with our human side, let's get on with what's troubling you?"

"Maybe I'd better clear the air first, Anne. If you think that exchange between us just now has jeopardized my ability to effectively finish writing Marc's memoirs, I'll give you everything I've done to date and refund your fee less my plane fare and the car rental charge. I know that now and then a lawyer and client have conflicts. Sometimes they can't do anything about it but we can. So, it's up to you. Do I go or do I stay?" I think that might have been from an old pop tune. Damn, I may be getting senile.

She reached over and softly placed her hand on his forearm.

"Bishop, you stay and finish your job. I like you even if you do have outmoded values. Besides, you may change your mind." She gave him a devilish smile.

That's what I'm afraid of.

He laughed. "Okay. Here's what's bothering me. Well, what was bothering me when I walked into the kitchen."

He told her his revelation about Phillip's old truck. It had a scrape on the passenger side bumper that could have been made when pushing Flint off the street.

"And, I understand that he was missing from the opening about the time Marc was being pushed off the road."

"You think he'd kill Marc for the value of the tax losses? Four hundred thousand dollars?" she asked.

"That's the problem. When Marc was killed, you hadn't said he could have the corporation. That's what I have to think about."

"I'd say."

"Here's one scenario. After Marc was killed, Phillip probably saw an opportunity to make some money off the company's tax losses if he could get the company. Let's assume he became afraid the interviewing I was doing for the memoirs would expose what he had in mind. So, he tried to stop me by sending hate messages and by blowing out of my back window," Bishop said.

"That seems logical, Bishop, but that doesn't seem enough to make him a murderer."

He shrugged. "True. But, that truck he drives at least suggests that he could have run Marc off the road. I just need somehow to find a motive. As you say, the opportunity to make money off the tax losses didn't come until after Marc had been killed."

She twisted her head with a grimace and agreed.

"Every time I chase my tail, I always end up with the same question. Why was he killed? I first thought a disgruntled developer or a husband whose wife Marc had taken a temporary liking to, but I haven't found much, hell, anything, to support that theory."

He shook his head in frustration.

She picked up her wine, took a sip and said, "I don't know if I told you or not, Bishop, but the closing's been moved to tomorrow at a title company's offices down town. The liquidation committee has sent two attorneys. Marc's company attorney will represent the company. My attorney will represent my interest as Marc's wife and as executrix. I'll be there to sign the documents. Why don't you come?"

He would. "After that, all that remains is what you will do with the company ... with its tax losses. Ordinarily, I'd say Phillip deserves some kind of fee for putting the tax losses on the table to make the company attractive to a buyer. However, in light of what he ... might have been trying to do, you'll have to search your conscience about that."

She stared at him and said, "He made a plausible argument. I'm not as cynical as you and Derek so I'll probably give him a good fee. He has the boy to raise and the boy's eye operation might not have been totally covered by insurance. Marc had insurance for the company but it carried a large deductible."

Being reminded of the boy's operation sent a flash through Bishop's thoughts.

Eli was almost four. He was born after Phillip came to work for Flint. Flint fathered Sarah's son. Did he father Phillip's as well? Would Linda have been that stupid? Sarah got pregnant because Flint said he always wanted a son. Why would Linda have gotten pregnant?

"Where'd you go?" she asked him. "You went all blank on me."

"I was thinking that Phillip's son might have been Marc's. If so, Phillip might have found out or guessed and decided to take his revenge. Kill Marc. And just to be sure that indiscretion by Linda stayed a secret, he tried to stop me from writing anything that could let that secret out of the bag."

"I don't buy that, Bishop. I'm sure Marc would have been more careful than that. I doubt seriously he'd knowingly father a bastard child especially if he'd be exposed somehow. He was very cautious ... extremely fearful of being sued. Lawsuits against him were 'not convenient' he used to say."

"Maybe," Bishop said. "But, I wonder." He was thinking about the lazy eye problem the boy was born with. Linda said the gene, or whatever, was carried by the male side of the family. What did Linda say about Phillip's side of the family having a history of lazy eye?

He told himself to dig out his notes and see.

"That beer did wonders for your thinking process. Maybe it did too much."

Bishop shrugged. "You're right. That last scenario probably doesn't make sense, but something has to. Marc was killed and somebody has been trying to stop me from writing about it."

"Maybe you need another beer."

He laughed. His glass was empty. "Could be. But first, I want to check my notes."

"Are you going to take me to dinner?" she asked.

"I am. How about the Marine Room for the high flyers or Denny's for the blue collar crowd. From the sublime to the ridiculous."

"I've only eaten at Denny's once. It wasn't bad. The food or the service."

So, that's where they went. Considering Denny's blue collar status, according to Bishop, they went in his rented car.

He had the senior's breakfast and she had a scrambled egg dish with vegetables. Both had decaffeinated coffee. Naturally, Anne turned heads, men's and women's, when they walked in.

"I haven't seen Derek today. What's he up to?" Bishop asked during dinner.

"He says he has a plan to make money. Something in sales. He said you put him onto it," she said.

"Me? I don't recall ... well, I did say he would probably do well in sales. Maybe he's trying to hire on with Wakefield's company."

"He won't say. Says it'll jinx him."

"How is Marc's mother doing?" he asked.

"I don't know. I haven't been by to see her since you got here. Too many things going on. I'll try to get by after the closing," she said.

"What's happening with your publisher?"

She laughed. "He finally got around to inviting me to bed. I asked him if he was married. He admitted that he was. That was the end of our relationship. He was a dud anyway. However, he's going ahead with my world signing tour. Cynthia, my daughter, is going to help with the publicity. Throw a little business her way. I made that a condition." "

"Congratulations. Does she favor you or Marc?"

"A little bit of both, I think."

He gave her a hug when they got back home. She cheated and turned it into a kiss, a long one. He cursed to himself but couldn't say he didn't enjoy it. A good reason to get the hell out of here.

He went to his room to check his notes from his interview with Linda.

The doctor had told her it was likely inherited from the male side of the family. Phillip couldn't remember if he had it or not and he couldn't remember it ever being talked about in their home.

"So, I'm nowhere unless..." He went to bed with that thought.

The next morning, he had a message on his phone. His client needed him for work. When could he get back?

He figured after the closing, he could fly back, catch up with his bank work and finish a draft of Flint's memoirs. The bank message would give him a good reason to leave.

\* \* \* \*

The closing was held in a downtown title company's conference room. As promised, the liquidation committee sent two lawyers. All the documents had been reviewed ahead of time. Anne's lawyer came as did another lawyer to represent the company's interest. Bishop and Derek also came but had little to say after introductions. Derek was all smiles however. Bishop assumed his smile had something to do with his plan to get into sales.

Anne had driven to the closing with him. Phillip was also there. He also seemed in good spirits. Bishop figured Anne must have been generous with her fee.

The lawyers for the committee agreed to let Phillip work out of Flint's building until it was sold. He agreed to cooperate with brokers showing the building to prospective buyers. There was no mention of tax loss carry forwards. Bishop figured Phillip enjoyed a silent sigh of relief.

Documents were slid across the table by the title officer for signing and initializing. The title officer, a lady with years of experience, would get everything recorded and title policies issued insuring the first lien position of the company formed by the liquidation committee to hold the property.

The committee would meet later to decide how to distribute the properties and projects to the banks on the committee. The details about how that would be done were not disclosed. After that, Flint's lender client would be out of business.

Business was concluded minutes before noon. They walked to the popular Grant's Grill for lunch and chatted as if they were old friends. And, why not, Bishop figured, all conflicts had been resolved.

In the afternoon, Bishop made reservations for a flight to Mississippi later that day. After he'd done that, he called Ellen.

"The Marc Flint Empire is no more, Ellen." He told her about the closing. "I'm going back to Mississippi to do some real work." He explained.

"Yeah, I remember. You told me about your cushy life last time you were out here."

"Old age, Ellen. One of the perks. You'll get there one of these days."

"Not if I keep hanging around you. Somebody with bad eyesight's likely to aim at you and hit me."

"Yeah. No more collard greens for you."

"I'll miss 'em. Soul food, my man. Soul food."

"Do you want a copy of the memoirs I'm writing? Flint's history?"

"Damn right I do. You may say something useful."

"For a change. Was that what you were thinking?"

"You said it, not me. Besides, I figure I made a contribution to 'em. Vis-a-vis that, I'm still working on that study we talked about. Looking at that man's truck 'n all."

"Let me know if you find anything."

"Count on it."

\* \* \* \*

He told Anne about the call from his client and his flight. "I expect to catch up in a week. I'll write my reports and then finish a draft of Marc's memoirs. I'll email you a copy to read then I'll come back and tie up a couple of loose ends."

"One we talked about," Anne said.

"Especially that one. I have a thought I need to explore. It may not be totally satisfactory, but it'll be enough for me."

She acted reluctant to see him go, but didn't object. From the look on her face, Bishop could tell she was reconciled to the fact that he wasn't going to weaken and sleep with her. He knew damn well that it would be a one-night kind of thing for her in any case. As attractive as she was, he wasn't interested. Kathy was the only woman he needed and the only one he wanted.

He called the bank manager in Mississippi and told him he was on his way.

"Get the files ready." He'd be by for them the next day.

He also called Kathy. He'd be by to pick her up that evening. Food would be something they could stop for on the way. Afterwards, they'd have gin and tonics – their drink together – and watch Indian Creek flow past the back porch of his cabin.

And, he was sure they would do more than that. He knew it and she did as well.

* * * *

Bishop and Kathy did enjoy the evening together. Her mother was doing well so Kathy spent the night. They fried eggs and bacon the next morning and eased into the day. The beavers were up before they were and already swimming in their pond, repairing mud huts and building new ones. The beaver population had increased, Bishop decided.

A herd of deer frolicked past on the pond dam. On the other side, they paused long enough to enjoy a cold drink of water from the creek.

About nine, Bishop drove her home so she could open the library on time.

He'd had no calls from other banks and assumed they didn't need any help from him. Since he had work to do, he didn't get into contact with the Campbells for tennis or for anything social.

He drove to Jackson to meet with the bank manager there and to pick up his assignments for the loans guaranteed by the Small Business Administration. His goal was to visit four borrowers a day. He had fourteen files requiring on-site inspections and discussions. As usual, the borrowers had been notified to have their financial statements ready.

About half the businesses referred to by the bank were doing well, so all Bishop had to do was get a general overview about the business and any future plans they had. He'd take pictures for the bank's file and go to the next borrower on his list.

For the businesses in trouble, as in being consistently late in their payments, Bishop had to do more work, even talk to other local businessmen to see if management might be the problem. The problems, he determined, were about fifty percent bad management and fifty percent poor business. For those with insufficient traffic to sustain the business,

Bishop advised them to cut overhead and see if they could survive on reduced income. If not, they should advertise for someone more creative to buy the business.

Four days later, he'd finished the inspections and had written his reports. He sent them by Federal Express to the bank manager, gave him a day to read them and then visited him in Jackson to discuss his findings.

The manager agreed with his recommendations. Two borrowers would receive default letters advising them to come up with money to reduce their loan to a level consistent with cash from their businesses.

* * * *

Bishop had lunch with the manager downtown to wrap up the assignment. Afterwards, he drove home to begin writing what remained of his draft of Flint's memoirs. By the end of the following day, he had finished. It turned out to be one hundred and five pages. He figured Anne would make changes and when he went back to La Jolla to finish his research, he'd make more.

He attached a copy to an email he sent to Anne.

"Read it over," he advised in his email. "Make any changes you like and email me the changes. I'll correct my copy or tell you why I disagree. After we've done with that, I'll fly back to finish it up."

His subconscious had come up with a couple of questions he needed answered. Remembering that Ellen wanted a copy, he emailed her and attached a copy.

In his email, he said, "Right now, Ellen, what I'm sending you is most likely confidential. In fact, I know some of it is. If you think you can't keep it confidential, I trust you not to use it. Can you reply and let me know?"

Fifteen minutes later, he received her email. "I kind of figured you'd dig up some dirt. I won't spread it around but if it looks like somebody dirty might have had a motive, I'll wander past like that Columbo character I used to watch on television and ask a dumb question. Actually, I still do watch him on one of those channels I had to buy a box for. Is that okay?"

He agreed so long as she didn't reveal why.

"Perish the thought, Bone. By the way, our forensics people did a quick study on the man's truck and Flint's Jeep. The rust didn't help a bit. We couldn't match it one way or the other. Our guys did say it was possible for the truck's bumper to have matched up with Flint's tires and run him off the street."

"With all those maybes, I doubt the DA will decide to give his staff the day off to celebrate the resolution of the case."

"That Mississippi air must be doing you some good. You got it right. I'll see you when you're next in town. If I get a brainstorm or a decent suspect, I'll let you know."

He thanked her.

That night, he and Kathy celebrated with the Campbells at the Country Club. It was prime rib night, a favorite of the club members so the dining room was jammed.

They asked about Bishop's activities in California. He told them about the murder of Marc Flint, the La Jolla developer whose life's story he been commissioned to write. In the process, he told about the attempts to get him not to write it.

Not much had changed in their lives. Seth's business had leveled out some. The economy had slowed and when it did, demand for new commercial buildings slowed with it. Sonja, his daughter, pretty much ran the business during slow periods allowing Seth time to spend with his wife. She came to dinner with her husband and son.

Bishop was pleased to see that Seth's wife, Beth, had fully recovered from the depression that had plagued her for years. Maybe having Seth at home more did the trick, Bishop thought. At one time, Seth was seriously considering getting a divorce. Bishop was certain he was glad he hadn't. He and Beth seemed to enjoy themselves at dinner.

As they were finishing, Chief Jenkins and his wife strolled in. Bishop and the Chief had gotten into it from time to time over one thing or another, usually a murder and had become friends. Bishop went over and said hello.

"Be damned, Bishop Bone," the chief said with a pat on the back. "It's been awhile. How's California?"

Bishop had told him what he had been doing, writing Flint's memoirs. So, he brought him up to speed as to where that stood.

Afterwards, as friends do, they promised to get together for dinner.

## CHAPTER 16

Bishop took a shower and was sound asleep when the phone rang. It was Anne.

"You got my email?" he asked, thinking that was why she'd called and wondering why she was calling so late. It was after two in the morning.

She said something he couldn't understand. From the stress in her voice though, he knew something was terribly wrong.

"What's wrong," he asked.

"It's Derek," she said. "He was killed. Shot in Balboa Park. A little after midnight."

The police had just called her.

"Damn, I'm sorry. I'm so sorry. You must be devastated."

She was. "Can you come out? I need someone with me I can trust."

He'd catch the morning flight and rent a car. She offered to pick him up but he refused. She was in no state to be driving in San Diego airport traffic, always bumper to bumper with nervous drivers anxious to get someplace.

Evelyn wasn't with him, thankfully. They'd had dinner, Anne said. "He said he was meeting somebody about a business deal. He swore it was a sure fire money-maker."

"Sounds mysterious," Bishop commented.

"It was whatever he'd been working on," she said. "He still hadn't told me anything. He did say it was going to pay off. He may have gotten some money already. He had a handful of bills one day when he came in. From what I could see, they looked like hundred dollar bills."

"Hmm, hundred dollar bills? That doesn't sound like business, Anne." Bishop was thinking it sounded more like drugs or ... blackmail.

He'd be there by noon. They'd talk more then.

*  *  *  *

Bishop parked on the street and walked to the Flints' front door. The house was as impressive as ever. "Imposing" was the word he used when he described it to himself. Hoping he would not have to return, he'd left his garage door opener behind. "I should have known better," he mumbled to himself as he stood there waiting for Anne to open the door.

When she saw him, she burst into tears and put her arms around him. "I'm so happy to see you, Bishop. I've needed you more than I thought I'd ever need anybody. Derek's murder hit me hard, especially coming so soon after Marc's. It floored me."

"I understand. I'm so sorry. I know he meant a lot to you."

"More than I knew. I had my differences with him but I never wanted anything to happen to him."

He put his arm around her waist and walked her down the hall.

"Can I get you a glass of wine?" he asked.

He could. She had already had one and pointed to her glass on the breakfast bar where she'd left it to answer the door. He refilled it and got his mug out of the freezer where she'd put it when he called from the airport.

He got a bottle of beer from the wet bar cooler and took it outside. They sat at the small table. It was not a day to enjoy the view. She sat deadpanned, mostly staring at him.

"What are the police saying?" he asked.

"They think it was a robbery. His wallet was gone."

"Did they say anything else?"

"Ellen Wasserman, came out with a couple of guys in uniform. They searched his room. I don't think they found anything."

"No money?"

"No. He had money that one day, but said he owed Evelyn. He might have paid her. I told Wasserman about it. She said she'd talk to Evelyn and she did. Evelyn called. She was in tears too. She couldn't believe it. Derek was getting his life in order she said. He had a deal going to make some decent money, he told her. He did pay her back what he owed her."

"It doesn't sound like a robbery," Bishop said. "But, I don't know of any business deal that would take Derek to Balboa Park that time of night. Unless he was into drugs. Selling drugs."

"What! No! He'd never do that! He never used drugs. Wasserman asked me the same thing. That was just not true."

"She was probably thinking about the money he had," Bishop said.

She shook her head.

"How was he shot, if you don't mind talking about it?"

She shook her head. "He … he was, God, it's so hard to accept. He was shot in the head. Once. In his car. Wasserman said nobody was around and nobody heard the shot. She said it was close range."

"Sounds like he was meeting somebody, Anne. My guess is, he was blackmailing somebody."

"Wasserman asked me about that. I told her he'd never told me anything about it if he was."

"I doubt he was selling drugs," Bishop said. "He might have seen somebody dealing and threatened to turn them in if they didn't pay. Maybe the Balboa Park meeting was to collect more money."

"That's so awful. More people get killed or die because of drugs. The police should do something to stop it."

"I think it's like the Dutch boy and the leaky dike. Every time they plug one hole, another leak pops up," he said.

She shook her head and drank half her wine. He figured he'd end up having to put her to bed but didn't figure it'd cause a problem for him.

"You know what I'm thinking?" Bishop said. "I'm thinking he figured out who killed Marc and was threatening them. It had nothing to do with drugs."

"How would he do that? You didn't. The police didn't either."

"I know, but sometimes people get lucky. They get a flash and they know they're right."

"Yeah, I suppose."

"I do wonder though how he could have gotten a flash when I've strained my brain and haven't come up with anything." He then remembered the loose end he wanted to tie down. His thoughts created a scenario that the loose end would be the ravel that would lead to the killer. But, it would have to wait until tomorrow. He was tired from the flight.

"Anne, why don't you lie down and rest some. I'll take you to dinner tonight. It won't be fun, but it'll get you out of the house and get you mind off Derek for a few minutes."

She agreed and went inside. She lay down on her bed. Bishop closed the door behind her.

\* \* \* \*

He parked his car in the garage and unpacked. Then, he called Ellen to find out if she knew anything.

"Bishop Bone," she said. "I knew you'd be calling. You're back in town aren't you? Come out here to stir things up. Get more people killed."

"All that and more, Ellen. Have you come up with anything?"

"I first figured he had decided to get into the drug business and somebody took exception. Those drug guys don't welcome competition."

"That's right," Bishop agreed.

"Before you say it, I don't think he was. It just didn't fit. Our sources never heard of him and he didn't say anything to his girlfriend or sister about drugs and there was no trace of drugs on him or in his car. We went over it with a fine-toothed comb."

"So, you backed into blackmail?" Bishop asked.

"I figured you'd get there too. Any ideas who? I read your memoirs. Nothing jumped out at me as pointing to a killer. I've been cogitating about how he figured out who killed Flint and put the bite on 'em."

"Great minds think alike, Ellen. I just wonder what he saw that I didn't."

"I'm standing in your shoes on that one, Bone. I do it for a living and I didn't get any bright ideas. I was living off what you fed me and I was losing weight."

"The truck thing is as close as I got to a decent clue. Phillip had motive ... well might have had. I have a thought I want to run down. That thought notwithstanding, he knew the company was closing. It's a stretch, but he could have figured with Flint out of the way, he could convince Anne to give him the company and he'd offer the tax losses to another developer."

"Lot of ifs in that, Bishop. Too many. I'd like to believe it but it just doesn't ring right."

"I agree. I got the impression when I talked to him that he didn't like Flint all that much, but he liked the money he was making. And with Flint still alive, they might have been able to stay in business. Flint had a reputation and knew how to make deals. Phillip wouldn't know one end of a deal from another. As he said, he was a numbers guy. That's about all he knew. I don't see him killing Flint for a pig in a poke. That's what the tax losses were at that point. He couldn't even be sure the liquidation committee wouldn't find them," Bishop said.

"I didn't wring it out like that, Bone, but my gut told me Phillip didn't make sense as the killer unless there was something else we didn't know about."

"That bothers me too. What did Derek find out that I should have spotted? I'm going to track down a couple of things. If I find anything, I'll pass it on."

"Yeah, Bone. I like the jobs you throw my way. Every now and then, you come up with something that makes sense. I always take credit for them, you know."

"Why, hell, Ellen, I know you do. Anybody who loves collard greens like you do … and like I do, wouldn't stop at using a loose idea some unsuspecting soul lays in front of them."

"Damned if you can't talk up a blue streak, Bone. I'll be seeing you," she said and hung up.

He hoped she was right about seeing him. If he found out what Derek knew, and didn't handle it right, he could end up like him.

\* \* \* \*

He checked on Anne. She was still asleep. He called Kathy and explained what he'd run into.

"What are you going to do?" she asked. "What can you do?"

"I don't know. Derek may have discovered who killed Flint, and was blackmailing him … or her. If he could do it, I should be able to. So, I'm going to retrace my steps and keep my eyes open. I'll keep you informed."

"Don't meet anybody in Balboa Park late at night," she said.

He laughed.

\* \* \* \*

He roused Anne at five. She took a shower and got dressed and looked like a New York model. He saw her and was stunned and felt like a bum in his khakis so he grabbed something decent from Flint's closet and put it on, a sports coat and slacks. Everything fit.

At her request, he drove the Tesla to the Marine Room for dinner. Most of the staff recognized her and were most courteous. As usual, heads turned as they walked into the dining room and found their table by the window. Waves splashed rhythmically against the restaurant walls below the window adding a dynamic to the setting.

"Exciting," she said with a nod at the waves. She was wearing her haughty beauty face, the one that came with just a trace of a smile.

They ordered. She wanted lobster. He went with the steak. Crab cakes for an appetizer. She asked for a white wine and recommended a red for him. He knew it'd be dry but he resolved to drink it with a smile.

"Have you been thinking?" she asked.

"Some. Let me ask you ... well, let me tell you something that's in the memoirs."

She interrupted to say she hadn't had a chance to read them.

"No matter." He told her about Eli's lazy eye and how it was probably inherited from his father.

"Linda said Phillip couldn't remember if he had anything like that. So, I'm wondering if Marc had the lazy eye. I'm going to ask his mother. She told me he had a problem when he was young and the boys made fun of him. Something to that effect."

She said she didn't know about a lazy eye when Marc was young. Marc had never talked about it.

The waiter brought the crab cakes and their wine.

"Tastes good," she said, taking a bite of the crab cakes followed by a sip of her wine. He did likewise, including the endorsement of both although it was difficult to drink the wine without making a face.

They picked up the conversation where they'd left it.

"You're thinking Marc's problem might have been ... the lazy eye?" Anne asked.

"Possibly. Who knows what the kids would have called him ... cross-eyed or something."

"I still can't believe Marc would have been gotten Linda pregnant."

"Maybe he wouldn't, but Sarah got around that, didn't she?" Bishop said.

"But, she wasn't married."

"When I was married, Anne, my wife knew when it was safe to have sex if you know what I mean. We never had an accident. What if Linda thought she was safe but was wrong? She could have told Phillip it was his."

"She should have been on the pill," she said. "I was."

They talked a bit about that. What if she forgot to take her pill?

Their orders came. His steak looked cooked to perfection. He didn't see how she could eat anything that looked like her lobster but kept that to himself. From the way she cut into it, he was convinced that it must have been good.

"What if Phillip wanted to have a baby?" he asked when they took a break from chewing. "And, Marc came along at the wrong time."

She shook her head. "Hmm. That might have happened. What a bummer if it did."

"I'll ask Marc's mother about the lazy eye thing."

"Good God! Hard to comprehend, Bishop. Two illegitimate children, both boys. Marc wanted a boy. He may have ended up with two. But, how does that lead to murder?"

"Not easily," Bishop answered. "First, Phillip would have to discover somehow that Eli wasn't his. I don't know how he could, but he might have. Then, he'd have to be so angry, he'd kill Marc ... for revenge."

That was what Bishop had accused Banker Ben of doing, killing Flint for having debased his daughter.

"Does Phillip strike you as a killer?" she asked.

"No, but you know the old saying. Still waters run deep. Who can say what might have gone through his mind when he found out."

"If he found out? You still have to bridge that big gap."

He agreed.

"Phillip a murderer. I can't believe it. And, I just gave the man two hundred thousand dollars," she said.

"Pretty good."

"Yeah."

They shared an apple tart with decaffeinated coffee for dessert. Freshly brewed, Bishop decided from the taste. They must have one of those Swiss machines.

Bishop found room for half a glass of beer on the balcony when they got home. She sat with him and sipped on a glass of wine but drank very little.

The view was breathtaking but neither of them said anything about it. Mostly they sat and thought. His thoughts were on the interview of Flint's mother the next day. He assumed hers were on Derek's death.

She didn't ask him to escort her to her room. For that, he was grateful.

\* \* \* \*

Bishop waited until after nine to visit Flint's mother. He was shown into the sitting room where Flint's mother, white haired and frail, sat in a wheelchair, staring into space as if waiting for something.

If I were in her shoes, I know what I'd be waiting for, Bishop thought. .

He walked over and introduced himself. To his surprise, she brightened immediately, smiled and said, "Of course, Mr. Bone. I'm so glad to see you again. How have you been?"

Her response made him glad he'd come regardless of what he would find out. They spent a couple of minutes talking about nothing in particular, the weather and politics mostly. Bishop marveled at her recall and awareness.

After a bit, she looked at him and asked, "Why have you come, Mr. Bone? Do you have more questions for me? About Marc? They say he's dead. Perhaps you told me that the last time you were here. He was a good boy. He always saw after me."

Bishop felt embarrassed. He didn't recall if he had told her or not. She knew however so somebody must have.

"He was a tremendous success, Mrs. Flint. As you recall, I've been writing his memoirs."

She did. "I want to read them when you're finished." He promised.

"What do you want to know?" she asked.

"You said when he was young, the other kids made fun of him. He got into fights. I think you said he had problems. Do you recall what they were?"

She nodded. "I do. He was born with a bad eye. They called it something else, but I don't remember what it was. The children, mostly the boys, made fun of him about it. They said he was cross-eyed. He'd go after them for it. We took him to a doctor who helped us straighten it out. I don't remember what we did, but it worked and my boy outgrew it. After that, if any of the boys even looked at him cross-eyed, he'd tear into them. I just made a joke, didn't I?" She laughed.

He joined her then asked, "Did Marc remember it when he got older?"

"Goodness me. Yes he did. We'd talk about it now and again when he'd come by. He didn't mind who knew it. I think he was proud that he got over it like he did."

"Did he talk about it in front of other people?" Bishop asked.

She shook her head and slumped in her chair. The caregiver watching over them hurried over. "I guess it's time to take her back to her room. I know she was glad to see you. Last time you were here, she talked and talked about it. She said you looked just like her son."

Bishop smiled. "Be damned. Other people have told me that. I wish I had his success to go with it."

She laughed. "He was something, that Mr. Flint, wasn't he?"

He was.

On the way back to the Flint's home, he called Ellen. "Ellen, I found out something that is interesting and wondered what you'd make of it."

"I guess I'd better sit down. Okay, I'm sitting, what is it?"

He referred her to the draft copy Flint's memoirs he'd sent her.

" I'm at page twenty," she said.

"Well, in about ten or so pages, you'll come across my treatment of an interview with Linda Marshall. Phillip Marshall's wife."

"Okay, I'll watch for it. Why are you wasting my time with that?" she asked.

He told her about the Marshall boy's lazy eye condition and how the doctors said it was probably inherited from his father.

"Linda told me Phillip didn't recall having anything like that when he was little and didn't remember his father or mother talking about it," he told her.

"I appreciate knowing that, Bishop. I really do, but –"

"The thing is this, Ellen. I just talked to Flint's mother. Flint was born with the lazy eye. Don't you see it? The Marshall boy was probably fathered by Flint. You know how he never hesitated to put himself about."

"Damned if you haven't come up with something that ties into Flint's murder. Phillip found out somehow and decided to take revenge. Is that your theory?"

It was. He also told her the story Anne had given him of the day of the La Jolla project's opening celebration. How Phillip had goaded Flint into playing three games of racquetball when the man was practically dead on his feet. He was wobbling as he worked the crowd before he spoke to them.

"Phillip knew he was a diabetic because his wife, Linda, had told him the night before," Bishop explained. "He made her wait to tell Flint until the next day. When Flint didn't die on the racquetball court, Phillip had her turn off her phone so Flint couldn't call her for the insulin injection he needed."

Ellen picked it up and said, "So, when Flint staggered out, you're saying Phillip followed him in that old truck he drives and ran Flint off the street."

"That's what I'm getting at."

"Damn, I think finally you may have stumbled onto a decent theory, Bone. Yep, I think that makes sense. The truck could have easily run him off the street, especially with him about to pass out."

"Hate drove him. And, when I started nosing around writing the memoirs, he was afraid I'd find out," he said.

"And, he'd be up shit creek," Ellen answered with a laugh.

"Precisely."

"Now, all we need to do is prove it. Any ideas?" she asked.

"We could run a DNA test on the boy. Compare it with Flint's. I'd guess there a hair or two left in his house. Maybe a fingernail or something. Or I could ask and see if Linda will admit it."

"It's Phillip Marshall we need the admission from. We need for him to admit he hated Flint enough to kill him or we need to find evidence to show he ran Flint off the street."

"To start with, I'd suggest that you go back over the people you talked to from the opening and pin down exactly when Phillip was gone from the opening."

"Wait a minute. How'd he know that Flint had the lazy eye thing when he was young? We have to link -"

"Phillip went with Flint to visit his mother. Flint would just pop in when he was out and about. Suppose Flint or his mother brought it up? Flint was apparently proud of the fact that he'd overcome it."

"Getting into some big ifs now, Bishop. I like your theory, but I suspect the DA will want a little more proof. I hate to think about Flint's mother being cross-examined. The jury would throw up their hands and vote for an acquittal without going into the jury room."

Bishop suddenly had another thought. "How about this, Ellen? Find out who does DNA profiles in town. Ask them if Phillip Marshall requested one."

"That's a decent idea, Bone. I'll get somebody on it. That'll help if we could tie that end down."

"Okay. If I come up with any other brilliant ideas, I'll call," Bishop said.

"Can you expedite the process?"

Bishop laughed and punched off.

# CHAPTER 17

Anne studiously dusted the tables and anything with a surface. Bishop figured it was busy work to stay ahead of her thoughts.

"Staying busy?" he asked as he walked past.

"Trying to. Sarah's father, Banker Ben Holliday, called me. He offered his condolences about Derek."

"Thoughtful of the man," Bishop replied.

"That's not all. He wants to come out for a visit this afternoon. Around three. That's one reason I'm running round with this dust cloth."

"Did he say why?"

"Well, yes. He did. He wants to talk about 'little Marcus,'" she said.

Bishop frowned. "Wonder why?"

She shook her head. "Maybe he wants to show pictures."

"Could be, but he doesn't strike me as being that grandfatherly."

"Me either but I told him he could come out," Anne said.

She asked Bishop if he'd stick around and give her moral support. The man scared her. His eyes were like daggers, she recalled from the times he'd been to the house. "Like he hated me. Most likely Marc, but he didn't soften the daggers when he looked at me."

Bishop told her he'd be there and sent into his visit with Mrs. Flint and his subsequent conversation with Ellen Wasserman, specifically the plan to find out if Phillip had requested DNA on anybody. Linking Phillip to Marc's murder and more than likely Derek's brightened her mood immediately.

"I'll be damned," she said. "You said it might be Phillip. I didn't believe it but what you're saying makes sense, if you can prove it."

The police would be able to bring Phillip in for questioning if Ellen could link Phillip directly to Marc's murder.

"Are you going to talk to Linda?" she asked. "Ask her if the boy is Marc's?"

He said he would wait until Ellen had completed her investigation before making that decision.

Derek was going to be buried the next day. Bishop told Anne he'd go with her. She doubted anybody else, except for Evelyn, would show up. Derek had about as many true friends as had Marc.

Derek wasn't a lovable character, Bishop thought. And, unlike Flint, he didn't use his charm to fool anybody. What you saw was what you got, and when you looked at Derek, you saw a selfish shit.

He'd recorded his notes from the morning and reread the draft of Flint's memoirs to see if his subconscious could come up with anything useful for Ellen and her quest to tie Phillip to Flint's murder.

At three precisely, the doorbell rang. He told her he'd get it and did.

"Mr. Holliday," he said and stuck out his hand.

"Bone? What are you doing here? I'd heard that you were back in Mississippi."

"I was but when Derek was killed, I came back to see if I could help Anne," Bishop said.

"Well, I had some private business to discuss with Mrs. Flint."

"I'm sure she won't mind if I sit in. In fact, she asked me to."

"It's private," Holliday said.

"Come on back. She's waiting," Bishop answered.

He hesitantly followed Bone down the hallway into the living room. Anne got up to greet him.

He looked at Bone with a frown and said, "My business is private with you, Mrs. Flint."

"I trust Bishop. He's a lawyer and is bound not to reveal anything that's said," she told him.

Holliday looked surprised. "I guess he is. I'd forgotten that. It was in the paper, I think. Okay."

She asked if she could get him anything. He said no and sat down.

He clasped his hands together, looked at her and said, "I want to talk about Marcus, my grandson. I'm sure you know by now that your late husband is the father."

She did without changing her facial expression which was totally blank and without emotion.

"I've discussed his future with Sarah. He's a charming little boy. Smart too. I want Sarah to bring him out for a visit. She could do it on a regular basis if you'd like," Holliday offered.

"I appreciate what you're proposing, Mr. Holliday. And, it might make sense to some people, but it doesn't to me. I don't think I'd want to see the boy," Anne said. "He'll always be a reminder of my husband's infidelity."

"That's too bad," Holliday said. "Because, I think you bear some responsibility for the boy's welfare. His schooling. Everything. He is your late husband's child. If he were alive, he'd do the right thing by the boy."

Anne looked at Bishop as if to ask is he saying what I think he's saying?

Bishop decided he was. "Are you suggesting that Anne pay for the boy's upkeep and education like he was one of hers?"

Holliday nodded. "Her husband fathered him. Sarah shouldn't have to pay for his future. Flint must have left you well off, Mrs. Flint. The least you could do is put aside some money for him. His education. It costs plenty to go to a decent college these days."

"Mr. Holliday," Bishop told him. "If you'll excuse my bluntness, that's the dumbest thing I've ever heard of. You have plenty of money. It's your grandson, no matter the father. I think if you'll consult your attorneys, you'll find that neither Anne, nor her husband's estate, have any legal responsibility for the boy. I'm sure he's a great boy and all that you say, but legally, Anne is not responsible."

As stingy as he apparently was, Bishop doubted the man would spend the money to try and make new law. He's out here trying to chisel money out of Anne. Flint hasn't been dead that long and she just lost her brother. What a bastard.

He ignored what Bishop had said and looked at Anne. "My question was addressed to you, Mrs. Flint. Mr. Bishop has no say in this matter. What is your response? Are you going to ignore your husband's son?"

"I think I've already given you my answer," she said. "However, I'll make it clear. I am going to do just that. I don't need to see the boy. He's not my child. I have no responsibility for him. I've already discussed it with my attorney. He agrees with Bishop.

"I'm sorry you have wasted your time. Frankly, I'm surprised and shocked that a man with your reputation would try to squeeze money out of me while I'm trying to recover from the death of my husband and my brother. What kind of man are you?"

"I believe a man should bear the responsibility for what he does, even if he's dead," Holliday said.

Bishop said, "I bet you foreclosed on lots of widows when you were starting out in banking, Mr. Holliday. Did you carry your Bible with you when you took possession of their houses?"

Banker Ben got up in a huff, pointed a finger at both of them said shouted. "You are both worthless sinners. You haven't heard the last of this matter. The Lord said, 'it would be better that a millstone be hanged around your neck and that you be cast into the sea to drown than to refuse care for a child.' The Bible says you will burn in hell for refusing this child's needs."

They were too stunned to reply. He reached into his coat pocket, pulled out an envelope and threw it in Bishop's direction. Over his shoulder he said, "If you won't obey the laws of God, maybe you will obey the laws of man."

He slammed the front door behind him.

Bishop looked at Anne who seemed to be in shock. "Damn! That was a display. Old Banker Ben. When somebody called him hard-nosed, they weren't joking. I'm just surprised he didn't bring his Bible to read from while he was trying to squeeze money out of you."

She shook her head in disbelief. "I thought I'd heard it all, but that man goes to the top of my list. When he started his harangue, I thought I must not be understanding him."

"You were," he said.

"Yeah. I gather. Thanks for setting him straight," Anne said with a big sigh.

"It was a pleasure. He is, excuse my language, an asshole."

"If you don't mind me saying, I agree with you. He is an asshole."

Bishop picked up the envelope and pulled out the letter inside. "From an attorney," he said. He read it quickly. "Basically, the letter addresses his question about your responsibility for Marc's illegitimate child. It says about what

I told you before. The attorney thinks the law is drifting in the direction of support for the child, but the case would probably end up in the Supreme Court and would be a very expensive case."

"You think he'll sue me?" She scoffed.

"It's not his call. It's Sarah's. I can see him putting pressure on her and I can see him putting up the money to file a suit for the principle of it. I don't think he likes to lose."

"Another one," Anne said, an indirect reference to her last husband.

"In some cases, the equity is on the side of the mother and child," Bishop added. "You know, a philanderer impregnates the woman and leaves laughing. 'Ain't none of mine.' And, the poor woman – that's usually the case – is left with the burden of raising an unwanted child.

"That is not the case here. Marc thought she was on the pill and she had been. She knew he would never divorce you and she had accepted that. It was her decision to have the child. She wanted it and hadn't even told Marc about it. So, I think the trial court would hold against Sarah if she files. However, I don't think she will."

"I hope you're right. I don't want to pay out large legal fees. It wouldn't be fair," Anne replied.

"No. I'd say not to worry about it. I'd be very surprised if Sarah would embarrass herself by filing a lawsuit for the world to know that she'd had an illegitimate child. Frankly, I'd be surprised if Holliday would want that. I think it's a bluff."

He folded the letter and handed it to her.

"It's a bit early," Bishop looked at her and said, "but, I think drinks on the patio are in order."

She agreed.

He had his regular beer in a frozen glass. She had her glass of red. Dry, Bishop assumed.

They talked more about the man's gall and couldn't resist a laugh as they recounted what he had proposed.

"He wants to enjoy the boy but wants you to support him," Bishop said. "He takes cheap to a new level."

"That must be why he's so successful as a banker. He wants every penny he can get," she said.

"Yeah. He waves the Bible around when it suits him. But, he likes to sound contrite when it doesn't cost him anything." He was remembering his interview with Holliday at his Banker's Hill townhouse, his talk about being a sinner for being rude and for hating Flint.

He scoffed. "He told me Marc killed himself when he committed adultery and the Lord saw to it."

"If he weren't so successful, I'd call him a nut case," Anne said.

"Maybe that's why he is so successful. He gets fixed on a notion and won't let it go. If he makes a loan, he won't rest until the borrower pays it off."

Derek's funeral was the next day.

\* \* \* \*

Derek's funeral was a graveside ceremony orchestrated by Anne with help from the funeral home. It was a morning funeral. A gray-haired man in robes, black and purple, stood by the coffin suspended by straps over the grave to say words. In his hand was a Bible. Some distance away, in black, stood four other men ready to assist in the ceremony should they be needed.

Green blankets covered the freshly disturbed earth. An elaborate coffin sat over the grave. One of Derek's old scarred-up surfboards leaned against it. Most of its coloring was long gone. It was short enough to be buried beside the coffin.

There was no tent. Anne didn't figure there'd be enough attendees to warrant one and for the same reason, there were no chairs. Everyone stood.

Evelyn, dressed appropriately in an understated gray dress and jacket, stood close to the casket and cried throughout. Anne, in black with a white blouse, stood beside her. Tears rolled down her face. Bishop was half a pace behind them. He thought she looked elegant, perfect for the occasion.

Phillip and Linda, with Eli, were there, somberly dressed. Their faces displayed no emotions. Eli was on his best behavior. Bishop wondered if Ellen had approached them with her questions. He'd find out later.

Cynthia and her family flew in from New York for the funeral but left shortly afterwards. Attesting to Derek's popularity, no one else attended.

Two large evergreen trees covered the site and attendees in shade. Birds frolicked and sang in their branches but stopped from time to time to perch forward on a branch in search of tiny, wiggling things liberated by the digging. But, the green blankets covering the earth, temporarily kept them from becoming bird-brunch.

Anne had arranged for a decent-sized head stone with Derek's name and the pertinent dates. The top of the brown, wooden casket was laden with flowers. Flowers also covered the ground around it.

A disc player, someplace out of sight, played music. One of the songs was Somewhere over the Rainbow by Judy Garland. One other was a spiritual instrumental. Sad, Bishop thought, but he knew that sad music was played at all funerals.

Bishop wore one of Flint's black suits for the occasion.

After three plays of Over the Rainbow, the man in robes opened his Bible and began to talk. He recounted Derek's good deeds, his love of people, his love of life and in particular his love of Evelyn. He gave a nod in her direction. She burst into tears.

Then, he read. "Listen, I will tell you a mystery: We will not all sleep, but we will all be changed in a flash, in the twinkling of an eye, at the last trumpet. For the trumpet will sound, the dead will be raised from their resting places and the saying that is written will come true: 'Death has been swallowed up in victory.'

"Where, O death, is your victory? Where, O death, is your sting? Thanks be to God. Who gives us victory over death through our Lord Jesus Christ. So to all those Derek left behind, do not let your hearts be troubled. You believe in God; believe also in Me. And, you will see Derek again.

"Jesus told us that my Father's house has many rooms; if that were not so, would I have told you that I am going there to prepare a place for you?

"So, Derek, Jesus has prepared a place for you and for us all and one day Jesus said that He will return and free you from the shackles of death and you shall live again."

The casket was lowered into the grave. Anne and Evelyn each picked up a handful of dirt and threw it on top. They thanked the man in robes for a fine funeral. He replied with a smiling nod.

Bishop led them away. Phillip and his family left at the same time and presumably went home. Nothing else was planned, no wake, no dinner, just the funeral.

"Derek would have wanted it that way," Anne had said.

Anne invited Evelyn to come home with her for a glass of wine as a last remembrance of her brother.

Bishop joined them on the patio.

"To Derek," Anne said and raised her glass. "We wish you were here." Then, she burst into tears. Evelyn also cried and the two women comforted each other.

Bishop sat down, sipped the dry wine and said nothing. His thoughts were on who might have killed Derek and why, though he was certain that whoever did it was being blackmailed.

After a while, Evelyn gave Anne and Bishop a tearful goodbye and left, presumably to go to back to the law office where she worked.

Anne excused herself to lie down.

Bishop went to his room to enter his notes into the computer. Even though he'd been there and witnessed Banker Ben's request for support, it was still difficult to believe.

The funeral, he figured, wouldn't merit much in Flint's memoirs but had to be included since Derek had been named numerous times in the memoirs. His death was the end of his story.

\* \* \* \*

Bishop's phone range during the noon hour. It was Ellen.

"Bone," she barked. "Are you going to buy me lunch or not?"

"I'm waiting for you," Bishop forced a jovial tone he didn't feel.

"Bread and Cie," she said. "I've got some updates I'll share with you. Not a hell of a lot, but worth a lunch."

"I'll be there in twenty minutes."

He pulled into the parking lot seconds before Ellen. She drove a black Chevrolet. Anyone with any kind of record or knowledge of the police establishment would have known it was a police car.

They ordered the day's special with coffee and sat down to wait for the food. The coffees were brought to their table almost immediately.

"Okay," Bishop said. "What updates?"

"Can't you see, Bone, I'm puttin' sugar in my coffee. Sometimes I think you ain't got a lick of sense. I'll talk after I've tasted it. Okay?"

"Son of a bitch, Ellen. I've just figured it out. Police people can only do one thing at a time. No wonder it takes so long for a crime to get solved."

"You know what you can kiss, Bone."

"I wouldn't know where to start." He smiled.

She smiled back.

"Okay. My coffee is just right. So, on to the updates."

Her staff had re-interviewed most of the people at the Apogee opening, even showed pictures. Not many people recognized Phillip at all. That was the problem. He was practically nondescript.

The entertainment manager remembered Phillip coming outside to talk with Derek and they left together. He didn't know where they went, but the beverage manager confirmed that both unloaded cases of champagne from a van. That only took a few minutes.

Ben Holliday also saw Phillip and his wife, even exchanged a few words but he wasn't paying attention to what they did afterward. He didn't see Phillip go in or out. He was tired and left the opening early.

Sarah was more helpful. She saw Phillip go outside where the musical group was setting up. She didn't see him come back but did see him dancing with his wife later. Sarah left soon after the music began.

Anne saw Phillip and Linda but only now and then. He could have been anywhere for any number of minutes the rest of the time. Phillip's wife, Linda, said he was with her most of the time and she was certain he never left her side for more than five or ten minutes a couple of times.

A couple of older men at the opening noticed Linda standing alone and made their way to where she stood. "A woman that good lookin' shouldn't be left alone," was what they said.

Phillip interrupted one guy's pitch, bringing drinks. She cut the other one short. The guy she'd cut short didn't see Phillip but knew he wasn't around while he was making his move. It took a few minutes – he didn't exactly measure how long – for him to accept the fact that she wasn't interested. He didn't know when he was making his move but knew it was after Flint had made his little speech.

She said, "The DA wasn't totally impressed but he did like the second guy's account. He also liked Sarah's version. Linda's recollection didn't bother him too much. A jury expects a spouse to lie.

"Did you talk to the mother so see if she ever talked about Flint's bad eye in front of Phillip?" Bishop asked, wondering is she'd corroborated what she'd already told him.

"No. We want you to be there when we do. She knows you and you can introduce whoever we send, probably me. That way we won't scare the hell out of the poor woman."

They decided to do it the next day about ten thirty in the morning. Ellen had been told that the ladies were up and about by that time. They had had their morning coffees and were most alert. As the day wore on, they grew tired and sleepy.

When they were well into lunch, Bishop asked, "Anything on the DNA?"

Ellen nodded and said, "I won't bore you with the details, but we did locate an outfit that admitted Phillip sent in two samples for analysis. They initially refused to tell us shit without a court order. Privacy laws. I told the snippy order taker if she didn't tell me what I wanted to know, I'd send a police van out there with half a dozen police officers who'd tear their place apart and shut them down for a week.

"She decided if I wouldn't tell anybody she'd give me the results of the tests. The two samples Phillip had submitted matched. The samples were not labeled but, we can assume one was for his son and the other for Flint. We can get a court order for results that we can introduce in court," she said.

"So, he knew the boy wasn't his. What was the date of the DNA report?" Bishop asked.

"Three months before Flint died, Bone. Good timing, don't you think?"

"I do."

"The DA did too," she said with a smile. "That's our best piece of evidence so far. I sent our forensics team back out to look at Flint's Jeep and Phillip's truck. We didn't mind if he saw us. I figured a little intimidation might help us out."

"Did he say anything?" Bishop asked.

"Just wanted to know what we were doing. My guys said he looked nervous but I don't think we could get that in front of a jury."

Bishop agreed and asked. "What'd they find?"

"They're willing to say there is a fit. His iron front bumper matches up with Flint's Jeep tire. They can't say it pushed him off the street, just that it could have. That uncertainty didn't bring a smile to the DA's face."

"No doubt. Did you talk to Linda?" he asked.

"We tried. She was always busy. I'm going to have her picked up and brought to my headquarters if she doesn't cooperate soon."

"Let me talk to her first. I have some standing. I'm still working on Flint's memoirs. Hell, I'll ask her if the boy is Flint's and what Phillip thinks about it."

She laughed. "I'd like to see the look on her face when you tell her Phillip knows she was sleeping with his boss."

By then, they'd finished lunch.

"So, we meet at the nursing home tomorrow at ten thirty?" he asked.

Ellen nodded. "See you then."

"I think tomorrow is Linda's day off. I'll drop by early on and see if she'll talk."

"Won't Phillip be there?" Ellen asked.

"He'll probably be at the office. The closing attorneys said he could use the office until it's sold. If he is there, however, I'll play it straight and talk about Flint's memoirs."

Before they parted company, he asked if they had anything new on Derek's murder. She didn't. They really weren't working on it.

"I figure if we solve Flint's, we'll solve Derek's."

## CHAPTER 18

When Bishop walked into the Flint home, Anne was in the kitchen doing something over a butcher block. She looked up when she saw him. "Where were you? I got up and you were gone."

Bishop told her about his meeting with Ellen. In turn, Anne told him about the call she'd gotten from one of Ellen's detective, trying to nail down the times Phillip was missing from the opening. She didn't figure she was helpful. She was too distracted by people asking her questions about Marc to notice what Phillip was or was not doing.

"I will be talking to Linda to see what she'll admit to and later to Mrs. Flint with Ellen to see what she remembers about Marc's lazy eye and who she might have told.

"I imagine Linda will not know anything, if you know what I mean."

He did.

"Mrs. Flint might know something if she's lucid." she said. "Sometimes she is. Sometimes she isn't. But, I understand that you have to find out."

"Right," he said. "If she can remember, it'll be one more bit of evidence that Phillip knew that Marc was sleeping with his wife. It would certainly point to why Phillip suspected Marc was the father. If she isn't, the DA can rely on the DNA reports that Phillip ordered. The results will show that he knew Marc was his son's father, before Marc was killed, presumably by Phillip."

"Well, good luck," she said. "I'm cooking pork chops for dinner. I coat the chops with fennel. Gives them a great taste. Our old chef used to cook 'em for Marc."

"Have you made any plans for the future? Your future?" he asked.

"Well, a friend I knew in college wrote me. He works in Palo Alto for a pharmaceutical company. He read about Marc dying. His wife died a couple of years ago. His children are on their own."

"Have you seen him lately? People don't always look like they did in college," he said.

"I've run into him from time to time. He stays in good shape. Plays tennis, has a good head on his shoulders. Likes my books. Says he does. That gives him an edge right there." She smiled, her good one.

"Sounds promising."

"I had another thought, but it didn't pan out." A second smile.

"Yeah. Too bad."

She returned to her task of preparing dinner. He updated his notes.

* * * *

The fennel-coated pork chops never tasted better, Bishop told her after dinner. From her smile when he said it, he knew she was pleased and had a right to be.

For desert, they had panna cotta again with sliced berries and decaffeinated coffee from her fancy machine. It was delicious both times.

Bishop helped clean away the dishes and stack the dishwasher.

They finished the evening on the balcony with after dinner drinks. He stuck with beer. She finished the half a glass of wine left over from dinner.

"I could get used to this," she told him and again put her hand on his arm.

While he enjoyed the touch, he wished she wouldn't. As he had told her, he was only human and each touch eroded his resistance.

When they stood to go inside, she kissed him full on the lips. Not one of those quick "hello" things. It was a serious kiss. He wondered if he could have avoided it and knew that he could. He should have anticipated it when she moved close.

"Thank you Anne. I'd better go to my room before I forget my manners."

"I don't mind if you do, Marc ... I mean Bishop." A slip of the tongue but understandable, he knew.

He went to his room.

It had been his plan to update Flint's memoirs but he couldn't quite shake the warmth of Anne's body close to his, her sensitive kiss. Damn. He thought of Kathy when Anne got too close.

"I'll be glad when I get out of here."

He took a shower and got ready for bed. He did call Kathy and hoped she didn't sense what had happened a few minutes earlier.

He woke several times during the night with Anne in his thoughts. He almost got up and went to her room around two o'clock but thankfully didn't.

Bishop remembered something Banker Ben Holliday said during their interview. He didn't recall what it pertained to, but he did remember the quote. "I'm glad I don't have that sin to atone for." And, Bishop was glad he didn't have the sin that was heavy in his thoughts to atone for. He did wonder if the sin was in the thinking about it. Probably is but what kind of man wouldn't think about it?

He didn't have an answer, but knew he wasn't the kind that couldn't.

The next morning after coffee and a roll, he drove to La Costa to see if he could talk to Linda. He got to their house around eight thirty. Damn, Phillip was in the driveway. He was backing out but stopped and went inside for something. Bishop pulled to the curb and parked. Seconds later Phillip reappeared in the doorway with Linda. They had a quick embrace and kiss. He got back into his car and drove away. Bishop ducked as Phillip drove past his car.

With the coast clear, Bishop parked in front of their house and went to the front door.

He pushed the doorbell and Linda appeared almost immediately. "What'd you forget?

Oh, it's you, Mr. Bone. You didn't call. I'm not expecting you. I'm not sure Phillip wants me talking to you again."

"I saw him leave."

"He's meeting with the bank people who made Marc a loan for the La Jolla project. He says the financials for the new company he's working for, look better than the ones he did for Marc."

"So the new company is keeping him on?"

"Yes. He used the money he got from the sale to invest in the new company. Anne's bonus or fee, whatever you want to call it. It won't be easy to push him around now."

"Like Marc did?"

She nodded. "We're kind of starting over. Fresh. He told me not to talk to you again."

"He probably did, but I think I need to ask you a couple of questions I missed last time. Won't take more than a few minutes. He won't know I've been here."

She appeared reticent, even looked down the street as if to wish Phillip back. After that pause, she shrugged and said, "Okay. Come in. I'm kind of in a hurry so you'll have to make it quick."

He followed her into the living room.

"I want to ask about Eli," he said.

"Eli. He's doing well. Recovered from the surgery. Still asleep."

"Not that question. I'm glad however. I wanted to ask about your relationship with Marc. From what I've heard, you had an affair with the man."

Her body visibly slumped. She practically fell into one of the living room chairs. "That's a lie."

"He told Anne," Bishop lied but didn't think he had anything to lose.

"He did what?"

"He told Anne about all his affairs. That's how they stayed together. He convinced her that the other women meant nothing to him," he said.

"I did not have an affair. Oh damn." She stared out the window into the back yard. "Okay, I did sleep with him a couple of times. He practically threatened to fire Phillip if I didn't. Or, he'd tell Phillip that I had. I didn't like it. I told him. I love Phillip. So, he didn't bother me after that. I didn't like him. Marc was arrogant and self-centered. And, he wasn't nearly the man in bed that Phillip is," Linda said as she wiped tears from her eyes.

"Did you tell him that?"

"Yes," she said.

It didn't sound convincing to Bishop but he let it go.

"Did you tell Phillip?" he asked.

"Good Lord no! Why would I do that? I love Phillip. I want us to stay together. Something like that would destroy us. He never liked Marc. Just the money and experience. It was more money than he'd ever made before. And, we got this house. He felt Marc was gifted, but he almost despised him. Maybe more than almost. Marc had a habit of lording himself over everyone he knew or met. Phillip put the financials together that enabled Marc to get money for the projects he took over but Marc barely seemed to notice."

What do I tell her about Eli? That Phillip knows the boy isn't his. That he had DNA tests run to prove it. That's why I came.

He decided. "I think Phillip knows Eli is Marc's son."

"What! He is not! What gave you that idea?"

Now what do I do? I think she's serious.

"How can you be sure? You slept with him at least twice." A couple of times means more than two usually.

"I am sure. A woman knows her menstrual cycles. She knows when she's fertile and when she's not. I kept up with mine. Phillip didn't like to use condoms. I knew when he didn't have to. God this is embarrassing to talk about."

That made some sense. He and his wife had done the same thing safely, but apparently Linda and Flint didn't. "A woman can make a mistake about that, can't they?" he said.

"I suppose, but we've been doing it for ages. I haven't made one yet."

Well, you made one. Little Eli.

"I think Phillip suspected because of something Flint's mother said one day when they visited."

She looked at him with a question on her face and slowly asked, "What? What did she say? What could she say about me and Phillip?"

"Not about you and Phillip. About Flint," he told her. "You see, Flint had the lazy eye condition when he was a kid. The other kids laughed at him, bullied him and called him cross-eyed. Doctors pretty much say it's inherited from the father. So, if Eli –"

She jumped out of her chair and shouted, "No! It can't be! The doctors aren't always right. Phillip didn't remember. His daddy might have had it. He might have had it. His parents are both dead. There's no way we could find out. Just because Marc had it doesn't mean Eli's his boy. It couldn't be! Oh God." She began to shake and sob like a little girl who'd just lost something dear, like her kitten.

"I'm sorry, Mrs. Marshall … Linda. I believe Eli is Flint's son and I believe Phillip knows." He wanted to tell her about the DNA tests, but considering how Ellen came by the information, elected not to do it.

Linda buried her face in her hands and cried, never looking up, never replying.

That's how he left her.

I feel like a real shit, but it's probably best that she knows. Phillip knows and he probably hates her for it. Maybe he'll forgive her. They say love conquers all. It'll have a pretty big hill to climb over this time.

Well, I only told her the truth. And, sooner or later Phillip is bound to bring it up.

What husband wouldn't?

He still had plenty of time to get to the nursing home, but he sped anyway. Maybe he wanted to put the scene with Linda behind him as quickly as he could.

* * * *

Ellen and a nondescript woman in a plain dress were waiting beside Ellen's old Chevy. She looked to be over sixty and matronly. Bishop supposed that was to put Mrs. Flint at ease.

Bishop greeted Ellen who introduced him to Joan, the woman standing beside her. They went inside. One of the volunteers for the day met them at the front door of the facility and escorted them into the drawing room where Mrs. Flint sat in a chair in her usual place, her white hair carefully groomed. She was wearing something a little dressier than usual. The volunteer had obviously prepared her for the meeting.

Bishop introduced Ellen and Joan then asked, "How are you this morning, Mrs. Flint?"

She was feeling fine. She'd had a good night's sleep and a delicious breakfast. It was oatmeal and fruit day and they "allowed me to have an extra cup of coffee."

Ellen and Joan joined in the small talk for a minute or so before Bishop, not wanting to wait too long for fear she'd tire, said, "Mrs. Flint, did I tell you I've been writing your son's memoirs?"

The white-haired lady smiled broadly and replied, "Oh yes. I remember. You've been by a couple of times. I always enjoy your company. You remind me of my Marc so much."

"Thank you Mrs. Flint. Well, today, I want to ask you some more questions about Marc. Do you mind?"

She did not.

"Remember you told me the boys used to make fun of him because he was, what they called, cross-eyed. He probably had something doctors today call the lazy eye."

She brightened, "Lazy eye. That was what I was trying to remember the last time you came in. That's what the doctor's called it back then!"

"I think you told me Marc talked about it sometimes when he visited."

"He did. He was proud that he overcame it. He said it made him strong."

Bishop took the picture of Phillip from Joan and handed it to Mrs. Flint. "This is a picture of Phillip Marshall. He worked for your son. Did he ever visit you with Marc? Do you remember him?"

She stared at the picture for several seconds. Her hand shook ever so slightly. She began to nod. Finally she said, "Yes, I do remember him. It's been awhile since he was here, but he did come with Marcus a few times. I can't remember how many."

"Now, Mrs. Flint, we'd like to know if you remember something else when they visited together."

"I'll try," she said earnestly and fixed her eyes on him.

"Do you remember if Marc ever talked about his lazy eye when Phillip was with him?"

"Oh, goodness me. You are asking me a hard question. Let me see. Right off I don't remember, but let me think about it. Let me see."

They waited while the little lady pondered the picture, looking up once or twice as it about to say something, only to lower her face once more to the picture.

"I'm sorry, I can't say for sure, but I'm pretty sure we did talk about it. I think Marc wanted the young man – he looked young to me – to know what he'd been through."

"Do you remember for sure, Mrs. Flint?" Ellen asked.

Mrs. Flint looked at her and said, "I don't know if I could swear to it, but Bishop asked me if I could remember and I think I do."

They thanked her.

Bishop promised to return for another visit. That pleased Mrs. Flint.

Outside, Ellen and Joan and Bishop discussed what they'd learned. It turned out that Joan was an attorney working in the DA's office but had dressed informally for the visit.

She spoke first, "I hate to think of the fun a defense attorney would have with her recollection, but I feel the jury would accept her testimony especially with some corroborating evidence."

"The DNA report," Ellen said.

Joan agreed.

"We're building a case, one little pebble at a time," Ellen said. They exchanged goodbyes. Ellen promised to be in touch.

He drove back to the Flints' cliff-side home for a late morning cup of coffee. Anne was out. She had said she would be for most of the day. It was her day to visit local bookstores to informally chat with readers and store personnel. "Good PR," she had told Bishop.

Mrs. Flint had offered them coffee but he'd refused. He knew under the circumstances he'd barely have tasted it anyway.

But, he did want a cup with a breakfast roll. Coffee always tasted better with a fresh roll. He drank it on the balcony deck and enjoyed the view down below.

Afterward, he updated his notes and entered the changes in his computer file. It was noon by the time he'd finished.

Ellen had said they weren't doing anything about Derek's murder so there wasn't anything else he could write about it. If Ellen found a murderer, he'd add that later.

He was thinking it might be time to catch a flight back to Mississippi. Anne seemed to have regained her composure; certainly if she was out doing "PR" work. And, she had an interested suitor apparently interested in taking Marc's place.

He was checking flights to Mississippi when the front doorbell rang. That was followed by a pounding.

"What the hell," Bishop hurried to open it. "Must be an emergency."

The pounding grew louder.

Bishop shouted. "I'm coming. I'm coming!"

He opened the door, half expecting to see a policeman coming to tell him something had happened to Anne. Instead, it was a red-faced Phillip in shirt sleeves with clenched fists. At the curb was their Audi. Inside were Linda and Eli. Both watched through the open car windows. Linda looked solemn and depressed. Eli was waving excitedly, shouting, "Mr. Boon."

"What –" Bishop said but Phillip interrupted shouting, "You slimy lowlife bastard!"

Bishop shook his head. "What the hell're talking about?"

"You know damn well what I'm talking about! You sneaked into my house this morning while I was out trying to make a living, you crooked son of a bitch! You upset my wife with your lies!"

With that, he pushed into the door, forcing Bishop to step back.

Bishop hadn't really appreciated how short Phillip was until then. He can't be much over five and a half feet tall. No more than a hundred and thirty pounds, but most of that is muscle.

Bishop figured the man was in good shape, playing racquetball as he did, according the Anne.

Phillip was wearing his glasses but with all the shouting and shaking of his head, they seemed ready to fall off. Screaming curse words and poking Bishop in the chest with his finger, he marched forward. Bishop retreated.

Mindful of Marsha's seal sculpture on a pedestal in the hall behind him, Bishop stepped to his left. It looked like he was going to have to fight the little shit if he couldn't get him calmed down.

He pushed the man back with both hands. The push caused Phillip's glasses to fall off his face onto the floor. With Bishop's weight advantage, it was relatively easy to force the smaller man backward. He'd fought little guys before. Most were in good shape, as was Phillip. He knew he could wear them down eventually but it was always a hard fight. They usually had quick hands. And, being short as was Phillip, Bishop couldn't duck under their punches easily and drive them back with his shoulders. He had to bob and weave and move from side to side to avoid as many hits as possible until he could get in a decent shot.

"You'd better settle down, Phillip. One of us could get hurt and I sure as hell don't want it to be me."

"You bastard!" Phillip replied and moved toward him, his fists clenching and unclenching. The fight was brewing like a pot of boiling water, bubbling over the sides.

Bishop stepped back again to see if he'd calm down. He didn't. Instead, the little rooster kept cursing and poking at his chest with his finger and sometimes his hands. It looked like it was going to be a wall jarring fight, Bishop decided. Fortunately there were fewer pictures hanging on that side of the hall.

Finally, in a last attempt to calm the man down Bishop said. "Listen to me you, Phillip. I told your wife that you knew Eli wasn't your son. I –"

"What do you know about my son? Were you there when we were having sex? You lied. You and Marc. Both liars! Both cheats and slimy bastards."

What the hell. Were both of them in denial?

"You ordered DNA reports on Flint and Eli," Bishop shouted. "You know they matched. You fucking know he's not your son so shut the fuck up!"

With that, Phillip stopped shouting and began swinging. He was like a windmill. Bishop backed up with his arms raised to catch most of the blows. A bunch got past and struck Bishop in the ribs and hurt. After one flurry, Phillip stepped back and shouted,

"That's just a sample. I'm gonna tear you a new asshole, you bastard. You'll wish they'd buried you instead of that Derek asshole!" He launched himself at Bishop again.

After a minute of Phillip's furious barrage, Bishop ran into him hard with his arms high and used his weight advantage to drive him toward the front door. As Phillip was pushed back, he dropped his arms to catch his balance. When he did that, Bishop let lose a right hand that caught Phillip hard on the side of his head. It sent a jolt up Bishop's arm all the way to his shoulder.

It also staggered Phillip but didn't put him down, He shook his head to clear it of the buzz Bishop's fist left inside. Bishop didn't wait, he followed his right with a looping left. That one caught Phillip a bit lower, on the jaw. It drove the smaller man to his knees, dazed.

As Phillip struggled to get to his feet, Bishop finished him off with a hard right hand that hurt because it was still aching from the first hit. He aimed it at Phillips jaw. It connected and Phillip fell sideways not quite unconscious but too far gone to put up any more fight.

Linda saw what had happened and ran inside to help her husband up. Bishop picked up the glasses and shoved them into the pocket of her dress. She stared at him with a hateful scorn.

Though barely conscious, Phillip was able to stumble toward the open car door. She pushed him inside and closed it. They drove off with Eli still watching from the back window as if trying to figure out why Mr. Boon had hit his daddy.

Bishop straightened the pictures on the hall walls. They weren't too askew. His main concern was Marsha's Little Angel sculpture, the seal with the baby's face and hands. Pushing back and forth, they had brushed against the pedestal and he was afraid they'd knock it off. They hadn't. It only required a bit of straightening.

With his right hand throbbing, he went into Anne's bathroom to look for ointment he could rub into his knuckles and bruised ribs to calm the pain. He found something that professed to do just that, calm joint pain, and rubbed a healthy layer into his aching places.

He also found a bottle of pills, the label of which swore to ease pain within minutes. He took one with a swig of beer from the refrigerator. He wasn't sure whether it was the pill or the beer, but his pain began to let up within a few minutes.

He went to his room and lay down until he heard noise in the kitchen. He knew it'd be Anne so he got up and went to tell her what had happened.

They discussed it on the patio.

"Linda was upset when I told her that Phillip knew Eli had been fathered by Marc," Bishop told Anne.

"I guess she was," Anne said. "Why did she let that happen?"

"She swore it was not possible. She said she used a kind of homespun system for avoiding sex when she was fertile. However, I did leave her crying so she might not have been as certain as she wanted me to believe."

"So, Phillip showed up here to straighten you out," she said with a nod toward his swollen right hand. "I smell the liniment."

He half laughed. "He did just that, unfortunately, he got the short end of the stick. Linda and Eli watched from their car. I tried to avoid a fight, but he was too upset and started swinging. We had the equivalent of a barroom brawl in the hall. He's a tough little shit. I got some bruises to go with my hand. Linda helped him to the car afterward. I was sorry his son had to witness it."

"You must have straightened up afterward," she said with a glance in the direction of the hall."

"I did. I don't know why but both of them are in denial about the boy. Who knows what Phillip's game is? He knows Eli is Marc's son. She has to suspect that he knows after what I told her, but I figure they're playing a game to stay married. She's certainly the best woman he could ever hope for."

"I thought that about Marc," she said with a note of sadness in her voice.

"People like Marc, act a part and they do what the part calls for."

"Do you?"

He almost said, not yet, but didn't. He just shook his head and changed the subject back to Eli, bringing in Ellen's investigation. He didn't tell her how he knew. Ellen's DNA information hadn't been officially subpoenaed yet.

"I'd kiss every bruise but I don't like the taste of whatever you put on them and you may take issue with me kissing your naked body." She added a flirty smile at the end.

He returned her smile and playfully added. "Right now, I'm not so sure. The heat of battle always leaves me in a randy mood."

She raised out of her chair with a smile.

"I was just joking, Anne. Well, kind of joking. I'm too bruised to do anything biblically forbidden anyway."

"I could do all the sinning. I haven't been to church since Marc and I got married."

He smiled. Damned if she wasn't a temptress.

He ignored what she'd said and told her about the visit with Mrs. Flint to ask if Marc had ever discussed his lazy eye problem during a visit and if Phillip was ever present. He had shown her Phillip's photo.

"Ellen and an attorney from the DA's office were there. Mrs. Flint thought she remembered that Marc had talked about the problem when Phillip was with him. He often did.

"Apparently he was proud of having overcome it. The DA's attorney wasn't overwhelmed with the prospects of having Mrs. Flint testify and cross-examined, but she'll just have to let the pieces lay where they fall."

"I think you're making progress," she said, ending the discussion.

She had come home for a bite of lunch before going out again. More bookstores waited, along with two libraries that had scheduled her for talks to mothers and children using her books.

## CHAPTER 19

Bishop went to his room for an extension to his rest break before calling Ellen. He had taken a couple of shots to the head and felt laying down might help clear the cobwebs. Anne came by and kissed him goodbye; on the lips.

"That's for doing a good job with Marc's memoirs," she said. "You've put a fresh coat of paint on him. You make him shine. I've been reading them. I emailed a copy to Cynthia. She'll love 'em. She knows he was a rogue. I'll see you later. Maybe we'll go out."

Her kisses lingered with urgency, he admitted as he tried to fall asleep. They were still in his thoughts when he woke up. They soon disappeared when he called Ellen. He was once more into the fray.

"Ellen I had a knock-down, drag out with Phillip a while ago," he said.

"I guess you'd better tell me about it," She said.

He began with his trip to La Costa and his talk with Linda; her reaction to his disclosure that Phillip knew the boy wasn't his at all, but Flint's.

"She emphatically denied the boy was Marc's, Ellen, even cried when I told her, but she did admit to sleeping with him a couple of times. Probably more. She swore she didn't like it and didn't like Flint. Told him so."

"Yeah," Ellen scoffed. "No woman wants to admit some man dominated her to the point of ecstasy. Don't give some arrogant bastard that satisfaction after he's had his way. I've been there. When I was younger. I'd rather die than let some smirking bastard know he'd controlled me like that."

"Not many women as savvy as you, Ellen. Half of them fall in love."

"I dare say. Why didn't you tell me about your trip north this morning while we were at the nursing home?"

"Why Ellen, I was thinking about you. I figured I'd tell you in private so if it turned out to be important, you could use it to further your career. It wouldn't do me a damn bit of good. I'll stick it in Flint's memoirs if I can find a place, but hell, as far as the world goes, I could have gotten the info from that skilled and dedicated detective, Ellen Wasserman."

"Damn, Bishop, that's uncommonly white of you. You don't mind if I throw a little bit of racism at you, do you? I don't permit anything thrown back, you understand?"

"Of course, I expect it. Hell, don't you know I'm living in Mississippi now. The left wing press would like nothing more than to have us wear a target on our backs." He laughed.

"Deservedly so, you act more like a redneck every day." She laughed back at him.

"Moving on" he said. "After I got back from the nursing home, Phillip showed up. He was mad as hell that I'd talked to his wife behind his back."

He related the details of his fist-to-fist encounter with Phillip, including how it finished up.

"Linda and the boy, Eli, had to watch it from the car," he said. "I don't know what he expected. I outweigh him by fifty pounds. I think his ego and rage overrode his common sense."

"I imagine he'll remember in the morning when he's nursing his headache and drinking his coffee through a straw," she said with a chuckle in her voice.

"So, where do you go from here?" he asked. "It's still a murder investigation. Nothing to do with me anymore.

I've finished writing Flint's memoirs and got a good review from his wife."

"I bet you did, you old stag."

"Now Ellen, don't go assuming facts not in evidence."

"I don't have to assume with some people," she said with a knowing laugh. "It's so obvious no evidence is needed. I've been dealing with the likes of men like you for a long time."

"It an evolutionary process, Ellen. It's bigger than me and there ain't a damn thing I can do about it. It's what makes for bigger and stronger and smarter people having to face the bigger and more complex problems of the future."

"Spare me the bootstrap crap, Bone. If you sleep with somebody, it's because you're horny and she's willin'."

He laughed. "For the record, Ellen, the review from Anne was verbal from start to finish. You can't possibly think a woman with as much money as she has or as beautiful as she is, would have anything to do with an ugly old bastard like me, do you?"

"Yeah, yeah. You ain't gonna trick me into defending you. I know that trick. Next thing I know, I'd be massaging your back."

He laughed. "Okay, Ellen. You got me dead to rights. So, what are you going to do?"

"I was hoping you had an idea or two," she said.

"If I were you, I'd get a warrant to search Marshall's house and office for guns. Specifically, a rifle and a handgun. I don't think you can lay the DNA on him until you have an official report. You can say you were told. He'll think I somehow got a copy."

"Unless we find a weapon, we don't have enough to make an arrest," she said.

"I agree but while you're searching his office, you can ask him where he was when Derek was shot. And, bluff him about people saying he went missing after Flint left. Maybe embellish about how he pushed Flint into playing racquetball knowing he might have a diabetic reaction and die on the court," he told her.

"He'll deny that," she said.

"He will, but he may start thinking you know something. You might spook him into making a mistake," he said.

"You've been watching too many television shows. Bad guys don't spook easy. And, they don't confess because the show's run out of time. Even so, I think I'll take your suggestion. If we get lucky and find the guns, we'll have the bastard."

"Let me know what you find out. I may head back to Mississippi. I don't have anything else to do out here," he told her.

"Call me before you go," she said. "I'll buy lunch. Put it on my expense report."

They both laughed.

\* \* \* \*

Bishop took a shower and got dressed into something casual – from Flint's closet – enough to have dinner in, hopefully someplace he'd like. The hot water of the shower made his hand feel better; that and the pill he'd taken.

He updated his notes and waited for Anne to come home.

While he waited, he called Kathy. Before they'd finished, he told her he thought he'd be able to fly home soon. He decided to wait until he was home to tell her about the fight.

"Not much else for me to do. The police are investigating both murders. They don't need me and I've finished Flint's memoirs for the most part. If the police get lucky and find the murderers before I get it printed, I'll add that. Otherwise, his wife can add it to the second edition."

"You think there'll be a second edition?"

"Got to be a best seller," he said with a chuckle.

\* \* \* \*

Anne came in near six o'clock. Her tour was a big success. She said readers lined up for her to sign their copies. And, at the libraries, mothers were primed with questions. How do you get your ideas? How long does it take to write a book? And, who did her illustrations?

She was practically dressed to go out, so they only hung around the house long enough for her to freshen up.

"My car or yours?" Bishop asked when she reappeared.

"I've been driving all day and my batteries are low so let's take yours." They got in Bishop's rental and backed out.

There was rarely any traffic on the street, but Bishop stopped for a look anyway. Nothing was coming so he turned right. In front of the house, he saw what looked like a shadow at the front door and being extra sensitive after his fight with Phillip, braked to an abrupt halt. That might have saved his life or hers. A shot rang out from the street above and ricocheted off the hood. Anne screamed and ducked.

He immediately gunned it. A second shot bounced off the top as he drove to the other side of the street, away from the shooter's angle. The shooter was obviously on the street above, the same street the shooter used to blow out his back window.

There were no other shots.

He stopped around the corner to see if anybody was still around and to check the car. He saw nothing and the car was okay except for the bullet mark in the hood and top. He got back in and cautiously drove around to the street where the shooter must have been. No one was around, no shooter and no witnesses.

He cursed out of frustration. "Second damn time. I wasn't watching. Damn."

"Thank goodness you were extra cautious," Anne said, talking about his sudden stop to check out a shadow at the front. The shadow was caused by street lights passing through a bush beside the house. A breeze had caused it to move.

They talked about making a police report but decided it was a waste of time. He'd call about the car the next day and let Ellen know. The shots pointed to Phillip. If she could find the rifle, it'd be over for him.

"You still want to go out?" he asked.

"More than ever," she said. "I want to get away from all the turmoil."

He talked her into the Olive Garden, unlimited soup and salad. It was great. They drank more than they should. Bishop passed it off to nervousness.

Naturally, they talked about being shot at. It would have been impossible not to. And, naturally, Bishop figured it had to be Phillip. Only now, he had a reason. The first time, there was some doubt as to why somebody would shoot out his back window. The motivation for the second shot was clear. Revenge.

*  *  *  *

He parked the car in the garage. She gave him a hug at her bedroom door without pushing it. He went to his room and emailed Ellen an account of the shooting. Seconds later, Anne appeared in the door. He'd left it open. She was wearing a scant bathing suit.

"I'm going to relax in the Jacuzzi. It's down below. I'll be disappointed if you don't join me."

She threw him one of Flint's bathing suits. "I'm sure it'll fit you."

Bishop wanted to sit in a Jacuzzi like he wanted an extra hole in the head. He just wanted to slide into bed early and get a good night's sleep, but she was standing there with a big, expectant smile on her face, waiting.

So, he picked up the bathing suit and changed.

They stopped in the kitchen for a glass of wine and a mug of beer. Bishop didn't need another beer either, but went along. He'd sip it slowly however.

They eased into the bubbling hot water, sat on seats, drank their drinks and made small talk. She related more of her stories from the day's tour. He mostly listened but couldn't help but notice the bubbles flowing around her almost naked body.

He reached back to put his mug on the Jacuzzi decking. When he turned back, she had taken off her top.

"I like to feel the bubbles," she said with a wicked smile.

"Anne, you know I … I don't want to get involved. My resistance is low just now."

He tried to look away but couldn't.

"Don't worry," she said. "I'm not going to attack you. Just relax."

He laughed. "You know that's not possible." He twisted out of the water, turned away from her and wrapped himself in a towel. "If you don't mind, I'm calling it a day … a night too. I'm sorry. I really am. Damn …" He shook his head as if that would get the scene out of his thoughts. It did not.

"I saw how sorry you were just now when you got out of the Jacuzzi. What was under that towel?" She laughed.

"Yeah. Well, I told you I was human."

"You just proved that."

He hurried away, went to his room, turned off his lights and slid into bed. He was asleep in minutes. The beer had caught up with him.

He awoke sometimes later. He felt something warm against him. Then, he felt Anne's lips against his and her naked body next to his and it was too damn late for him to do anything about it.

Finally, he fell back asleep but when he woke the next morning, Anne was still in bed with him and he remembered what he had done. He cursed himself but knew he couldn't change anything.

She kissed him and held him close for a few seconds. "You were great, Bishop. Your woman is a lucky woman." She rolled out of bed and went to her room.

"I'll see you for breakfast in thirty minutes," she told him from the door, still totally nude.

He cursed himself again but knew he'd enjoyed every minute of it. It was something he'd have to somehow put behind him, if he could He smelled the bacon before he reached the kitchen. Once there, he saw Anne at the stove.

"Bacon and eggs," she said over her shoulder. "With English muffins. I figured it'd be a welcome change."

"They're my favorite. I may have said. It's what I order when I go to Denny's."

He walked to where she stood and put his hands on her arms. "Ordinarily, I'd give you a kiss after last night. I won't hedge about last night though. It was beautiful. And, wonderful. But, –"

"I know, nothing has changed. I'd be disappointed in you if it had."

"Well, I do have another taint on my soul, but if I was going to put a taint on it, I couldn't have picked a better one."

She laughed.

"You are beautiful … no, that's not enough," he told her. "You have a kind of haughty, look of rejection on your face that drives men wild trying to overcome it. I saw it when you opened the door the first time. And, I've seen it every damn day I've been here. But, since I've been here, I've seen the other side of you, what lies under the surface of your haughty look. You have a tenderness about you that, to me, is more compelling than what most people see on the surface. I guess it was inevitable that my resistance would weaken."

She turned and kissed him on the cheek. "I'm glad it did. You know you remind me of Marc. So my affection for you, since you walked in the door, is the affection I had for Marc.

" I don't know if there's enough chemistry between us, independent of Marc, to sustain a relationship. I only know how much I enjoyed being with you last night. It meant more to me than you could ever guess. It was like … well, I think I can finally let Marc go. I believe I finally have closure. I thank you."

He kissed her back. "I understand. I truly do. I don't think I'll consider the evening a taint after all. How can an act of pure love be considered sinful?"

They enjoyed a full English breakfast. While it did not come close to what they enjoyed the night before, it was nevertheless great.

Ellen sent an email. Her "people" had already been out. They found where the shooter lay in the grass to make the shot. From the impression in the grass, they deduced that the shooter had a slight frame.

Having heard that bit of information, Bishop immediately jumped to Phillip as the shooter.

They figure he or she parked their vehicle in front of where they lay to block anyone happening past from seeing.

They found no witnesses who saw anything but that was not surprising. The little street was a short stub that was only occasionally used for overflows.

Ellen said they were placing a notice in the Light and Tribune asking for anyone who drove on the street that night to come forth. She wasn't optimistic but it was standard procedure. Often people who might have seen something didn't want to get involved.

Like Bishop had done, she also fingered Phillip as the shooter. They were going ahead with their plan to get a search warrant for Phillip's house and the office.

Bishop sent an email back thanking her. He wasn't optimistic that their searches would find anything. Phillip wasn't stupid. He'd know a search might be forthcoming and hide anything incriminating. Bishop's next question was: where would he hide a weapon?

He called the car rental company about the car. They asked if he could bring it in. He could keep it unless it bothered him. They just wanted to inspect it to make sure it wouldn't be a hazard to drive.

\* \* \* \*

Ellen had said it might take a couple of days of police work to finish their investigation so Bishop decided to visit Sarah unannounced at the bank. He wanted to ask her reaction to Banker Ben's miserly try to squeeze money from Anne for little Marcus.

Most likely he's told her to avoid me at all costs, he thought.

He wandered into the bank a few minutes after one o'clock. He carried a briefcase to give the impression he was making a business call. It wasn't necessary. When he walked in, she was in her office pouring over a stack of papers.

He knocked on her door and walked in before she could say "no."

By the frown on her face, he knew he had been right. Banker Ben had put the word out. Do not talk to Bishop Bone.

"I'm busy right now," she said, touching the papers on her desk. "Loan application I'm reviewing. I have a deadline. Sorry. You should call for an appointment anyway."

"I just have one question," he said and asked it before she could refuse. "You father visited Anne Flint the other afternoon and asked for money to support little Marcus. Was that your idea?" He knew it wasn't, but wanted to let her know what the man had done.

"What? Dad asked for money? Why? He said you had made a personal attack, verbally, on him and I wasn't to talk to you. He didn't say anything about … asking for money. I have enough money to support my child. I don't want anything from Anne Flint. Marc thought she was not a loving woman. I don't want her messing up my son."

"I thought you felt that way," he told her. "Your dad offered visitation rights in exchange for money."

"What? I can't believe he'd do that. I don't think he did! You're making that up," she said.

"No, I'm not," he answered. "Why would I lie? I'm not involved with the Flints except to write Marc's memoirs. You can ask Anne. She was as shocked as I was. Your dad spouted Bible verses, claiming Anne was going to hell if she didn't do the Lord's work and put money aside for the boy."

Her facial expression indicated that she believed him. "I'm going to talk to Dad about that. I will not have him interfering that way."

"Do that," Bishop said. "I also think he's considering filing a lawsuit. His attorneys anyway. Of course he'd need for you to actually file it."

"File a lawsuit!" she said, practically shouting. "Why? Are you trying to con me out of something? If you are, I'll have you arrested before you can blink twice. I've seen your kind before."

I bet you have. His name was Marc.

"I'll be leaving you now, but here's the letter your Dad left behind. He probably didn't think I'd give it to you." He handed it to her and waited.

She opened it and began to read. Her face showed her shock.

A few minutes later, she folded it and handed it back. "I apologize, Mr. Bone. Of course you are not trying to con me out of anything. But, what are you looking for?"

"I told Anne that I didn't think you'd do anything so ... well, dumb as to file a public lawsuit for all to know what had happened between you and Flint."

She shook her head.

"I just wanted to be sure. I think your dad gets wound up in the Bible now and then and takes the wrong slant. I doubt seriously if he or you would ever be short of money for your son," Bishop said.

"Goodness no! I already have a trust fund set up for him. He has a little eye problem we're having to deal with but the doctors think it can be handled by an eye patch, maybe some drops."

"Lazy eye," Bishop said.

She looked at him sharply. "Lazy eye! How'd you know? Have you been snooping around?"

He gave a dry laugh. "No. Flint had lazy eye when he was young. He had to overcome it and said it gave him the strength to do all the things he later did in life. Since lazy eye is inherited from the father, I deduced that your son might have that same condition."

His visit was over. He'd found out what he'd come to find out. The money squeeze was Holliday's idea and it wasn't likely to go any further. He knew that would relieve Anne. He'd also verified that lazy eye was indeed inherited from the father and that Eli was certainly Flint's boy, no matter how much Linda and Phillip might argue otherwise. The DNA results were valid.

"I can see why Phillip might want to deny it," he said to himself. "If he admitted it, he'd have to admit that Flint slept with his wife, more to the point, that his wife had slept with Flint and that he was not ready to face even with DNA proof in his hands. And, Linda was just flat out wrong. She was fertile," he told himself. "Sometimes, I think I don't understand people at all.

And, I have to throw myself in that pot." He was thinking about the Jacuzzi affair.

Why did I do that? Easy to ask that question the day after.

His phone range before he reached the Flint's garage. Ben Holliday was on the other end shouting. "You are a vile, blasphemer of lies, Bone. You have slept in the house of the devil and you have become evil. You have stolen and violated God's commandments. Thou shall not steal. And you will pay for your sin."

"Hold on, Holliday," Bishop interrupted the man's diatribe. "What the hell are you talking about? I've told no lies and I haven't stolen anything. If you'll pardon my expression, Mr. Holliday, you're full of shit."

"You intruded on my daughter and told her lies. You stole her love from me when you placed a barrier between our love for each other. And you will burn in hell for that!"

"Okay. I get it. You're pissed because I told her about your miserly attempt to shakedown Anne Flint. You won't give it up will you? You were wrong then and you're wrong now. Personally, I think you need help."

"Lawyers are the devil's instrument for evil. The world would be better off if you were all dead."

"Sure, if we were dead and some bank, like yours, makes a bad loan and then tries to force the poor borrower to pay it back, you'd like it if the borrower didn't have an attorney to stand up for him. Is that how you made all you money, beating up on poor borrowers who couldn't afford an attorney?

"I've been nice to you, well, as nice as I could, but I'll tell you, Mr. Holliday, you can go straight to hell. You spout the scripture verses and you want to act holier than thou, but you're a living example of evil, hiding behind the banner of the Bible. Get help before the people in white coats, waving nets, show up to take you away."

"You – "

Bishop punched the end button.

He could imagine the man standing in his office with steam coming out of his ears, staring at his phone. Nobody ever hangs up on Banker Ben. Unfortunately, he can't foreclose on me.

He would have told Anne, but she was not to be found. So, he made a cup of coffee and drank it in his room while he added Holliday's outburst to his notes. Flint's memoirs are growing and are taking on some real drama.

Ellen called as he rinsed his cup in the kitchen sink. "Bone, I thought I'd bring you up to date. We got a search warrant. Anything requested by anybody in La Jolla gets priority. So, we tore Marshall's house and office apart. He

bitched the whole time. His wife did too. They both swore he'd never had a rifle or a gun and wouldn't allow any guns in the house with a little child. My, my, they were indignant."

"You found nothing."

"Not a damn thing. No box of shells. No rifle, no scope, no handgun. We also checked with every gun dealer in town. Marshall, neither one, has bought a weapon at any of them. No way could we check on-line sellers."

"Tell you what, Ellen," Bishop said. "Check the back window of the truck to see if there are any traces of a gun rack. I figure you'll find an outline. Then, get the license plate to the DMV and find out the last owner before Flint's company. I'm betting they took the truck with one of the projects they took over and re-registered it in Flint's company name. If you get that far, call the guy and see if he had a rifle hanging on the back window. I'll check with Anne to see if Flint ever brought one home or ever talked about one. If not, we can conclude that Phillip ended up with it."

"That all sounds well and good, Bone, but what good does it do us? Hell, we still won't have it. Where else can we look?"

"Let's take it one step at a time, Ellen. I'll do some thinking about where else you can look. Knowing there is a rifle, and I believe there is, gives me an incentive to find it."

"Yeah. I feel the same way. I'll jump through the hoop for you one more time, Bone. I hope it pays off. Now and then, I get tired of dancing to your tune, Bone."

"Come on, Ellen, you like to dance."

"Just not always to your tune. I have my own music." She hung up.

He hung his coffee mug in the cup rack sat down to think. Where would Phillip hide a weapon? Would he have thrown it away? That's a possibility. Why keep it? In case he needed it again?

Anne came in. He told her what Sarah had to say about her father's attempt to squeeze money out of her for Flint's illegitimate son.

She was relieved. "Thank goodness. I can't imagine what it'd cost to fight a suit backed by Banker Ben. He has more money than anybody in town."

"More money than God," Bishop quipped.

"At least."

"He called and practically accused me of being Satan. If he didn't quite get that far, it was only because I hung up on him before he could."

"He may be a bit unhinged," she said what Bishop had been thinking.

"My thought too."

He told her Ellen had searched Phillip's home and the office for a rifle but had found nothing. He had hoped they'd also find the gun that killed Derek, the theory being that Derek was shot because he was blackmailing Phillip.

"He most likely threw the rifle away or hid it where they'll never find it. The gun too, if he used it to shoot Derek," she said, fighting back the tears.

"Yeah," Bishop said. "I don't suppose Marc said anything about a rifle or gun? Or ever brought one home?"

"No. We never even talked about having a rifle. Marc bought me a .25 Caliber automatic. I keep it locked in my desk downstairs in case I have a break-in while I'm working. We have a security system to protect me. However, I don't turn on when you're in the house." She said with a smile.

"Glad to be of service," Bishop said.

"No complaints so far," she said.

"Just thinking out loud," Bishop said. "Derek might also have been blackmailing Phillip about the tax losses he was concealing from you and the liquidation committee."

"Wouldn't that have implicated me as well?" she asked.

"Only slightly, if at all," he answered. "You're not the chief financial officer and you're not an accountant. If it ever comes up, you can say that Phillip came to you after the closing and told you about a windfall. That should keep you out of it."

"What does your police friend think about that?" she asked.

"We haven't discussed blackmail or Derek's murder," he said. "She's thinking he tried to murder me when he shot at the car because I rattled his case about their boy being fathered by Marc. I figure what really upset him was having to face the fact that his wife slept with Marc."

"I can imagine, Bishop. Marc said he fought him tooth and nail on the racquetball court. He had been taking lessons from a local pro, Marc said."

"It wouldn't take much for me to conclude that Phillip, in effect, tried to kill Marc on the racquetball court the day of the opening. Linda had told him Marc's blood sugar was dangerously high. Phillip might have goaded him into playing, hoping he'd drop dead."

"When he didn't, do you think he followed Marc in his truck and ran him off the road?" she asked.

"That's the theory Ellen and I have been working on. So far without much success."

They agreed to go to the Japanese noodle café that evening. Ellen had told Bishop she was instructing the La Jolla patrol to drive down the lane looking down at the Flint home from time to time to see if any cars were parked there or if any suspicious characters were around.

Bishop doubted Phillip would take a chance at another shot anyway. "He's either thrown the rifle away or hidden it someplace he thinks is safe. Even so, I'll take a long look up there before we drive out."

"Let's go before dark," Anne suggested.

"Good idea," Bishop agreed. "Anybody'd be stupid to take a shot at us in daylight."

Anne had some mail she needed to get to the post office and a couple of errands. They'd go to the restaurant when she came back.

He called Ellen to see if she had any news. "Have you cracked the case yet, Ellen?"

"Did you hear a big whoopee coming from City Hall?"

He hadn't.

"I'll tell you what we have," she said.

The forensics group determined that there had been a gun rack on the back window. They found an outline. "Thank you for that suggestion, Bone."

They tracked down Earnest Wagner the prior owner. Indeed, he had owned a rifle. His company had anyway. When Flint kicked him out and took over, he also took his rifle. It was in the company's name.

"It pissed him off, but he said, it only cost two hundred dollars so he didn't make much of a fuss about it. 'Sides, he said, talking like he did, 'Flint had this big goon with him. There was no scope on the rifle. So, if your guy used one, he had to buy it later,'" Ellen told Bishop. "Any more ideas about where Marshall might have hidden it?"

"I'm still thinking about it. I'll see what I can come up with overnight and call you in the morning. I thank you for having the roving patrol keeping an eye out for us. I saw a car roll past here today."

"I have to keep my main man safe," she said.

## CHAPTER 20

Bishop and Anne had an uneventful dinner at the noddle café including only a single carafe of hot sake. After they returned home, he went directly to his room and Anne went to hers. No Jacuzzi that night.

Maybe she has had closure, Bishop thought. He updated his notes and went to bed. But, about two o'clock that morning, he had an idea and got up and emailed Ellen.

* * * *

Bishop and Anne had the usual for breakfast, coffee and rolls and conversation. No bacon and eggs that morning. She had places to go and wasn't too chatty. He was really out of options. The only thing left was to hear from Ellen. If his email didn't produce fruit, he'd think about flying home.

At ten, Ellen called. "We've been out following up on your midnight ideas. My phone dings when I get an email. Did you know that?"

"No. Mine may but I ignore it."

"Well, I can't. So, I got up and read your ideas."

"Sorry," he said

"Don't be. I'm getting to like 'em. We've already been out to the La Jolla project and talked to the pick-up crew. They're under contract with the holding company set up by the liquidation committee. All the units were sold at auction. The committee made a bundle from that project."

"Right. What'd you find out?"

"Nothing yet. That's why I called. I thought you might want to go with us. We have a construction shack at the La Jolla project to search and we found the storage yard, your second idea. Flint's company rented a storage unit there."

"I'd love to come."

She'd pick him up in thirty minutes. First La Jolla. If they didn't find anything there, they'd try the storage bay.

They drove to the La Jolla project. The pick-up crew consisted of eight men completing the last of the landscaping, putting out plants, adjusting sprinklers and lights. The storage shed Ellen wanted to see was a temporary building set up at the back of the project in what would be open space eventually. It was about twenty feet square with a large door to permit tractors and electrical buggies easy access.

Having been alerted that they were on the way, the foreman for the crew met them in front of the building. Bishop and Ellen introduced themselves. Another police car pulled up behind them and four uniformed officers hopped out and walked over.

Ellen explained to the foreman what they were looking for. He nodded and told them to search all they wanted. He hadn't seen anything that resembled a weapon, rifle or handgun. She waved her crew inside. Bishop stayed close to her and followed her around.

He didn't want to contaminate any evidence they found. Over the next two-and-a half hours, they turned the place inside out and found nothing.

"Any other facilities around here the company could have used for storage?" she asked the foreman.

He shook his head. "No. Not related to construction. There might be something close to the meeting room where they held the opening. They keep dishes, folding tables, other things like that in there for meetings. I have a key."

They followed him to the room which he unlocked. Inside were the things he'd described including napkins and rolls of paper towels. The room was not nearly as large as the storage shed so it didn't take as long to search and determine that no rifle was hidden there.

Bishop and Ellen were visibly disappointed. It had seemed like a good idea. Ellen sighed. She looked at Bishop and as if knowing what he was thinking, said, "You get used to disappointment in this business, Bishop. Let's us get to our next rendezvous with destiny. Maybe the gods will favor us there."

Yeah, he thought, and maybe not. Damn. Nothing's working.

\* \* \* \*

Someone had arranged for a security guard to open the gate at the storage yard. He was standing to one side as they drove past. Likewise, the storage unit had been unlocked for them. Ellen, Bishop and the four police officers got out of their vehicles and went inside. Along one wall was a stack of, what appeared to be, blankets for cushioning things being transported in truck beds. Storage boxes, some empty, some not, lay stacked along another wall. Small tools lay on benches here and there. Two hand-pulled wagons and a dolly sat in front of the benches. A couple of tables were propped against the stack of empty boxes.

"Get at it," Ellen shouted. Bishop watched as the officers looked into the boxes, behind the tables and under the cushioning blankets.

One of the officers said, "Be damned!" He pointed. At the bottom of the stack of blankets was a long object wrapped in plastic. To Bishop and everyone else, it looked like a rifle and it was. A barrel poking out of one end of the wrapping showed what it was. It did not have a scope, however.

"Okay," Ellen said. "Bone, you lucked out again. Be careful, I don't want any fingerprints smudged."

The officers carefully lifted the wrapped rifle from its hiding place into a box and placed it in the trunk of their car. Ellen told them something. Bishop assumed they were taking it to be fingerprinted.

They searched more for a scope but didn't find one.

"We have the slugs we dug out of the side of Flint's house and the one from the back of your rental car," she said. "We'll be able to tell if that rifle shot them. And, if we're lucky, Phillip Marshall's prints will be on it someplace. And, we'll have him at least for attempted murder."

She was smiling as was Bishop. Finally a break in the case. She drove him home and promised to call as soon as they had anything.

Bishop joked about her next promotion and interviews and television spots.

She passed it off, but he could tell that she was happy.

\* \* \* \*

A courier hand delivered a letter to him from Holliday's attorney demanding that he cease and desist from "stalking Sarah or a criminal complaint would be filed."

He laughed when he read it. "Ridiculous. No way would the statute be that broadly interpreted. The attorney is obviously pandering to a difficult client for a fee and to keep him happy."

He threw the letter in the trash.

"What a crock. The man totes a Bible and spouts Bible verses against sin and sinners, but consults with "evildoers" when it suits him."

\* \* \* \*

Anne was pleased as well that they had found a rifle, when she came home.

"Phillip!" she said. "That's hard to believe. Kind of the mild mannered type. Who would ever suspect him of shooting at anybody? And, they think he killed Marc too?"

"They think it. I do too, but unless he confesses ... or Linda somehow incriminates him, they still don't have any proof linking him to Marc's death. I know they'll be trying to piece enough bits and pieces to do that, but from what I know, they'll have a hard time convincing a jury."

"What are you going to do? Go back to Mississippi?"

"Yes. I'll wait around a couple of days in case they want to talk to me. And, I'm sure I'll come back for the trial but after I update the memoirs, there's not much left for me to do out here."

She gave him her sweet smile. "We could take a getaway trip someplace to celebrate and relax while you're waiting."

"Tempting, Anne, but you know I can't do that." He also smiled. "Besides, I don't think my heart could handle another Jacuzzi frolic. I still remember the last one."

She did too.

They had a late lunch snack together and enjoyed it on the balcony. Although Bishop had sat out there numerous times lately, this was the first in a long time that he had actually enjoyed the view.

Recently he had been distracted about finishing up Flint's memoirs and the problems he'd been having so he could get home and resume his normal life ... with Kathy. He missed her more than ever.

During lunch he told her about the latest from "old Banker Ben." They both had a laugh about it. She wanted to see the letter. He dug it out of the trash can and gave it to her.

Anne went into her office to work on her latest. She told him she had been racing for the curtain – meaning it was almost finished - but had been too distracted lately to think creatively.

"My publisher's pressing me for a draft," she told him.

\* \* \* \*

Bishop went to his room and called Kathy. "Looks like I'm finished out here." He told her about the morning's events, the searches and the discovery of the rifle they were certain had been used to shoot at him.

"They'll test it and let me know. If they don't need me, I'll book a flight home. I've missed you, sweetheart. I can't wait to see you ... and hold you close to me."

She felt the same way. "I've been afraid you were growing roots out there. Your emails, even your telephone calls have seemed distracted."

He apologized. "No doubt. I've been getting it from all sides." He told her about his call from Holliday and the letter. "The man's certifiable. He picks and chooses something from the Bible to give credence to what he wants to say."

She was aghast. "How old is he? He sounds like he has a touch of dementia."

"I wouldn't be surprised."

"I'd leave him alone, Bishop. His daughter too."

"I intend to. I only talked to his daughter to make sure she wasn't behind his attempted shake-down of Anne. She wasn't."

"Anne? That's the first time you've called her that. Does that mean anything?"

He laughed and hoped it was convincing. "Nothing at all. She got tired of me calling her Mrs. Flint."

She laughed. "Let me know when you have a flight."

"I will."

After the call, he sat down to do a final update of Flint's memoirs. He had to add more about Phillip when he was first introduced into Flint's history so the reader would know him better by the time they'd zeroed in on him as the killer.

"I wish he'd confess to Derek's murder as well," Bishop said to himself after he'd finished. "That'd tie it up."

He heard nothing from Ellen and knew not to call her and have her rant about being disturbed. She'll call when she has something.

Anne had said earlier she'd bought fresh halibut for dinner. He knew it was a fish of some sort, but wasn't sure he'd ever eaten it. He had confessed to her that he was not a big fish eater. She'd told him how healthy fish were and that he should eat it more often.

"I guess we get fresh fish in Mississippi. I just don't know what kind and I hate the smell of the things."

"Get 'em fresh. They don't smell if they're fresh."

And, the dish she served that night didn't smell and tasted delicious.

"I may have to change my view of fish," he told her. "This was delicious."

She smiled, not the haughty smile she used to reject or keep people at bay. It was the one she showed to people she liked or at least knew very well.

On the balcony after dinner, they relaxed with drinks on the balcony. She talked about her friend from the Bay area. He hinted about coming down for a couple of days beginning with the weekend. His company was seriously considering moving to the San Diego area. It had been offered incentives to move.

She didn't try to keep the excitement out of her voice. At the end of what she had said, she touched his arm, as she often did, looked him in the eyes and said, "I will miss you, Bishop. These past few weeks have been great tonic to me. Don't be offended, but it's been like having Marc with me again, only better."

He said he understood and actually did somehow. "At first, I kept you at arm's length, Anne. I was working for you but the more we were together the more I saw the real person you are. From what I've learned about your husband, I'm not sure he completely appreciated you. He probably loved you in his own way, but I think he could have given more of himself."

She got up and kissed him and sat back down.

"I … you didn't … that wasn't necessary. I was just telling you what I felt … after I got to know you better," he said.

"And, I was just showing my appreciation. I don't think you minded."

He shook his head. "No, I didn't. I'll have some soul cleansing to do when it's over though."

She laughed. "Not too much, I hope. I won't ever forget."

He knew it'd be difficult for him as well, but knew Kathy would make it happen once they were back together.

The day ended. It had been a good one.

He went to bed and wasn't awakened by a warm, inviting body. He told himself he was glad.

\* \* \* \*

The next morning, Ellen called with news. "No fingerprints on the rifle. Not even a smudge. But, the slugs were fired by the rifle. Earnest Wagner said it was the rifle Flint took away with him the day he took his company so we arrested Phillip on suspicion of attempted murder. Now, we have to build a case. We don't have a rifle scope but at the distance involved, we don't think a decent shooter would need a scope. The DA approved the arrest. He thanks you. I told him we had been working together, like we did in the Shores murders case."

"Maybe you'll get another promotion," Bishop said."

"Only if we get a conviction. A murder conviction for Flint's murder, would do the trick. Attempted murder on an out of towner … probably not."

"I think that amounts to discrimination or profiling or something popular that's going around. I wish I had a liberal friend I could consult," he said.

"You're consulting with one now." She laughed.

"Okay. What's next?" he asked.

"Now, we do our calling and interviewing and snooping. Somebody will be grilling Marshall, trying to get him to confess, telling him how much easier it'll be on everybody if he does. No messy trial. The usual police routine."

"Yeah. I watch BBC television shows too," Bishop said.

"A lot of it is what actually goes on," she said.

"It sounds like it. Kathy wants me home. When do you think I can get out of here?"

"Ah, now you're asking me to look into the crystal ball. How the hell do I know? I don't know how long it's gonna take to track down all the loose ends, Bone. I'd say give us a week. I reckon you could fly home for a week, if your carnal instincts are bothering you. I'll call you when it's time to come back."

"That'd suit me."

"Shouldn't take more than a day for you to get back. The DA might want to interview you. He likes to eyeball his witnesses. See how they'll do under cross-examination by a hotshot defense lawyer. By the way, Marshall has retained the best defense attorney in town, Washington Carver. That's what he claims he does, carves up hostile witnesses."

"I've heard of him. Must be costing Phillip his savings," Bishop said.

"Their house is not on the market. They intend to fight. He says he's innocent."

"That's why we have trials, to find out. I think I'll go home. I'd appreciate a call now and then with updates. A conviction for attempted murder is okay, but I'd like to know if you are able to link him to Flint's murder … or Derek's for that matter."

"Yeah. Well, as you know, there's still some doubt about Flint's death. It may not have been murder. Remember. Our forensics people still say it was possible the Jeep was run off the road. It was mostly your doings to get that out of them so we still have it on our books as a maybe," she explained.

"I think, maybe you should rethink it," he said.

"We'll rethink it when we have more proof. I haven't seen you walk in with any that wouldn't get me demoted," she joked.

"A man filled with as much hate as Phillip sure as hell wouldn't have hesitated to kill Flint or Derek."

"That may be, Bishop. You have a decent track record but the DA won't take a case to trial on your track record. We still have to get him away from the opening long enough to have done it. And, we don't have a damn thing linking him to the Derek murder."

"The way I look at it, Ellen, is this. I pointed to the killer but you guys are holding the guns. It's up to you to bag the game."

"For what it's worth to you, Bishop, down here we've doped out your approach to getting results. You stick your nose into people's business until you make somebody mad enough to take a poke at it. When they do that, you grab 'em by the jugular until they confess. You get good press around here. But, we have to go by the rules. We have to dot the I's and cross the T's, legally."

He thanked her. She's probably right, but it sure gets hard on the nose at times, poking it into people's business.

"I've got things to do in Mississippi," he told her.

"I can imagine the things you've got to do, Bone. Don't sugarcoat it with me. I know you."

Bishop laughed at her perception.

\* \* \* \*

He called the airlines and got a flight for the next day. Then, when he went upstairs for his mid-morning coffee, he told Anne.

She wasn't pleased but she accepted it. And, he supposed, she did have another option, her friend from the Bay area.

Once that was settled, he called Kathy. She'd pick him up at the local airport. It was an early flight so they could have dinner out and he'd catch her up with all his news.

She was waiting for him at the gate. Other passengers paused to take a look at the "couple" in the close embrace.

* * * *

They went to a place not far from his cabin for dinner, Catfish Charley's. It served great hamburgers, with more French fries that one human could eat, cole slaw that any grandmother would envy and good coffee. Also, it seemed that wherever they looked they saw somebody they knew.

"It's like one big family around here," Bishop said. Kathy agreed.

After that feast, they went back to his cabin and relaxed on the back porch to the music playing in the speakers he'd mounted on trees in the woods around it. He played a CD with Shostakovich's Second Waltz. Indian Creek was ablaze in green from his submerged lights.

The next morning, over breakfast, he suggested that she call in sick or something to give them a day to catch up.

"I already did that yesterday when I knew you'd be flying in." She smiled. "After last night, I wouldn't have been fit to work anyway."

"Good. We'll drive down to McHenry and pick up a pecan pie for desert tonight." McHenry was a small community on the highway to the Mississippi Coast. The Pecan House that specialized in pecan pies and other pecan delights and gifts was in an old Cajun style shack with a bathroom in what looked like an old fashioned outhouse.

"I'm cooking tonight," she said. "Salad and lentil soup. That should get your mind back to Mississippi."

"Sweetheart, last night got me back to Mississippi, body and soul."

"I'm relieved. I was afraid somebody had convinced you that California was your new home. Who's that detective you're always going on about?"

"Ellen Wasserman. Ellen is a friend, of sorts. I like working with her because she doesn't beat around the bush, but she's happily re-married and has a happy home."

He wasn't sure of that but knew it'd fit. Next time he saw Ellen, he'd ask about her family situation. She may have said, but he'd forgotten if she had.

# CHAPTER 21

"Dinner was outstanding," he told her. The croutons she added to the lentil soup put it over the top, he had said. Dessert was a slice of the pecan pie they'd picked up at the Pecan House. They ate it with fresh coffee. Sleeping wasn't a problem.

Kathy spent the night with him. She'd arranged for someone to check on her mother who had complained that she was okay by herself, but Kathy wanted to be sure. She left after breakfast the next day to go to work.

Bishop made his usual inspection of the cabin and his land. He did some pruning and some cleaning up but nothing much had to be done. He called Seth to see if they needed a fourth for tennis. They did, that afternoon. That was a welcome break. He caught up on their news and they caught up on his.

"Yours is much more exciting," Sonja said over drinks at the country club lounge after their two set match. Bishop, suffering from jet lag and a lack of sleep, was on the losing end of two sets. He didn't mind and didn't offer an excuse.

The next day, he called his bank clients and picked up a couple of assignments.

Things had been somewhat slow so he hadn't been missed. He took the files from the bank and went out in quest of a challenge. He didn't find one. The borrowers whose files he'd been given were ready with the financial reports and good news. Business was improving and they gave him checks to bring their loans current.

He stopped by Chief Jenkins' office to say hello and to buy him a beer.

"I've missed my fishing trips out to your place," Jenkins said.

"We'll catch up," Bishop promised.
Jenkins thanked him.

\* \* \* \*

Bishop went home, wrote reports and delivered the reports and check to the banks the next morning.

Ellen called late that afternoon about the Flint investigation. "Okay, here's my update. My progress report," she said.

She told him what they had been doing. They made a surprise search of Phillip's home and office hoping he would have relaxed and taken the handgun that killed Derek from where he'd hidden it, back home. He hadn't.

"We figure he threw the thing away. He doesn't have a real alibi for that night but we can't tie him to the murder. His wife says he was in bed at the time of the murder. We don't have anything that says otherwise."

Phillip denied shooting at anybody with the rifle. He said he hadn't seen it since Flint brought it back from the take-over of Wagner's project. He didn't want the thing hanging in the truck so he'd taken it down and left it in the office.

He swore he didn't know how it got into the storage bin. Nobody came forth to say otherwise. But, the DA was satisfied that he was the last person to have been seen with it before Ellen had found it.

Not only that, it was definitely the rifle used to shoot at Bone and he had a motive, Bone's threat to his family. He felt the jury would buy his case. A strong part of the DA's case was Phillip's attack on Bone at the Flint's home after he'd told the man's wife that Phillip knew about her affair with Flint and more importantly, that Eli was Flint's son. Phillip's bonus that year was to be given in evidence to show that Flint knew about the boy and was trying to make amends in his own way.

"He'll introduce the DNA reports and he'll let Mrs. Flint testify. The defense attorney will tear into her, but the DA figures the jury will be offended if he tears too hard."

Bishop agreed.

"You'll testify about your meeting with him at the office, how he was reluctant to let you interview his wife. You'll testify to your interviews with his wife, the lazy eye thing, her affair with Flint and your disclosure to her that Phillip knew Flint fathered his son."

"A decent case," Bone said. "A bit speculative, but decent."

"And, we have two witnesses who'll testify that Linda told them shortly after Flint's death that she'd told Phillip about Flint's blood sugar reading and his likely diabetes. She also told the witnesses that she'd told Phillip that Flint had better take it easy or risk a stroke or something worse. Phillip then goaded Flint into playing an extra racquetball game when he was already tired, according to what Anne Flint says Flint told her at the opening. That, the DA thinks, will be convince the jury that Phillip wanted Flint dead."

"I didn't think he was going to charge Phillip with Flint's murder. In fact, last time we talked, you weren't sure it was murder."

"We still aren't. I'm just giving you our briefing summaries. He still wants something definitive in the way of proof. We have a couple of witnesses who'll testify that Phillip was 'probably' gone for more than fifteen or twenty minutes a couple of times. One of those is Anne Flint."

"So, you'll jump from his hate of Flint to the forced racquetball games that didn't kill him to the opportunity to run him off the road with his truck to finish the job."

"That's the thinking. The DA says the attempted murder case – on you - is stronger but he wants to file murder against him for Flint. I'm waiting and we're still investigating. We've impounded the truck for more studies."

"Well, you have been busy," Bishop said.

"We don't fool around, Bishop. You got your beavers to look after, we've got our criminals."

"I feel better with the beavers."

"I would too. The DA would like you back out here for a couple of interviews. I think he wants to pick your brain about Phillip and how he might have run Flint off the road. He figures you'll tell him things the defense will bring up. He wants to be ready for it."

Bishop didn't want to go back until the trial but Ellen was insistent.

"You see, Carver's pushing for a settlement of the attempted murder charge. He wants probation for Phillip. He says you drove him over the edge with your claims about his wife. He became unbalanced and tried for a second time to warn you off. He has no record, works hard, has a family to support, all that bull. He blames it all on you."

"People usually do. Hell, it's better than accepting blame for something. It's his fault."

"His wife is running all over town saying the same thing. She's called me half a dozen times, the DA, the mayor, anybody who'll take her call. Her husband never tried to kill anybody. He didn't kill Flint and only wanted to scare you off because you were threatening his family. It's playing well with the public. Old Ben

Holliday has publically proclaimed his support for her. He's putting up money for Phillip's defense and is asking for donations."

"No doubt, he doesn't like me because –" Bishop stopped short of disclosing Flint's fathering of Sarah's boy. That's privileged information. "He doesn't like me because I don't kiss his pinky ring when I ask him questions."

"Well, there's no doubt that he doesn't like you one damn bit. In one interview and I'm reading now. He said that he had dealt with you and that you are ruthless and insensitive to the feelings of others. 'Bone is not to be trusted. Anything he says should be looked at critically. Like Marc Flint, the man he's writing about, he is a purveyor of filth and evil. I was not surprised that Flint died.

'The Lord punishes those who sin against others. Flint and now this man, Bone, have sinned against others. Phillip Marshall is one man Bone is sinning against. I ask all of San Diego to stand with me and reject Bone's charges against this innocent man. I say to you all, the world would be a better place if all those who sin against righteousness were removed by a higher power than us.'" She continued to read. "The man is unhinged,"

Bishop said. "He sounds like he believes he's the second coming. He's getting close to being sued by me. He'll have to show how he came up with his slanderous rants."

"Maybe not the second coming, Bishop, but he's like a God in financial circles around San Diego. Practically everybody who is anybody owes him money. And, what he's saying is playing well to prospective jurors and Carver knows it. I think the DA is seriously considering negotiating some kind of plea bargain with them. What you say might convince him to hang in there, even file murder charges against Phillip."

Bishop wasn't sure he could add anything to what they already knew, but would fly back.

"Give me a couple of days to square things around here," he said.

"Sounds okay to me," she told him. "I want to interview a couple more witnesses about Phillip's missing minutes at the grand opening. We're still looking for somebody who saw him visit the storage bin after your car got hit. We have a couple of leads we're tracking."

He hung up and called Anne. "Have you heard what Holliday's saying?"

She had. "He's acting crazy but people are donating money for Phillip's defense. I've had calls asking for money, if you can believe it. Editorials are expressing support for Phillip and condemning you."

He told her Ellen wanted him to fly back and talk to the DA. "He's apparently being pressured to negotiate some kind of lenient plea bargain with Phillip."

"What? The man tried to kill us! As far as I'm concerned, he killed my husband! Plea bargain? I can't believe it."

"Holliday is behind it all because I told Sarah about his miserly scam to get you to support Marc's illegitimate son. I think she called him and raised hell and he blames me for it."

"He's been making the papers. Front page a couple of times."

"Amazing how people get excited when they just hear one side of a story," Bishop said.

"Are you coming back?" she asked.

"I don't know. I'm not sure I can add anything to what the DA already knows from Ellen Wasserman. However, she thinks if I talk to him he'll see I only have one head and what I say makes sense as opposed to the diatribe Holliday is throwing at me," Bishop said.

"She may be right. Certainly, if he's considering a plea bargain, I'd encourage you to come back and do all you can to stop that. We should have a trial and let everybody know what a twisted little shit Phillip Marshall really is."

"Right now, considering the damage Holliday has done, I'm not sure they can even seat an unbiased jury," he said.

"That's distressing, Bishop. Almost depressing is how some nutcase with a little influence could cause a miscarriage of justice. Phillip tried to kill us and probably killed Marc with that old truck he drives. And, you say the DA's considering a reduced sentence," Anne said.

"Yep. I'm surprised people haven't been marching in front of your house. If I were there, they probably would be. Would you want to be subjected to that? If I come back, it might be better if I stayed in a hotel for the few days it'd take for me to talk to the DA. I think I'd also want to give an interview to the Light and Tribune. Give my side of the story," he said.

"That's a good idea, Bishop. That's what Marc would do for sure. He never took a hit without hitting back. I guess that's why we hit it off like we did. You're so much like him. But, if you fly back, you'll stay here. Nobody's going to intimidate me either!"

"Okay. I appreciate getting your point of view. I'll see what I have going on here. If there's nothing pressing, I'll fly back. First thing I'll do is call the newspapers. Next, I'll call on the DA."

She thanked him.

He sent an email to Holliday's attorney objecting to the man's public accusations against him. "He is very close to defaming me and I know he has assets enough to respond to a judgment. I'm an attorney in good standing in California so having to prosecute a lawsuit won't be a burden to me. In fact, I'll enjoy deposing your client. He won't have a hell of a lot of time for bank work and not much for Bible thumping either. This is my good faith attempt to have the man stop with his public rabble-rousing at my expense. One more outburst and you'll get a complaint."

That night, he told Kathy what had been going on in California and the call he'd gotten from the detective he'd been working with. "She wants me to come back and talk to the DA before he caves in to public pressure and lets the guy who shot at me go free."

"Sounds like you've stirred up a hornet's nest," she said. "I don't think you have a choice. You have to go."

He grimaced and said, "Yeah. I think you're right. I was hoping you'd argue with me. I'd rather be here with you than out there. I did what I was paid to do."

"You never back away from a fight Bishop. That's one reason I love you. Go out there and straighten them out."

Kathy cooked dinner for them, chicken and dumplings with turnips and cornbread. The rest of the evening they sat on the porch and talked about Lawton and what had been happening there.

She drove home later.

\* \* \* \*

Bishop was on a plane for California the next morning. He drove his rented car to La Jolla. Anne was glad to see him and cooked one of his favorites, pork chops coated with fennel for dinner.

Apparently the new cook didn't make it either.

He slept fitfully that night, awaking off and on to think about what he would do the next day.

It seemed to him that he was having to fight a fight that wasn't his but one he'd inherited. Remind me not to write any more memoirs, he thought before he finally fell asleep for the last time.

In the morning, he had an email reply from Holliday's attorney. He adamantly rejected Bishop's claim of defamation. According to his email, Bishop was a public figure and public criticism of the nature of the criticism made by Ben Holliday was not actionable.

Bishop's reply was, "I believe that's a conclusion about a question of fact before it has been decided. We'll see what you think after the matter had been litigated and I start executing my judgment."

Bishop received no reply to his email. And while Holliday's public claims about Bishop didn't stop entirely over the next few days, it did diminish in intensity.

* * * *

Bishop called the Light and the Tribune and asked if the papers wanted to interview him. They jumped at the chance. Both said they didn't think he was in town. They had been told he had gone back to Mississippi. He assured them that he was back and anxious to clear the air from the crap "Banker Ben" had been polluting it with. They agreed to send reporters to the Flint's home at ten that morning.

Anne said she'd like to be present if he didn't mind. He welcomed her.

He showered and put on his khakis after considering whether to wear something of Flint's that would be more formal. "The hell with it," he'd said. He felt more comfortable in khakis and that was what he put on.

Anne told him he looked ready for a fight.

"If they come for one, they'll get one," he promised.

\* \* \* \*

At a few minutes before ten, they heard noises outside, talking and the sounds of equipment bumping other equipment. Bishop answered the doorbell. A young lady in casual dress stood in the doorway. She introduced herself as a reporter for the Light. He didn't catch her name.

In her hand was both a notepad and a handheld recorder but that wasn't what Bishop was really looking at. Behind her all the way to the street were, he estimated, eight or nine others, men and women, including at least one television crew. He deduced that from the camera they held. Others had brought handheld cameras. The television crew had a video camera mounted on a tripod.

Damn, the word must have spread about.

"Well," he told the assemblage. "Come on in." He led them into the living room where Anne stood. Her face also showed surprise at the number of people who had shown up.

Like Bishop, she'd dressed understated to avoid attracting attention for the wrong reason. The meeting was to rebut what Holliday had been saying. She and Bishop had dressed to keep the focus on that. Seeing their numbers, she looked toward the dining room table and the chairs.

"Chairs, if you need them," she said, pointing in that direction.

"Also," she said. "Coffee if anybody wants a cup." She waved toward the coffee machine. Mugs had been set out in front of it.

None took her up on either the chairs or the coffee. They had had coffee already and preferred to stand for the interview. Bishop did also. He felt his juices flowed better when he was standing. It took him back to his trial days.

Anne sat down in a soft chair to watch.

When they had all assembled and formed a half circle around him, he said, "Why don't I start with an introduction and then let you ask questions?"

They shook their heads to show their agreement.

He told them how he came to be involved with the Flint family; how, after Marc Flint was killed, Anne asked him to write Flint's memoirs. In order to do that, he decided he needed to talk to anybody who had significant contact with him. That included other builders whose projects had gone into default and were taken over by Flint at the request of Flint's lender client, The New Opportunity Bank.

"The bank is now being liquidated," he explained with some details about the process.

He gave the names of Larson and Smith and included Larson's two investors. Bishop said he'd talked with all but one investor who was not available. He also told the reporters that he'd had a number of conversations with Flint's mother who had been most helpful.

"In addition, I talked to Flint's broker, Terry Wakefield, who was handling the sales of homes Flint was building and had built. He was very helpful with information about how Mr. Flint went about his business as well as how Phillip Marshall helped Mr. Flint.

I'm sure you know by now, Mr. Marshall was Mr. Flint's chief financial officer."

Impatient nods all around. Reporters rarely exhibited patience.

Bishop continued. "The La Jolla project was probably Marc Flint's crowning achievement so I talked to the lender who provided the construction loan. That was Sarah Webster and her father, Ben Holliday, otherwise known about town as Banker Ben. "

One reporter raised her hand to speak but Bishop waved her off saying, "I'm almost finished. Be patient. I'll answer every question you have in good time."

She shrugged and lowered her hand.

"Most of Flint's staff had been let go by the time I came out here since his arrangement with his client called for all of his projects to be transferred to a holding company. I won't go into the details because I don't think it's relevant to this meeting. In any case, Phillip Marshall would be the best person to talk to about that. I did talk to Mr. Marshall and a representative of Flint's lender client about the business and what was happening to it. I gave you its name. I was gathering information for Flint's memoirs. I thought my interviews with both men went well. I saw no animosity."

The reporter raised her hand again and asked, "When did you decide Flint's death was murder, not an accident."

Bishop sighed. "Okay, I guess my introduction is over. After I'd interviewed Flint's widow, Anne ..."

He pointed in Anne's direction. "I looked at the site of the incident and saw marks on the curb that suggested a struggle by Flint to stay on the street. Later I looked at his Jeep and saw some strange marks on the driver's side of the Jeep, on the wheel primarily. The marks suggested that another vehicle had pushed him off the street which even in his weakened condition, his diabetic condition, he'd fought. I thought a vehicle with big wheels and hydraulic lifters could have done it. I've seen them around town."

Bishop paused for a look around the room. He had their attention.

He added, "Flint eventually lost the battle and his Jeep rolled down the incline and he died. The police forensics team could not confirm specifically that his Jeep was run off the street but agreed with a strong probability that it had been."

Another reporter said, "You were guessing."

"No. A guess is without logical support. I had logical support."

"Why are you accusing Phillip Marshall? Do you have logical support for your accusations?"

"Ah, now we get to it. I'm glad you brought that up. I've never accused Marshall of anything, certainly not running Flint off the street. The police do all the charging, not me. A car I had rented was shot at twice, the last time Anne Flint was in the car with me. The first shot was meant as a warning, a call informed me. The second was probably meant to kill and might have had I not stopped suddenly."

"Why did you implicate Marshall in those shots?" another asked.

"I had noticed the imprint of a gun rack on the back window of that old truck he drives and figured he might have had a rifle at one time. I told the police what I'd seen. They investigated and found out that the truck was one Flint had acquired with a defaulted project. It had a rifle mounted on the back window when it was acquired. Marshall was seen with the rifle by one of Flint's construction workers. And, the rifle was found in one of Flint's storage units. The police have determined that it was the one that fired the shots at me. The police concluded that Marshall fired the rifle at me and charged him with attempted murder."

He had deliberately embellished a bit on the facts, but figured by then Ellen would have found someone who'd seen Phillip with the rifle. And, she had. One of Flint's construction workers had seen the rifle mounted on the back window of the truck he drove. Another had seen him with it at the storage unit.

"Why do you think Marshall would want to shoot you?"

"I wondered that myself. He knew I was writing Flint's memoirs. Maybe he was worried I might uncover something in Flint's past that could reflect unfavorably on him. I really don't know. All I know is what I've been told by the police and what I've read in the papers. I assume all the facts will be disclosed during the trial."

"Mr. Holliday accuses you of lying about Marshall to boost interest in the book you're writing, Flint's memoirs."

"I've read what he's been saying. You'll note that he hasn't given you one bit of evidence to support his charges. He loves to quote the Bible and point fingers, but he never backs up anything with proof. Also, let me tell you this. I get nothing from the book if Mrs. Flint elects to sell it. And I will not write anyone else's memoirs. So, I have no reason to do anything to boost interest."

The cameras rolled and flashed and reporters made notes.

Another said, "He's heading up a citizen's group trying to free Marshall. What do you say about that?"

"Thank goodness we're a free country and a private citizen can do that. I'm also thankful that our judicial system has strict rules about criminal charges. They have to be decided by a court, with or without a jury, not by people making wild, unsupported claims to the media. The facts will be disclosed during the trial of Mr. Marshall by witnesses under oath who will be cross-examined by the defense attorney, Washington Carver, I understand. One of the best. Mr. Marshall will have a fair trial."

"Mr. Holliday claims you are ... excuse me Mrs. Flint, but he says you are sleeping with Mrs. Flint and plan to step into Mr. Flint's shoes. He has also said that is a sin against the Bible. And, that's why you're pushing the case against Phillip Marshall, to gain Mrs. Flint's favor. How do you answer that claim?"

Bishop laughed. "That is such a blatant lie, it makes me laugh. I am not a student of the Bible, but I don't think I'm sinning against any of the covenants of the Bible by writing Flint's memoirs and by trying to stay alive while I'm doing it."

A reporter interrupted to ask about "sleeping with Anne,"

Bishop reply was loud and rapidly given. "Specifically, I am not interested in any relationship with Anne Flint and have never been! I am engaged to be married in Mississippi and as soon as this mess is over, I will. I am not sleeping with Anne Flint. She's here so why not ask her?"

The reporter who had just asked the question turned to Anne and did ask.

Anne said, "I'm still mourning the deaths of my husband whom I loved very much and my brother." She lowered her head and pretended, Bishop's assessment, to wipe tears from her eyes. "Having a relationship with anybody is too ridiculous to even consider. I'm too depressed to do much more than make it through each day. Mr. Bone came out here at my request to write Marc's memoirs. I regret that he has been shot at and harassed. As far as I know, his only interest in me has been what I can tell him about Marc so he can finish what I'm paying him to do. I have no interest in him other than that. I don't know why Mr. Holliday has made that claim but I can tell you he is totally wrong."

Actually, she did know but didn't say. She knew Holliday was making the fuss he was, because she and Bishop had rejected his demand to support Sarah's son. Adding fuel to that fire was Bishop's disclosure to Sarah about Holliday's demand. To disclose all of that would only embarrass Sarah and she hadn't been a part of Holliday's Biblical diatribe.

Anne's rebuttal pretty much ended the interview. Some of the reporters packed up and left immediately. They had a story and they wanted to get it back to wherever they came from as soon as possible.

A few of the others engaged in small talk with Anne and Bishop, the latter to a lesser extent. One reporter did ask if he was the Bishop Bone who'd been involved in the La Jolla Shores murders awhile back. He said he was and answered a couple of questions about the murders, primarily about the people involved.

When the conversations lulled, Bishop said, "If you want to talk again, call me," he said and gave them his phone number.

When he opened the door to let the others out, he was met by Linda and her son, Eli, She was sobbing and she looked as if she hadn't slept in a week. And probably hadn't, Bishop decided.

The little boy appeared bewildered but managed a smile and a "Hello Mr. Boon."

Bishop patted his head and returned his greeting. "Mrs. Marshall," he said. "What is the matter?" He knew, but decided it would be better if he asked.

"Oh, Mr. Bone. Please Mr. Bone. Please withdraw your complaint against Phillip. He didn't kill Marc. I know he didn't. He was standing by me all the time except when he and Derek unloaded two cases of champagne."

The reporters still there could scarcely believe their luck. The television guy began taping the scene without worrying about a tripod. He just held the camera and taped away. The others snapped pictures and listened.

"Mrs. Marshall, Linda, it's not up to me."

"Mr. Holliday says you're railroading Phillip. You have a vendetta against him. Why, Mr. Bone? We've never done anything to you."

"I know you haven't, Linda. I-"

"Why did you hit my Daddy, Mr. Boon?"

"I'm sorry, Eli. I didn't want to hit him." But, what could I do? He was trying to kill me.

He looked at Linda and said, "I don't have a vendetta against anybody. That's just Holliday shooting off his mouth because I don't let him push me around."

"Can't you help me, Mr. Bone? I think you're a good man. I know Phillip. You just made him go crazy saying what you did." She glanced at Eli.

Bishop knew she was talking about Marc fathering her son.

She continued. "I don't know if he did anything, like shoot at you, but I know he didn't kill Marc. I know it. He was with me. He's doesn't like to mingle with a crowd. So, when we're out like we were at the opening, he stays close to me. Can you help me? I'm desperate. I love Phillip. And, he loves me!"

Bishop was about to say something, but she interrupted. "And, Mr. Bone, he loves HIS son. Eli, his son."

She burst out crying loudly, stopping only long enough to wipe away her tears.

"Don't cry Mommy," the little boy said as he tugged at her leg. Then, he began to cry. The reporters were eating it up.

Bishop began walking her back to the Audi. As he walked, he told her, "Linda, I have nothing to do with any charges brought about by Flint's death. That would be up to Anne to file charges if the police ever get around to charging anybody. I don't know why Holliday is saying what he is. I'll be talking to the DA, probably tomorrow. I'll tell him what you've told me. That's the best I can offer."

She turned and hugged him. The reporters got shots of it.

Eli let go of his mother's hand and hugged Bishop's leg. "Thank you, Mr. Boon."

"You're welcome, Eli."

They walked away. He bid the reporters a goodbye and went inside.

## CHAPTER 22

Bishop shut the front door behind him and breathed a loud sigh of relief. He called to Anne, "It's too early for strong libation, but I'd love a fresh cup of coffee."

"I'll get it," she said. "I want one too."

"Can you put a little cream and sweetener in mine? Take the bitter edge off the morning."

She would.

"Think we'll make the evening news?" she asked when they were seated.

"When Linda and Eli showed up, a spot on the evening news was practically guaranteed. I expect she was tipped off."

"Did you mind?"

"No. I know this whole thing has been a trial for her. But, I had nothing to do with it. I didn't shoot at anybody with a rifle."

\* \* \* \*

The next morning Bishop called the DA's office to set up a meeting with the DA. He got no argument from the secretary. It was like they were expecting a call from him.

He showed up exactly at ten, the time he had picked. The secretary showed him into a small conference room and offered coffee which he declined. Half a minute later, a tall, distinguished man with gray hair and glasses strolled in. He was well dressed in a dark suit, no vest and appeared to be in excellent shape.

He stuck out his hand. Bishop stood briefly for the handshake.

"Mr. Bone. I'm Steve Callahan, the DA. I'm pleased that you called. I was about to call you."

"You go first," Bishop said, palms up.

The man shook his head. "No, you go ahead. You called first."

So, Bishop gave him the "jury trial" closing argument he would have given if he had been the prosecuting attorney in the Phillip Marshall case. Primarily, he reviewed the facts against Phillip as if they had been presented and proven.

The DA nodded. "I agree. You get my vote, but as you no doubt know from all the hullabaloo Banker Ben's been throwing out, I've been catching hell from my constituents."

"No doubt," Bishop agreed.

"The man hasn't said anything that makes a lick of legal sense, but he's raised over a hundred thousand to defend Marshall," the DA said.

"And Carver's already lining up his expert witnesses. I can tell you that you'll catch hell when you take the stand. Carver's gonna tear you a new one."

"I gather he'll try."

"Hell, I expect the courtroom to stand and cheer when he ... tries. Ordinarily, I might assign the case to a junior attorney, but with Carver jumping up and down screaming prejudice and bias and injustice, I'll have to take it on myself, unless we can find some way out of the thing. You got any ideas? I know of you. You have a good reputation for having a level head. Detective Wasserman speaks highly of you."

"She's a good detective. I always enjoy working with her."

He shook his head and said, "Oh, by the way, I saw your televised interview last night. You did a good job. And, you're right, old Holliday hasn't offered a damn thing but Bible verses to support his claim that you're out to get his now-good-friend Phillip Marshall. My grapevine tells me his bank turned Marshall down for a loan to develop a couple of low income properties. But, now, he's got the red-ass to turn a simple case into a persecution."

"I think he has a hidden agenda but I'm not sure what it is," Bishop said. Of course, he knew, but didn't say. Holliday couldn't get over the fact that Flint had impregnated Sarah, his beloved daughter and had violated a Biblical

commandment while he did. And, since Flint was dead, Bishop had inherited the blame somehow.

"That's my take as well. I'm going to ask Detective Wasserman to see what she can find," the DA said.

Bishop said, "I guess you saw Marshall's wife on the televised interview. She came in late."

He had.

"Well, she practically admitted that Phillip shot at me."

"I agree."

"She seemed more concerned about a possible charge against him for murdering Flint," Bishop said.

He acknowledged that as well, adding, "The news video showed her crying at your front door with the little boy by her side. Damned effective. I wonder who set that up."

"Who knows?" Bishop asked. "Somebody though."

"They're talking about running Banker Ben for mayor. Can you believe that? All the man has ever done in his life, besides thump his Bible, which he's seems to be getting worse at or louder at these days. Damn, I lost my train of thought. Oh, I remember. All he's ever done is make loans and foreclose on anybody who's a day late."

"Mayor?" Bishop asked. "Damn, I'm glad I don't live here. Hell, he'll probably hold prayer meetings between council meetings."

The DA shook his head and asked, "So, any ideas how we can solve our ... my little problem? You'll be gone."

"I'm assuming you don't have a damn thing to tie Marshall to Flint's murder," Bishop said. "That's the big case, not the attempt on my life."

The DA shook his head. "We don't have a damn thing. Not a scintilla of evidence. The police can't even say for sure if it was murder."

"I figured. Frankly, the fright I had when the bullets hit the car pales beside the injury the Marshall's son, Eli, and his mother, Linda, would suffer if Marshall is convicted and sent to prison."

He agreed.

"I guess I'm a prime witness. What if I withdrew my charges?"

The man's relief showed on his face like a cool breeze on a hot day. "Would you? He tried to kill you, according to Detective Wasserman. That's a serious charge."

"On the human side of things, he doesn't have a record. They have one child, the boy, Eli. Confidentially, Marshall was upset because I told his wife that he knew the son he loved wasn't his. I think he didn't want to face the truth and went crazy to block it out," Bishop said. "He and his wife are in denial about it."

"Be damned. I was wondering about what triggered the thing, the shooting. Most men would have gone out and gotten a divorce lawyer if they found out something like that. Fought it out in court to avoid child support. Leave the child with a stigma he might never overcome.

So, I agree, it'd probably be in the best interest of everybody if they stayed together."

"One thing does bother me," Bishop tapped the table as he said it.

"What?"

"Old Banker Ben has been collecting money. Not even Carver has had time to spend it all. Just between me and you, I'd hate for that money to end up in a bank account in Banker Ben's bank."

"I see what you're getting at. I think I could negotiate something with Carver about that. I'd say Marshall should get that money ... no, better than that. I think that money should go into a trust fund for the boy."

"Great idea. That way, if they ever do split, the boy will have enough to get a couple of years in a decent college."

Wrapping up the meeting, the DA said he'd call Carver for a meeting. If it went well, he'd call a press conference and announce his decision to withdraw the charges against Marshall. Since Marshall hadn't been charged with Flint's murder, the DA could still file that charge if "Wasserman can find solid evidence to link Marshall to the murder."

"I appreciate your help, Bishop. I'm not sure I'd have done the same had I been in your shoes. Having somebody shoot at me and walk away without having to pay the price would leave me with a bad taste in my mouth."

"I agree. The only reason I can is because I won't be around here much longer. I have a life in Mississippi that I have to get back to."

The DA reached across the table to shake Bishop's hand. "Thank you," he said.

"Maybe that poor woman will stop crying now," Bishop said. "You should have seen the look on her face and her son's face. I felt like hell."

"Makes me think we're doing the right thing."

Bishop wondered if Anne would agree. He'd find out.

* * * *

He told her what had transpired at the DA's office and how they agreed to resolve the case against Marshall in such a way that they could still file against him if they found proof that he killed Marc.

She wasn't broken up about it. Sure, she might have been killed, but Bishop was the likely target. It scared her but she'd suffered no lasting harm.

"What are they doing about Marc's murder and Derek's?"

"I don't know. Ellen was hoping the charge against Phillip would spread out and pick up the murder charges but it didn't go that way."

"Because of Holliday," Anne said.

"I think he played a large part. He got Linda all worked up that I had a vendetta against them. How in the hell he came up with that one, I'll never know."

"He wanted his pound of flesh for Sarah's son," she said. "You stopped it and he wanted revenge."

"Best explanation I've heard. He's a vindictive son of a bitch," Bishop said.

"He's calling you and Marc evil blasphemers but he's the only evil thing I've seen. And, I've seen it firsthand. I still can't believe the gall of the man, trying to get me to pay for something his daughter orchestrated. Marc didn't know anything about it!" Anne said with a note of despair in her voice.

Bishop agreed.

"Are you going home?" she asked. "Nothing for you to do around here. They don't need your testimony. I guess you'll finish up Marc's memoirs."

"That's right," he said. "I'll talk to Ellen and wind things up. Looks like I'll end up with almost two hundred pages for Marc's memoirs. Hell, I could make the names fictitious and make it into a decent murder mystery."

"You'd have to have a murderer. Who would you pick?" she asked.

He laughed. "I'll have to reserve judgment on that one. Maybe my subconscious will come up with an idea. Maybe my subconscious side will discover some evidence that says Phillip did it."

"Don't you wish? Don't I?" she said.

She had a dinner engagement. She didn't say with whom and he didn't ask. He assumed it was with her Bay Area friend. So, he'd eat alone. And, that meant a senior's breakfast at Denny's.

* * * *

He updated his Flint files and called Kathy. "I have to meet with the detective I've been working with. Unless she can come up with a reason for me to stay longer, I should wrap things up within a few days."

That made her happy. Next, he called Ellen to see if she had a reason to keep him there.

"I know all about it," she said. "The DA called and told me. Wanted to see if I objected. You think I would? I know which side my bread's buttered on. And, I sure as hell don't want Ben Holliday as mayor. I'd never get another raise."

He suggested that they meet at Denny's for dinner. She asked. "Have you come down in the world?"

"I like Denny's. I've never had a bad meal there."

"I'm just kidding you, Bone. I eat there all the time. Love it. I'll see you there at five thirty."

\* \* \* \*

The first thing she asked when they sat down was, "What the hell got in old Holliday's craw to make him come after you like he did? Practically every day, he's been holding press conferences and reading Bible verses condemning you to hell for one sin or another.

You and Marc Flint are both sinners and both deserve to burn in hell."

The waiter came for their orders before Bishop could answer her question. Both got senior breakfasts. She wanted extra bacon with hers. Both asked for coffee.

When the waiter was out of hearing range, Bishop answered her question. "I know why, Ellen, but I can't tell you. I'm legally bound not to talk about it. I will tell you that it had nothing to do with the Marshalls or the case we had against him. He was using that as an excuse."

"Damn good one, Bishop. He was beatin' the shit out of you in public with it. Hey, it's not like you to hold out on me. Tell me."

"I know and if it in anyway affected the case or had any bearing on anything, I'd tell you, legal ethics notwithstanding. I crossed him in a personal matter and he couldn't get over it."

"I sure wish you could tell me."

"I may one of these days, but not right now. It'd leak out and I'd be on the hot seat."

"I understand, I think. I don't guess you know, but Carver and the DA are going to have a joint press conference in the morning to announce the resolution of the Marshall case. They worked it out this afternoon. Marshall will plead to a misdemeanor for breach of the peace, no fine. The fund for his legal defense will be put in trust for his son's education. Of course we know about the son, don't we?"

"That we do, Ellen."

"When you going home?" she asked.

"In a day or two. I want to talk to Anne about Flint's memoirs. Does she want revisions or is it okay as I've written it? I've added to it since I wrote the first draft. Something seems to happen every day. Holliday's diatribe has to get into it," Bishop said.

"He'll be taking credit for getting the charges against Marshall reduced to nothing," she said.

"Maybe so, but people will forget his name by the time of the next election. And, the more people see of him, the less they'll like him. He has an abrasive personality," Bishop said.

Ellen agreed.

Their food came. Coffee had already come. They were ready for refills.

"I want a copy of the final thing."

"Ellen, you'll get the first copy off the presses."

"I have to open a file on Flint and Derek. Murder investigation. Starting new. And, you'll be back in Mississippi eatin' fried possum and turnip greens."

"Yep. You'll have to come down to see me one of these days."

"You count on it. Just get me a pass from your local KKK Chapter." She grinned.

"Of course. I see the Grand Dragon all the time," Bishop joked. "We drink our bootleg whiskey out of a fruit jar."

She laughed. "You're so full of horse manure, Bone, I'm surprised your eyes don't turn brown."

He laughed and continued, "By the way, changing the subject, did you see my so-called press conference?"

"I did. You did yourself proud, my man, especially with Marshall's wife and her little boy. I thought you did superb."

"Thanks. One thing I said when we were inside the house triggered a thought process and left me with a question."

"For me?" she asked.

He nodded.

"Don't keep me on pins and needles. Ask me. You know I've re-married. Happily too so I hope it's not that kind of question." She laughed.

He laughed too. "No, but it is about our good friend, Banker Ben. It just occurred to me. You never told me what kind of Jeep he was driving that day, the day Flint was killed."

She frowned and thought about it for a couple of seconds before answering. "I don't reckon I know. I sent a rookie out to the dealer to ask if the Jeep had any damage. He reported back that there was no substantial damage, a few scratches and dings. He never told me what kind of Jeep it was. How many kinds are there?"

"Lots. Tell you what, Ellen, why don't you meet me out there about ten in the morning. I'll need some official authority to ask about anything."

"Are you going to tell me or do I have to wait?"

"If you don't mind, I'll ask you to wait until we get there. I want to think about the ramifications some more before I get you all excited."

"Heaven forbid that you'd do anything like that. I wouldn't be able to sleep all night. Now, I won't be able to sleep wondering what it is you want to ask. If it was anybody but you, you know where I'd tell them where to stick their secret questions."

"I know, Ellen and I appreciate your patience. This is my last question and I'll be flying home. I'm just curious about what Banker Ben with all his money, was wheedling out of the dealer."

"Anything you're curious about, I'm curious about. Usually your curiosity means more work for me and more work might lead to a promotion."

"I doubt it's as serious as that. This time, I'm really just curious. Flint drove a soft top Jeep that I'd call old timey and he and Holliday butted heads. I want to see what he drove."

"Sounds like a waste of time, but I'll be there. You can buy the coffee afterward. Starbucks!"

## CHAPTER 23

Bishop's phone rang that evening. There was no name on the monitor. He took the call. It was Linda Marshall.

"Mr. Bone," she said in her shy, little girl voice.

"Yes," he said, expecting a tirade of some sort.

"Phillip and I and Eli, too, want to thank you. We assumed you had something to do with the DA dropping the charges against Phillip and setting up the trust fund for Eli."

"I shouldn't comment one way or the other," he said, not wanting to get into a discussion with either of them. "But, thank you. I wish you both well, all three of you, the best for the future. I hope everything works out for you."

She told him Phillip was enjoying his position in the company that had acquired what was left of Flint's old company. It was ready to begin development of the two properties acquired from the liquidation committee. A bank,

not Holliday's, had committed to a construction and development loan.

"Phillip is a lucky man to have a wife like you, Linda. And a son like Eli."

She thanked him again.

\* \* \* \*

Bishop met Ellen in the lobby of the Jeep dealership in town. She had been given the name of the technician they needed to see about Jeeps that had been consigned.

"Ricky Newman?" Ellen asked a blue uniformed man at the service center. He pointed toward another guy in blue overalls holding an oil stained cloth and looking under the hood of a Jeep.

They walked over. Ellen showed her credentials and introduced Bishop as someone assigned to observe their investigation.

Broad enough to cover a football stadium, Bishop concluded.

"Bishop has a couple of questions he'd like to ask," she said with a gesture in Bishop's direction.

The man turned to Bishop. "Fire away."

"We'd like to see the kind of Jeep you consigned to Benjamin Holliday."

"Sure. We have a couple on the lot. Actually, if you wanted to see the one we consigned to Mr. Holliday, it just came back yesterday afternoon. I was just going to log it in."

That'd be perfect, Bishop and Ellen told him. They followed him to the end of the bay where sat a black, four door Jeep with hydraulic lifters and oversized tires.

"Ain't this a beauty?" he asked.

"It is," Bishop replied. "Did you inspect it after Holliday returned it?"

"Ah, no. Purv, that's what we called Purvis. Purv was supposed to have inspected it. He's no longer with us. His approach to work was to smile at it till it went away. So, when one of these consignments was brought in, he'd give it a quick walk around, smile and say. 'Looks good.' Customers loved him."

"Did he miss anything?" Bishop asked.

"I'm not sure when he missed it, but I'll show you what he should have picked up."

He walked them around the oversized Jeep and pointed out scratches and scrapes here and there. "We don't know when these were picked up 'cause old Purv never did a decent job of inspecting. The boss most likely would have let 'em go, but we're supposed to point 'em out. The boss takes it from there. For example, look at this." He walked them around to the front passenger side tire.

"See these cuts," he ran his fingers along a number of grooves in the tire. "I don't know when they happened, but when we put 'em on the lot to sell, the buyer's gonna want a discount on this tire and this scrape on the fender."

Bishop and Ellen bent over for a closer look. "If I didn't know better, I'd say somebody ran into something. Cut the tire and scraped the fender."

The guy agreed. "The Jeep is drivable and the damage is superficial but we shoulda caught it."

Bishop shook his head in agreement.

They thanked the man and walked outside to their cars.

"Starbucks across the street," Ellen said. "You've got something on your mind. Over coffee is a good place to let it out."

"Yeah. My treat," Bishop said.

"You damn right it is. Getting me out here for nothing."

They walked across the street and ordered cappuccinos and warmed rolls.

She looked at Bishop and said, "I know what you're thinkin'. You're thinking Banker Ben cut that tire and scraped the fender when he ran Flint off the road."

Bishop gave her comment half a nod.

"Right. I thought so. Let me tell you something, Bone. I wouldn't ever propose filing charges on that kind of speculative evidence. Ain't no way in hell we can prove Holliday did that damage. No way! Coulda been any of the other consignees, Bone. Think in another direction."

"I agree with you Ellen. I was thinking in another direction."

"You're not thinking about bluffing old Ben, are you?"

"No. I doubt he could be bluffed," he said. "He's stared too many tough guys down to be bluffed. He does the bluffing. 'Cause he's got what the other side wants ... the money."

"So, all I'm gonna get outta this trip is a cup of coffee?" she asked.

"Not necessarily. We both think Holliday made those tire cuts and scraped the fender when he ran Flint off the street. We just have to convince him that we can prove it," Bishop said.

"I bet you got some notion about how to do just that," Ellen said.

He outlined his notion to her.

After a loud sigh, she pushed back from the table where they sat and said, "Damn, Bishop, if you can't come up with some real lulus. But, you know what, it won't cost us a dime to try it out." She said it with a big smile.

They finished their coffees and went back to the Jeep dealership.

\* \* \* \*

Bishop picked up the other thing he needed from Walmart and told Ellen to be ready.

"If it works, I'm gonna ask for a promotion. If it fails, I'm gonna blame you. The DA likes you so I can skate by on that."

"That's okay with me. I'll be on a plane before the shit hits the fan."

Bishop drove to the Flint's home and told Anne what they were planning. "Sounds risky to me, Bishop," she said.

"It could be a bit but I'll be on alert." He also told her he needed something from her and needed her help.

She was agreeable. "I'm excited," she said. "I never thought I'd do anything like that."

He called Ellen and they put the plan into effect. Later that afternoon, it was done except for the write-up. Bishop did that after dinner. All that was left was the execution. The question was when and how. And, the bigger question was whether it would work.

\* \* \* \*

The next morning, Bishop picked up his phone and dialed Banker Ben's number.

"Holliday," the man barked into his cell phone.

"Bone here," Bishop replied, matching the man's tone and brusqueness.

"Bone, you slimy purveyor of filth and lies. If I saw you burning on the street, I wouldn't piss on you to put out the flames. I wish you to hell."

He hung up.

"Hmm," Bishop muttered.

He called again.

"Holliday."

"You'd better listen to me you pompous ass. I know you ran Flint off the street and I can prove it. I-"

Holliday hung up without answering.

*This is going to be harder than I expected.*

He told Ellen about his trouble ending with, "I'll have to try a different approach." He explained what he would try next. "Some risk, but ..."

"There's always a risk. Hell, give it a try. Might work. It can't hurt. Calling ain't getting it apparently," she said.

So, Bishop sat down and composed a letter. Then, he put it in an envelope and took it to the front desk at the Seville.

"This is for Mr. Holliday. It is important that he get it immediately. Can you see to it?" Bishop asked.

The lady at the desk nodded and said, "I think he's up there. I'll take it up right now."

Bishop thanked her and went back to the Flint's to wait.

An hour later, when Bishop was about ready to pull the plug on the idea, his phone rang.

"This is Holliday. What is this lie? Are you threatening to blackmail me you lowlife lawyer? You're not fit to walk among real people!"

"Blackmail? No indeed. I have a flight out tomorrow and I thought you might find what I sent you as intriguing as I did. You seem interested in justice. I thought you'd want to see what I found in Derek's desk."

"You're a troublemaker, Bone. I don't believe anything you touch. It would be a divine intervention were you to be struck dead where you stand. You deal in lies and destruction. Your world is evil. And evil will be destroyed and banished from this earth by our Lord when next He comes."

"The Lord'll have a lot of work to do when He comes. I'll be way down on His list. You'll be right at the top."

Holliday grumped and said, "Blasphemers like you will be the first to be sent into the fires of hell."

"We'll have to wait for that, won't we? Well, enjoyed talking with you, Holliday. I'm going to take what I sent you and the rest of what I found to that police detective I've been working with. She'll probably be glad to get it."

"This blurred copy you sent me doesn't show anything. Maybe two Jeeps, maybe not. You'll be wasting her time," Holliday said.

"Probably but I don't have anything else to do. I'm finished in San Diego, thanks to you and your smear campaign. Besides, the police may have the technology to figure out the tag number of the black Jeep. Who knows what they'll find?" Bishop asked.

"Your name is mud at city hall and it'll stay that way. I have clout downtown. I'll tell them you're just out to cause more trouble," Holliday said immediately.

"Not so, Holliday. If I give it to them, I'll look like a good citizen doing his duty. My name won't be mud after that. I just had an idea. You could give it to them. You could take credit for helping them with Flint's murder if anything came of it. On the other hand, if it's you in that black Jeep, the video wouldn't do you any good. Looking at it that way, I guess your name would be mud, big time. Don't you think?"

"What video?" Holliday asked.

"I don't guess I told you about the video. The video was on an iPhone in Derek's desk. I downloaded one frame and copied it. That's why it's so grainy. The video is much clearer."

"I don't like you Bone. I didn't like Flint and now, you've taken his place. One dead disciple of evil replaced by another one."

"Personally, I think the video might be worth some money in the right circles. For example, if somebody thought they could use the video in an election smear campaign, they'd probably pay money for it. Say, somebody running to be re-elected Mayor," Bishop said.

"Money? You're going to sell it?" Holliday asked.

Now we're talking business.

"Why shouldn't I sell it? I'd say the value of a high office like the mayor of San Diego, would be worth at least a hundred thousand. The video should be enough to win the voters over, I believe, don't you? Think of all the kickbacks and political corruption available to the winner of an election like that."

"A hundred thousand! You are a greedy, worthless piece of dog shit, Bone."

"Even a worthless piece of dog shit has needs, Holliday. Mine run to a hundred thousand. I'll never be seen around here again."

There was silence from Holliday's phone.

"I don't even know if you have a video. And, I don't see how it'd be worth anything to me."

"You're probably right. What made me think you might be interested is something I heard. I heard your name is being bandied about as a candidate for Mayor. I also heard that you had a black Jeep on consignment when Flint died. Yours was just like the one in that blurry picture. Even if the one in the picture isn't the one you had, I bet the voters would think it was. You know how fickle voters are. And, you know what else, I bet the police, especially that black detective, would jump all over that picture. She could haul you in and get herself a promotion for knocking off a big dog like you, Holliday."

I didn't think he'd talk this long. I think he's interested. Got him on the hook. Now, I have to pull him in.

"That's not the Jeep I had. I'm not afraid of anything you can do, Bone. No one –" He interrupted himself.

Almost gave it away, didn't you. No one was behind you. Was that what you wanted to say?

After taking a loud breath, Ben continued. "As I was saying, no ... well, nobody's going to listen to anything you say. I've made certain of that. You picked the wrong man to cross."

Covered himself.

"I didn't cross you, Holliday. You crossed yourself. I think you murdered Flint. Revenge for what he did to your daughter. Let me see now. What does the Bible say about murder? Isn't that a violation of one of the cardinal commandments? Or, have you lent enough money to buy your way into heaven regardless of the evil you have done?"

"Are you blaspheming me, Bone? You are not fit to lick my boots. What have you ever done for anybody? Nothing. All you've done in your life is cause trouble. I've been a pillow of respect in my community."

"I think I'm about to punch a hole in your pillow."

"You ... you won't punch anything! I'm going to pay you the money you've demanded to get rid of an evil blight growing in San Diego. I'll use my connections to track down the Jeep. I'll give what I find to the police. They wouldn't believe anything you give them, anyway. You're an evildoer, Bone. You steal from everybody. The Lord will deal with you."

"Maybe He'll want the video!"

"You're taking the Lord's name in vain, Bone, and you'll pay for it on judgment day. I'll meet you tonight at the Mount Soledad Park to see what you have."

"Twelve midnight."

"No, I'll be in LA until late. How about two o'clock in the morning. I'll bring the money you've demanded. Your blackmail."

"I object to that term. I'm selling you campaign information."

"I'll see it before you get a dime!"

"Of course. I'll be waiting."

"You slimy, worthless, blight on the human race."

"I like you too, Holliday."

Click.

He called Ellen. "He bit. Finally. I'm to meet him at two in the morning by the cross on Mount Soledad."

"Damn, I never thought it'd work. That's a fitting place to meet a Bible-toting son of a bitch like Holliday. But, two o'clock! Damn the man's a masochist," she said.

"I thought so too. I think he sees Soledad as a place the Lord will deliver me to hell. Using one of his disciples of course."

"I know which one Holliday has in mind. How're you going to prevent it? I hate funerals," she said.

"I'm not sure. How fast are you?" he asked.

"Not that fast. I'll have to park some distance away. There are no streets that close to Soledad Park. You'd better figure out how to stall," she said. "I'll need time to get there."

"I'll think of something," Bishop said.

"I'm serious. If he is a killer, he wouldn't hesitate to get rid of you. Remember Derek? Right now, I'd say

Holliday killed him, notwithstanding his upstanding citizen protests. "

"Yeah. I bet Derek threatened to tell the world that his pristine daughter gave birth to a bastard child. He couldn't stand that news getting out," Bishop speculated.

"Banker Ben would have had a hell of a time explaining that away," Ellen said. "I don't imagine he had to think very long about what to do. Eliminate the messenger. Derek had to go."

"Poor bastard thought he could deal with a snake. Derek didn't know the man had fangs. The son of a bitch needs to be put away. Only problem is, I'm not sure he's mentally fit to stand trial. I think he's bordering on Alzheimer's," Bishop said.

"Might account for his strange behavior," she said. "See you tonight. I hope."

"I'm with you on that," Bishop said.

\* \* \* \*

At a quarter to two, Bishop rolled to a stop facing the street beside the wall of pictures and written descriptions of service men and women who'd given their lives for their country. He got out for a look around. There was nobody else around.

"I hope Ellen can hear me," he whispered. They had agreed that she would not signal or do anything that might tip Holliday off. He hadn't seen her car when he drove in but he wouldn't have if she parked in a residential area.

"It'd be my luck that she got hung up in traffic or worse, an accident. I'll plan on there being no back up."

He figured Holliday would be carrying the same weapon he used to kill Derek. If I'm right. Ellen'll never let me live it down if I'm not. Old Holliday might be setting up an arrest for blackmail.

Bishop had tentatively decided that Holliday killed Derek. It seemed a safe assumption based on the impression he'd come away with after his telephone conversation with Holliday. And, meeting with a man that was probably a killer and without decent backup, didn't leave him with a comfortable feeling. He was also uncomfortable about the other alternative. Was Holliday innocent?

He made a decision. And, for certain, is Holliday planning to let me walk away with a hundred thousand dollars of his money.

He waited.

At a minute to two, a car drove slowly by on the street facing the Park. It was just barely visible from where he had parked. He saw a figure inside but couldn't make out who it was or what it was. Has to be Holliday.

The car drove by again before disappearing down a residential street, then another. After that, it stopped someplace out of sight.

Must have parked someplace or it's not Holliday after all. Damn! However, he was reassured that no other suspicious cars were about, as in, police cars to arrest him for attempted blackmail.

A minute later, a man appeared on the street into the Park. He was heavyset like Holliday, in dark clothes with his head covered by a dark bucket hat. In his left hand was a bag.

The money! Looking good! Bishop let out a big breath.

The man saw Bishop's car and walked around the cross, away from where Bishop had parked. Checking to see if I brought anybody.

Half a minute later, he came up behind Bishop's car. As he drew closer, Bishop could see it was Holliday. Even in the shadow of the bucket hat and the scant lighting of the parking lot, his face appeared grim and determined. He paused at the back window of Bishop's car, looked inside to verify that indeed it was Bishop and no one else. He opened the passenger side door and got in.

"Let me see the video you claim you have. There's no way anybody could claim I was in that Jeep. No one could have seen my Jeep. I wasn't there. You're trying to blackmail me. You want to steal my money! I won't let you."

"I thought I was trying to help you stay out of jail, Holliday. Now you're accusing me of breaking the law. Well, I'll tell you, now that you're here, how I came to have the video. It had nothing to do with Derek or his iPhone. I just claimed to have Derek's video of you running Marc's jeep off the road to get your attention. I know you killed him to stop him from telling the press about your daughter's bastard child."

"You're a lying son of a bitch," Holliday said and made a move like he was going to hit Bishop. Bishop readied himself, but Holliday relaxed and said. "So, how'd you get the video you say you have, the one I haven't seen? You probably don't have anything! You lying blasphemer!"

He reached for the door handle but stopped when Bishop said, "Might want to see what I do have, old buddy."

Holliday released the door handle and sat back, his face a mask of hate.

Bishop said, "Phillip Marshall hated Flint because guess what, Flint forced Marshall's wife to sleep with him and guess what, she got pregnant, just like Sarah. I'll tell you something else. The boy was born with the same lazy eye condition Sarah's boy has. That condition, I'll educate you a bit, is inherited from the father."

"The man deserved to die. He should never have been born," Holliday said. "That goes for you as well."

"I don't think you or I have the right under the Bible or under the laws that govern us to decide that."

"You belong in the grave with him and the other thief, Anne Flint's brother. He was as slimy as you and Flint," Holliday said almost with a hiss.

"Nobody can say you don't go out and do the Lord's work. You kill anybody you decide is evil, but let me finish. Marshall hated Flint and found out Flint had diabetes. His wife's a nurse and she ran a blood test on Flint and found out the day before the grand opening of Flint's La Jolla project."

"I read the newspaper reports about Flint's death."

"I bet you did. Unfortunately, the reports didn't tell it all. Let me tell you what you don't know and some things you do. Marshall first tried to kill Flint on the racquetball courts but couldn't. Flint was too tough. So, when Flint left early, Marshall got into his old truck with its big metal bumpers and hurried to catch up with him. He intended running him off the road, just like you did."

"I was carrying out the Lord's wish," Holliday said, kind of a slip of tongue. Bishop was glad to hear it.

"Well, Marshall rounded that curve up there and guess what he saw? He saw you and your big Jeep, catching up with Flint's. Flint was weaving all over the road because he was having little diabetic seizures, about to pass out."

Holliday interrupted. "Nobody was on that street! ... when I drove home."

"Ah, don't you wish. When he was catching up with you and Flint, your Jeep was trying to run Flint off the street. He pulled back and took the video on his iPhone. You were doing his work. He didn't get it all because he was afraid you'd see him. He gave it to me when I dropped my charges against him. Well, his wife actually gave it to me. A Christian thing to do, don't you think?"

Holliday scoffed. "You're a lying heathen. You don't have a video."

"I don't? How about this?"

With that Bishop picked up the iPhone from the caddy between the seats and turned it on to show the video he, Anne and Ellen had made using Jeeps borrowed from the Jeep dealer.

Holliday stared at the few seconds of video. His mouth dropped open. He stared at the last frame of the video and said haltingly. "There was nobody. I didn't see another car or truck. I know it! I'm sure no one was behind me. You can't see me in that thing." He gestured at Bishop's iPhone. "You can't even make out the tag."

"Not clearly but what do you want to bet the police lab will be able to make it out, the tag? They can take that and run it back to the Jeep dealer who consigned the Jeep to you. They'll have you, Holliday. Murder in the first degree. It'll be … lethal injection, I guess now, for you. I wonder if they'll let you take you Bible into the chamber with you. No matter. Do you think you'll go to heaven?" Bishop asked with cynicism hanging onto every word.

"I can't say I've ever hated anybody more than you, Bone. I hated Flint for what he did to my lovely, sweet daughter. I hate you for carrying on in his place. I'll give you the money. I don't ever want to see you again."

He reached into the bag he'd brought with him. Bishop was instantly alert but the man's hand held only a packet of hundred dollar bills from what Bishop could see in the dim parking lot lighting.

"That's not a hundred thousand," Bishop said.

"You're going to get it all!" He reached back into the bag. Bishop was thinking the man was going to pay after all. But, he was wrong. When the man's hand next emerged it was holding an automatic.

But, Bishop was ready for it and grabbed Holliday's gun hand. With some effort, he shoved it to one side. But Holliday was already squeezing the trigger. Bishop felt the burn of the bullet passing within an inch of his arm. He tried shoving the gun farther away but Holliday resisted. The second bullet barely missed Bishop and slammed into the door panel. Bishop pushed Holliday's arm up and locked his arm to prevent the huge man from lowering it. Two more bullets went through the car's roof. Although Holliday was probably not in great shape, he was strong and he outweighed Bishop by plenty.

The struggle caused Bishop's face to break out in a sweat that ran down into his eyes, stinging them. But there wasn't anything he could do but hang onto Holliday's arm. He felt his arm weakening so he grabbed Holliday's arm with his other hand for extra support. It helped. Bishop wondered where in the hell Ellen and her troops were. Holliday used his weight to press down on Bishop's arm. Even with both arms pushing Holliday's arm upward, Bishop felt like his were being crushed.

Desperation made him remember that he'd brought a gun, Anne's automatic. It was under his leg. With a surge of adrenalin, he released his right hand from Holliday's gun hand and reached for Anne's automatic. He had a difficult time getting a grip on it because

Holliday was struggling like a mad man and was using his strength to push Bishop's arm aside. He managed to fire two more shots before Bishop could raise his gun from the seat and push it against Holliday's head.

He said, "One more shot and I'll shoot you."

Holliday's answer was to swing his gun around and fire another shot that missed Bishop's head by less than an inch. Bishop pulled the trigger but in the struggle, missed Holliday's head and hit him in the shoulder.

"Stop! Police!" he heard Ellen shout.

'Bout damn time! Bishop thought.

Her shouting didn't matter. Bishop's shot had taken the wind out of Holliday's attack. He was crying out in pain with blood spurting out all over, drenching Bishop's shirt.

"Get an ambulance," he told Ellen. "The man's bleeding to death."

"One's on the way. We were afraid you were being shot. Had to park way the hell away."

"It was damned close."

Bishop touched his arm and felt no blood. Likewise, though his jaw burned, it had not been hit.

Ellen told him she'd gotten it all on tape. The only thing the man didn't confess to was Derek's murder but she was betting Holliday's gun would be the gun used to kill Derek and it was.

## CHAPTER 24

As it turned out, it didn't matter much if he'd confessed to murdering Derek. Holliday died on the way to the emergency room.

The next day, Bishop returned the rental. The car company couldn't believe Bishop's story but accepted it with Ellen's corroboration.

"Three cars, the man destroyed," an executive at the company had said.

"He gets no more cars from us."

Bishop hoped he'd never have the need for another rental car.

He talked to Sarah afterward. She wasn't friendly but she said she understood. "Dad has been acting funny for a while. He may have been Alzheimerish. You didn't help any, Mr. Bone. You put pressure on him. Well, I guess to be fair, it started with Marc. Then, the baby."

He left her crying.

Anne was apparently getting along with her Bay Area friend. His company had relocated to San Diego so they were seeing more of each other. She hugged Bishop goodbye at the airport and kissed him hard on the lips. "I'll never forget our Jacuzzi night, Bishop. It was wonderful." Tears came into her eyes.

He couldn't disagree with her. He didn't want to. It was wonderful. A secret memory of their time together.

The final draft of Flint's memoirs was two hundred pages. It had been picked up by a small publisher, one she knew through her books, and published. With all the publicity that surrounded his death and the aftermath, it sold very well. Anne sent him a bonus.

Ellen emailed him later. Indeed, she was being considered for another promotion. His last call was from Linda Marshall. She told him she was pregnant.

"Phillip is enjoying his work with the new developer. They are getting ready to break ground on two projects."

Bishop was betting their next baby would not have the lazy eye condition.

Once he was back in Mississippi, he sent Mrs. Flint a bouquet of flowers, thanking her for her help in finding her son's killer. He was embellishing but who was to know or care. He was sure it made her feel good and necessary.

Kathy didn't care about any of that. She just cared that Bishop was back, and they were having their afternoons together, sitting on the back porch enjoying a beer and watching the beavers work in their pond across the creek.


## THE END

Made in the USA
Las Vegas, NV
22 October 2022